HALFWAY to the Grave

Jeaniene Frost

Copyright © Jeaniene Frost 2007
All rights reserved

Excerpt from *One Foot in the Grave* © Jeaniene Frost 2008

The right of Jeaniene Frost to be identified as the author of this
work has been asserted by her in accordance with the
Copyright, Designs and Patents Act 1988.

First published in Great Britain in 2010 by
Gollancz
An imprint of the Orion Publishing Group
Orion House, 5 Upper St Martin's Lane, London WC2H 9EA
An Hachette UK Company

5 7 9 10 8 6

A CIP catalogue record for this book is available
from the British Library

ISBN 978 0 575 09377 5

Printed in Great Britain by
Clays Ltd, St Ives plc

www.jeanienefrost.com

www.orionbooks.co.uk

The Orion Publishing Group's policy is to use papers that are
natural, renewable and recyclable products and made from wood
grown in sustainable forests. The logging and manufacturing
processes are expected to conform to the environmental regulations
of the country of origin.

HALFWAY
TO THE
GRAVE

To my mother,
Who always believed in me,
Even when I didn't.

ONE

I STIFFENED AT THE RED AND BLUE LIGHTS flashing behind me, because there was no way I could explain what was in the back of my truck. I pulled over, holding my breath as the sheriff came to my window.

"Hi. Something wrong?" My tone was all innocence while I prayed there was nothing unusual about my eyes. *Control yourself. You know what happens when you get upset.*

"Yeah, you've got a busted taillight. License and registration, please."

Crap. That must have happened when I was loading up the truck bed. Speed had been of the essence then, not daintiness.

I handed him my real license, not the fake one. He shone his flashlight back and forth between the identification and my face.

"Catherine Crawfield. You're Justina Crawfield's girl, aren't you? From the Crawfield Cherry Orchard?"

"Yes, sir." Politely and blandly, as if I didn't have a care in the world.

"Well, Catherine, it's nearly four A.M. Why are you out this late?"

I could tell him the truth about my activities, except I didn't want to sign on for hard time. Or an extended stay in a padded cell.

"I couldn't sleep, so I decided I'd drive around."

To my dismay, he ambled to the bed of the truck and shone his light in it.

"Whatcha got back there?"

Oh, nothing unusual. A dead body under some bags and an ax.

"Bags of cherries from my grandparents' orchard." If my heartbeat were any louder, it would deafen him.

"Really?" With his flashlight he poked at a plastic lump. "One of 'em is leaking."

"Don't worry." My voice was almost a squeak. "They always leak. That's why I carry them in this old truck. They've stained the bottom of it red."

Relief crashed through me when he ceased his explorations and returned to my window.

"And you're driving around this late because you couldn't sleep?" There was a knowing curl to his mouth. His gaze took in my tight top and disheveled hair. "You think I'm going to believe that?"

The innuendo was blatant and I almost lost my cool. He thought I'd been out sleeping around. An unspoken accusation hung between us, nearly twenty-three years in the making. *Just like your mother, aren't you?* It wasn't easy being illegitimate in a town so small, people still held that against you. In today's society, you wouldn't think it mattered, but Licking Falls, Ohio, had its own set of standards. They were archaic at best.

With great effort I restrained my anger. My humanity tended to shed like a disposable skin when I got angry.

"Could we just keep this between us, Sheriff?" Back to

the guileless blinking of my eyes. It had worked on the dead guy, anyway. "Promise I won't do it again."

He fingered his belt as he considered me. His large belly strained against the fabric of his shirt, but I refrained from comments about his girth or the fact that he smelled like beer. Finally he smiled, exposing a crooked front tooth.

"Go home, Catherine Crawfield, and get that taillight fixed."

"Yes, sir!"

Giddy with my reprieve, I revved up the truck and drove off. That had been close. I'd have to be more careful next time.

People complained about having deadbeat fathers or skeletons in their family's closets. For me, both were really true. Oh, don't get me wrong, I hadn't always known what I was. My mother, the only other person in on the secret, didn't tell me until I was sixteen. I grew up with abilities other children didn't have, but when I asked her about them, she'd get angry and tell me not to talk about it. I learned to keep things to myself and hide my differences. To everyone else, I was just weird. Friendless. Liked to wander around at strange hours and had odd pale skin. Even my grandparents didn't know what was in me, but then again, neither did those I hunted.

There was a pattern to my weekends now. I went to any of the clubs within a three-hour drive to look for some action. Not the kind the good sheriff thought I was into, but another brand. I'd drink like a fish and wait to be picked up by that special someone. One I hoped I could end up planting in the backyard, if I didn't get killed first. I'd been doing this for six years now. Maybe I had a death wish. Funny, really, since technically I was half dead.

Therefore my near miss with the law didn't stop me from going out the following Friday. At least this way, I knew I was making one person happy. My mother. Well, she had a right to hold a grudge. I just wished it hadn't spilled over to me.

The club's loud music hit me like a splash, jerking my pulse to its beat. I made my way carefully through the crowds, seeking that unmistakable vibe. The place was packed, a typical Friday night. After I wandered around for an hour, I felt the first stirrings of disappointment. There appeared to be only people here. With a sigh, I sat at the bar and ordered a gin and tonic. The first man who tried to kill me had ordered it for me. It was now my drink of choice. Who said I wasn't sentimental?

Men approached me periodically. Something about being a single young woman screamed "Screw me" to them. Politely and somewhat impolitely I turned them down, depending on how persistent they were. I wasn't here to date. After my first boyfriend, Danny, I never wanted to date again. If the guy was alive, I wasn't interested. No wonder I had no love life to speak of.

After three more drinks I decided to cruise the club again, since I was having no luck being bait. It was nearly midnight, and so far there had been nothing aside from alcohol, drugs, and dancing.

Booths were tucked in the far corner of the club. As I passed in front of them, I felt a twinge of charged air. Someone, or some*thing*, was near. I stopped and did a slow circle, attempting to ferret out the location.

Out of the light and obscured by shadows, I saw the top of a man's head bent forward. His hair was nearly white under the intermittent lighting, but his skin was unlined. Hollows and contours became features as he looked up and spotted me staring at him. His brows were distinctly darker than his hair, which appeared to be light blond. Those eyes were dark as well, too deep for me to guess a color. His cheekbones could have been chiseled from marble, and that flawless diamonds-and-cream skin gleamed from under his shirt collar.

Bingo.

Pasting a false smile on my face, I sauntered over with the exaggerated walk of someone drunk and plunked myself down on the opposite seat.

"Hello, handsome," I said in my most alluring voice.

"Not now."

His tone was clipped, with a distinct English accent. I blinked stupidly for a moment, thinking maybe I *had* drunk too much and misunderstood him.

"Excuse me?"

"I'm busy." He sounded impatient and mildly annoyed.

Confusion raged in me. Could I have been wrong? Just to be certain, I reached out and ran a finger lightly over his hand. The power nearly jumped off his skin. Not human, all right.

"I was wondering, um . . ." Stumbling over my words, I searched for an enticing phrase. Frankly, this had never happened before. Usually his kind were easy pickings. I didn't know how to handle this as a true professional would.

"Want to fuck?"

The words burst out, and I was horrified at myself for saying them. I barely managed to avoid clapping a hand over my mouth, never having used *that* word before.

He glanced back with a curl of amusement on his lips, having turned away after his second refusal. Dark eyes raked me appraisingly.

"Bad timing, luv. Have to wait until later. Be a good bird and fly away, I'll find you."

With a flick of his hand, he dismissed me. Numbly I got up and walked away, shaking my head at the turn of events. *Now* how was I supposed to kill him?

In a daze I went to the ladies' room to inspect my

appearance. My hair looked okay, albeit its usual startling crimson shade, and I wore my lucky top, which had led the last two guys to their doom. Next I bared my teeth at my reflection. Nothing was stuck in them. Lastly, I raised my arm and sniffed near the crease. No, I didn't smell bad. What was it, then? A thought occurred to me. Could he be gay?

Reflectively I considered it. Anything was possible—I was proof of that. Perhaps I could watch him. Follow him whenever he tried to pick someone up, male or female. Decision made, I headed out with renewed determination.

He was gone. The table he'd been crouched over was empty, and there was no trace of him in the air. With growing urgency I searched the surrounding bars, the dance floor, and the booths again. Nothing. I must have dawdled too long in the bathroom. Cursing myself, I stalked back to the bar and ordered a fresh drink. Although alcohol didn't dull my senses, having a drink was something to do, and I was feeling very unproductive.

"Beautiful ladies should never drink alone," a voice said next to me.

Turning to give a rebuff, I stopped short when I saw my admirer was as dead as Elvis. Blond hair about four shades darker than the other one's, with turquoise-colored eyes. Hell's bells, it was my lucky night.

"I hate to drink alone, in fact."

He smiled, showing lovely squared teeth. *All the better to bite you with, my dear.*

"Are you here by yourself?"

"Do you want me to be?" Coyly, I fluttered my lashes at him. This one wasn't going to get away, by God.

"I very much want you to be." His voice was lower now, his smile deeper. God, but they had great intonation. Most of them could double as phone-sex operators.

"Well, then I was. Except now I'm with you."

I let my head tilt to the side in a flirtatious manner that

also bared my neck. His eyes followed the movement, and he licked his lips. *Oh good, a hungry one.*

"What's your name, lovely lady?"

"Cat Raven." An abbreviation of Catherine, and the hair color of the first man who tried to kill me. See? Sentimental.

His smile broadened. "Such an unusual name."

His name was Kevin. He was twenty-eight and an architect, or so he claimed. Kevin was recently engaged, but his fiancée had dumped him and now he just wanted to find a nice girl and settle down. Listening to this, I managed not to choke on my drink in amusement. What a load of crap. Next he'd be pulling out pictures of a house with a white picket fence. Of course, he couldn't let me call a cab, and how inconsiderate that my fictitious friends left without me. How kind of him to drive me home, and oh, by the way, he had something to show me. Well, that made two of us.

Experience had taught me it was much easier to dispose of a car that hadn't been the scene of a killing. Therefore, I managed to open the passenger door of his Volkswagen and run screaming out of it with feigned horror when he made his move. He'd picked a deserted area, most of them did, so I didn't worry about a Good Samaritan hearing my cries.

He followed me with measured steps, delighted with my sloppy staggering. Pretending to trip, I whimpered for effect as he loomed over me. His face had transformed to reflect his true nature. A sinister smile revealed upper fangs where none had been before, and his previously blue eyes now glowed with a terrible green light.

I scrabbled around, concealing my hand slipping into my pocket. "Don't hurt me!"

He knelt, grasping the back of my neck.

"It will only hurt for a moment."

Just then, I struck. My hand whipped out in a practiced movement and the weapon it held pierced his heart.

I twisted repeatedly until his mouth went slack and the light faded from his eyes. With a last wrenching shove, I pushed him off and wiped my bloody hands on my pants.

"You were right." I was out of breath from my exertions. "It only hurt for a moment."

Much later when I arrived home, I was whistling. The night hadn't been a total waste after all. One had gotten away, but one would be prowling the dark no more. My mother was asleep in the room we shared. I'd tell her about it in the morning. It was the first question she asked on the weekends. *Did you get one of those things, Catherine?* Well, yes, I did! All without me getting battered or pulled over. Who could ask for more?

I was in such a good mood, in fact, that I decided to try the same club the next night. After all, there was a dangerous bloodsucker in the area and I had to stop him, right? So I went about my usual household chores with impatience. My mother and I lived with my grandparents. They owned a modest two-story home that had actually once been a barn. Turned out the isolated property, with its acres of land, was coming in handy. By nine o'clock, I was out the door.

It was crowded again, this being a Saturday night. The music was just as loud and the faces just as blank. My initial sweep of the place turned up nothing, deflating my mood a little. I headed toward the bar and didn't notice the crackle in the air before I heard his voice.

"I'm ready to fuck now."

"What?"

I whirled around, prepared to indignantly scald the ears of the unknown creep, when I stopped. It was *him*. A blush came to my face when I remembered what I'd said last night. Apparently he'd remembered as well.

"Ah yes, well . . ." Exactly how did one respond to that? "Umm, drink first? Beer or . . . ?"

"Don't bother." He interrupted my hail of the bartender and traced a finger along my jaw. "Let's go."

"Now?" I looked around, thrown off guard.

"Yeah, now. Changed your mind, luv?"

There was a challenge in his eyes and a gleam I couldn't decipher. Not wanting to risk losing him again, I grabbed my purse and gestured to the door.

"Lead the way."

"No, no." He grinned chillingly. "Ladies first."

With several glances over my shoulder, I preceded him into the parking lot. Once outside, he looked expectantly at me.

"Well, get your ride and let's be off."

"My ride? I—I don't have a ride. Where's *your* car?" I fought to remain cool, but I was inwardly rattled. This was all off my normal routine and I didn't like it.

"I drove a bike here. Fancy a ride on it?"

"A motorcycle?" No, that wouldn't do. No trunk to carry his body in, and I wasn't about to balance it on the handlebars. Plus, I didn't know how to ride one. "Umm, we'll take my vehicle instead. It's over there."

As I walked to the truck, I reminded myself to stagger. I hoped he'd think I had been pounding the booze.

"Thought you didn't have a ride," he called after me.

I stopped short, turning back at him. Crap, I had said that.

"I forgot it was here, is all," I lied breezily. "Think I drank too much. You want to drive?"

"No, thanks," was his immediate response. For some reason, his strong English accent grated on me.

I tried again with a lopsided smile. He had to drive. My weapon was in my right pants leg, since I was always in the passenger seat before.

"Really, I think you should drive. I'm feeling woozy. I'd hate to wrap us around a tree."

It didn't work.

"If you just want to beg off until another night . . ."

"No!" There was desperation in my voice, which raised his eyebrow a notch. "I mean, you're so good-looking and . . ." What the hell did one say? "I really, *really* want to get it on."

He stifled a laugh, dark eyes glittering. A denim jacket was casually thrown over his collared shirt. Under the streetlights, his cheekbones looked even more pronounced. I had never seen such perfectly chiseled features before.

He looked me up and down, his tongue tracing the inside of his bottom lip.

"Right, then, let's be off. You're driving."

Without another word, he climbed into the passenger seat of the pickup.

Left with no other option, I got in the driver's side and pulled away, heading for the highway. Minutes ticked by, but I didn't know what to say. The silence was unnerving. He didn't speak, but I felt his eyes as they moved over me. Finally I couldn't stand it anymore and blurted the first question that came to mind.

"What's your name?"

"Does it matter?"

I glanced to my right and met his eyes. They were so dark brown they could have been black. There was that cool note of challenge in them again, almost a silent dare. It was disconcerting, to say the least. All the other ones had been perfectly willing to chat.

"I just wanted to know. Mine's Cat." I exited the freeway and turned onto a nearby gravel road leading to the lake.

"Cat, hmmm? From where I sit you look more like a Kitten."

My head jerked around and I shot him an annoyed look. Oh, I was going to enjoy this, all right.

"It's Cat," I repeated firmly. "Cat Raven."

"Whatever you say, Kitten Tweedy."

Abruptly I slammed on the brakes. "You got a problem, mister?"

Dark eyebrows rose. "No problem, pet. Have we stopped here for good? Is this where you want to shag?"

There went that pesky flush again at his bluntness.

"Um, no. A little farther up. It's prettier there." I steered us deeper into the woods.

He gave a low chuckle. "I just bet it is, luv."

When the truck stopped at my favorite rendezvous spot, I glanced over at him. He sat exactly as he had been, immobile. There was no way I could go for the surprise in my pants yet. Clearing my throat, I gestured toward the trees.

"Don't you want to go outside and . . . shag?" It was a strange word, but much better than *fuck*.

A quick grin lit his face before he responded. "Oh no. Right here. Love to do it in a truck."

"Well . . ." Damn, what now? This wouldn't work. "There's not much room." Triumphantly I began to open my door.

He didn't budge. "Plenty of room, Kitten. I'll stay here."

"Don't call me Kitten." My voice was sharper than romance dictated, but I was seriously aggravated. The sooner he was truly dead, the better.

He ignored me. "Take off your clothes. Let's see what you've got."

"Ex*cuse* me?" This was too much.

"You weren't going to shag me with all your clothes on, were you, Kitten?" he taunted. "Guess all you'll need off is your knickers, then. Come on. Don't take all bloody night."

Oh, I was going to make him sorry. I hoped this hurt like hell. With a superior smile, I looked back at him.

"You first."

He grinned again with a flash of normal teeth. "Shy bird, are you? Didn't peg you for the type, what with walking up to me and practically begging for it and all. How about this? We'll do it at the same time."

Bastard. It was the filthiest word I could think of, and I chanted it in my mind as I warily stared at him while unbuttoning my jeans. He nonchalantly loosened his belt, unbuckled his pants, and pulled out his shirt. The action revealed a taut pale belly that was hairless until it met his groin.

This was way further than I'd ever let things progress before. I was so embarrassed, my fingers shook as I peeled off my jeans while reaching inside them.

"Look here, luv, see what I have for you."

I glanced down and saw his hand close around himself before quickly looking away. The stake was almost in my hand, all I needed was another second . . .

It was my modesty that did me in. When I turned to avoid seeing his groin, I missed his hand clenching. His fist moved unbelievably fast to connect with my head. There was a flash of light followed by shooting pain, and then silence.

†wo

SOMETHING SEEMED TO BE DIGGING AT MY brain. With agonizing slowness I opened my eyes, squinting at the unshaded lamp nearby. It made the sun seem pale in comparison. My hands were above me, my wrists ached, and the pain in my head made me immediately lean forward and throw up.

"I thawt I thaw a putty tat."

The mocking voice caused my pain to dissipate in a rush of terror. When I saw the vampire close by, I shuddered.

"I *did*, I *did* thee a putty tat!"

Finished with his Tweety Bird imitation, he grinned unpleasantly at me. I tried to scoot back and realized my hands were chained to a wall. Both my feet were also cuffed together. My top and pants were gone, leaving me in only my bra and underwear. Even my trademark gloves were missing. *Oh God*.

"Now, then, luv, let's get down to business." The bantering left his tone and his eyes hardened into pools of dark granite. "Who do you work for?"

This surprised me so much, it took me a moment to answer him. "I don't work for anyone."

"Bollocks." He bit the word out precisely, and I didn't have to know what it meant to guess he didn't believe me. I hunched when he moved nearer.

"Who do you work for?" With more menace.

"No one."

My head snapped back as he slapped me. Tears came to my eyes, but I held them there. I was going to die, but I didn't have to grovel.

"Go to hell."

Immediately there was another ringing in my ears. This time I could taste blood.

"Once again, who do you work for?"

Spitting it out, I blazed up at him defiantly. "No one, ass-munch!"

He blinked in surprise, and then rocked on his heels and laughed so loudly my ears rang. Regaining control, he leaned in until his mouth was inches from my face. Fangs gleamed in the light.

"I know you're lying."

His voice was a whisper. He lowered his head until his mouth brushed my neck. I held myself rigid, praying for the strength not to plead for my life.

Cool breath blew on my skin. "I know you're lying," he continued. "Because last night I was looking for a bloke. When I spotted him, I saw the same lovely red-haired girl who'd been rubbing on me leaving with him. I followed, thinking I'd sneak up on him while he was occupied. Instead, I watched you plug a stake in his heart, and what a stake!" In front of my stricken eyes, he dangled my modified weapon triumphantly. "Wood on the outside, silver on the inside. Now, *that's* made in America! Poof, down goes Devon! Yet it didn't stop there. You plopped him in the trunk and drove to your truck, where you chopped his bleedin' head off and buried him in pieces. Then you went home whistling a merry tune. How in the bloody hell could you do that, hmm? You don't work for anyone? Then why, when I take a deep whiff here"—he put his nose against my collarbone and inhaled—"do I smell something other than human? Faint, but unmistakable. *Vampire.* You've got a boss, you do. Feeds you some of his blood, right? Makes you stronger and faster, but still only human. Us poor vamps never see it coming. All we see is . . . food."

With one finger, he pressed lightly on my jumping pulse.

"Now, for the last time before I forget my manners, tell me *who* your boss is."

I looked at him, knowing his would be the last face I ever saw. Bitterness briefly coursed through me before I pushed it aside. There would be no complaints. Maybe, maybe the world would be a better place for what I'd done. It was all I could wish for, and so I'd die telling my executioner the truth.

"I don't have a boss." Each word was poison. There was no need to be polite. "You want to know why I smell like a human and a vampire? *Because that's what I am.* Years ago, my mother went on a date with what she thought was a nice guy. He turned out to be a vampire, and he raped her. Five months later there was me, premature but fully developed, with a whole slew of funky abilities. When she finally told me about my father, I promised her I'd kill every vampire I found to make up for it. To ensure no one else suffered what she had to. She's been afraid to leave her home ever since! I hunt for her, and the only thing I regret about dying now is that I didn't take more of you with me!"

My voice rose until I screamed the last part, hurling the words in his face. I closed my eyes and braced for the killing blow.

Nothing. No sound, no strike, no pain. After a moment I peeked to see him standing exactly where he'd been. He tapped his chin with his finger and looked at me with an expression that could only be described as thoughtful.

"*Well?*" Fear and resignation strained my voice to the breaking point. "Kill me already, you pathetic suck-neck!"

That earned me an amused glance. "Ass-munch. Suck-neck. You kiss your mum with that mouth?"

"Don't you talk about my mother, murderer! Your kind isn't fit to speak of her!"

A ghost of a smile hovered on his lips. "Bit of the pot calling the kettle black, isn't it? I've seen *you* do murder. And if what you're telling me is true, you're the same kind I am."

I shook my head. "I am nothing like your kind! You're all monsters, preying on innocent people and caring nothing about the lives you wreck. The vampires I killed attacked me—it was their bad luck I was ready for them. I might have some of this cursed blood in my veins, but at least I was using it to—"

"Oh, stick a sock in it already," he interrupted me with an irritated tone you'd use to scold a child. "You always ramble on so? No wonder your dates went right for your throat. Can't say as I blame them."

Speechless, I gaped at him. With absolute clarity I understood the phrase *adding insult to injury.* First he'd slapped me soundly, now he was going to slander me before murdering me.

"I hate to interrupt your sympathy session over the other dead vampires, but are you going to be killing me soon or what?" *Brave words*, I thought. At least it beat sniveling.

Faster than I could blink, his mouth was at the pounding pulse in my neck. Everything inside me froze as I felt the unmistakable graze of teeth. *Please don't let me beg. Please don't let me beg.*

Abruptly he leaned back again, leaving me trembling in relief and fear. One eyebrow cocked upward at me.

"In a hurry to die, are you? Not before you answer a few more questions."

"What makes you think I will?"

A curl of his mouth preceded his response.

"Believe me, you'll like it much more if you do."

I cleared my throat and tried to slow my heartbeat. No need to keep ringing the dinner bell for him.

"What do you want to know? Maybe I'll tell you."

That little smirk widened. Nice to know one of us was having a good time.

"Brave little Kitten, I'll give you that. Right, then. Suppose I believe you're the offspring of a human and a vampire. Almost unheard of, but we'll get back to that. Then let's say I believe you troll clubs hunting us evil deads to avenge your mum. The question remains, how did you know what to use to kill us? It's not an open secret. Most humans think good old wood will do it. But not you. You're telling me you've never dealt with vampires before, except to kill them?"

In the midst of all that was occurring, my life over and a horrible death looming in front of me, I spoke the first words that popped into my mind.

"You got anything to drink around here? Nothing with clots in it, I mean, or that can be classified as O-negative or B-positive. Hmm?"

He let out an amused snort. "Thirsty, luv? What a coincidence. So am I."

With those frightening words, he pulled a flask out of his jacket and placed the rim against my lips, tilting it. My manacled hands were useless, so I wrapped my teeth around it and used them for leverage. It was whiskey and it burned slightly going down, but I kept swallowing until the last drop trickled down my throat. Sighing, I released my bite and let the flask drop back into his hand.

He held it upside down, apparently bemused by its lack

of contents. "If I'd known you were such a lush, I'd have given you the cheap stuff. Going to go out with a bang, are you?"

I shrugged as much as my raised arms would allow.

"What's the matter? Did I ruin my flavor for you? I'm sure I'll be turning over in my grave worrying that you didn't like how I tasted. I hope you choke on my blood, you jerk."

That drew more laughter. "Good form, Kitten! But enough stalling. How did you know what to use if no vampire told you?"

Another modified shrug. "I didn't. Oh, I'd read a hundred books or more about our . . . your kind after hearing about my father. They all varied. Some said crosses, sunlight, wood, or silver. It was pure luck, really. One night a vampire approached me at a club and then took me for a drive. Of course, he couldn't have been nicer, right up until he tried to eat me alive. I made up my mind that I was going to kill him or die trying, and the big cross dagger was all I had on me. It worked, though it took a bit of doing. So, presto, I knew about silver. Later I found that wood didn't work at all. Got myself a nice scar on the thigh to prove it. That vamp laughed when he saw my stake. Clearly, he wasn't afraid of wood. Then when I was making caramel apples it occurred to me to hide the silver in something a vampire would think was harmless. It didn't seem like such a stretch. Most of you are so busy eyeing my neck, you don't see me pull out my pointy friend. There you have it."

He shook his head slowly back and forth as if uncomprehending. Finally, he fixed piercing eyes on me and burst out, "Are you telling me bloody caramel apples and books taught you how to kill vampires? Is that what you're saying?"

He started to pace in short, rapid lengths. "It's a damn good thing most of the recent generations are nearly illiterate or we'd all be in serious trouble. Blimey!" Throwing back his head, he laughed in rich, deep peals of mirth. "That's the funniest bleedin' bit I've heard in decades!" Still chuckling, he returned until he was next to me again.

"How did you know he was a vampire when you saw him? Did you know, or did you not find out until he tried to have an artery party?"

Artery party? Well, that was one way to put it. "Honestly, I don't know how I knew. I just did. For starters, your kind looks different. All of you do. Your skin looks . . . ethereal, almost. You move different, more purposefully. And when I'm near you, I feel it in the air, like static electricity. Happy now? Heard what you wanted?" Desperately I tried to hang on to my courage, but this chattering was eating away at it. Being flippant was all I had left.

"Almost. How many vampires have you killed? Don't lie to me, or I'll know it."

Pursing my lips, I considered lying despite the warning. Would it be better if he thought I'd only killed a couple? Maybe it wouldn't make any difference. If he could tell I was lying, perhaps he'd do more than just kill me. There were so many things worse than death. . . .

"Sixteen, including your friend from last night." Honesty won out.

"Sixteen?" he repeated in disbelief, looking me over thoroughly again. "Sixteen vampires you took out yourself with nothing but a stake and your cleavage? Makes me ashamed of my kind, it does."

"And I would have killed more if I hadn't been too young to get into bars, since they're vampire trolling ground, not to mention all the time I had to take off when my grandfather got sick," I flared. So much for trying not to make him angrier.

In a flash he was gone, leaving me staring at the spot where he'd just been. He certainly moved fast. Faster than any vampire I'd seen. I cursed my earlier impatience. If only I'd waited until the next weekend to hunt again. If only.

Left alone, I craned my neck to see where I was. With a start, I realized I must be in a cave. There was the sound of dripping water in the background, and it was dark even for my eyes. The single bald lamp only shone light in the immediate vicinity. The rest was blackness as complete as my nightmares. I heard slight echoes of him in the distance, how far away I had no idea. Seizing my chance, I wrapped my fingers around the braces holding me and pulled downward with all of my strength. Sweat popped out on my brow, my legs clenched with effort, and I channeled every muscle toward that singular goal.

There was a creak of metal in stone, a rasp of chains clanging together, and then the only light was suddenly switched off. Laughter from the darkness made me sag in defeat.

"Oh, sorry about that. Those won't budge. They're not going anywhere—and neither are you. Good of you to try, though. Hate to think your spirit's broken already. Not much fun in that."

"I hate you." To avoid sobbing, I turned my face away from his direction and closed my eyes. *Our Father, who art in Heaven, hallowed be Thy name . . .*

"Time's up, luv."

Thy kingdom come, Thy will be done . . .

My eyes were closed, but I felt him move closer until he pressed lengthwise next to me. Unable to help it, my breath came in short hard pants. His hands moved to my hair, and he smoothed it back from my neck.

. . . on earth as it is in Heaven . . .

His mouth sealed on my throat, tongue circling my thundering pulse in a deliberate manner. My back cut into the wall as I tried to disappear into the rock, but the cold hard limestone offered no escape. I felt the pressure of pointed, sharp teeth at my exposed and vulnerable artery. He was nuzzling my neck the way a hungry lion nuzzled a gazelle.

"Last chance, Kitten. Who do you work for? Tell me the truth and I'll let you live."

"I told you the truth." That high-pitched whisper couldn't be mine. The roaring of blood in my ears was deafening. Were my eyes still closed? No, I could see a faint green glow in the darkness. Vampire eyes.

"I don't believe you. . . ." Softly spoken, yet falling with the weight of an ax.

Amen. . . .

"Bloody hell, look at your eyes."

So deeply had I fallen into the fervent prayer, I hadn't felt him pull back. He stared at me with fanged mouth open in disbelief, his face illuminated in the new green glow of my eyes. His brown ones were now that penetrating shade as well, and matching rays of emerald connected one shocked gaze to another.

"Look at your bloody eyes!"

He gripped either side of my head as though it would spin off. Still in a fog from teetering on the brink of mortality, I mumbled my response.

"Don't need to look at them, I've seen them. They change from gray to green when I'm upset. Happy now? Going to enjoy your meal more?"

As if my head were scalding, he released me. I sagged in my chains, the adrenaline abandoning me and leaving dizzying lethargy in its wake.

The sound of his pacing bounced off the stone walls.

"Bugger, you're telling the truth. You have to be. You have a pulse, but only vampires have eyes that glow green. This is unbelievable!"

"Glad you're excited." I peeked at him through my hair, which had tumbled back onto my shoulders. In the near-complete darkness I saw he was definitely worked up, his steps brisk and full of energy, eyes fading from feeding green to snapping brown.

"Oh, this is perfect! In fact, it could come in right handy."

"What could come in handy? Either kill me or let me go already. I'm tired."

He spun around, beaming, and clicked the lamp back on. It cast the same harsh light it had previously, flowing over his features like water. He looked ghostly beautiful under its blanket, like a fallen angel.

"How would you like to put your money where your mouth is?"

"What?" To say I was baffled didn't begin to describe it. Seconds ago I was a nick away from eternity, now he wanted to play guessing games.

"I can kill you or let you live, but living comes with conditions. Your choice, your pick. Can't let you go without conditions, you'd just try to stake me."

"Aren't you the smart one?" Frankly, I didn't believe he'd let me go. This had to be a trick.

"You see," he continued as if I hadn't spoken, "we're in the same boat, luv. You hunt vampires. *I* hunt vampires. Both of us have our reasons, and we both have our problems. Another vampire can sense me whenever I'm close, so that makes it bleedin' difficult to stake 'em without them expecting the try and running. *You*, on the other hand, put them completely at ease with that juicy artery of yours, but you aren't strong enough to bring down the really big fish. Oh, you may have beaten some green ones, probably no older than twenty years, tops. Barely out of their nappies, as it were. But a Master vampire . . . like me . . ." His voice dropped to a scathing whisper. "You couldn't bring me down with both stakes blazing. I'd be picking you out of my teeth in minutes. Therefore, I propose a deal. You can continue to do what you love the most—killing vampires. Yet you will only hunt the ones I'm looking for. No exceptions. You're the bait. I'm the hook. It's a capital idea."

This was a dream. A very bad, bad dream, brought on by liver poisoning from too many gin and tonics. Here it was, a deal with the devil. At what price my soul? He watched me expectantly and threateningly all at the same time. If I said no, I knew what would happen. Save the glass, waitress, I'm drinking from the bottle! Happy hour, with my neck on tap. If I said yes, I'd be agreeing to a partnership with pure evil.

His foot tapped. "Don't have all night. The longer you wait, the hungrier I get. Might change my mind in a few minutes."

"I'll do it." The words flew out without thought. If I gave them thought, they'd never be spoken. "But I have a condition of my own."

"Do you?" That made him laugh again. My, what a jolly guy. "You're hardly in a position to demand conditions."

My chin stuck out. Pride or peril, take your pick. "Just challenging you to put *your* money where your mouth is. You said I wouldn't last minutes against you, even with both weapons. I disagree. Unchain me, give me my stuff, and let's go. Winner takes all."

There was a definite spark of interest in his eyes now, and that sly smile was back on his lips. "And what do you want if you win?"

"Your death," I said bluntly. "If I can beat you, I don't need you. As you put it, if I just let you walk, you'd come after me. You win, and I play by your rules."

"You know, pet," he drawled, "with you chained there, I could just have a nice long drink out of your neck and go about my business as usual. You're pushing your luck quite a bit saying this to me."

"You don't seem the type that likes a boring drink out of a chained artery," I boldly countered. "You seem like the type who likes danger. Why else would a vampire hunt vampires? Well? Are you in, or am I out?" My breath sucked in. This was the moment of truth.

Slowly he walked over, letting his eyes slide all over me. With a raised brow, he pulled out a metal key and dangled it in front of me. Then he inserted it firmly into the center of my manacles and twisted. They fell open with a clink.

"Let's see what you've got," he said finally. For the second time that night.

THREE

WE FACED EACH OTHER IN THE CENTER OF A large cavern. The ground underneath was uneven, just rocks upon rocks and dirt. I was dressed again, sans gloves, the stake and my special cross dagger in my hands. He had laughed again when I demanded my clothes back, saying the jeans didn't have give and they would cost me fluidity. Tartly I responded that, fluidity or no, I wasn't battling him in my underwear.

There were more lights strung up around the area. How he had electricity in this cave was beyond me, but that was the least of my concerns. Underground as we were, I had no idea what time it was. It could already be dawn, or still be deep in the night. Briefly I wondered if I'd ever see the sun again.

He wore the same clothes as before, fluidity apparently not a concern for him. His eyes snapped with eagerness as he cracked his knuckles and rolled his head around his shoulders. My palms were sweaty with trepidation. Maybe the gloves would have been a good idea after all.

"All right, Kitten. Because I'm a gentleman, I'll let you have the first try. Come on. Let's do this."

Without further encouragement I charged him, moving as fast as I could with both weapons pointed murderously. He whirled in a semicircle that left me sailing past him, chuckling infuriatingly as he did so.

"Going jogging, pet?"

Catching myself, I glared at him over my shoulder. God in heaven, but he was fast. His movements were almost a blur to me. Gathering my courage, I feinted a broad overhead right swing. When he raised an arm to block, I swiped low with my left hand and slashed him before getting a devastating kick to the midsection in return. Doubled over, I saw him examine his garment with a slight frown.

"I liked this shirt. Now you've gone and ripped it."

I circled again, breathing slowly to combat the pain in my stomach. Before I could blink, he came at me and punched the side of my head, hard enough for me to see stars. In mindless defense I kicked, punched, and stabbed at whatever was near me. The returning blows came heavily and rapidly. My breathing was ragged and my vision swam as I lashed out with all of my strength. The room suddenly spun as I was thrown backward, rocks cutting into my skin.

He stood about ten feet from where I was sprawled. Clearly, in hand-to-hand combat, I was outclassed. I felt like I'd been dropped off a cliff, and there were hardly any marks on him. With a sudden flash of inspiration, I flung my cross. It flew with incredible speed and sank into his chest but too high, too high.

"Bloody hell, woman, that hurts!" he snarled in surprise, snatching it from his chest.

Blood flowed from the wound before stopping abruptly, as if a faucet had been turned off. Contrary to popular belief, vampires did bleed red. I was dismayed, being down to only one weapon and not even having slowed him. Bracing myself, I sprang to my feet, moving with heavy steps.

"Had enough?" He faced me and sniffed the air, once. I blinked in confusion, never having seen a vampire breathe before. I was panting furiously. Sweat was dripping off my brow.

"Not yet."

There was another blur of motion, and then he was on me. I blocked blow after blow and tried to score some of my own, but he was too quick. Fists landed on me with brutal force. Desperately I jabbed the stake into whatever was nearest, but it always missed his heart. After ten minutes or so that seemed like eternity, I fell to the ground for the last time. Unable to move, I gazed at him through swollen eyelids. *I don't have to worry about his terms*, I thought dully. I was dying from my injuries.

He loomed over me. Everything was colored red and fading.

"Enough now?"

I couldn't speak, couldn't nod, couldn't think. As my answer, I passed out. It was the only action I was capable of.

There was something soft underneath me. Floating, I was floating on a cloud and covering myself with its fleece. I burrowed farther inside when it spoke to me in irritated tones.

"If you're going to take all the covers, you can bloody well sleep on the floor!"

Huh? Since when was a cloud both annoyed and *English*?

When I opened my eyes, I saw with horror that I was in a bed with the vampire. And yes, apparently I had the entire blanket wrapped around me.

Shooting upward as though burned, I immediately banged my head on the low ceiling.

"Owww . . ." Rubbing the sore spot, I glanced around in revolted fear. How did I end up here? Why wasn't I in a coma from the beating? In fact, I felt . . . fine. Aside from the mild concussion I had surely just given myself.

I backed as far into a corner as I could manage. There didn't seem to be any visible exit to this small limestone chamber. "Why am I not in a hospital?"

"I healed you," he replied blandly, as if we were discussing tea.

Numb with fear, I checked my pulse. God, he hadn't turned me, had he? No, my heart pounded strongly.

"How?"

"Blood, of course. How else?"

He leaned back on his elbows, eyeing me with impatience and weariness. He had changed into a new shirt, from what I could see. I didn't even want to know what was under the sheet.

"Tell me what you did to me!"

With a roll of his eyes at my hysteria, he fluffed his pillow and then hugged it to him. It was such a human gesture, it was uncanny. Who knew vampires cared if their pillows were fluffed?

"Gave you a few drops of my blood. Figured you wouldn't need much, what with your being a half-breed. You probably heal fast naturally, but then you were banged up a bit. Your own fault, of course, having suggested that stupid match. Now, if you don't mind, it's daylight and I'm knackered. Didn't even get a meal out of all this."

"Vampire blood *heals*?"

He shut his eyes as he answered me. "You mean you didn't know? Blimey, but you're ignorant about your own kind."

"Your kind is not my kind."

He didn't even flinch. "Whatever you say, Kitten."

"Would too much blood turn me? How much is too much?"

That got an eye opened balefully at me. "Look, school's out now, luv. I'm going to sleep. You're going to shut up. Later, when I'm awake, we'll go over all of these niceties while I prepare you for our arrangement. Until then, let a fellow get some rest."

"Show me the way out and you can sleep all you want." Again I looked around for an exit, finding nothing.

He snorted in derision. "Sure thing. Hows about I fetch your weapons for you as well, then I'll just close my eyes while you plug holes into my heart? Not bloody likely. You're in until I let you out. Don't bother trying to escape, you'd never make it. Now I suggest you get some rest, because if you keep me awake much longer, I'm going to want breakfast. Understand?" He closed his eyes again with finality.

"I'm not sleeping with you." Indignation filled my tone.

There was a brief tussling on the bed, and then a sheet hit me in the face.

"Sleep on the floor, then. You're a cover hog anyhow."

Left with no other alternative, I lay down on the cold stone ground. The sheet didn't do much to keep out the chill, let alone provide any padding. I maneuvered around, hopelessly trying to find a softer spot before giving up and cradling my head on my arms. At least this was better than being in bed with that thing. I'd sooner sleep on nails. The silence of the room was somehow soothing. One thing was for certain, vampires didn't snore. After a while, I drifted off.

It could have been hours, it seemed like minutes. A hand none too gently shook my shoulders and that dreaded voice sounded in my ears.

"Rise and shine. We have work to do."

My bones gave an audible creak of misery when I stood and stretched. He grinned at the sound.

"Serves you right for trying to kill me. Last bloke who did that ended up with much more than a stiff neck. You're right lucky you're useful, or you'd be nothing more than a flush in my cheeks by now."

"Yeah, that's me. Lucky." I felt bitter instead, trapped in a cave with a homicidal vampire.

He wagged a finger at me. "Don't be glum. You're about to get a first-class education in nosferatu. Believe me, not many humans get to learn this stuff. But then again, you're not really human."

"Stop saying that. I'm more human than I am . . . thing."

"Yes, well, we'll find out just how much shortly. Move away from the wall."

I complied, not having much choice in this small room and not wanting to be close to him. He stood in front of the stone wall where I'd been sleeping and grasped either side of the rock. With ease, he lifted the slab completely off the ground and set it to the side, exposing a crevice big enough to walk through. So that was how we entered this tomb.

"Come along," he threw over his shoulder, stepping through it. "Don't dawdle."

As I squeezed through the narrow opening, a sudden twist of my bladder reminded me that I was still very much dependent on my organs.

"Um . . . er, I don't suppose . . ." To hell with the niceties. "Is there a bathroom in here? One of us still has functioning kidneys."

He stopped short, arching an eyebrow at me. There were thin streams of light coming from the limestone ceiling, making crisscrossed patterns of illumination throughout the cave. Daytime, then.

"Do you think this is a bloomin' hotel? What, next you'll be wanting a bidet?"

With infuriated embarrassment, I ground out, "Unless you like it messy, I suggest you show me an alternative, and fast."

A noise that sounded very much like a sigh came from him. "Follow me. Don't trip or twist anything, damned if I'll carry you. Let's see what we can come up with. Sodding woman."

As I clambered after him, I comforted myself with mental images of him writhing helplessly under my stake. The visual was so clear, I almost smiled as he led me toward the sounds of water.

"There." He pointed to a cluster of rocks that appeared to hang over a small inner stream. "That water runs downstream. You can climb on those rocks and do your business."

I hurried over, and he called out with an edge to his tone, "By the way, if you're thinking you'll just jump off and swim out of here, it's a bad idea. That water's about forty degrees and snakes over two miles before it exits these caves. You'd be suffering from hypothermia long before then. Not a nice way to be, shivering and lost in the dark, delusions setting in. Besides, you'd have broken our agreement. I'd find you. And I would be really, really displeased."

The grim note in his voice made the words sound more lethal than the cocking of a gun. Despair pricked me. I *had* been thinking of doing that.

"See you in a bit." He turned around and walked a short ways away, his back to me. Sighing, I climbed up the rocks and balanced while answering nature's untimely call.

"I suppose toilet paper's out of the question?" I called out flippantly.

There was a bark of laughter in reply. "I'll put it on my shopping list, Kitten."

"Stop calling me Kitten. My name is Cat." Finished, I

lowered myself down until I again stood on somewhat
solid ground. "What's yours, by the way? You never told
me. If we're going to be . . . working together, at least I
should know what to call you. Unless you simply prefer
answering to profanity, of course."

There was that sly curl to his lips again when he faced
me. His feet were planted apart and his hips tilted slightly
forward. Pale hair hugged his head in tight waves. Under
the pinholes of light around him, his skin positively
glowed.

"My name is Bones."

"First things first, luv. If you're going to be truly good at
killing vampires, you need to know more about them."

We sat on boulders facing each other. The dim light in
the cave from the shafts of sun had a vague strobe effect. It
had to be by far the strangest moment of my life, sitting
across from a vampire calmly discussing the best ways to
kill one.

"Sunlight doesn't do anything but give us a bad sun-
burn. Our skin won't explode in flames like it does in the
movies, and we won't turn into bits of crispy chicken.
However, we do like to sleep in the day because we are
most powerful at night. That's an important point to remember. During the day we are slower, weaker, and less
alert. *Especially* at dawn. By dawn, you'll find most vampires tucked into whatever they call a bed, which as you
could tell from last night doesn't necessarily mean a coffin. Oh, some of the old-fashioned ones will only sleep in
coffins, but most of us sleep in whatever's most comfortable. In fact, some vamps will have coffins staged in their
lair so some Van Helsing wannabe goes there first while
the vampire sneaks up on them. Done that trick a time or
two myself. So if you think throwing up the blinds and letting the sun stream in will do the trick, forget it.

"Crosses. Unless they're rigged up like yours, crosses don't do much more than make us laugh before we eat you. You seem to know that one yourself, so we'll move on. Wood, as you are also aware, might give us splinters and piss us off, but won't stop us from ripping your throat out. Holy water . . . well, let's just say I've had more damage done to me by someone throwing dirt in my face. The whole religious thing is bunk when it comes to hurting our kind, got it? Your only advantage is that when a vampire sees that special stake of yours, they won't be put off."

"Aren't you afraid I'll use this information against you?" I interrupted. "I mean, why should you trust me?"

In all seriousness he leaned forward. I leaned back, not wanting to be any closer to him.

"Look, pet. You and I are going to have to trust one another to accomplish our objectives. And I'll make this very, very simple: If you so much as look cross-eyed at me and I even *wonder* if you're thinking about betraying me, I'll kill you. Now, that might not scare you, being the big brave girl you are, but remember this: I followed you home the other night. Got anyone you care about in that barn of a house? Because if you do, then I suggest you make nice with me and do as you're told. If you cross me, you'll live long enough to see that house burned to the ground with everyone still inside. So if you ever make a go for me, you'd better be sure you finish me, understand?"

Gulping, I nodded. I understood. Oh God, did I ever.

"Besides"—his voice brightened like a spring day—"I can give you what you want."

Doubtful. "What could you possibly know about what I want?"

"You want what every abandoned child wants. You want to find your father. But you don't want a happy reunion, no, not you. You want to kill him."

I stared at him. He'd spoken aloud what I hadn't even

allowed my subconscious to whisper, and he was right. It was the other reason I hunted vampires, to kill the one who fathered me. More than anything, I wanted to do that for my mother. If I could, I would feel I had in some small way atoned for the circumstances of my birth.

"You . . ." I could barely speak with all the thoughts flying through my mind. "You can help me find him? How?"

A shrug. "For starters, I might know him. Know a great many undead types, I do. Face it—without me, you're looking for a needle in a fangstack. Even if I don't personally know him, I already know more about him than you do."

"What? How? What?"

He held up a hand to stop my babbling. "Like his age, for example. You're twenty-one, right?"

"Twenty-two," I whispered, still reeling. "Last month."

"Indeed? Then you have the wrong age as well as the wrong address on that fake license of yours."

He must have gone through my purse. Well, it made sense; he'd also stripped me when I was unconscious. "How do *you* know it's a fake?"

"Didn't we just cover this? I know your real address, and it's not the one on that license."

Oh crap. That defeated the purpose of why I'd gotten the phony ID to begin with, in case I ever lost against a vampire and he rifled through my things. I hadn't wanted one to be able to track down my family. That had been the thought, anyway. Stupid me never expected a vampire to follow me home.

"Come to think of it, pet, you are a liar, possessor of false identification, and a murderer."

"Your point?" I snapped.

"Not to mention a tease," he continued as if I hadn't spoken. "Foulmouthed, as well. Yep, you and I will get along famously."

"Bollocks," I said succinctly.

He grinned back at me. "Imitation is the sincerest form of flattery. But back to the subject. You said your mum carried you for, what, four months? Five?"

"Five. Why?" I was more than a little curious as to his reasoning. What did that have to do with how old, or how undead, my father was?

He leaned forward. "See, it's like this. When you're changed, it takes a few days for some of the human functions to cease completely. Oh, the heartbeat stops right off and the breathing as well, but some of the other things take longer. Tear ducts still work normally for the first day or so before you cry only pink due to the blood-to-water ratio in our bodies. You might even piss once or twice to get it out of your system. But the main point is that he still had swimmers in his sacks."

"Ex*cuse* me?"

"You know, luv. *Sperm*, if you want to be all technical about it. He still had living sperm in his juice. Now, that's something which would only be possible if he'd been newly changed. Within a week at most. Right off, then, you can pinpoint almost exactly how old he is, in vampire years. Add that to any recent deaths around that time and place matching his description, and bingo! There's your dad."

I was stunned. Just as promised, in a few seconds he'd given me more information than my mother had known all of my life. Maybe, just maybe, I'd stumbled onto a gold mine. If through him I could learn more about my father *and* killing vampires, and all he wanted in return was to pick the targets . . . well, then, I could stomach it. If I lived long enough.

"Why do you want to help me find my father? In fact, why do you kill other vampires? They're your own kind, after all."

Bones stared at me for a moment before replying. "I'll help you find your father because I reckon you hate him more than you do me, so it'll keep you motivated to do what I say. As for why I hunt vampires . . . you don't need to bother about that now. You have more than enough to concern yourself with. Suffice it to say some people just need killing, and that goes for vampires as well as humans."

I still didn't know why he wanted me to work with him in the first place. Then again, maybe it was all a lie and he was biding his time, intending to rip my throat out when I least suspected it. I didn't trust this creature, not for a moment, but right now I had no choice but to play along. Find out where this led to. If I was still alive in a week, I'd be amazed.

"Back to the subject at hand, luv. Guns don't work on us, either. There are only two exceptions to that rule. One, if the bloke is lucky enough to shoot our necks in two and our heads topple off. Decapitation *does* work; not many things can live without a head, and a head is the only part on a vampire that won't grow back if you cut it off. Two, if the gun has silver bullets and enough are fired into the heart to destroy it. Now, that's not as easy as it sounds. No vampire will stand still and pose for you. Likely he'll be on you and the gun shoved up your arse before any real damage is done. But those silver bullets hurt, so you can use them to slow a vamp down and then stake him. And you'd better be quick with that silver, because you'll have one very brassed-off vampire on your hands. Strangulation, drowning, none of that does anything. We only breathe about once an hour for preference, and we can go indefinitely without oxygen. Just a breath now and then to put a dab of oxygen in the blood and we're sound as a pound. Our version of hyperventilating is to breathe once every few minutes. That's one way to tell a vamp is tiring. He'll start to breathe a bit to perk up. Electrocution, poisonous gas, ingestible poisons, drugs . . . none of those work. Got it? Now you know our weaknesses."

"Are you sure we can't test some of those theories?"

He wagged a finger at me reprovingly. "None of that, now. You and I are partners, remember? If you start to forget that, maybe you'd best remember the things I just mentioned would work really well on you."

"It was a joke," I lied.

He just gave me a look that said he knew better. "The bottom line is that we are very hard to put down. How *you've* managed to plant sixteen of us in the ground is beyond me, but then the world never lacks for fools."

"Hey." Piqued, I defended my skills. "I would have had you in pieces if you hadn't made me drive and then sucker-punched me when I wasn't looking."

He laughed again. It transformed his face into something I just realized was very beautiful. I looked away, not wanting to see him as anything but a monster. A dangerous monster.

"Kitten, why do you think I made you drive? I had you pegged five seconds after speaking with you. You were a novice, green to the gills and, once off your routine, helpless as a babe. Of course I sucker-punched you. There is only one way to fight, and that's dirty. Clean, gentlemanly fighting will get you nowhere but dead, and fast. Take every cheap shot, every low blow, *absolutely* kick people when they're down, and then maybe you'll be the one who walks away. Remember that. You're in a fight to the death. This isn't a boxing match. You can't win by scoring the most points."

"I get it." Grimly enough, I did. In this he was correct. It was a death match every time I confronted a vampire. Including this one.

"But now we're off topic. We've covered our weaknesses. On to our strengths, and we have many. Speed, vision, hearing, smell, physical strength—all are superior to a human's. We can scent you long before we see you, and we can hear your heartbeat a mile away. In addition to that, all of us have some form of mind control over humans. A vampire can suck a pint of your blood and seconds later you won't even remember seeing one. It's in our fangs, a little bitty drop of hallucinogen that, when combined with our power, makes you susceptible to suggestion. Like, for example, someone didn't just suck on your neck but you met a bloke and had a chat and now you're sleepy. That's how most of us feed. A little dab here and a little dab there, and none the wiser for it. If every vampire killed to eat, we'd have been outed from our closet centuries ago."

"You can control my mind?" The thought horrified me.

His brown eyes suddenly bled to green and his gaze drilled into mine.

"*Come to me*," he whispered, yet the words seemed to resound in my head.

"No fucking way," I said, chilled at the sudden urge I had to do it.

Abruptly, his eyes were brown again and he threw a cheery grin my way.

"Nope, appears not. Good on you, that'll come in handy. Can't have you getting all weak-minded and forgetting your goals, can we? Probably it's your bloodline. It doesn't work on other vampires. Or humans who imbibe of vampire blood. Guess you have enough of us in you. Some humans are immune to it also, but only a very small percentage. Have to have extraordinary mind control or natural resistance not to let us in and meddle about. MTV and video games have solved that problem as far as most of humanity goes. That, and telly, as it were."

"Telly?" Who was that?

He grunted in amusement. "Television, of course. Don't you speak English?"

"You sure don't," I muttered.

Shaking his head, he frowned at me. "Daylight's burning, luv. We have a lot to cover. We've gone through the senses and the mind control, but don't forget our strength. Or our teeth. Vampires are strong enough to break you in half and carry the pieces with a finger. We can throw your car at you if we want to. And we'll rip you apart with our teeth. The question is, how many of our strengths do you have in you?"

Hesitatingly, I began to tick off my abnormalities.

"I can see very well and darkness doesn't affect me. I see as well at night as in the day. I'm faster than anyone I know, humanly speaking. I can hear things from far away, maybe not as far as you can. Sometimes in my room at night I could hear my grandparents downstairs whispering to each other about me. . . ."

I stopped, judging from his look that I'd revealed too much about personal issues.

"I don't think I can control anyone's mind. I've never tried it, but I think if I could, people would have treated me differently." Dammit, there I was opening up again.

"Anyways," I went on, "I know I'm stronger than the average person. When I was fourteen, I beat up three boys, and they were all bigger than me. That was when I couldn't hide anymore from the fact that something was very wrong with me. You've seen my eyes. They're different. I have to control them when I'm upset so other people don't see them glow. My teeth are normal, I guess. They've never poked out funny, anyhow."

I glanced at him through lowered lashes. I'd never spoken of my differences to anyone like this before, even my mother. It upset her to know about them, let alone discuss them.

"Let me get this straight. You said at fourteen you truly realized your uniqueness. You didn't know what you were before? What did your mum tell you about your father when you were growing up?"

That was a very painful subject, and I felt a shudder go through me at the memory. A vampire was hardly the person I ever thought I'd be talking to about this.

"She never mentioned my father. If I'd ask, as I did when I was little, she'd change the subject or get angry. But the other children let me know. They called me a bastard from the time they could speak." I closed my eyes briefly, the shame still stinging. "Like I said, when I hit puberty I started to feel . . . even more different. So much worse than when I was a child. It got harder to hide my weirdness, like my mom told me to. I liked the night most. I'd wander for hours in the orchard. Sometimes I wouldn't even sleep until dawn. But it wasn't until those boys cornered me that I knew how bad it was."

"What did they do?" His voice was softer, almost gentle.

In my mind I could see their faces as clearly as if they stood before me.

"They were shoving me around again. Pushing me, calling me names, the usual stuff. That didn't set me off. It happened almost every day. But then one of them, I can't remember which, called my mother a slut, and I lost my temper. I threw a rock at him and busted his teeth out. The others jumped me, and I beat them. They never told anyone what happened. Finally, on my sixteenth birthday, my mother decided I was old enough to know the truth about my father. I didn't want to believe her, but deep down, I knew it was true. That was the first night I saw my eyes glow. She held a mirror up to my face after stabbing me in the leg. She wasn't being mean. She wanted me upset so I could see my eyes. About six months later, I killed my first vampire."

My eyes stung with unshed tears, but I wouldn't cry. *Could* not cry in front of this thing who had made me retell what I'd tried to forget.

He stared at me in a very peculiar way. If I didn't know

better, I would say there was empathy in his gaze. But that was impossible. He was a vampire, they didn't do compassion.

Abruptly I stood. "Speaking of my mother, I have to call her. She'll be worried sick. I've come home late before, but I've never been out this long. She'll think one of you blood-suckers killed me."

That caused his eyebrows to fly into his hairline. "Your mum knows you've been luring vampires with promises of shagging and then killing them? And she allows you to do this? Blimey, I thought you were joking when you said she knew you were putting a dent in our population. If you were *my* child, I'd have you nailed inside your room at night. Don't understand people nowadays, let their kids do anything."

"Don't speak about her that way!" I burst out. "She knows I'm doing the right thing! Why wouldn't she support that?"

His eyes bored into mine very steadily, clear dark pools of brown. Then he shrugged. "Whatever you say."

Suddenly he stood in front of me. I hadn't even had time to blink, he was so fast.

"You've got good aim when you throw things. Found that out last night when you chucked your cross at me. Just think, a few inches lower and you might have been planting daisies over my head by now." He grinned as if amused at the mental image. "We'll work to improve your speed and accuracy. You'll be safer if you can kill from a distance. You're too bloody vulnerable up close."

He grasped me by the upper arms. I tried to pull away, but he held on. Iron bars would have had more give.

"Your strength leaves much to be desired. You're stronger than a human man, but probably as weak as the weakest vampire. We'll have to work on that as well. Also, your flexibility is shit and you don't use your legs at all when you fight. They're valuable weapons and should be treated as such. As for your speed, well . . . that might be hopeless. But we'll give it a go anyhow. The way I figure it, we have about six weeks before we can get you out in the field. Yep, five weeks of hard training, and one week to work on your looks."

"My looks?" Outrage filled my voice. How dare a dead man critique me? "What's wrong with my looks?"

Bones smiled condescendingly. "Oh, nothing *horribly* wrong, but still something that needs fixing before we send you out."

"You—"

"After all, we're going after some big fish, luv. Baggy jeans and a mediocre appearance won't cut it. You wouldn't know sexy if it bit you in the arse."

"By God, I am going to—"

"Quit blathering. Didn't you want to call your mum? Come with me. My cell phone's in the back."

Mentally I performed all sorts of tortuous acts on his bound and helpless body, but in reality I bit my tongue and followed him deeper into the cave.

FOUR

HARD TRAINING. THOSE WERE THE WORDS HE used to describe the brutal, agonizing, death-defying ordeals even the military wouldn't inflict on their most hardened troops.

Bones ran me through the forest at speeds cars couldn't sustain. I stumbled over fallen trees, rocks, roots, and natural potholes until I was too exhausted to even vomit. Passing out didn't excuse me from my tasks, either. He'd simply keep dousing icy water on my face until I came to again. I practiced throwing knives until my knuckles cracked and bled. His response? To uncaringly toss me some Neosporin and tell me not to get it on my palms or it would ruin my grip. His version of weight lifting? Hefting stone boulders repeatedly, gradually increasing their size and density. StairMaster? That would be climbing up the cave inclines with large rocks strapped to my back.

After one week, I threw off all of his artificial impediments and refused to go farther, stating had I known his intentions beforehand I would have gladly chosen death.

Bones just smiled at me with his fangs extended and told me to prove it. Seeing that he was serious, I reapplied my outfittings and trudged wearily onward.

By far, though, the most grueling activity was up close with him. He stretched my limbs until tears poured down my face, chiding me all the while for my lack of flexibility. Then, during our hand-to-hand combat, he'd knock me into a state of unconsciousness that all the icy water in the world couldn't revive. I would wake up with the taste of his blood in my mouth, just to repeat the procedure all over again. To say I fantasized about killing him every second of every day was an understatement. Yet I got better, I had no choice. With Bones, it was either improve or die.

My first indication of increased stamina came after my second week of training. Bones and I fought and I actually didn't pass out. He still beat me soundly, but I remained conscious throughout. It was a mixed blessing. I had my dignity from not going night-night in the middle of our battle, but then was awake when he fed me his blood.

"Disgusting," I spat after being cajoled and then threatened into putting his bloody finger in my mouth. "How can you things live off that?"

The words left my lips without forethought, as had many before them.

"Necessity is the mother of all appetites. What you need in order to survive, you learn to love," he replied shortly.

"All this blood better not turn me into a vampire. That was *not* our deal."

I felt uncomfortable arguing with his finger jammed in my mouth, and I moved my head backward until it slid wetly out. It was almost a sexual gesture. I blushed as soon as the thought flitted through my mind. He caught the flush, of course. No doubt the reason behind it as well, but just wiped his hand on his shirt.

"Trust me, luv, you aren't having nearly enough blood to

turn you into a vampire. Since you fret about it all the time, however, I'll tell you how it works. First, I'd have to drain you to the very point of death. There's a trick to that, taking enough blood without taking too much. Then, stuffed full of your blood, I'd open my artery for you and let you drink it right back out of me. All of it, and then some. There's a trick to that, too. You have to be strong to make other vampires, or your would-be protégée sucks you dry and kills you while he or she is changing. New vampires are harder to get off an artery than a starving babe off a juicy teat. These measly drops of blood I'm feeding you aren't doing more than healing your injuries. They're probably not even enough to enhance your strength. Now, will you stop griping every time you have to lick a few bits off my pieces?"

That *really* caused me to color at the visual that skipped across my subconscious. Seeing it, he ran an aggravated hand through his hair.

"Now, that's another thing you have to stop doing. You turn red as a sunset at the slightest hint of innuendo. You need to be playing the part of an aggressive, *horny* woman! No bloke's going to believe that when he says boo and you faint from embarrassment. Your virginity's going to get you killed."

"I'm not a virgin," I countered, and then nearly did faint as predicted.

His dark brows went up. I turned away, sputtering, "Can we change the subject, please? We're not girlfriends at a slumber party. I don't want to be discussing this with you."

"Well, well, *well*," he drawled, ignoring my plea. "Kitten's catted around, has she? The way you act, I'm surprised. Chap waiting patiently for you to finish your training? Must be quite a lad, to get you all hot and bothered. Again, didn't peg you for the experienced type, but then again, you did offer me a taste when we first met.

Makes me wonder now if you planned on staking me before or *after* you got your itch scratched. What about the other vampires? Did they die with a smile on their—"

I slapped him. Or tried to. He caught my wrist and held it, and caught the other one when I whipped my left palm toward his cheek.

"Don't you dare talk to me that way, I've heard enough of that crap growing up. Just because my mother had me out of wedlock, our stupid old-fashioned neighbors thought that made her a slut, and me, too, by default. And not that it's any of your business, since you've probably raped villages full of women, but I've only been with one person. He dropped me like a bad habit right afterwards, so that was enough to cure me of any desire I had to duplicate the sexual escapades of my peers. Now, I mean it, I don't want to talk about this again!"

I was panting in pent-up fury over the wound he'd unknowingly ripped open. Bones released my wrists, and I rubbed them where his fingers had dug into my skin.

"Kitten," he began in a conciliatory tone, "I apologize. But just because your ignorant neighbors took their prejudice out on you, or some pimply-faced teenager pulled a one-nighter—"

"Stop it," I interrupted, terrified I was going to cry. "Just stop it. I can do the job, I can fake sexy, whatever. But we are not discussing this."

"Look, luv—" he tried again.

"Bite me," I snapped, and walked off.

For once, he didn't offer to take me up on the invitation, and he didn't follow me.

At the start of the fourth week, Bones announced we were taking a field trip. Of course, it wasn't an afternoon jaunt to the local museum. No, he had me driving along a narrow road at midnight with no idea where we were headed. He'd

given me the barest direction—turn here, turn there, etc.—
and I was nervous. We were in a very rural area, no streetlights along the road. If you wanted to suck someone's neck
dry and then dump the body, this would be an ideal place.

Then again, if he'd wanted to suck my neck dry and
dump my body, the cave was a pretty ideal place as well.
Considering all the times I'd been unconscious after our
training bouts, he could have dined on me before if he'd
wanted to. I wouldn't have been able to stop him. Hell, I
wouldn't have been able to stop him when I was awake. I
had yet to win a single round between us, to my dismay.
Bones was so damned strong and fast, fighting against him
was like trying to put a leash on a lightning bolt.

"Turn left here," Bones said, jarring me from my
thoughts.

I read the name on the sign. Peach Tree Road. It didn't
look like it led anywhere.

"You know, *partner*," I said as I made the turn, "you're
being very secretive. When are you going to tell me what
this field trip is about? I take it you didn't just get a sudden
urge to go cow tipping."

He snorted. "No, can't say that I did. I need some information from a man who lives out here."

The way he said it made it sound like the person wouldn't
be happy to see him. "Look, I refuse to be a part of killing
any humans, so if you think you're going to interrogate
this guy and then bury him, you're wrong."

I expected Bones to challenge me or get angry, but he
started to laugh.

"I'm serious!" I said, stomping on the brakes for emphasis.

"You'll get the joke soon enough, luv," he replied. "But
let me set your mind at ease. For one, I promise not to lay
a single hand on the fellow, and for another, you'll be the
one talking to him."

That surprised me. I didn't even know who the guy was, let alone what questions to ask.

An eyebrow arched at me. "Will we be driving again anytime soon?"

Oh. I let off the brake and hit the gas, jolting the truck forward. "Do I get any more details than that? Like, some background on him and what you want to know?"

"Of course. Winston Gallagher was a railway worker back in the sixties. He also had a side business of making moonshine. One day, a fellow bought one of Winston's products and then was found dead with it the next day. Winston might have mistaken the alcohol content for that batch, or the sot drank too much. Either way, it all ended the same. Winston was found guilty of murder and condemned to die."

"That's outrageous!" I exclaimed. "With no motive or proof of malice aforethought?"

"'Fraid the judge, John Simms, wasn't big on the idea of innocent until proven guilty. He also doubled as the executioner. Right before Simms hanged him, however, Winston swore he'd never let him have another night's peace. And since that day, he never has."

"He hung him?" I repeated. "The man you want me to speak to?"

"Pull over at that NO TRESPASSING sign, Kitten," Bones directed. I did, my mouth still open in disbelief. "Winston won't speak to me, since our kinds don't get along. He'll talk to you, though. But I warn you, he's about as cheerful as you currently are."

"What part of this am I not understanding?" My tone was waspish. Bitchy, me? "Did you or did you not say that judge hanged him?"

"Swung him right from the tree jutting over that cliff," Bones affirmed. "If you look, you can still see rope marks in it. A good many people lost their lives on that wood, but don't bother speaking to any one of them. They're residual. Winston's not."

I picked my words carefully. "Are you telling me Winston's . . . a ghost?"

"Ghost, specter, phantom, take your pick. What's most important is he's sentient, and that's rare. Most spooks are only replays of their former selves. Not able to interact, just doing the same thing over and over, like a record stuck on a turntable. Blimey, I'm dating myself; no one uses records anymore. Point is, Winston was so mad when he died, part of his consciousness stayed on. It's also due to location. Ohio has a thinner membrane for separating the natural from the supernatural, so it's easier for a soul to stay behind instead of crossing over. This particular area's like a homing beacon. Five cemeteries forming a pentagram—really, what were they thinking? It's a road map for spirits, is what it is. Thanks to your bloodline, you should be able to see them, whereas most humans can't. You should also be able to feel them by now. Their energy's like a voltage in the air."

He was right. I'd felt an invisible hum as soon as I'd turned onto this road, but I thought maybe my leg had fallen asleep or something.

"What kind of information could a vampire possibly want from a ghost?"

"Names," Bones said succinctly. "I want Winston to give you the names of any young girls that have recently died around these parts. Don't let him tell you he doesn't know, either—and I'm only interested in deaths by unnatural causes. No car accidents or diseases."

He didn't look like he was kidding, but I had to ask. "Is this some kind of a joke?"

Bones made a noise that was almost a sigh. "I wish it were, but it isn't."

"You're serious? You want me to go to a cemetery and ask a *ghost* about dead girls?"

"Come, now, Kitten, is it really so hard for you to believe in ghosts? You're half vampire, after all. I wouldn't think ghosts would be such a stretch of your imagination."

Put like that, he had a very good point. "And ghosts don't like vampires, so I guess I shouldn't mention my mixed lineage. Do I get to know why ghosts don't like vampires, by the way?"

"They're jealous, since we're as dead as they are, but we can do as we please while they're forever stuck as a hazy apparition. Makes them right cranky most of the time, which reminds me . . ." Bones handed me a bottle of something clear. "Take this. You'll need it."

I held it up and swished the liquid around. "What is it? Holy water?"

He laughed. "For Winston it is. That's white lightning. Pure moonshine, luv. Simms Cemetery is right past that line of trees, and you might have to bang about a bit to get Winston's attention. Ghosts tend to nap frequently, but once you've got him up, be sure to show him that bottle. He'll tell you whatever you want to know."

"Let me get this straight. You want me to go stomping through a graveyard brandishing a bottle of booze to rouse an unrestful spirit so that I can interrogate him?"

"That's it. And don't forget this. Pen and paper. Make sure to write down the names and ages of every girl Winston tells you about. If he can include how they died as well, so much the better."

"I should refuse," I muttered. "Because interrogating a ghost was *not* part of our agreement."

"If I'm right, this information will lead to a group of vampires, and hunting vampires *is* part of our agreement, isn't it?"

I just shook my head as Bones gave me the pen, a small spiral notepad, and the bottle of illegal liquor. A vampire was having me go out and wake the dead. Guess it proved

I wasn't psychic, because if someone had told me four weeks ago that I'd be doing this, I would never have believed it.

Simms Cemetery at midnight wasn't a soothing place. It had been hidden from the road by thick bushes, trees, and that rocky cliff. True to Bones's description, a tree still protruded over the precipice, and there was also a large evergreen in the midst of the dilapidated headstones. Seeing some of the dates clarified his earlier comment about Winston being a railway worker in the sixties. He'd meant the 1860s. Not this past century.

A figure behind me made me whirl with a little scream, my hand whipping out a knife.

"Are you all right?" Bones immediately called out. He was waiting out of sight beyond the cemetery, with the explanation that this way none of the *dead* dead would see him. The thought of vampires and ghosts not getting along was just too weird. Even in the afterlife, different species still couldn't play nice?

"Yeah . . ." I said after a beat. "It was nothing."

It wasn't, in fact, but it didn't require help. A hooded, shadowy form swept past me, literally floating over the cold earth. It went to the edge of the cliff and then disappeared with a faint sound, like a whispered scream. I watched in fascination as moments later it returned out of nowhere and walked the same path, culminating with another ghostly wail.

To my left, the indistinct outline of a woman was bent over another headstone, sobbing. Her clothing wasn't of this era, from the hazy glimpses I could catch of it, and then she, too, faded into nothingness. For a few minutes I waited, and then her outline blurred into view again. Soft, almost inaudible cries came from her until they, and she too, vanished once more.

A record stuck on a turntable, I thought with dark appreciation. Yeah, Bones had given a pretty accurate description of it.

In the corner of the cemetery, there was a headstone with barely visible etched letters, but I saw a W and a T in the first name, while the last one started with a G.

"Winston Gallagher!" I called loudly, rapping on the frigid stone for emphasis. "Come on out!"

Nothing. A breeze made me tighten my jacket while I shuffled my feet and waited.

"Knock, knock, who's there?" I said next, driven to absurdity by what I was doing.

Something moved at the edge of the trees behind me. Not the cloaked phantom, who was still traveling the same unaltered path, but almost a fuzzy shadow. Maybe it was just the bushes rustling in the wind. I returned my attention to the grave at my feet.

"Oh, Winsssttonnnnn . . ." I cooed, fingering the bottle inside my jacket. "I've got something for youuuu!"

"Cursed, insolent warm baggage," a voice slithered on the air. "Let's see how fast she can run."

I stiffened. That didn't sound like any person I'd heard before! The air in my vicinity got colder all at once even as I turned toward that voice. The shadow I'd previously observed stretched and changed, taking form, revealing a male in his fifties with a barrellike belly, squinting eyes, brown hair overrun with gray, and untrimmed whiskers.

"Hear that, do you?" Another odd keening came out of him, eerily echoing. He shimmered for a second, and then the leaves near where he hovered scattered in a burst of concentrated air.

"Winston Gallagher?" I asked.

The ghost actually looked over his shoulder, as if expecting to see someone behind him.

I put more stress into it. "*Well?*"

"She can't see me . . ." he said, presumably to himself.

"The hell I can't!" I marched over in relief, anxious to get out of this creepy place. "Is that your headstone? If the answer's yes, then tonight's your lucky night."

Those squinty eyes narrowed further. "You can see me?"

Was he this thick when he was alive? I wondered irreverently. "Yeah, I see dead people. Who knew? Now let's talk. I'm looking for some newly deceaseds, and I heard you could help."

It was almost funny to watch those transparent features change from incredulity to belligerence. He didn't have facial muscles anymore, needless to say. Was it just the memory of them that made his scowl form?

"Get out of here or else the grave will swallow you and *you'll never leave!*"

Boy, did he make it sound intimidating. If he had anything to threaten me with, I'd have been concerned.

"I'm not afraid of the grave; I was born half in it. But if you want me to get out of here"—I turned as if to go—"fine, but that means I'll just have to throw this in the nearest trash can."

Out of my jacket came the clear bottle with the lightning bolt. I almost laughed when his eyes fastened on it as though they were magically welded. This had to be Winston, all right.

"Whattt'ssss that you've got there, mistress?"

He drew the first word out in a lustful hiss. I popped the cork, waving it under where his nose appeared to be.

"Moonshine, my friend."

I was still uncertain how Bones thought I was supposed to bribe him with this. Pour some on his grave? Hold the bottle inside his disembodied form? Or splash him with it?

Winston made another keening noise that would have chilled anyone near enough to hear it.

"Please, mistress!" Gone was his hostile tone, replaced instead with one of desperation. "Please, drink it. Drink it!"

"Me?" I gaped. "I don't want any!"

"Oh, let me taste it through you, please!" he begged.

Taste it through me. Now I knew why Bones hadn't mentioned how to entice Winston before. That's what I got for trusting a vampire even in the littlest thing! I gave the ghost an irritable look while promising myself revenge on a certain pale-skinned, room-temperature creature of the night.

"Fine. I'll drink some, but then you're going to give me names of young girls who've died around here. No car accidents or diseases, either. Murders only."

"Read the paper, mistress, why do you need me for that?" he barked. "Now drink the 'shine!"

I was so not in the mood to be pushed around by another dead person. "Guess I've caught you on a bad night," I said pleasantly. "I'll just leave you alone and be on my way. . . ."

"Samantha King, seventeen years old, passed last night after being bled to death!" he trumpeted. "*Please!*"

I didn't even have to ask for him to specify a cause of death. He must want that liquor real bad. I wrote the specifics down on my notepad and then tipped the bottle to my mouth.

"Mother of God!" I choked moments later, hardly noticing Winston's entire form diving through my throat like he'd been shot from a gun. "Arghh! That tastes like kerosene!"

"Oh, the sweetness!" was his enraptured reply as he came out the other side of my neck. "Yessss! Give me *more*!"

I was still coughing, and my throat burned. Whether that was from the liquor or the ghost was anyone's guess.

"Another name," I managed to get out. "Then I'll have more."

Winston didn't need to be told twice any longer. "Violet Perkins, age twenty-two, died last Thursday of strangulation. Cried the whole way up."

He didn't sound particularly sad for her. A hand waved impatiently at me, its edges blurry. "Go on!"

One deep breath later and more moonshine went down the hatch. I coughed just as much as before, my eyes watering.

"Why would anyone pay for this swill?" I gasped when I came up for air. My throat was almost throbbing when Winston exited it and he floated back in front of me.

"Thought you'd taken my 'shine from me forever, didn't you, Simms?" Winston shouted at the passing hooded phantom. It didn't react. "Well, look who's drinking while you're condemned to eternally wander off that cliff! This nip's for you, old John! Carmen Johnson, twenty-seven, bled to death ten days ago. Drink, mistress! And this time, swallow like a woman, not like a gurgling babe!"

I regarded him with amazement. Out of all things, liquor seemed to be what he missed the most. "You're dead and you're still an alcoholic. That's so dysfunctional."

"A bargain's a bargain!" he belted. "Drink!"

"Prick," I muttered under my breath as I eyed the bottle unhappily. This stuff made gin taste like sugar water in comparison. *You're going to get Bones back for this*, I swore to myself. *And not just with a silver stake. That's too good for him.*

Twenty minutes later, my notepad had thirteen more names on it, the bottle was empty, and I was swaying on my feet. If I wasn't so dizzy, I'd have been amazed at all the girls who'd been murdered the past couple months. Hadn't the new governor just been bragging on TV about how the crime rate was way down? The names on my list sure seemed to indicate otherwise. Tell those poor girls the crime rate was down, I'd bet they'd all disagree.

Winston lay on the ground, his hands over his belly, and

when I let out an extended burp, he smiled as though it had relieved his diaphragm also.

"Ah, mistress, you're an angel. Sure there's not a drop left? I might have remembered one more person. . . ."

"Up yours," I said rudely with another belch. "It's empty. You should tell me the name anyway, after making me drink all that sewage."

Winston gave me a devious smile. "Come back with a full bottle and I will."

"Selfish spook," I mumbled, and staggered away.

I'd made it a few feet when I felt that distinct pins-and-needles sensation again, only this time it wasn't in my throat.

"Hey!"

I looked down in time to see Winston's grinning, transparent form fly out of my pants. He was chuckling even as I smacked at myself and hopped up and down furiously.

"Drunken filthy pig!" I spat. "Bastard!"

"And a good eve'in' to you, too, mistress!" he called out, his edges starting to blur and fade. "Come back soon!"

"I hope worms shit on your corpse!" was my reply. A ghost had just gotten to third base with me. Could I sink any lower?

Bones came out from behind the bushes about fifty yards away. "What happened, Kitten?"

"You! You tricked me! I never want to see you *or* that bottle of liquid arsenic again!"

And I chucked the empty moonshine jug at him. Or tried to. It missed him by a dozen feet.

He picked it up in astonishment. "You drank the whole bloody thing? You were only supposed to have a few sips!"

"Did you say that? Did you?" He reached me just as I felt the ground tip. "Didn't say anything. I've got those names, so that's all that matters, but you men . . . you're all alike.

Alive, dead, undead—all perverts! I had a drunken pervert in my pants! Do you know how un*san*itary that is?"

Bones held me upright. I would have protested, but I couldn't remember how to. "What are you saying?"

"Winston poltergeisted my panties, that's what!" I announced with a loud hiccup.

"Why, you scurvy, lecherous spook!" Bones yelled in the direction of the cemetery. "If my pipes still worked, I'd go right back there and piss on your grave!"

I thought I heard laughter. Or maybe it was just the wind.

"Forget it." I tugged on his jacket, leaning heavily. It was that or I was going to fall. "Who were those girls? You were right, most of them had been killed by vampires."

"I suspected as much."

"Do you know who did it?" I slurred. "Winston didn't. He just knew who they were and how they died."

"Don't ask me more about it, because I won't tell you, and before you even wonder, *no*, I had nothing to do with it."

The moonlight shining down made his skin even creamier. He was still staring off in the distance, and with his jaw clenched, he looked both fierce and very beautiful.

"You know what?" Suddenly, very inappropriately, I began to giggle. "You're pretty. You're *so* pretty."

Bones glanced back at me. "Bloody hell. You'll hate yourself in the morning for saying that. You must be absolutely pissed."

Another giggle. He was funny. "Not anymore."

"Right." He picked me up. The leaves made small crunching sounds under his feet as he carried me. "If you weren't half dead, what you just drank would kill you. Come on, pet. Let's get you home."

It had been a long time since I'd been in a man's arms. Sure, Bones might have carried me before when I was unconscious, but that didn't count. Now I was very aware of his hard chest against me, how effortlessly he held me, and how really *good* he smelled. It wasn't cologne—he never wore any. It was a clean scent that was uniquely his and it was . . . intoxicating.

"Do you think I'm pretty?" I heard myself ask.

Something I couldn't name flashed across his face.

"No. I don't think you're pretty. I think you're the most beautiful girl I've ever seen."

"Liar," I breathed. "He wouldn't have done that if I was. He wouldn't have been with *her*."

"Who?"

I ignored him, caught up in the memory. "Maybe he knew. Maybe on some deep, *deep* level, he could sense I was evil. I wish I hadn't been born this way. I wish I hadn't been born at all."

"You listen to me, Kitten," Bones cut me off. In my rant, I'd almost forgotten he was there. "I don't know who you're taking about, but you are *not* evil. Not one single cell of you. There is nothing wrong with you, and sod anyone who can't see that for themselves."

My head lolled on his arm. After a minute, my depression lifted, and I began to giggle again.

"Winston liked me. As long as I have moonshine, I've always got a date with a ghost!"

"I hate to inform you, luv, but you and Winston don't have a future together."

"Says who?" I laughed, noticing that the trees were tilted sideways. That was weird. And they seemed to be spinning as well.

Bones lifted my head up. I blinked. The trees were straight again! Then all I could see was his face as he leaned very close.

"I say."

He seemed like he was spinning also. Maybe everything was spinning. It felt that way.

"I'm drunk, aren't I?"

Since I'd never been drunk before, I needed clarification.

His snort tickled my face. "Impressively so."

"Don't you dare try to bite me," I said, noticing his mouth was only a few inches from my neck.

"Don't fret. That was the furthest thing from my mind."

The truck came into view. Bones carried me to the passenger side and deposited me on the seat. I slumped, tired all of a sudden.

His door shut, and then the engine vibrated to life. I kept shifting to get comfortable, but my truck didn't have an extended cab and the interior was cramped.

"Here," Bones said after several minutes, and pulled my head down to his lap.

"Pig!" I screamed, jerking up so fast, my cheek banged on the steering wheel.

He just laughed. "Isn't *your* mind in the gutter? You shouldn't be so quick to label Winston a drunken pervert. Pot calling the kettle black, if you ask me. I only had the most honorable of intentions, I assure you."

I eyed his lap and the extremely uncomfortable truck door, weighing my options. Then I flopped back down and put my head on his thigh, closing my eyes.

"Wake me when we get to my house."

FIVE

It WAS WEEK FIVE. I TRUDGED INTO THE CAVE, wishing Bones would just beat me unconscious again instead of what I knew was coming. My makeover, courtesy of a vampire.

He wasn't perched on his usual boulder. Maybe he was still sleeping. I was about ten minutes early. It didn't take as long this time to give my mother the latest in a long line of lies about where I was going. The first few weeks, I told her I'd taken a job waitressing, but with always being broke, I knew I had to get more inventive. At last I settled on telling her I'd signed up for an intensive exercise program people took to prepare for boot camp. She'd been aghast at the thought of me being exposed to the military, but I assured her that all I wanted was the training to help with my extracurricular activities. Very extracurricular activities, since killing vampires was on no college course I'd read about.

"Bones?" I called out, traveling further into the cave.

A whoosh of air came from above me. I pivoted on one

leg and struck out forcefully with the other, knocking my attacker to the side. Then I ducked in time to avoid the fist that shot toward my skull, and backflipped out of range from the next lightning punch.

"Very good!" The pleased voice belonged to my undead trainer.

I relaxed. "Testing me again, Bones? Where did you come from, anyway?"

"There," he replied, pointing up.

I followed his gesture and saw a small crevice in the rock about a hundred feet up. How in the world had he gotten up there?

"Like this," he answered my unspoken question, and propelled himself straight upward as though he'd been yanked on a string.

I was openmouthed. Five weeks and he'd never done anything like that before.

"Wow. Neat trick. Something new?"

"No, luv," he said as he plummeted down with grace. "Something old, like I am. Remember, just because a vampire isn't in front of you doesn't mean he's not right on top of you."

"Got it," I murmured. Five weeks ago I would have blushed like crazy. Now I didn't even blink at the possible innuendo.

"Now, then, let's move on to our final phase. Turning you into a seductress. Probably going to be our most difficult yet."

"Gee, thanks."

We reached what was the makeshift family room, which was rather normal-looking, if you didn't count the limestone and stalagmite walls. Bones pirated electricity from a nearby power link and rerouted it cleverly into the cave. Thus he had lamps, a computer, and a television plugged in by the sofa and chairs. He even had a space heater for when he tired of the cave's natural mid-fifties temperature. Hang a few paintings and add some decorative throw pillows, and it could be a subterranean feature in *House Beautiful*.

Bones grabbed his denim jacket and led me back toward the entrance of the cave.

"Come on. We're going to a salon, and I expect this will take a while."

"You can't be serious."

I looked with a mixture of revulsion and disbelief at my reflection in the full-length mirror Bones had propped up against the wall. Five hours at Hot Hair Salon had given me an exact understanding of what it was like to go through the washer and dryer. I'd been washed, waxed, plucked, snipped, blown dry, manicured, pedicured, sloughed, exfoliated, curled, primped, and then covered in shades of makeup. I hadn't even wanted to look at myself by the time Bones had returned to pick me up, and I'd refused to speak to him on the way back to the cave. Finally seeing the end result made me break my silence.

"There is no way I'm going out in public like this!"

It seemed while I was being tormented at the salon, Bones had been out shopping. I didn't ask where he got the money from, images of old folks with their necks bleeding and their wallets missing dancing in my head. There were boots, earrings, push-up bras, skirts, and something he swore to me were dresses but only looked like pieces of dresses. I was wearing one of those now, a bright green and silver number cut about four inches above my knees and *way* too low in the front. That, combined with my new leather boots, curled hair, and makeup, made me feel like a twenty-dollar whore.

"You look smashing." He grinned. "Can't hardly stop myself from ripping your clothes off."

"You think this is funny, don't you? This is all a big . . . *bloody* chuckle-fest to you!"

He sprang forward. "This isn't a joke, but it is a game. Winner takes all. You need every advantage you can get. If some poor undead fellow is busy looking at these"—he flipped the material of my dress outward to get a peek before I slapped his hand away—"then he won't be looking for this."

Something hard was pressed against my belly. I wrapped my hands around it and squared my shoulders.

"Is that a stake, Bones, or are you just happy with my new dress?"

He gave me a grin that was filled with more innuendo than an hour's worth of conversation.

"In this case, it's a stake. You could always feel around for something more, though. See what comes up."

"This better be part of that dirty-talk training, or we're going to give this new stake a go."

"Now, pet, that's hardly a romantic rejoinder. Concentrate! You do look great, by the way. That bra does wonders for your cleavage."

"Slime," I spat, resisting the urge to glance down and see for myself. Later, when he wasn't looking, I'd check it out.

"Moving on, Kitten. Put the stake in your boot. You'll find there's a loop for it."

I reached down and found a leather circle inside each boot. The stake fit snugly inside, concealed yet within easy reach. I'd wondered where I was supposed to hide a weapon in this skin-tight dress.

"Put your other one away as well," he instructed me. Complying, I was now outfitted as Cat, the Vampire-Killing Slut.

"That loop was a great idea, Bones."

The compliment flowed off my tongue, and I regretted it

at once. He didn't need praise. This wasn't a friendship, it was a business arrangement.

"Done it myself a time or two. Hmmm, still something not right, something missing. . . ."

He walked in a circle around me. I held still as he scrutinized my every angle. It was nerve-wracking, to say the least.

"I've got it!" he declared suddenly, snapping his fingers in triumph. "Take your knickers off."

"What?" Did that mean what I think it did?

"Your knickers. You know—panties, underwear, muff-huggers, nasty nets—"

"Are you out of your mind?" I interrupted. "This is where I draw the line! What does my *underwear* have to do with anything? I am not flashing my . . . my crotch at someone, no matter what you say!"

He spread his hands toward me in a conciliatory way. "Look, you don't have to flash anyone anything. Believe me, a vampire will know right off without you showing him that your box is unwrapped."

Pushing the crude imagery out of my mind before I exploded, I jumped right in with both feet. "And just how's he supposed to know that? No panty lines?"

"The scent, pet," he replied instantly. That did it. My face must have been every shade of crimson. "No vamp in the world could mistake that. Like dangling bloomin' catnip in front of a kitty. Bloke gets a good whiff of—"

"Will you stop?" I fought to alleviate my intense embarrassment. "I get the picture! Stop drawing it, okay? God, but you are—are . . . profane!"

With anger as a buffer, I could look him in the eye again.

"I hardly see how that's necessary. You've got me dressed in these screw-me clothes, I'm all dolled up with hair and makeup, and I'm going to burn their ears off with dirty talk. If that isn't enough to get them to take me for a ride, then I think it's hopeless."

He stood very still the way vampires do, utterly motionless. It creeped me out when he did that, because it let me know how foreign our two species were. I had half of that contamination. Half of that blood flowed in my veins. His face was thoughtful—we could have been discussing the weather. The hollows and planes of his cheekbones were reflected from the overhead light. He was still the most chiseled man I'd ever seen.

"It's like this, luv," he responded at last. "You look right fetching now with your new togs, but suppose a fellow prefers blondes? Or brunettes? Or likes 'em with a little more meat on the arse? These aren't greenhorns looking for the first available artery. These are Master vampires with discriminating tastes. We might need something to tip the scales, as it were. Think of it as . . . advertising. Is it really that difficult for you? You know, with a vampire's natural sense of smell, it's not like he can't sniff you out in the first place. Blimey, I can tell right off when you've got your monthlies, knickers or no knickers. Some things you just—"

"All right!" *Inhale slowly, exhale slowly. Don't let him see how he's traumatized you with the thought of him scenting out your period.* "I get your point. Fine, I'll do it, when we go out on Friday. Not before. I'm not negotiating on this one."

"Whatever you say." He sounded amenable, but it was a lie. Everything was done his way. I only pretended to win some battles. "Now, then, let's get on to the nasty speak."

We sat at a table opposite each other. Bones held my hands despite my protest, arguing that if I flinched or twitched repeatedly, it would be a dead giveaway. Pun intended. Between my expressions and my hand movements, he had his lie detector test. For every blush and recoil I gave, it would be ten miles running through the woods with him chasing me. I was determined not to take that nature jog from hell.

"You look luscious, pet. The only thing that could make your mouth more beautiful is if it were wrapped around my cock. I wager you could start my heart again. I'd like to bend you over just to hear how loud you can scream. I bet you like it rough, you'd like me to tear into you until you can't beg anymore. . . ."

"My, my, someone hasn't been laid in a while," I mocked, proud of myself for not running out of the room.

It wasn't just his words, or the little circles his thumb traced on my palm. His eyes were dark and heated as though lit from within, looking right into mine with a knowing stare that made every word more intimate. Filled with promise and threat. His tongue flicked out to trace the inside of his lower lip, making me wonder if he imagined doing all of the things he described. It took all of my will-power to hold his gaze.

"I'll take your breasts inside my mouth, licking your nipples until they turn dark red. They'll do that, luv. The more I lick and the more I nibble, the darker they'll get. Let me inform you of a secret about vampires—we direct where the blood goes in our bodies, for as long as we want it to be there. I can't wait to find out how you taste, and you won't want me to stop even after I've completely exhausted you. You'll think you were on fire, your skin will burn. I'll suck all of your juices out of you. And then I'll drink your blood."

"Huh?" Understanding dawned about the sequence of the last two lines, and with it came a sudden mental image of him doing *that* to me.

A flush scorched across my cheeks in the next instant. Mortified, I snatched my hands away and stood so abruptly the chair fell over.

Taunting laughter followed me.

"Oh, Kitten, you were doing so well! Guess you just couldn't pass up a nice stroll in the woods. Beautiful night for it, I smell a storm coming. And you wonder why I had you pegged as an innocent. I've met nuns who were more promiscuous. I knew it would be the oral stuff that did you in, I would have bet my life on it."

"You don't have a life, you're dead."

I was trying to remind myself of that. Listening to his explicit detailing of everything he could do to me—not that I would ever *let* him, of course!—had made that a hard point to remember. I shook my head, trying to clear it of the images dancing in it.

"That's a matter of opinion. In fact, if you judge by senses and reflexes, I'm as alive as any human, just with a few more upgrades."

"Upgrades? You're not a computer. You're a killer."

He rocked back on the two legs of his chair, easily balanced. He wore a charcoal-gray pullover that hugged his shoulders and skimmed his collarbone. Black pants were nearly a staple with him; I wondered if he owned any other color. The dark colors only accented his light hair and pale skin, making them even more incandescent. This was no accident, I knew. Everything was deliberate with Bones. With those incredible cheekbones and his ripped physique, he was stunning. And dangerous, yet somewhere along the line I'd lost most of my fear of him.

"You're a killer, too, luv, or did you forget that? You know, those who live in glass houses shouldn't throw stones, and all that rot. Really, Kitten, why so shy on our former topic? Didn't that sodding chap who shagged you kiss you everywhere first? Don't tell me the wretch neglected foreplay."

"Not unless you count him taking his clothes off as *foreplay*." Goddamn Bones, and damn Danny Milton as well.

Maybe one day I could look back and not feel a sting. "Can we not talk about that? It hardly puts me in the proper mood."

Something cold flashed across his face, but his voice was light. "Don't fret over him, pet. If I meet him, I'll snap him in half for you. No, we won't speak of him any longer. Ready to go back to the table now? Or do you need a few more minutes to cool off?"

There was that insinuating tone again, making simple words sound graphic.

"I'm ready. I just wasn't prepared before." I sat back at the table and slid my hands into his waiting grip. "Go on. Give it your best shot."

He grinned with a slow sexy twist of his lips and the fire leapt back into his eyes.

"*Love* to give it my best shot. Let me tell you just how I'd do it. . . ."

Two hours later, my ears were burned to twin crisps, and I owed him forty miles. Bones was in high spirits. Why wouldn't he be? He had just hypothetically fucked me into incomprehension. Tartly I asked him if he wanted a cigarette when he was finished, and he informed me with a laugh that he'd quit smoking. Heard it wasn't good for his health. God, the man amused himself with his own jokes.

I used one of the cave's small enclosed areas as a changing room to strip out of the harlot's dress and put on my jogging clothes. Bones always collected on his bets, never mind that there was now a thunderstorm out. We were going for our little tortuous run in the woods. With my hair rolled into a bun to avoid it lashing me in the face, I squeezed out from behind the rocks to find him waiting for me. He gave me a once-over, and that cocky twist returned to his lips.

"There's the Kitten I know and love. Felt like you'd been

away for a while, with how different you looked. Ready for a romp in the rain?"

"Let's get this over with. It's nearly nine o'clock and I'd like to get home. After this evening, I feel like I have to wash."

"Well, luv"—we had reached the mouth of the cave, and the rain came down in torrents—"I aim to please. One shower, coming right up."

The run was brutal, as expected. He even had the nerve to laugh behind me the whole way. When I climbed into my truck, I was soaking wet and exhausted. It was an hour-and-a-half round trip every day I went to the cave, and the truck was a gas guzzler. Bones was going to have to start contributing to my travel expenses, because I wasn't going to use more of my college money on gas.

The lights were out at the house when I pulled in, and the rain had slowed to a drizzle. I took my shoes off and headed straight for the bathroom. Once inside, I removed all of my clothes and ran a hot bath.

As I sank into the water, I closed my eyes. Everything ached from the run. For a few moments I just sat, allowing myself to relax. The steam from the water caused moisture on my upper lip and I wiped it away, startled when the brush of my fingers caused an unexpected tightening in my belly.

I tried it again, never having done this before and imagining my fingers were not my own. Gooseflesh broke out on my body and in a completely surprising reaction, my nipples hardened.

I cupped my breasts next, gasping at the increased sensation. The water felt like it caressed me as well now, in the most intimate of places. I skimmed the outsides of my thighs, amazed at the ripples of enjoyment that followed. Then I ran a hand along the inside of my thigh, stopped guiltily for a moment, and reached lower.

A soft moan escaped. With my eyes closed, open mouth breathing in warm humid air, I let my fingers move a little faster, a little faster. . . .

. . . *feel your tight wet box wrapped around me, pulling me deeper inside you* . . .

Bones's words stole through my mind and I snatched my hand away as though burned. "Oh, *shit!*"

I jumped out of the tub, slipped on the wet tile, and fell with a crash to the floor.

"Sonofabitch!" I shouted. Great, that was going to leave a mark. There'd be a bruise the size of my stupidity.

"Catherine, what happened?"

My mother was outside the bathroom door. The thump or my shout must have woken her.

"It's okay, Mom, I just slipped. I'm fine."

I dried off with a towel while lashing myself under my breath.

"Stupid, stupid, stupid, thinking about a vampire. What is wrong with you? What is wrong with you?"

"Who are you talking to?" Apparently my mother was still outside the door.

"No one." No one intelligent, that's for sure. "Go back to bed."

After changing into a pair of pajamas, I carried my dirty clothes downstairs and put them in the washing machine, reminding myself to start a load in the morning. When I went into the room I shared with my mother, I found her sitting up in her bed.

That was different. She was usually asleep by nine every night.

"Catherine, we have to talk."

She couldn't have picked a worse time, but I stifled a yawn and asked her what she wanted to talk about.

"Your future, of course. I know you waited two years to start college so you could help out after Grandpa Joe had his heart attack, and you've been saving for another two years so you can transfer to Ohio State University from the community college here. But soon you'll be leaving. Living on your own, and I'm worried about you."

"Mom, don't worry, I'll be careful—"

"You can't forget you have a monster inside you," she interrupted me.

My mouth tightened. God, she'd picked a *great* time to go into this! *You have a monster inside you, Catherine.* Those were the opening words she'd used when I was sixteen to tell me what I was.

"I've been scared for you since I found out I was pregnant," she went on. The lights were off, but I didn't need them to see the tension in her face. "From the day you were born, you looked just like your father. Then each day after that, I watched your abnormalities grow as you did. Soon you'll leave, and I won't be there to watch over you anymore. You'll have only yourself to make sure you don't become like the monster who sired you. You can't let that happen. Finish school, get your degree. Move out of town, make some friends, it'll be good for you. Just be careful. Don't ever forget you're not like everyone else. They don't have evil in them trying to break out like you do."

For the first time in my life, I wanted to argue with her. To tell her that maybe there wasn't any evil in me. That my father could have been bad *before* he turned into a vampire, and my unusualness made me different, but not half evil.

Even as the denial sprang to my lips, however, I choked it back. It hadn't escaped my notice that our relationship had dramatically improved since I started killing vampires. She loved me, I knew, but before that, I'd always felt like a small part of her also resented me for both the circumstances of my birth and the repercussions of it.

"I won't forget, Mom," was all I said. "I won't forget, I swear to you."

Her features softened. Seeing that made me glad I hadn't argued. There was no need to upset her. This was a woman who'd raised the child of her rapist, and in this small town, she'd been alienated just for having a baby out of wedlock. No one even knew the horrible truth behind her pregnancy. As rough as that was, to top it off, I had hardly been a normal child. She didn't need me lecturing her on right and wrong.

"In fact," I went on, "I'm going out Friday to hunt again. I'll probably be home late. I—I have a good feeling I'll find one."

Yeah. Did I ever.

She smiled. "You're doing the right thing, baby."

I nodded, swallowing back the guilt. *If she found out about Bones, she'd never forgive me. She wouldn't understand how I could have partnered with a vampire, no matter the reason.*

"I know."

She lay down in her bed. I got in mine as well and tried to fall asleep. But fears of my changing perspective and who was responsible for it kept me awake.

Six

FRIDAY FINALLY ARRIVED. FOR THE PAST FIVE days, I experimented with makeup and different hairstyles to turn myself into more appetizing bait. The goody bag from Hot Hair Salon had been filled with cosmetics, gels, hair spray, hair clips, nail polish, you name it. Bones also bought me curling irons and hot rollers. After dolling myself up, I would spar with him in full slut gear, preparing myself to fight in a short dress.

Now Bones waited for me by the entrance of the cave, a rarity. From the looks of him, he was already dressed for the evening. Black long-sleeved shirt, black pants, black boots. With his light skin and hair, he looked like an archangel dipped in coal.

"Now, you're clear on all the details, right? You won't see me, but I'll be watching you. When you leave with him, I'm going to follow you. Anywhere outside is fine, but do not, I repeat, *do not* let him take you inside any buildings or houses. If he tries to force you inside one, what do you do?"

"Bones, for God's sake, we've been over this a thousand times."

"What do you do?" He wasn't about to give up.

"Hit the pager in the watch, Mr. Bond, James Bond. You'll come running. Dinner for two."

He grinned, squeezing my shoulder. "Kitten, you have me pegged all wrong. If I go for your neck, I have no intention of sharing."

Although I would never admit it, having a small safety net like that made me feel better. The watch was rigged with a tiny pager that would only send a series of beeps to Bones, but if it went off, it meant my ass was in jeopardy.

"Are you ever going to tell me about who I'm after? Or do I find out later if I've staked the wrong guy? You've been pretty secretive about the whole identity thing. Afraid I'd rat you out?"

That previous smile was wiped from his face, replaced by an expression of complete seriousness.

"It was better for you not to know beforehand, pet. That way no accidental slips. Word can't get out if word isn't spoken, right?"

He followed me to the partially enclosed space where he kept my slutty clothes and accessories. It was amazing how many places a cave held. As near as I could figure, this one was half a mile long. I went inside the makeshift dressing room and put the privacy screen in place with a pointed look. Changing clothes in front of him was not going to happen. The screen didn't impair conversation, however, so I answered him as my clothes came off.

"It amuses me to think of you worrying about my Freudian slips. Maybe you didn't hear me the other times I told you, but I don't have any friends. The only other person I talk to is my mother, and she's being kept far out of this loop."

As soon as the words left my mouth, a hollow feeling

grew in my chest. It was true, too true. As twisted as it was, Bones was the closest thing to a friend I'd ever had. He might be using me, but at least he was up front about it. Not sneaky and deceitful like Danny had been.

"All right, luv. His name is Sergio, though he might well give you another one. He's about six-one, black hair, gray eyes, typical vampire skin. Italian is his first language, but he's fluent in three others as well, so his English has an accent. He's not very beefy. In fact, he may even look soft to you, but don't let it fool you. He's almost three hundred years old and more powerful than you can imagine. Also, he's a sadist, likes 'em young, real young. Tell him you're underage and that you snuck in with a fake ID, it'll only switch him on more. You also can't kill him straightaway, because I need some information from him first. That's everything. Oh, and he's worth fifty thousand dollars."

Fifty thousand dollars. The words echoed through my mind. And to think I'd been prepared to argue with Bones over pocket change! The words kept resounding, and with them an important detail that had never been revealed before.

"Money. So *that's* why you hunt vampires. You're a hit man!"

I was so amazed by this new information, I opened the screen while only wearing my bra and panties.

He cast a leisurely look down the length of me before meeting my eyes.

"Yeah, that's right. It's what I do. But don't fret. You could also say I'm a bounty hunter. Sometimes my clients want 'em back alive."

"Wow. I just thought we were going after people who had pissed you off."

"And that was enough for you to kill for, someone who might have looked at me cross-eyed? Blimey, but you're not particular. What if I were chasing some nice sweet thing that'd never hurt a fly? Still be all right with it then?"

I snapped the screen shut and found my mother's words coming out of my mouth.

"None of you are nice sweet things. You're all murderers. That's why it didn't matter. Point me at a vampire and I'll try to kill it, because at one time they've done something to deserve it."

It was so silent outside the screen, I wondered if he'd left. When I peeked, he was still standing where he'd been before. A flicker of emotion passed over his face before it became blank again. Suddenly uncomfortable, I retreated back inside to don my revealing costume.

"Not every vampire is like the ones who killed those girls Winston told you about. It's just your bad luck to be living in Ohio at this particular time. There are things going on you don't know about."

"Winston was wrong, by the way," I said smugly. "I looked up those girls' names the next day, and none of them were dead. They weren't even missing. One of them, Suzy Klinger, lived in the town next to mine, but her parents said she moved away to study acting. What I don't know is why Winston would make that up, but far be it for me to understand the mental workings of a ghost."

"Bloody hell!" Bones almost shouted. "Who did you talk to, aside from Suzy Klinger's parents? The police? Other families?"

I didn't know why he was so worked up. It's not like there *had* been multiple homicides, after all. "No one. I entered their names online at the library's computer and when nothing came up, I looked in a few local papers and then called Suzy's parents saying I was a telemarketer. That was it."

Some of the tension drained out of him. At least he wasn't clenching his fists anymore.

"Don't go against what I tell you to do again," he said in a very calm tone.

"What did you expect? For me to forget about over a dozen girls being murdered by vampires because you *told* me to? See, this is just what I'm talking about! A human wouldn't act like that. Only a vampire could be that cold."

Bones folded his arms. "Vampires have existed for millennia, and though we have our villains among us, the majority of us just have a sip here and there, but everybody walks away. Besides, it's not like your kind hasn't made its mark for ill on the world. Hitler wasn't a vampire, was he? Too bloody right. Humans can be just as nasty as we are, and don't you forget it."

"Oh, come on, Bones!" Dressed now, I pulled back the screen and started fixing hot rollers into my hair. "Don't give me that crap. Are you telling me you've never murdered someone innocent? Never drank the life out of someone when you were hungry? Never forced a woman who said no? Hell, the only reason you didn't kill *me* the night we met was because you saw my eyes glow, so sell that smack to someone who's buying!"

His hand flashed out. I braced myself, but all he did was catch a falling curler. Without blinking, he rolled it back into my hair.

"Think I'd strike you? You really don't know as much as you claim to. Aside from teaching you how to fight, I'd never lay a harsh hand on you. As for the night we met, you did your level best to kill me. I thought you were sent by someone, so I smacked you and threatened you, but I wasn't going to kill you. No, I would have sipped from your neck and green-eyed you until you told me who they were. Then I would have sent you back to the shit with your limbs broken as a warning, but I promise you this—at no point would I have forced myself on you. Sorry, Kitten. Every woman I've been with has wanted me to be there. Have I killed any innocents in my time? Yeah, I have. When you've lived as long as I have, you make mistakes. You try to learn from them. And you shouldn't be so quick to judge me on that. No doubt you've killed innocents as well."

"The only people I've killed were vampires who tried to kill me first," I said, rattled by his nearness.

"Oh?" Softly. "Don't be so sure. Those blokes you killed, did you wait for them to try to bite you first? Or did you just assume because they were vampires and they'd gotten you alone, they intended to murder you? Ignoring the very real likelihood that they were there because they'd thought a beautiful girl was hot to shag them. Tell me—how many of them did you kill before they'd even shown you their fangs?"

My mouth dropped even as immediate denial echoed in my brain. *No. No. They'd all been trying to kill me. They had. Hadn't they . . . ?*

"Whether they showed their fangs or not doesn't change the fact that vampires are evil, and that's enough for me."

"Bloody mule-headed woman," he muttered. "Then if all vampires are the filth you claim them to be, why wouldn't I just pry your legs open now and take out some of my evil on you?"

He was too strong for me to stop him, if he decided on that course of action. I glanced at my stakes, but they were too far away on the floor.

Bones saw me looking and a sardonic snort escaped him.

"You never have to fret about it. Told you, I don't come in unless invited. Now hurry up. You have another murderous fiend to kill."

He was gone in a whoosh of air that left me trembling. *Great, I'd offended my backup. Smart. Real smart.*

We drove separately to avoid being seen together. In fact, I didn't see him at all after our little spat at the dressing table. He'd left me a note telling me he'd be watching and to proceed with the plan. On my way to the club, I was inexplicably upset by what had happened. After all, what I'd said was right, wasn't it? Okay, maybe every vampire I'd killed hadn't been going for my throat, true. Some of them had been pretty focused on my cleavage, in fact. But they would have tried to kill me, wouldn't they? Bones might act different, but *all* vampires were bad.

Weren't they?

The music greeted me with its loud pumping beat. Same vibrations, different songs. According to Bones, Sergio would probably put in an appearance in about an hour. I seated myself at the bar, making sure I had a clear view of the doorway, and ordered a gin and tonic. Aside from that half gallon of moonshine, alcohol seemed to make me calmer instead of inebriated. Bones said it was due to my bloodline. He should know—he could knock back bottles of whiskey without even a twitch. On the plus side, it added to the helpless female image to look drunk.

It had been a while since my last gin and tonic, so I promptly had it refilled by the attentive bartender when I was done. His eyes had been undressing what little clothing I was wearing since I'd walked in. Good to know Bones knew what he was about when it came to picking bait apparel. We'd see if it worked as well with the monsters.

As the hour dragged on, it became apparent that the bartender wasn't alone in his admiration of my new look. After refusing offer after offer of drinks or dancing, I had passed the flattered stage and gone into the irritated one. My God, I must look easy. No less than a baker's dozen had made a go at me.

The vampire came through the door with the gliding stealth only the undead could manifest. Judging from his height and black hair, it had to be Sergio. Even though he wasn't well muscled or overly handsome, his grace and aura of confidence had more than a few feminine eyes following him as he made his way through the throngs of people. In a nonchalant manner, I sipped my drink and stretched my legs, crossing them while rubbing one calf against the other. The bar I was at was elevated and in direct sight of the entrance, so he had a good view of me over the heads of the other patrons. Out of the corner of my eye I saw him pause, stare, and change direction. Headed now straight toward me.

The seat next to me was occupied by an older man staring fixedly down my dress, but the vampire never hesitated. With a flick of his hand, Sergio dislodged him from his chair. "Go," he commanded.

The other man walked away with his eyes glazed over. Mind control. Bones had warned me about that.

"Thank you," I remarked. "If he'd have drooled any more, the bartender would've had to mop the floor."

"Who can blame him?" The smooth accented voice flowed over my ears. "I can't take my eyes off you, either."

I smiled and took a deep sip of my drink, letting the liquid roll around inside my mouth before swallowing. He didn't miss a motion of it.

"I seem to have finished my drink."

I looked at him expectantly. He gestured to the bartender and a fresh one was poured.

"What's your name, my young beauty?"

"Cat," I replied, this time letting my tongue linger on the edge of my glass before swallowing another long draught.

"Cat. What a coincidence. I love pussies."

The double-entendre was so bald, I was glad Bones had put me through that dirty-talk test or I'd have blushed right then. Instead, I raised a brow in perfect imitation of his trademark.

"And you are, my pussy-loving new friend?" Kudos to me, not a hint of a flush.

"Roberto. Cat, I must say, you look far too young to be gracing such a place."

I leaned forward conspiratorially, opening my dress to spectacular proportions. "Can you keep a secret? I'm not really twenty-one. Actually, I'm nineteen. My friend loaned me her ID, we look kind of alike. You won't tell, will you?"

From his expression, he was downright delighted. "But of course I will keep your secret, sweet one. Is your friend with you night?"

The question sounded innocent, but I knew what it meant. *Will anyone miss you if you leave?*

"No. She was supposed to meet me, but she hasn't shown up yet. Maybe she met someone, you know how it is. You just forget everything else around you."

He covered my hand with his and I almost gasped. Ten more points for Bones. Sergio's power nearly crawled up my arm. None of the other vampires but one had felt like this, and look where he'd gotten me.

"I know what you mean," he said, squeezing my hand.

I smiled seductively and squeezed back. "I think I do, too."

Less than thirty minutes later we were out the door. I made sure to drink multiple gin and tonics beforehand, so there was valid reason for me to be staggering in his eyes. Sergio kept up a steady stream of innuendo about pussies, cream, and licking that would have shocked me into bolting if it hadn't been for Bones. Damn him, but it was turning out he'd come in handy.

Sergio drove a Mercedes. Never having been in one before, I kept up a line of suggestive compliments about how I loved the interior. Especially the backseat. So roomy.

"This leather feels wonderful," I purred, rubbing my cheek against the cushion of the passenger seat. "That's why I wear the gloves and boots. Love the way it rubs against my skin."

The tops of my breasts were straining against my push-up bra. Sergio grinned, showing a crooked front tooth he'd managed to conceal at the bar.

"Stop doing that, little pussycat, or I won't be able to drive. How about we go to my place instead of that club I told you about?"

Warning. "No," I breathed, getting an angry look in return. Clearly he didn't expect to be disagreed with, but there was no way we were doing that. Thinking fast, I caressed his arm. "I don't want to wait that long. Pull off somewhere. Kitty needs a tongue bath." *Ick*, my mind protested, but as incentive I rubbed my hands across my stomach and down to skim my outer thighs.

He bought it, hook, line, and sinker. Too well.

Sergio kept one hand on the steering wheel and reached over to run his other hand along my leg. It climbed higher up my thigh and toward his goal with relentless determination. As instructed, I wasn't wearing any underwear. The thought of his fingers touching me there sent a wave of revulsion through me. Quickly, I grabbed his hand and stuck it in my cleavage instead. Better there than the alternative.

"Not yet." Anxiety made me breathless. Hopefully he would think it was desire. "Pull off. Pull off now."

The sooner I had a stake in him, the better. His hand seemed happy where it was, but just in case, I unfastened my seat belt and climbed over the seat.

He gave me a surprised look. I wrapped my arms around him from behind, licking the side of his ear. *Double ick*. "I'm waiting, Roberto. Come and get me."

The car swerved to the shoulder of the road. Damn, we weren't even in the woods yet. I hoped someone wouldn't drive by while we were decapitating him. That would be hard to explain.

"I'm coming, pussycat," Sergio promised, and then his teeth clamped on my wrist.

"Motherfucker!"

The word flew out of my mouth in a yelp as he bit me savagely.

"You like this, pussycat?" he snarled, sucking at the blood pouring from my forearm. "Slut. Whore."

Furious, I unsheathed my stake with my free hand and plunged it into his neck. "Didn't your mother tell you not to talk with your mouth full?"

A howl escaped him and he let go of me to grab the stake. I yanked my arm out of his mouth, tearing it more, and went for my other stake.

In a flash, he was in the backseat. Sergio loomed over me, but I kicked out hard and scored a direct hit to his groin. Another pain-filled bellow shook the car.

"Bitch! I'm going to rip out your throat and fuck your bleeding neck!"

Not wanting him to get anywhere near my neck, I brought my knees up as a barrier when he flung himself on me. With my boots so close, I managed to extract the other stake and then ram it in his back.

Sergio flew out of the car, smashing through the doorframe as though it were paper. I charged after him, needing to retrieve one of my weapons. A blow knocked me sideways as soon as I cleared the door. I rolled to avoid the kick aimed at my head and sprang to my feet.

Sergio lunged at me again—and then was yanked backward by the vampire who seemed to materialize behind him. Bones held him roughly, one hand on the stake in his neck, the other gripping the one in his back.

"About time," I muttered.

"Hallo, Sergio!" Bones said cheerfully, giving a vicious jerk to the stake in Sergio's neck.

There were a few sickening gurgles before Sergio spoke. "Filthy bastard, how'd you find me?"

It amazed me he could talk at all with half his throat laid open. Bones tightened his hold on the stake in Sergio's back next, digging it deeper until it must have been grazing the other vampire's heart.

"I see you've met my friend. Isn't she just wonderful?"

Blood was running in rivulets down my arm. I ripped off one of my sleeves and wrapped it around the wound, which throbbed in accordance with my pulse. Even with that, I managed to get a grim satisfaction out of the look on Sergio's face when his eyes swung back to me.

"You. Set me up." Incredulity filled his voice.

"That's right, *pussycat*. Guess you won't be giving me that tongue bath after all." There was a piece of me that was startled by my coldness, and another that gloried in it.

"She is something, isn't she?" Bones went on. "Knew you couldn't pass up a pretty girl, you worthless sod. Isn't it fitting that now you're the one who's been lured into a trap? What, did you grow short on funds so you had to go out for dinner instead of order in?"

Sergio went still. "I don't know what you say."

From his expression, he did know. Well, I didn't have a clue.

"Of course you do. You're his best client, from what I hear. Now, I have just one question for you, and I know you're going to answer me honestly, because if not"—he gave another twist of the stake in Sergio's back—"I'm going to be really unhappy. Do you know what happens when I'm unhappy? My hand twitches."

"What? What? I tell you! I tell you!" His accent was thicker now, almost incoherently so.

Bones smiled a truly frightening smile. "Where's Hennessey?"

A petrified look came over Sergio's face. If it were possible, he blanched even paler than his vampire white.

"Hennessey will kill me. You don't cross him and live to brag about it! You don't know what he'll do if I talk. And you kill me anyway if I tell you."

"See, mate." Twist, turn, yank. "I promise I won't kill you if you tell me. That gives you a chance to run from Hennessey. But I swear to you, if you don't tell me where he is"—another thrust of the stake, and Sergio let out a high-pitched wail—"you'll die right here. Your call. Make it now."

He had no choice, it was clear on the doomed vampire's face. Defeated, his head slumped forward and a single sentence emerged from his bloody mouth.

"Chicago Heights, south side of town."

"Thanks ever so, mate." With a cock of his eyebrow, Bones turned his attention to me. "This your stake, luv?"

He ripped the one out of Sergio's back and threw it at me. Catching it in midair, I met his eyes with perfect comprehension.

"You promised! You promised!"

Sergio whimpered as I advanced, my torn arm clutched to my chest. It was amazing how frightened he was at the thought of his own death when minutes ago he'd been delighted to hasten mine.

"I did. She didn't. Got something you want to say to him, Kitten?"

"No," I answered, and shoved the stake into Sergio's heart. My hand went into his chest with the momentum and I jerked back, shaking his thick dark blood off in disgust. "I'm done talking to him."

SEVEN

BONES WAS FAR MORE EXPEDITIOUS in disposing of a body than I'd been. He had Sergio wrapped in plastic and tucked inside the trunk within a few minutes, whistling to himself all the while. Meanwhile, I sat with my back against the car applying pressure to my wrist. He squatted down next to me after he'd closed the trunk with a bang.

"Let me see it," he said, reaching out to me.

"It's fine." Tension and pain made my voice sharp.

Bones ignored that and pried my fingers off the wound, undoing my makeshift bandage.

"Nasty bite, tore the flesh around the vein. You'll need blood for that."

He pulled a switchblade out of his pocket and started to press the tip against his palm.

"Don't. I said it's fine."

He just gave me an irritated glance and scored the blade along his palm. Blood welled up at once and he clamped it against my resisting forearm.

"Don't be irrational. How much did he take?"

My wrist actually tingled as his blood mingled with mine. The magic of healing, in real time. Somehow it seemed almost as intimate as when I had to lick blood off his fingers.

"About four good pulls, I guess. Stabbed him in the neck as fast as I could to get his mind off it. Where were you, anyway? I didn't see a car behind us."

"That was the idea. I drove my bike but kept back far enough so Sergio wouldn't know he was being followed. Bike's about a mile from here down the road." Bones nodded toward the nearby trees. "I ran that last part through the woods so there'd be less noise."

Our heads were only inches apart and his knees were pressed against mine. Uncomfortable, I tried to scoot back, but the car door left nowhere to go. "I think the car's ruined. The rear door is in scraps."

Indeed it was. Sergio had mangled it beyond belief. A wrecking ball would have done similar damage.

"Why did he go for your wrist, if you were both in the backseat? Couldn't get to your neck?"

"No." Inwardly I cursed at the memory. "He got frisky in the front seat and tried to feel me up, thanks to you and the no-panties idea. I wasn't about to let that happen, so I climbed into the back and put my arms around him from behind so he wouldn't get suspicious. Stupid of me, I know now, but I didn't even think of my wrists. Every other vampire had always gone for my neck."

"Yeah, including me, right? The car swerved off the road so fast, I thought you two were already sprawling inside. What made him pull off so erratically then?"

"I told him to come and get me." My voice was flippant, but the words hurt. He'd come and gotten me, all right. A question suddenly leapt to mind.

"Is he okay back there in the trunk?"

Bones chuckled. "You want to keep him company?"

An evil glare accompanied my retort. "No, but is he really gone? I'd always cut off their heads to be sure."

"Critiquing my work? Yeah, he's really gone. Right now we need to get out of here before some nosy driver pops alongside and asks if we need help." Releasing my wrist, he examined the wound. The flesh was already closed together as if by invisible stitches. His hand no longer even bore a mark. "That'll hold you. We need to move this vehicle."

I stood up and again looked at the mangled car. Not only was the door hanging by a mere few scraps of metal, but there was a fair amount of blood in the front area from my wrist and Sergio's neck.

"How I am supposed to drive in this wreck? Any cop that sees this car is going to pull me over!"

He grinned that cocky smile of his. "Don't fret. Have it all worked out." From out of his jacket he pulled a cell phone.

"It's me, we're finished. Looks like I'm going to need that lift after all, mate. You'll like the ride, it's a Benz. Needs a little body work on the door, though. We're on Planter's Road, just south of the club. Step on it, right?" Without saying goodbye, he hung up and turned his attention back to me.

"Sit tight, Kitten. Our ride will be here in a minute. Don't worry, he's nearby. Told him I might have a use for him tonight. Course, he was probably figuring on it being a little later in the evening." He paused, giving me a knowing look. "You left with him right quick, didn't you? He must have been quite pleased with you."

"Yeah, real happy. Color me flattered. Seriously, Bones, even if you tow this car there's still too much blood in it. And you didn't listen to me about bringing cleaning materials. This thing could have been at least mopped up."

He moved closer to pull my arm out for another inspection. There was only a thin red line of healed skin now, but after satisfying himself with its condition, he still didn't let me go. Avoiding his gaze didn't prevent me from feeling its weight.

"Trust me, luv. I know you don't, but you should. You did a smashing job tonight, by the way. That stake in his back was just a thought away from his heart. It slowed him, as did the one in his neck. You would have had him even if I wasn't here. You're strong, Kitten. Be glad of it."

"Glad? That's not quite the word I'd use. Relieved? You could say that. Relieved I'm alive and there's one less murderer prowling around for naïve girls. But glad? Glad would be if I never had this lineage. Glad would be if I had two normal parents and a bunch of friends, and the only thing I'd ever killed was time. Or if even *once* I had been to a club just to go dancing and have fun instead of ending up staking something that tried to kill me. That's glad. This is just . . . existing. Until the next time."

I pulled my hand away and moved off a few feet to put some distance between us. A wave of melancholy coursed through me at the things I had just mentioned that would never be mine. Sometimes it was frightening to feel old at twenty-two.

"Rot." The single word broke the silence.

"Excuse me?" How like a vampire, to have no sympathy.

"Rot, I said. You play the hand you're dealt just like everyone else in this bloody world. You have gifts people would kill for, no matter that you scorn them. You have a mum who loves you and a nice house to go home to. Sod your backwoods neighbors who look down their ignorant noses at you for your lack of a father. This world is a big place and you've got an important role to play in it. Think everyone goes around whistling about the life they lead? Think everyone is given the power to choose the way their fate goes? Sorry, luv, it doesn't work that way. You hold the ones you love close and fight the battles you can win, and *that*, Kitten, is how it is."

"What would you know about it?" Bitterness made me brave, and the words flung out of my mouth.

Surprisingly, he threw back his head and laughed before he seized my shoulders, moving closer until his mouth almost touched mine.

"You . . . haven't . . . the . . . slightest . . . *inkling* of what I've been through, so don't . . . tell . . . me . . . what I know."

There was thinly veiled menace in the way he deliberately spoke each syllable. My heart started to pound, and I knew he could hear it. His grip loosened until his fingers no longer dug into my skin, but his hands remained. God, he was close . . . so close. Unconsciously I licked my lips, and a jolt went through me as I saw his eyes follow the movement. The air fairly crackled between us, either from his natural vampire energy . . . or something else. Slowly his tongue snaked out and caressed his bottom lip. It was mesmerizing to watch.

A horn blaring made me jump nearly out of my skin. My heart caught in my throat as an eighteen-wheeler slowed down and parked just ahead of us. The noise of the axles releasing and brakes locking sounded deafening in the suddenly quiet night.

"Bones . . . !" Frightened of discovery, I was about to say more when he walked up to the vehicle and called out a greeting.

"Ted, you buggering bastard, good of you to arrive so quickly!"

It might have been me, but I thought I detected a note of insincerity in his voice. Me, I wanted to throw my arms around this Ted and thank him for interrupting what could have been a very dangerous moment.

A tall skinny man climbed down from the trailer and

gave a grinning reply. "I'm missin' my shows because of you, buddy. Hope I didn't interrupt nothin' between you and that gal. Two of you looked awful cozy."

"No!" It escaped me with all the denial of a condemned soul. "Nothing going on here!"

Ted laughed and walked around to the damaged side of the car, poking his head inside and wrinkling his nose at the sight of the blood.

"Sure . . . I can see that."

Bones arched a brow at me in silent challenge, causing me to look away. Then he clapped his friend on the shoulders.

"Ted, old chap, the car is yours. Just need to get a piece out of the boot and then we're golden. Drive us to the place, we'll be done by then."

"Sure thing, bud. You'll like the back. It's air-conditioned. Some boxes to sit on, or you could ride in the car. Come on, now. Let's put this baby to bed."

Ted opened the back of the trailer. It was equipped with stabilizing clamps to fasten a car onto. I shook my head in admiration. Bones really had thought of everything.

When Ted lowered the steel ramp on the back, Bones jumped into the Mercedes and drove it straight onto the clamps. After a few adjustments were made, the car was secure. Then Bones left to get his motorcycle, returning in a few minutes to put it in the trailer on its side. When he was finished, he grinned down at me.

"Come on, Kitten. Your taxi's waiting."

"We're riding in back?" Frankly, the thought of being alone in a confined space with him frightened me, and not for concern of my arteries.

"Yeah, here. Old Ted doesn't want to risk being seen with me. Values his health, he does. Keeps our friendship a secret. Smart bloke."

"Smart," I muttered as I climbed into the trailer's

interior. Ted closed the door with a decisive click and sound of a lock turning. "I envy that."

I refused to sit back in the car where my blood stained the seats and a body lay in the trunk. Instead, I was as far away from Bones as the tight interior of the truck's trailer could manage. There were crates toward the front, filled with God knows what, and I huddled into a ball on one of them. Bones perched contentedly on a similar box as if he hadn't a care in the world.

"I know this isn't a concern for you, but is there enough oxygen in here?"

"Plenty of air. Just as long as there isn't any heavy breathing." His brow arched as he spoke, while his eyes told me loud and clear that he hadn't overlooked an instant of our earlier moment.

"Well, then I'm safe. Absolutely safe." Damn him for the knowing twist of the lips he gave me in reply. What would I have done if he'd moved closer before? If he'd separated that last inch between our mouths? Would I have slapped him? Or . . .

"Shit." Oops, said that out loud.

"Something wrong?"

That half smile still curled his lips, but his expression was serious. My heart started to beat faster again. The air seemed to close in around us, and desperately I searched for something to break the tension.

"So who's this Hennessey you were asking about?"

His expression became guarded. "Someone dangerous."

"Yeah, I gathered that. Sergio seemed pretty scared of him, so I didn't think he was a Boy Scout. I take it he's our next target?"

Bones paused before answering, seeming to choose his words.

"He's someone I've been tracking, yes, but I'll be going after him alone."

My hackles rose at once. "Why? You don't think I can handle it? Or you still don't trust me to keep this secret? I thought we covered this already!"

"I think there are certain things you'd do well to stay out of," he replied, evasive.

I switched tactics. At least this topic cut the strange mood from earlier. "You said something about Sergio being Hennessey's best client. What do you mean by that? What did Hennessey do to whoever hired you? Do you know, or did you just take the contract on him without asking?"

Bones let out a soft noise. "Questions like that are why I won't tell you more about it. Suffice it to say there's a reason why Ohio's been such a hazardous place for young girls lately. It's why I don't want you chasing after vampires without me. Hennessey's more than just a sod who bleeds someone when he can get away with it. Beyond that, don't ask."

"Can you at least tell me how long you've been after him? That can't be top secret."

He caught the snippiness in my tone and frowned. I didn't mind. Better to be arguing with each other than, well, *anything* else.

"'Round eleven years."

I almost fell off my crate. "Good God! He must have a *real* fancy price on his head! Come on, what did he do? He pissed off someone rich, obviously."

Bones gave me a look I couldn't decipher. "Not everything is about money."

From his tone, I wasn't getting anything else out of him. Fine. If he wanted to play it that way, fine. I'd just try later.

"How did you become a vampire?" I asked next, surprising even myself with the question.

A brow arched.

"Want an interview with the vampire, luv? It didn't turn out too well for the reporter in the movie."

As I murmured, "I never saw it. My mother thought it was too violent," the humor of it made me laugh. Bones grinned as well, and cast a meaningful look toward the car.

"I can see that. Good thing you didn't watch it, then. Heaven knows what might have happened."

Laughter fading, it occurred to me that I really did want to know, so I looked at him pointedly until he let out an acquiescing noise.

"All right, I'll tell you, but then you'll have to answer one of my questions. Got an hour to burn anyhow."

"Is this quid pro quo, Dr. Lecter?" I scoffed. "Fine, but I hardly see the point. You already know everything about me."

A look of pure heat was shot my way and his voice lowered to a whisper. "Not everything."

Whoa. Back came that awkwardness in a flash. Clearing my suddenly dry throat, I fidgeted until I was scrunched up even smaller.

"When did it happen? When you were changed?" *Please just talk. Please stop looking at me that way.*

"Let's see, it was 1790 and I was in Australia. I did this bloke a favor and he thought he was returning it by making me a vampire."

"*What?*" I was shocked. "You're Australian? I thought you were English!"

He smiled, but with little amusement.

"I'm a bit of both, as it were. I was born in England. It's where I spent my youth, but it was in Australia that I was changed. That makes me part of it as well."

Now I was fascinated, my earlier consternation forgotten. "You have to go into more detail than that."

He settled back against the side of the trailer, legs casually splayed in front of him. "I was twenty-four. It happened just a month after my birthday."

"My God, we're almost the same age!" As soon they were out, I realized the absurdity of the words.

He snorted. "Sure. Give or take two hundred and seventeen years."

"Er, you know what I mean. You look older than twenty-four."

"Thanks ever so." He laughed at my obvious chagrin, but put me out of my misery. "Times were different. People aged far more rapidly. You bloody folks don't know how good you have it."

"Tell me more." He hesitated, and I blurted out, "Please."

Bones leaned forward, all serious now. "It's not pretty, Kitten. Not romantic like the movies or books. You remember you told me you slugged those lads when you were young because they called your mum a whore?.Well, my mum *was* a whore. Her name was Penelope and she was fifteen when she had me. It was fortunate that she and the madam of the place were friendly, or I never would have been allowed to live there. Only girl-children were kept at the whorehouse, for obvious reasons. When I was little, I didn't know there was anything unusual with where I lived. All the women doted on me, and I would do house chores and such until I got older. The madam, her name was Lucille, later inquired as to whether or not I wanted to follow in the family business. Several of the male customers who were so inclined had taken notice of me, for I was a pretty lad. But by the time Madam approached me with the offer, I knew enough to know I wouldn't want to perform such activities. Begging was a common occupation in

London then. Thieving was as well, so to earn my keep, I began to steal. Then when I was seventeen, my mum died of syphilis. She was thirty-three."

My face paled considerably listening to him speak, but I wanted to hear the rest. "Go on."

"Lucille informed me two weeks afterwards that I had to go. Wasn't bringing in enough quid to justify the space. It wasn't that she was cruel, she was simply being practical. Another girl could take my room and bring in three times the money. Again she offered me a choice—leave and face the streets, or stay and service the customers. Yet she added a kindness. There were a few highborn women she was acquainted with that she'd described me to, and they were interested. I could choose to sell myself to women rather than men. And so that is what I did.

"The girls at the house trained me first, of course, and it turned out I had a knack for the work. Lucille kept me in high demand and soon I had quite a few regulars among the blue bloods. One of them ended up saving my life.

"I was still picking pockets, you see. One unlucky day, I pulled the purse off a toff right in front of a bobby. Next thing I knew, I was in chains and up before one of the meanest hanging judges in London. One of my clients heard of my predicament and took pity on me. She persuaded the judge through carnal means that sending me to the new penal colonies would be just the thing. Three weeks later they shipped me and sixty-two other unlucky buggers to South Wales."

His eyes clouded, and he ran a hand through his hair reflectively.

"I won't tell you about the voyage except to say it went beyond any misery man should ever have to endure. Once we were at the colony, they worked us literally unto death. There were three men I became mates with—Timothy,

Charles, and Ian. After a few months, Ian managed to escape. Then, almost a year later, he came back."

"Why would he come back?" I wondered. "Wouldn't he have been punished for running away?"

Bones grunted. "Indeed he would have, but Ian wasn't afraid of that anymore. We were in the fields slaughtering cattle for beef jerky and the hides when we were set upon by the natives. They killed the guards and the rest of the prisoners except Timothy, Charles, and me. That's when Ian appeared among them, but he was different. You can guess how. He was a vampire, and he changed me that night. Charles and Timothy were changed as well by two other vampires. Though three of us were changed, only one of us asked for it. Timothy wanted what Ian offered. Charles and I didn't. Ian changed us anyway because he thought we would thank him later. We stayed with the natives for a few years and vowed to return to England. It took us nearly twenty years to finally get there."

He stopped and closed his eyes. At some point in his story I'd uncurled myself from my ball and sat staring at him in amazement. He was absolutely right, it wasn't a pretty story, and I *hadn't* had any idea what he'd been through.

"Your turn." His eyes opened to stare right into mine. "Tell me what happened with that sod who hurt you."

"God, Bones, I don't want to talk about that." I hunched defensively at the memory. "It's humiliating."

That dark gaze didn't waver. "I just told you that I used to be a thief, a beggar, and a whore. Is it really fair for you to cry foul over my question?"

Put like that, he had a point. With a shrug to hide my continued pain, I summarized it briskly.

"It's a common story. Boy meets girl, girl is naïve and stupid, boy uses girl and then hits the road."

He just arched his brow and waited.

I threw up my hands. "Fine! You want details? I thought he really cared for me. He told me he did, and I fell for his lies completely. We went out twice, and then the third time he said he had to stop by his apartment to get something before we'd go to this club. When we got there, he started kissing me, telling me all this crap about how special I was to him. . . ." My fingers clenched. "I told him it was too soon. That we should wait to get to know each other better, that it was my first time. He disagreed. I—I should have hit him, or thrown him off me. I could have, I was stronger than he was. But . . ." I dropped my eyes. "I wanted to make him happy. I really liked him. So when he didn't stop, I just stayed still and tried not to move. It didn't hurt as much if I didn't move. . . ."

God, I was going to cry. I blinked rapidly and took in an uneven breath, pushing back the recollection. "That's about it. One miserable time and then he didn't call me anymore. I was worried at first—I thought something bad might have happened to him." Bitter laugh. "The next weekend I found him making out with another girl at the same club where we were supposed to go. He told me then that he'd never really liked me and to run along because it was past my bedtime. That same night, I killed my first vampire. In a way I owe it to being used. I was so upset I wanted to either die or murder someone. At least having some creature try to rip out my throat guaranteed me one or the other."

Bones didn't make any of his usual mocking quips. When I dared to meet his eyes again, he was simply staring at me, no scorn or judgment on his face. The silence stretched, seconds into minutes. It filled with something unexplainable as we kept looking in each other's eyes.

The sudden jostling of the trailer broke the trance as the vehicle ground to a stop. With a slight shake, Bones leapt down from his perch and headed to the rear of the car.

"We're nearly at the place, and there's still work to be done. Hold open that bag for me, Kitten."

His normal jaunty tone was back. Perplexed by the earlier moment, I joined him at the rear of the trailer.

Bones unwrapped Sergio from his plastic shroud as cheerily as a child ripping through wrapping paper on Christmas. I was holding a kitchen-sized garbage bag and wondering what he was up to.

It didn't take long to find out. With his hands, he twisted Sergio's head off as cleanly as if it were the top on a soda bottle. There was a sickening crunch, and then the withering cranium was unceremoniously dumped into the bag.

"Yuck." I thrust the bag back into his hands. "You take it."

"Squeamish? That lump of rotting skull is worth fifty thousand dollars. Sure you don't want to cradle it a bit?" He smiled his familiar mocking smile, the old Bones again.

"No, thanks." Some things money just couldn't buy, and my spending more time with that head was one of them.

The rear of the trailer opened with a creak and Ted appeared in the artificial light.

"We're here, bud. Hope you both had a smooth ride." His eyes twinkled as he looked back and forth between the two of us.

Instantly I was defensive. "We were *talking*."

Ted grinned, and I saw Bones hide a smile as he turned to face his friend.

"Come on, mate. We've been driving for, what . . . fifty minutes? Not nearly enough time."

They both laughed. I didn't, seeing nothing amusing at all.

"Are you finished?"

Sobering, Bones shook his head. "Stay in the trailer for a minute. Something I have to take care of."

"What?" Curiosity killed the cat; I hoped for better results.

"Business. Got a head to deliver, and I want you to stay out of it. The less people know of you, the better."

Made sense. I sat on the edge of the trailer with my feet dangling and then peeled back the cloth to inspect my wrist again. The wound was completely healed, the skin coapted together around the edges and unscarred. There was such a vast difference between vampires and humans, even half-breeds like myself. We weren't even the same species. So why did I tell Bones things I'd never told anyone else? My mother didn't know what happened with Danny, for example. She wouldn't have understood. She wouldn't have understood a *lot* about me, in fact. I hid more from her than I told her, if I were being honest, and yet for some reason, I told Bones things that I should hide.

After about thirty minutes of contemplating this and chipping the polish off my nails, Bones reappeared. He jumped into the trailer, untied his bike, and carried it one-handed to the ground.

"Hop on, pet. We're finished."

"What about the car? Or the torso?"

I climbed behind him, wrapping my arms around his waist for leverage. It was disconcerting to be pressed so close to him after that near miss earlier, but I didn't want to peel myself off the asphalt if I fell. At least he'd given me a helmet, although he didn't wear one himself. One of the advantages of being already dead.

"Ted's taking the car. Got a chop house that he runs for 'em. It's how he makes his living, didn't I tell you?"

No, he hadn't, not that it mattered. "And the body?"

He sped off, leaving me clutching him at the sudden momentum as the motorcycle weaved onto the road.

"Part of the deal. He plants him for me. Less work for

us. Ted's a smart fellow, keeps his mouth shut and minds his business. Don't fret over him."

"I'm not," I shouted over the wind. Actually, I was tired. It had already been a long night.

It was a two-hour drive back to the cave, and we arrived shortly after three A.M. My truck was parked about a quarter mile away from the entrance as usual, since the vehicle couldn't navigate the rest of the way. Bones pulled to a stop at the truck, and I jumped off the motorcycle as soon as it quit moving. Motorcycles made me nervous. They just seemed such an unsafe way to travel. Vampires, of course, didn't share my trepidation of a broken neck, limbs, or skin sloughed off on the pavement. The other reason for my haste was simple—to be away from Bones as quickly as possible. Before any further attacks of stupidity overwhelmed me.

"Off so soon, pet? The evening is young."

He looked at me with a glint in his eye and a devilish curl to his lips. I just collected my keys from their hiding place under a rock and heaved wearily into the truck.

"Maybe for you, but I'm going home. Go find yourself a nice neck to suck on."

Unperturbed, he uncurled himself from the bike.

"Going home wearing that dress with blood all over it? Your mum might worry at seeing you that way. You can come inside and change. Promise I won't peek." The last part was accompanied by an exaggerated wink that made me smile despite my watchfulness.

"No, I'll change at a gas station or something. By the way, since this job is done, when do I have to come back here? Do I get a break?"

I was hoping for a break not only in training, but also in the time spent in his company. Maybe my head needed to be examined, and some time away would help accomplish that.

"Sorry, Kitten. Tomorrow night you're on again. Then after that I fly to Chicago to see my old friend Hennessey. With luck, I'll be back on Thursday, because Friday I have another job for us. . . ."

"Yeah, I get it," I said disgustedly. "Well, you just remember I'm starting college next week, so you'll have to cut me some slack. We might have an arrangement, but I've waited too long already to get my degree."

"Absolutely, pet. Fill your head with volumes of information that will never apply in real life. Just remember—dead girls pass no exams, so don't think you're going to neglect your training. Don't fret, though. We'll work it out. Speaking of that, here you go."

Bones drew out a wide opaque plastic bag from inside his jacket, which had looked considerably fuller than normal, come to notice. Rifling through it for a moment, he pulled out a wad of something green and held it out to me.

"Your share."

Huh? I stared at the multiple hundreds in his hand with disbelief that turned to suspicion.

"What's this?"

He shook his head. "Blimey, but you're a difficult chit! Fellow can't even give you money without you arguing. *This*, luv, is twenty percent of the bounty Sergio had on his head. It's for your part in him *losing* his head. See, I reckon since I don't pay anything to the IRS, I may as well give their cut to you. Death and taxes. They go hand in hand."

Stupefied, I stared at the money. This was more than I could earn in six months of waitressing or working the orchards. And to think I had been worried about draining my savings on gas! Before he changed his mind, I shoved the cash in my glove box.

"Umm, thanks." What did one say? Words left me at the moment.

He grinned. "You earned it, pet."

"You just got a big chunk of change yourself. Are you finally moving out of the cave?"

Bones chuckled. "Is that why you think I stay there? Out of lack of funds?"

His clear amusement made me defensive. "Why else? It's not a Hilton. You have to pirate electricity and you wash in an ice-cold river. I didn't think you did that just because you liked seeing your parts shrink!"

That really made him laugh. "Concerned for my bits and pieces, are you? Let me assure you, they're fine. Of course, if you don't take my word for it, you could always—"

"Don't even think about it!"

He stopped laughing, but there was still a gleam in his eyes. "Too late for that, but back to your question. I stay there because it's safer, primarily. I can hear you or anyone else coming from a mile away, and I know it like the back of my hand. Be difficult for someone to ambush me without my turning it around on them. Also, it's quiet. I'm sure there have been many times the background noise from your house has kept you awake. And besides, it was given to me by a friend, so I check on it when I'm in Ohio and make sure all's well, like I promised him."

"A friend gave you the cave? How do you *give* someone a cave?"

"His people found it hundreds of years ago, so that makes it theirs as much as anyone can claim anything they don't walk around in. Used to be a winter residence of the Mingoes. They were a small tribe of the Iroquois nation, and they were one of the last Iroquois still in the state when the Indian Removal Act of 1831 was put into effect. Tanacharisson was a mate of mine, and he chose not to go to the reservation. He hid at the cave after the last of his tribe was forcibly removed. Time went by, he saw his people and culture being irrevocably destroyed, and he decided he'd had enough. He painted his body for battle and went off on a suicide mission against Fort Meigs. Before he did, though, he asked me to look out for his home. Make sure no one disturbed it. There are bones of some of his ancestors back in the far part of it. He didn't want the whites desecrating them."

"How terrible," I said softly, thinking of that lonely Indian making his last stand after seeing everything he loved disappear.

He studied my face. "It was his choice. He had no control over anything except how he died, and the Mingoes were very proud. To him, it was a good death. One befitting the legacy of his people."

"Maybe. But when death is all you have left, it's sad no matter how you cut it. It's late, Bones. I'm leaving."

He touched my arm then, and his features were very serious.

"About what you told me earlier, I want you to know it wasn't your fault. Bloke like that would've done the same to any girl, and no doubt has before and since you."

"Are you speaking from experience?"

It flew out before I could stop myself. Bones let his arm drop and he stepped back, giving me another unfathomable look.

"No, I'm not. I've never treated a woman in such a manner, and most especially not a virgin. Like I said before— you don't have to be human to have some behaviors be beneath you."

I didn't know what to say to that, so I just hit the gas and drove away.

Eight

It occurred to me the next morning that
I had a few hours with nothing to do and money to
spend. The combination of both had never happened before. Energized by the thought, I ran upstairs to shower
again and get dressed. Showers were all I'd taken lately,
since baths had proven to be slightly dangerous.

After a blissful trip to the mall, I was shocked when I
glanced at my watch and saw that it was after six. My, how
time flew when I wasn't killing something. It was too late
to drive home and give my mother an excuse about tonight,
so I settled on calling her. I lied—again—and told her I'd
run into a friend and would be seeing a movie and having
a late dinner. I hoped whatever occurred tonight wouldn't
take too long. It would be nice to spend a weekend evening
at home for once.

Speeding to arrive late anyway, I leapt from the truck
as soon as I pulled into the familiar grotto. Paranoid, I'd
taken my packages with me. It would be just my luck for
someone to break in and steal my purchases, even at the

edge of the woods. By the time I'd sprinted the remaining mile to the entrance, I was almost out of breath.

Bones was waiting near the opening with a scowl.

"Took your sweet bleedin' time, I see. Oh, but I suppose everything in those bags is for me, so all's forgiven. Guess I don't have to wonder where you've been."

Oops. Suddenly it occurred to me that arriving with an armful of presents bought with his money while not getting him anything might be construed as rude. Covering my faux pas, I straightened my shoulders in feigned offense.

"Actually, I did get you something. Here. It's for . . . umm, your aching muscles and pains."

I handed him the massager I'd bought for my grandfather, realizing too late the stupidity in the gesture. Vampires didn't *have* aching muscles or pains.

He looked at the box with interest.

"Well, well. Five speeds. Heat and massage. Deep, penetrating action. Sure this isn't yours?" That dark brow arched with volumes of meaning, and none of them therapeutic.

I snatched it back.

"Just say so if you don't want it. You don't have to be so crude."

Bones gave me a pointed look. "Keep it and give it to your gramps like it was intended. Blimey, but you're a bad liar. Good thing you manage to pull it off with the marks."

Exasperated already, I fixed him with a scathing look.

"Can we get on to business? Like the details about tonight?"

"Oh, that." We descended deeper into the cave. "Let's see, your bloke's over two hundred years old, naturally brown hair, but he changes his color periodically, talks with an accent, and is very quick in combat. Good news is, you can keep your knickers on. He'll be smitten with you on sight. Any questions?"

"What's his name?"

"He'll probably make one up, most vampires do, but his name is Crispin. Get me when you're ready. I'll be watching telly."

Bones left me at my makeshift dressing room, and I flipped through the dozen or so skank-wears he'd bought me until I pulled out a halter dress that almost skimmed the knees. Still too tight, but at least my boobs and butt didn't hang out of it.

An hour of hot rollers, makeup, and high-heeled boots later, I was ready. Bones lounged sideways across the weathered chair, avidly watching Court TV. He loved the channel. Somehow, seeing a criminal get such a kick out of that program disturbed me. His favorite comment was that victims had less than half the rights of the offenders.

"Hate to pry you away, but I'm ready. You know, places to be, etc."

He glanced up in mild pique. "This is a good part. They're about to deliver a verdict."

"Oh, for God's sake! You're worried about a verdict on a murder case when we're about to commit one! Doesn't that strike you as a little ironic?"

Suddenly he was in front of me, uncurling himself with the speed a striking rattler would envy.

"Yes, it does, pet. Let's be off."

"Aren't you driving separately?" We never rode together, to avoid people making the connection.

He shrugged it off.

"Believe me, you'd never find the place. It's a different sort of club, very particular. Come on, let's not keep the gent waiting."

Different sort of club. That was the biggest understatement I'd ever heard. It was far off the main highways, down a twisting back road that looked seldom traveled, and inside an industrial warehouse that was soundproofed.

To the outside observer, it was simply another blue-collar industry building. Parking was around the back with only one narrow way in or out between tall trees that acted as a natural gate.

"What is this place?"

My eyes bugged even before we approached the door. There was a line of people waiting for entry. Bones simply passed by them while pulling me along up to the female at the door who I assumed was the bouncer. She was as tall and broad-shouldered as a linebacker, with a face that would have been beautiful except for its preponderance of masculinity.

"Trixie, missed you," Bones greeted her. She actually had to bend down to return his kiss on the cheek.

"Been a while, Bones. Heard you'd left these parts."

He grinned and she returned it, showing gold incisors in her smile. Nice.

"Don't believe everything you hear. That's how rumors get started."

We slipped through the door, to the consternation of the waiting patrons. It was dark inside, with low beams of reduced light making brief flashes across the ceilings, and immediately I knew what kind of a "different" club it was.

There were vampires everywhere.

"What the hell is this?"

My whisper was low and savage, because plenty of things here had great hearing.

Bones waved an unconcerned hand to encompass the general surroundings.

"*This*, luv, is a vampire club. It doesn't even really have a name, although the locals call it Bite. All sorts of things come in here to mix and mingle comfortably, not having to hide their true natures. Why, right over there you have some ghosts at the bar."

My vision swung to where he gestured. Damned if there

weren't three transparent men sitting (sort of) on barstools, looking for all the world like a couple of regulars from *Cheers*. Well, *Cheers Macabre*, maybe. The energy that vibrated off the inhuman inhabitants made my entire body feel like it touched a live wire.

"My God . . . there's so many of them. . . ."

And there were. A couple hundred, at least.

"I hadn't known there were that many vampires in the *world* . . ." I went on in disbelief.

"Kitten," Bones said patiently, "'round five percent of the population is undead. We're in every state, every nation, and we have been for a very long time. Now, I give you, there are certain areas where you'll find more of us. Ohio happens to be one of them. I told you it has a thinner line separating the natural and the paranormal, so the whole region gives off a faint charge. The younger ones love that. Find it invigorating."

"You're telling me my state is . . . a vampire hot spot?"

A nod. "Don't feel too unlucky. There are dozens around the globe."

Something brushed past, and my radar went haywire as I craned my neck to see who, or what, had just slipped by.

"What was that?" I whispered, having to press my mouth nearly to his ear to be heard. They were a noisy bunch of immortals.

"What?" He glanced in the direction I stared.

"That." Impatiently. "That . . . thing. It's not a vampire, I can tell, but it's definitely not human. What is it?" *It* being of male gender, though I wouldn't have been sure of anything, and looking human but not quite.

"Oh, him. He's a ghoul. Flesh-eater. You know, like *Night of the Living Dead*, only they don't walk so funny or look as hideous."

Flesh-eater. My stomach heaved at the thought.

"Here." He pointed to the bar. There was an empty seat

near the ghosts—or would the politically correct term be living-impaired? "Wait there, have a drink. Your bloke will show up soon."

"Are you crazy?" My mind couldn't compute fast enough all of the reasons not to do as directed. "This place is crawling with monsters! I don't want to be an appetizer!"

He laughed low. "Trust me, Kitten. See all the normal people waiting to get in? This is a special place, like I said. Mostly vamps and ghouls, but also humans as well. That's part of the lure. The humans that come here are handpicked or they wouldn't know about it. They come to mingle with the undead, and even to get some blood extracted. Believe me, there are those who get off on it. Whole Dracula thing, y'know. But there is a strict etiquette here. Absolutely no violence on the premises and only willing feedings. Can human nightclubs say the same?"

With that, he melted off into the crowds, leaving me with no choice but to sit where he said and wait for my victim. How was I supposed to spot him here? It looked like *Creepshow* met Studio 54.

The bartender, a vampire, asked me what my pleasure would be.

"Leaving," I snapped, then realized how rude that was. "Uh, sorry . . . um . . . do you have gin and tonic? You know . . . for normal people?" All I needed was a flesh spritzer, or a Bloody Mary the likes of which I'd never forget, to make my night complete.

The bartender laughed, showing teeth without a hint of fang. "First time here, honey? Don't be nervous, it's perfectly safe. Unless you leave with someone, of course. Then you're on your own."

How comforting. After assuring me the drink contained nothing more than regular gin and tonic—he showed me the bottles to allay my suspicion—I gulped it down as though it were a magic elixir that could make the whole place disappear. It was delicious, better in fact than any I'd had before. The bartender, whose name was Logan, smiled when I complimented him on it and informed me that after a hundred years, one got rather good at the trade.

"You've been a bartender for a hundred years?" Goggling at him, I quaffed another healthy sip. "My God, why?"

A casual shrug. "I like the work. You meet new people, get to talk a lot, and don't have to think. How many jobs can you say that about?"

How many, indeed. Certainly not mine.

"What do you do, young lady?" he inquired politely.

Kill vampires. "I, ah, go to school. College, that is."

Nervousness made me sputter. Here I was, having a casual conversation with a vampire in a club full of ungodly things. Where had my life gone wrong?

"Ah, college. Study hard, it's the key to success." With that advice and another quick smile, he turned away to take an incoming order from a ghoul across the counter. This was too weird.

"Hello, there, pretty girl!"

The voice made me turn around, and two young men grinned at me in a friendly way. From their looks and heartbeats, I knew they were human. Wow, what a relief.

"Hi, how ya doing?" I felt like someone in another country who met a stranger from her hometown and was inordinately glad to see people with pulses. They gathered around me, one on either side of my chair.

"What's your name? This is Martin"—he gestured to the brunette with the boyish smile—"and I'm Ralphie."

"I'm Cat." Smiling, I shook hands with both of them. They eyed my glass with interest.

"Whatcha drinkin'?"

"Gin and tonic."

Ralphie was about my height of five-seven, not tall for a man, and he had a sweet smile. "Another gin for the lady!"

he bellowed importantly to Logan, who nodded and brought a fresh glass.

"Thanks for the offer, boys, but I'm kind of . . . waiting for someone." As much as I liked having my own kind around me, still there was a job to be done and they would hinder my plans.

They each groaned theatrically.

"Come on, one drink! It's hard to be the fleshies around here, we have to stick together."

The entreaty so clearly mirrored my own thoughts that I relented with another smile.

"One drink. That's all, okay? What are you two doing here, by the way?" They both looked my age and way too innocent.

"Oh, we like it here, it's exciting." Martin bobbed his head up and down like a bird, watching as Ralphie again gestured to Logan for another refill.

"Yeah, exciting enough to get you killed," I warned them.

Martin dropped his wallet when he fumbled for the money for my gin, and I got down to help him pick it up. They looked too gullible by half. Giggling, Ralphie handed me my drink with a flourish.

"*You're* here. You can't say you don't understand."

"You don't want to know why I'm here," I muttered, more to myself than to them. With a slight salute, I raised my glass. "Thanks for the drink. Now you'd better go."

"Aren't you going to finish it?" Ralphie asked with almost childish disappointment.

I opened my mouth to respond, but a familiar voice beat me to it.

"Sod off, wankers."

Bones loomed threateningly behind them, and they gave him one frightened look before scampering off. He slid into the seat next to me after shoving its occupant aside. The person left, unoffended. Guess it wasn't that uncommon.

"What are you doing here? What if *he* comes in?" My voice was a low hiss as I pretended not to look at him for the benefit of anyone watching.

He simply laughed that infuriating chuckle of his and held out a hand.

"We haven't met. My name is Crispin."

I ignored the hand extended to me and whispered furiously to him out of the corner of my mouth, "I don't think that's funny."

"Don't want to shake my hand, do you? That's not nice manners. Didn't your mum teach you better?"

"Will you stop?" I'd passed the point of furious and headed straight into enraged. "Quit playing! I have a job to do. The real Crispin's going to be here and he'll be put off by your blathering! God, don't you have any sense?" Sometimes he was too cheeky for his own good.

"But I'm not lying, pet. My name *is* Crispin. Crispin Phillip Arthur Russell III. That last part was merely a bit of fancy on my mum's part, since clearly she had no idea who my da was. Still, she thought adding numerals after my name would give me a bit of dignity. Poor sweet woman, ever reluctant to face reality."

It occurred to me with mounting anxiety that he wasn't kidding. "*You're* Crispin? You? But your name——"

"Told you," he interrupted. "Most vampires change their name when they change from human. Crispin was my human name, just as I said. Don't go by it much anymore, because that bloke is dead. When Ian turned me, he laid me in the natives' burial grounds until I rose. For hundreds of years they'd buried their dead in the same place, and not too deeply, either. When my eyes opened for the first time as a vampire, all I saw about me were bones. I knew it was what I was then, for from bones I rose and Bones I became, all in that night."

The imagery was haunting, but still I persisted. "Then what kind of game are you up to? You want me to try and kill you, is that it?"

He laughed indulgently. "Blimey, no. In fact, this is all your doing."

"My doing? How could I have anything to do with . . ." looking all around, adequate words failed me. "*This*?"

"You said last night when you were moaning about your life that you'd never been to a club just to have fun and go dancing. Well, pet, this is it. Tonight you and I will drink and dance and absolutely murder no one. Consider it your night off. You will be Cat and I will be Crispin, and you'll send me home with a dry mouth and aching balls just like you would if we'd never met before."

"Was this all some trick to get me to go on a date with you?" With a scowl I drank my gin, courtesy of the two human boys who had run for the hills after one dirty look.

His eyes glowed with dark lights and that sly curl returned to his lips.

"Let you keep your knickers on, though, didn't I? Can't even appreciate the little things, you can't. Come on, luv, finish your drink and let's dance. Promise I'll be the perfect gentleman. Unless you request otherwise."

I set my glass on the counter.

"Sorry, *Crispin*, but I don't dance. Never learned how. You know, whole lack of a social life and all that."

His eyebrows nearly swept his hairline. "You've never been dancing? That deflowerer of yours never even took you out for a twirl? Bloody sod."

The memory of Danny continued to smart. "Nope. I don't dance."

He shot me a measured look. "Now you do."

He practically hauled me to my feet, ignoring my protests and vain attempts to pull free. When we were well inside the hoard of human and inhuman gyrators, he spun me around until my back was to him. He had one arm wrapped around my waist while the other still gripped my hand. His body was pressed along the length of mine, hips intimately touching front to rear.

"I swear if you try anything . . ." My threat was drowned out in the music pumping and noise around us.

"Relax, I'm not going to bite." Laughing at his own joke, he began to sway in time to the beat, hips and shoulders rubbing against mine.

"Come on, it's easy. Move the way I do, we'll start you out slow."

Out of lack of other options except to stand there stupidly, I followed the line of his body, mimicking his movements. The pulsating beat seemed to jerk my nerve endings like invisible puppet strings, and soon I undulated against him of my own accord. He was right, it was easy. And sexy as hell. Now I knew how a snake felt when the charmer played his flute, slavishly twisting along to the music. Bones whirled me around to face him, still gripping my hand as if fearing I would bolt.

He needn't have worried. I was curiously enjoying myself. The lights and sounds seemed to blur together. All of the bodies brushing by us made me feel drunk from their collective energy. It was a heady feeling, to let my body move any way it wanted, directed by the rhythm and nothing else. I raised my arms and let my head fall back, surrendering to the sensation. Bones slid his hands to my waist, lightly holding me, and a mischievous impulse surged through me. He had blackmailed me, beaten me, and forced me to endure unbelievable rigors of training. Time for a little well-deserved payback.

I splayed my hands across his chest, seeing his eyes widen, and brought him closer until our bodies touched and my breasts rubbed against him. Then I gave a slow twist of my hips against his as I'd seen another dancer do.

His arms tightened around me, yanking me to him until we were molded together. One hand crept up to tug my head back, and I smiled smugly at him.

"You were right, it's easy. And I'm a fast learner."

My body was still curled around his, taunting him. This was so unlike me, but something felt as though it had taken over. My earlier concerns were a faint memory not even worth dwelling on. The lights caused deep hollows to form under his cheekbones, making them look even more pronounced. The heat in his eyes should have made me break free and run, but all it did was entice me.

"Playing with fire, Kitten?"

His mouth grazed my cheek as he spoke directly in my ear to be heard above the noise. His lips were cool against my skin, but not cold. My head spun, my senses reeled, and in reply my tongue crept out and licked his neck with a long wet stroke.

The shudder went all through him. Bones pressed me so close that his body ground into mine, jerking my head back with a thick handful of hair until our eyes locked. What had started out as a game was now an open challenge, as well as a direct threat. Any further action would bear results, it was clear from the way his gaze smoldered into mine. All of this should have frightened me, but it was as if my mind were incapable of rational thought. He was a vampire, a hit man, and had almost killed me . . . and nothing mattered more than the feel of him. I licked my lips and didn't pull away, and it was all the invitation he needed.

His mouth came down onto mine, slanting across without difficulty, since I moaned at the first touch. It had been so long, *so long* since I'd kissed someone and not been faking it. The last time had been with Danny, and the scant desire I'd felt then was nothing compared to the searing flash of heat in me now. His tongue caressed my lips briefly before twining around mine and seeking my depths with ruthless sensuality. My heart pounded so fiercely I knew he could feel its pulse in my mouth as I responded, pulling him closer and digging my nails into his back. Bones deepened the kiss further until he sucked on my tongue. Everything inside me began to throb with need. I returned the gesture with more strength, drawing on his tongue with erotic hunger. There was a distinct hardness to him as he rubbed his hips against mine in a wave of friction that caused a near-excruciating clench in my loins.

He only pulled away to snap at someone when we were rudely jostled for no longer dancing, leaving me to gulp in breaths of air. My legs felt almost rubbery and lights danced in my head. Bones propelled me toward the far wall until we were clear of the dance floor, tumbling my hair in my face from the speed of his action. He brushed it back to kiss me again, and this kiss was better than the one before. His whole body seemed to be poured into his searching mouth. He finally pulled away, but didn't go far.

"Kitten, you need to make a decision. Either we stay here and behave or we leave now and I promise you"—his voice dipped lower and the words fell against my lips—"if we leave, *I won't behave.*"

His mouth closed over mine once more, lips and tongue expertly evoking a response. My self-control was still somewhere away on vacation and my arms went around his neck because I simply wanted more. His back was to the wall and one hand was in my hair while the other was low, dangerously low on my back. Fingers kneaded my flesh through the thin material of the dress, holding me so close, every movement he made stroked me. After another few dizzying minutes, he broke the kiss to whisper almost raggedly in my ear.

"Decide now, luv, because I can't take much more of this before I make up your mind and carry you off."

The room seemed fuzzy, the lights dimmer, and there was a far-off noise in my head. None of those things seemed important, however, except for Bones. His body felt as hard and sinewy as a racehorse's, and his mouth on mine made me want to scream with lust. There wasn't a single part of me that wanted to be anywhere but with him.

"Bones . . ." I couldn't begin to articulate the need.

Unexpectedly his whole body stiffened, and he looked over my shoulder with tension ringing off him.

"Bloody frigging hell, what is he doing here?"

He seemed to freeze in my arms, face hardening as though turned to stone.

Confused, I squirmed to look behind me. "Who? Who's here?"

"Hennessey."

Nine

MY MIND COULDN'T SEEM TO KEEP UP WITH current events. "I thought Sergio said he was in Chicago. He's supposed to be in Chicago!"

Bones muttered a foul curse and straightened, spinning us around until his back was to the door.

"Do you think Sergio lied to us?" I persisted.

He shook his head as if to clear it.

"Keep your eye on him, luv. Black hair. Mustache, thin beard, dark skin, tall. Wearing a white shirt, see him?"

I leaned my head against Bones's shoulder and scanned the faces until I found one that matched.

"Got him."

"Sergio didn't lie," Bones answered my earlier question grimly. "That means somehow Hennessey got word that he's gone missing. He knew Sergio was in this area, so he's poking around here for answers. He's no doubt rightly worried about what Sergio would have said to whoever made him disappear."

"Well, whatever the reason, he's here. Let's go for him."

"No."

The single word surprised me. "No? Why not? He just got dropped into our lap!"

His expression was ice, and he kept his voice low. "Because he's a bloody treacherous sod and I don't want you anywhere near him. You're going straight home as soon as he's away from the door. I'll handle this myself."

My head cleared enough for me to be pissed.

"You know, for someone who keeps telling me to trust him, you sure don't extend the same courtesy. I thought tonight was a regular job, so I'm all staked out and ready to roll. I took on vampires before you, remember? All by myself and without someone to hold my hand through it. Now I have training and backup, and you still want me to turn tail and run? Don't kiss me like a woman if you're going to treat me like a child."

Bones stared down at me with frustration. "This isn't about treating you like a child. Bugger, I clearly don't see you that way! Look, I told you Hennessey's not just a bloke who goes out and snatches up a girl when his tummy grumbles. He's in another league, Kitten. He's a very bad sort."

"Then quit arguing and let's go get him," I said, softly but firmly. "He sounds just like the kind of person I'd love to take out."

Bones didn't say anything for a moment, then he let out a resigned noise.

"I don't like this, not at all, but . . . fine. We'll go for him. So much for a night off. If anything goes wrong, anything at all, you hit that panic button. Now, here's what we'll do. . . ."

He outlined the plan quickly and I picked a place near the bar where Hennessey just sat, keeping myself within eyeshot. Actually, I still felt a little dizzy, not that I'd told Bones. He'd have pulled the plug on this for sure if he knew. God, had it been so long since I'd been kissed, a few smooches were enough to throw off my equilibrium? Just to be safe, though, I ordered a Coke instead of my usual gin and tonic. Maybe my resistance to alcohol wasn't as strong as I'd thought.

After about five minutes, Hennessey glided over. It amazed me how vampires seemed to be drawn to me. Certainly there were plenty of other pretty human girls milling about with veins just as big and juicy as mine. Bones told me once there was something about my skin that was eye-catching, some glow that still looked human but also a touch vampiric. He said it was like a homing beacon.

"I haven't seen you here before, Red. May I sit down?"

Wow, manners. Usually vamps just plunked down next to me, ready or not. After a faint inclination of my head in the affirmative, he sat next to me, regarding me with hooded blue eyes.

"Can I buy you a drink?"

Hmmm, two for two on politeness. With feigned regret, I smiled at him.

"Sorry, but I'm kind of here with someone. Wouldn't want to be rude."

"Ah, I see." He settled back into his chair but made no effort to vacate it. "Husband, perhaps?"

The thought of being married to Bones made me nearly choke on my next swallow of soda. "No. A first date, actually."

Hennessey smiled and spread out his hands in a harmless manner.

"First dates. They can be quite something, can't they? Either perfume or poison, with usually no in between. Tell me, if I may be so bold—which one is it for you?"

With a slightly embarrassed look to my face, I leaned in an inch. "If I had to answer now, I'd say poison. He's a bit . . . arrogant. Full of himself. I just hate that, don't you?"

My smile was all innocence as inside I laughed at my

chance to disparage the man who was going to kill the vampire opposite me at the earliest opportunity.

Hennessey nodded in agreement.

"That can be bothersome. It is always better to speak less and not more of oneself, don't you agree?"

"I couldn't agree more. What did you say your name was?" This one would have to be handled delicately, no crude potty-mouth with him. Boy, for someone that Bones had described as practically sprouting horns, Hennessey seemed almost . . . charming.

He smiled. "Call me Hennessey."

"Don't mind if I do, mate. Been a while, hasn't it?"

Bones appeared behind me, leaning down to kiss my cheek. I flinched out of genuine habit and it was perfect. The picture of the bad-first-date syndrome. Out of the corner of my eye I saw Hennessey's mouth tighten.

"Bones. What an unexpected . . . surprise. This lovely young woman can't be with you. She's far too well mannered."

Well, score one for the bad guy.

Bones gave Hennessey a look laden with threat. "You're in my seat."

"Bones," I chided him as if aghast, "you're being rude. This nice man was just keeping me company while you were away."

"Yes," Hennessey purred, looking at Bones with a gleam. "Can't expect to leave such a pretty thing alone for long, old chap. Some monster might just . . . snatch her up."

"Funny you should say that." There was an ugly undercurrent in his voice I hadn't heard before. Whatever had happened between them, Bones *really* didn't like him. "I hear that's your specialty."

Hennessey's eyes narrowed. The tension between them thickened. "Now, where would you ever hear something like that?"

Bones smiled with coldness. "You'd be amazed at the things people can find if they dig deep enough."

I looked at both of them. It seemed like any second, they'd quit the verbal exchange and go right for each other's throats.

Logan leaned across the bar and tapped the edge of my forgotten glass. He'd apparently picked up on their malevolent vibe as well.

"Not here, gentlemen. You know the rules."

Hennessey looked at Logan and waved an airy hand. "Yes, I know. Pesky ordinance, that, but one must abide by the rules of the house when one visits."

"Cut the fancy talk," Bones said sharply. "It doesn't suit you. That is my chair and she is my date, so back off."

"Excuse me." In a perfect imitation of outrage, I stood up and faced Bones. "I don't know how you're used to talking with other girls, but I will not be referred to in the third person as if I'm not even here! You don't own me, this is our first date. And I wouldn't have even gone out with you if you hadn't kept begging me." I bit back a grin as Bones blanched in indignation at that. "Our date is *over*. I'll call a cab. In the meantime, you can get lost."

Hennessey laughed. "You heard the lady. You know the rules. Only willing companions here, and she is clearly not willing. As she said, get lost."

Bones took it with thinly concealed wrath.

"Let's be men about this. Why don't we go outside and settle this, you and me? Been a long time coming."

Hennessey's eyes gleamed. "Oh, we'll settle this, mark my words. Not right now, but soon. You've been meddling where you shouldn't for too long."

What did that mean? I wondered. I'd have to ask later.

"Oohhh, I'm shakin' in me boots," Bones mocked. "Another time, another place, then. Looking forward to it."

With those last threatening words, he stalked off.

Pretending to be shaken, I grabbed for my purse and began to throw money on the table.

Hennessey stopped me with a beseeching hand on my arm. "Please, stay and have a drink with me. I feel responsible for what happened, but I must tell you it was for the best. That is a ruthless man."

As if reluctant, I sat back down.

"Okay, a drink. Maybe I owe it to you anyways for getting rid of that creep for me. My name is Cat, by the way. Bones forgot to introduce us." My smile wobbled for effect.

He kissed my hand.

"A true pleasure, Cat."

Hennessey coaxed me back into ordering alcohol, and so I had another gin and tonic. After three more, I pleaded to be excused to the ladies' room and left him at the bar. That residual dizziness still clung to me. Everything around me looked slightly altered, almost fuzzy around the edges. Time to switch back to Coke.

The bathroom was on the other side of the club, and once exiting it I saw Bones on the imitation balcony. His back was against the glass wall that separated us. I wanted to give him an update while I had the chance, so I quickened my pace and crossed through the people until I came to a door on the opposite side of the balcony he was on.

There was a woman in front of him. Her arms hung loosely at her sides and Bones gripped her shoulders. His mouth was on her neck, and the glow of vampire green shone from his eyes. I froze, transfixed, and watched as his throat worked, swallowing occasionally. The girl didn't struggle. In fact, she was half sagged against him.

His eyes suddenly lifted to look straight at me. Helpless to glance away, I stared as he continued to feed. After a few moments, he pulled his mouth from her neck. Surprisingly it was only a little red. He must be a dainty eater. With his gaze still locked to mine, he sliced his thumb on a fang and then held it to her neck. The two holes closed at once, and then vanished.

"Off you go," he instructed her.

With a lethargic smile she obeyed, walking right past me without batting an eye.

"Didn't your mum tell you it's rude to stare at someone when they eat?"

The casual tone to his voice shook me from my stupor.

"That girl . . . she's okay?" She certainly hadn't looked mortally drained, but then again, I was no expert.

"Of course. She's used to it. That's what most of them are here for, I told you that. They're the menu, with legs."

Bones came closer, but I retreated a step. He saw it and frowned.

"What's wrong? Look, the girl's fine. It's not like you didn't know I was a vampire. Did you just think I never fed?"

The thought was so repellent to me I'd never dwelled on it one way or the other. Witnessing the scene just now had been the bucket of icy water I needed.

"I came to tell you we're hitting it off. Probably be leaving in about twenty minutes." Absently, I began to rub my head. It had started to spin again.

"Are you feeling all right?"

The absurdity of the question made a bark of laughter escape me.

"No, I am not all right. Very far from it, actually. Earlier I kissed you, and now I just watched you make a Slurpee out of a girl's neck. Add to that a headache and it makes me not in the least *all right*."

He moved closer, and again I backed away. "Don't touch me."

Muttering a curse, he clenched his hands but stayed put.

"Fine. We'll talk about this later. Go on back, before he starts to get antsy."

"We won't talk about it later," I coldly stated while walking back toward the door. "In fact, I never want to speak about it again."

I was still rattled when I sat back down next to Hennessey, but I plastered a smile on my face and promptly ordered another gin and tonic. *Damn the Coke, full speed ahead!*

Hennessey reached out and grasped my hand. "What's wrong, Cat? You look distressed."

I debated lying but then thought better of it. He might have glimpsed me speaking to Bones, although he wouldn't have been able to hear us in this racket, so I didn't want to make him suspicious.

"Oh, nothing, really. I ran into Bones on my way back from the bathroom, and he said a few less-than-gentlemanly things. Guess it just upset me, that's all."

Hennessey withdrew his hand and stood, a smile of perfect politeness on his face. "Would you excuse me? I suddenly feel the need to renew an acquaintance."

"Please don't," I blurted, not wanting to have started a fight. Well, not yet.

"I'll only be a few minutes, my dear. Just to let him know his rudeness wasn't appreciated." He left me there with my mouth still forming protests. Annoyed, I swallowed the rest of my tonic, and was about to order another one when Ralphie and Martin sidled up.

"Hey, there! Remember us?"

Their smiles were so genuinely artless I felt a reluctant answering tug of the lips.

"Hello, boys."

They stood around me, one on either side again.

"Is that your date?" Ralphie asked, goggle-eyed.

"No. Yes. Well, he kind of is now. My other one didn't work out, so this guy is keeping me company." I was as vague as possible on any details that could somehow endanger them later. "He just went off for a little macho showboating, probably be gone about ten minutes. When he comes back, you scatter, okay?"

"Sure thing," they chorused.

Martin held out a drink in his hand with a shy smile.

"It's a gin and tonic, like you ordered before. After you had one, I tried them. They're good!"

The boyish delight on his face was infectious, and my smile broadened.

"Here," he said importantly. "It's a fresh one. I'll wait for the bartender for another."

"Why, thank you."

After raising it in salute, I took a long draught. It was slightly more bitter than the other ones I'd had. Maybe it was made by a bartender not as skilled as Logan.

"Delicious." Hiding my grimace, I took another drink so their feelings wouldn't be hurt.

They glanced anxiously at me and back and forth between themselves.

"Do you want to see my car?" Ralphie asked, eyes wide and intent. "It's a new Porsche, totally loaded. It's so cool."

"Yeah," Martin chimed in. "You gotta see it, it's really trick!"

From out of his pants Ralphie pulled keys, one with the Porsche insignia. "I'll let you drive it."

Their combined glee at the vehicle made me wistful. When had I ever been so excited over a car? Then again, I'd never owned a Porsche. Money must be a neat thing to have.

With a firm shake of my head, I set my glass down. My mind had begun to whirl again. It was definitely time to go back to the soda.

"Sorry, guys. Can't leave my date. Wouldn't be proper."

Complete sentences were something I couldn't seem to wrap my mind around. I was anxious to get on with the plan so that I could go home and sleep. Sleep sounded wonderful to me right now.

Ralphie tugged my hands, and Martin gave my shoulders a push. I blinked at them in confusion and sat up straighter. Or tried to.

"Hey. Don't get pushy. Sorry, but I said no."

"Come on," Ralphie urged, still pulling at my hands. "Just for a second! Hurry, before he comes back!"

"No!"

Now I was pissed. Everyone was trying to get me to do things I didn't want to do. That I should never be doing, no matter how good they felt. . . .

I pushed Ralphie off with enough force to make him stumble backward.

"You have to leave now."

They exchanged glances again, surprised. Apparently girls really must like the Porsche. They were stunned they'd been refused.

"Go." Putting more threat into my voice, I swiveled in my seat to turn my back to them. "Bartender," I called out wearily, and Logan appeared after a minute. "Do you have any Tylenol?"

Hennessey and I left fifteen minutes later. When he'd finally returned, I felt like complete shit. All I wanted to do was sleep, and I couldn't until we finished him off. Abruptly I suggested we leave and go to a different club, saying that I wanted to avoid another run-in with Bones. He accepted without hesitation and we were soon driving out of the narrow parkway in his loaded Mercedes. Was it a vampire thing, to own a Mercedes?

My head spun, and I could barely keep up with his pleasant conversation as he drove. In the back of my mind I wondered what my problem was, but it seemed too hard to concentrate. My eyes fluttered closed for a moment before I snapped them open. What was wrong with me?

"Too much to drink, Cat?"

For once, I wasn't faking when I answered him with slurred words.

"Y-you don't understand. . . ." Talking became difficult, and the first pangs of warning shot through me. Something was very wrong. "I can hadddle . . . *handle* my drink."

Hennessey smiled.

"I disagree. Perhaps we should journey to my place, where you can lie down and rest. You look too indisposed to go to another club."

"No . . . noooo. . . ." Vaguely I knew that would be bad, but I was having trouble remembering why. Who was this man in the car, anyway? How had I gotten here? My mind drifted away.

"I think so. You'll feel better for it."

Ignoring me, he was ignoring me! He was going to take me to his house, and something bad was going to happen. What was bad? Where was I? Had to get him to stop, to pull over. Then . . . I'd run away. Yes. Run away. And sleep.

"You have to stop," I slurred, horrified at the dark colors encroaching on the edge of my vision. A dull ringing began to sound in my ears.

"No, Cat. We'll stop at home."

He continued on the same route. We were nearly out of the country roads and would soon be on the freeway. Something inside me knew to prevent him.

"I'm going to throw up," I warned, and it wasn't an empty threat. My stomach heaved dangerously. Gagging, I leaned toward him.

The car screeched to a halt so fast the air bags should have deployed. "Not in the car!" he gasped, leaning over me and opening my door.

At once I spilled out onto the ground, retching as promised. Some of it splattered my dress and I heaved until my stomach felt stripped of its contents. Above me, I could hear Hennessey make a sound of disgust.

"You've gotten it all over yourself! Now I can't let you back in the car. You'd ruin the seats!"

This pleased me, but only a little, since I couldn't remember where I was or why I didn't want to go back into the car.

Suddenly I was moving, and painfully. He grabbed me by the hair and dragged me off the road into the trees as I tried to struggle. This was bad, it was very bad. My legs felt like boulders. Too heavy to move. My arms weren't much better, but I futilely slapped at him with no strength. He finally came to a stop and reached behind my neck to unfasten my halter. The dress dropped to my waist, leaving only the strapless bra covering my chest.

"Beautiful," he sighed, and undid the strap to bare my breasts.

"Don't."

I tried to scoot away, but my legs wouldn't work. Hennessey knelt over me, careful not to get dirty, and pushed my hair aside. At once his face transformed into glowing eyes and fangs. One hand cupped my breast, squeezing roughly, while the other held my head. Slow tears leaked out of my eyes as I sat trapped, unable to move or think. There was something that could help me, something . . . if I could only remember what it was.

A sharp pain in my neck made me gasp. Oh God, he bit me! He was drinking me! My legs kicked weakly, and my watch tangled in his hair as I tried to push him away. A dim flicker of memory remained, fading fast with every hurtful pull of his mouth. There was something about my watch. . . .

My vision blackened, but before darkness claimed me, I pushed a button.

Ͳεπ

SOMETHING WAS PRESSED AGAINST MY MOUTH.
Liquid spilled into it and rushed down my throat so fast I
choked, coughing. From far off I heard someone speaking
to me, shaking me, and the fluid pitilessly continued to pour.
I swallowed to prevent drowning in it, then the voice became clearer and I could see again.

Bones was behind me, clutching me to his chest. We
were sprawled on the ground. One arm held me to him and
his other wrist was shoved against my mouth. It was his
blood overflowing into me.

"Stop that, you know I hate that." Spitting out the remaining mouthful, I tried to push away, but he tightened
his grip, twisting around so he could see me.

"Bloody hell, you're all right. Your heart slowed for a
minute. Scared the wits out of me."

As my vision slowly cleared, I could see a dead vampire
in front of me. His head was twisted mostly off, and one
eye hung out of its socket. The flesh shriveled back against
the bones in the traditional way after true death, but the

face wasn't Hennessey's. It was someone I'd never seen before.

"Where's Hennessey?" My voice was only a murmur. Although my eyes and ears worked, my mind still rotated.

Bones gave a snort of disgust behind me.

"Blasted sod ran off. I was already on my way to you when I got your page. I pulled Hennessey off you, and we started to go at it when the bloody boot opens and this fellow pops out. He'd been hiding there as Hennessey's bleedin' bodyguard. Bloke jumped me and Hennessey took off. The bugger put up a hell of a fight, too. When I finished with him, I checked on you. That's when I saw that you were barely breathing and opened a vein. You really should have more, you're still pale as death."

"No." My response was soft but firm. Already I was afraid I'd had too much, remembering all the swallowing. Ugh.

"What happened back there? I thought you were just pretending and taking it far to goad me. Worked as well, that's why I was almost on him when your page went off. Did he catch you off guard?"

Although he no longer fed me, he still had his arms around me. A part of me protested, especially since I was naked from the waist up, but I was too exhausted to mention it. Forcing my mind to work, I thought back over the events. It was like cotton had replaced my brain.

"Um, I don't know. We got in his car and I started feeling sick. . . . No, that's wrong. I felt sick before, at the club. It started when we were dancing. Somehow I felt drunk. Everything was blurry and the lights seemed far off. . . . After a while it got under control, but when I left, it came back three times as bad. I couldn't move. My legs wouldn't work and my mind . . . I couldn't think. I even forgot about the watch until it got caught in his hair. Do you think he drugged me? Could he have known what we were up to?"

Bones pulled me back enough to look into my eyes. What he saw made him curse.

"Your pupils are dilated enough to belong on a corpse. You've been drugged, all right. You say you felt it before he showed up, when we were dancing? That doesn't make sense...."

His voice trailed off and like a brick, the truth hit me. Once again I saw the guileless smiles of Ralphie and Martin while holding out a glass.

"It wasn't him." *Come see my Porsche, come on outside....* "It was those kids. Ralphie and Martin, the ones you told to scram when we first arrived. They handed me a drink then and later when Hennessey went to find you. Those little pricks, they tried to pull me out to their car, they looked surprised when I wouldn't come...." Suddenly I was dizzy again, and my vision swam for a moment.

"You need more blood." It was a statement, and through the fog I waved him off.

"No. No. I'll be fine. I just need to sleep."

The landscape tipped, and when I opened my eyes I was lying on the ground with a familiar jean jacket under my head. Bones was about a dozen yards away, digging a hole.

The moonlight illuminated his skin, and there was a lot to illuminate. He'd taken his shirt off, and it reflected on the diamonds-and-cream flesh it seemed to caress. Without his shirt he looked even more chiseled. Long lines connected his collarbone, his shoulders appeared broader without clothing, and the hard line of his stomach was interrupted only by pants. Hollows and muscles rippled with his effort, and it was the loveliest sight I'd ever seen.

"Where is your shirt?" Apparently I'd spoken aloud instead of just wondered it in my mind, because he turned and answered me.

"You're wearing it, luv."

Leaning over, he picked up the dead vampire with one hand and plunked him in the hole, piling dirt on top of him.

"You're absolutely stunning without it, you know that . . . ?" My internal monologue was all off, since evidently I'd been audible again.

He paused to grin at me, teeth flashing in the night.

"It hasn't escaped my notice that you only compliment me when you're intoxicated. Makes you right more agreeable, it does."

He finished with a last slap of the shovel against the dirt and walked over to me. My vision still fluttered in and out.

"You're always gorgeous," I whispered, reaching out a finger and trailing it down his cheek as he knelt over me. "Kiss me again. . . ."

Nothing felt real. Not the ground underneath me, or his mouth once again moving over mine. A noise of disappointment escaped me when he lifted his head, disentangling himself from my arms.

"Why did you stop? Is it because I taste bad?" Some part of me remembered I'd thrown up recently.

He smiled, brushing his lips across mine once more. "No. You taste like my blood, and I want you unbearably. But not like this. Let's get you safely tucked in. Up you go."

He lifted me in his arms. "Bones," I sighed. "Know something? I'm not afraid of you, but you scare me. . . ." His outline blurred again.

"You scare me, too, Kitten," he might have replied, but I couldn't be sure. It was all black again.

My mother lay behind me with her arms wrapped around me, and I snuggled into her embrace. She never held me, and it felt good. She mumbled something and her voice was low and deep. Her arms were firmly muscled, and her chest pressed alongside my back . . . was rock-hard.

My eyes flew open, and for the second time in my life I woke up in bed with a vampire. This time was infinitely worse, because all I wore was a shirt and panties and he . . .

A scream tore out of my throat. Bones leapt up, head swiveling around to spot the danger. Immediately I looked away, because I'd spotted the danger, all right. Color rose in my face and I squeezed my eyes shut.

"What's wrong? Someone here?" His voice was insistent and deadly.

Mutely I shook my head, wracking my brain as to how I'd ended up here. The last thing I remembered was lying on the ground and kissing him. . . .

"Bones." My teeth ground, but I had to know. "Did you and I . . . did anything happen between us? I don't remember. You have to tell me the truth."

He made an exasperated noise and I felt the bed give under his weight as he climbed back in. I scooted off at once and peeked at him through my lashes until I was sure the sheet covered him below the waist.

He gave me a look of thinly veiled annoyance. "You think I'd shag you while you were passed out cold? Think I'm no better than those two buggers who doctored your drink? Your dress was half ripped off and covered in vomit, no less, so I put a shirt on you and brought you here. Then I went back to the club."

"Oh." Now I felt foolish and wanted to defend my misassumption. "But then why are you naked?"

"Because after I was finished with your little boys and looked around futilely for Hennessey, it was dawn. I was knackered and had blood on my clothes, so I stripped them off and fell into bed. You certainly weren't doing anything but snoring and taking all the bloomin' covers again. Didn't really pause to think about it, sorry." The sarcasm dripped off every word, but his earlier sentence chilled me.

"How did you finish with the boys? What happened to Ralphie and Martin?"

"Fretting about them, are you? So typically American, more concerned about the criminals than the victims. Didn't ask if they found a new friend to play with, did you? Didn't ask about what happened to her. No, you're too anxious over their welfare."

"They drugged someone else? Is she all right?" If he meant to shame me, he'd succeeded.

His eyes drilled into mine.

"No, pet. She is not all right. Since you didn't go down after two doses of their juice, they tripled the quantity. While you were off getting your neck munched on, they were merrily picking out another lass. It was their stupidity to drive her only a mile away from the club. When I went back, I came upon them in a van in the trees and smelled the filthy sods inside. One was shagging the poor girl while the other waited his turn. Course, they didn't realize she was already dead from too much drugs. I tore the doors off and snapped the spine of the lad doing the rooting. This scared the other one right good, as you can guess. I spoke to him a bit first to make sure he'd nothing to do with Hennessey. He sang, said he and his pal made sport of slipping girls drugs and then shagging them before dumping them wherever. Liked to pick vampire clubs and such, because girls who frequented those places tended not to report any crimes. He got real upset when I told him the girl was dead. Cried and said they weren't supposed to die, only lie there. Then I ripped his throat out and drank what was left. After that, I went to the club and reported them to the owner. They don't take to activities like that around their place, it draws unwanted attention. Did those snits a favor by killing them quickly. The owner would have drawn it out for weeks as a warning to any other human stupid enough to try that trick."

Feeling ill, I sat on the edge of the bed and lowered my head. That poor girl, what a tragedy. Hearing how Bones had killed Ralphie and Martin still put a chill through me. Did they deserve it? Yes. Should Bones have done it? I didn't have the answer.

"What did you do with her?"

"Drove the van away after dumping the lads' bodies at the club and parked it off the highway. Someone will find it, see who it's registered to, and make the assumption that after they'd raped her and she overdosed, they split. Well, one of them, as it were. There was blood inside the interior. Coppers will reckon the same bloke who killed them both ran off. It won't be the first time something like this has happened."

"At least her parents will find out about her and not have to wonder for the rest of their lives."

I grieved for that unknown family who would get that terrible phone call. My head dropped to my hands, pounding with a headache. After all that happened, it was a small price to pay.

"Hennessey. What do you think he'll do? Do you think he'll try something, or keep running?"

Bones gave a humorless laugh.

"Hennessey knows I'm after him now. He's suspected it, but he's finally got his proof. He'll try something, all right. But when and where, I have no idea. He might lie low for a bit, or he might come after me straightaway. I don't know, but it's not over."

"It's my fault Hennessey got away. God, I was so stupid not to notice that something was wrong until it was too late. . . ."

"It's not your fault, Kitten."

Hands settled on my shoulders as he slid nearer, and belatedly, it occurred to me that one of the ways I'd acted oddly was to make out with him. Now here we were in bed, with him naked and me nearly so. Not smart.

I got out of bed and turned my back to him, wanting to put more distance between us. It was the drugs that had made me kiss him, the drugs. Repeating it over and over made me feel better.

"Bones, I—I have to thank you. You saved my life. I passed out right after pushing that button, and he would have bled me dry. But you know the only reason I . . . was so forward with you was because of the chemicals they slipped me. You know that, right? Of course, I don't blame you for taking me up on it. I'm sure it meant nothing to you. I just wanted you to know it meant nothing to me as well."

My back was still to him, and I desperately wished for more clothes. It was too dangerous to be trapped with him without thirty layers of armor on.

"Turn 'round." His voice was filled with something I was afraid to decipher. Whatever it was, it wasn't happy.

"Um, can you move that stone so I can get out of here and just—"

"Turn *around*." Now I knew what was in his voice. Threat.

Slowly I faced him.

Without warning he was in front of me, only inches away, still totally nude. My face flamed, but I kept my eyes determinedly upward. That was almost as bad. The expression in his made me tremble.

"I'm really not comfortable with you being naked," I said, struggling for a normal tone and failing.

His brow arched. "Why should it unsettle you, pet? After all, you just said I meant nothing to you beyond mere gratitude. And you've seen a man's body before, so don't pull that blushing act with me. What could be bothering you, then? I know what's bothering *me*." The smoothly bantering tone changed to a low, furious growl. "What's bothering *me* is that you dare to stand there and tell me what I do and do not feel about last night. That kissing you and holding you meant nothing to me. Then, to top it all off, that you were only reacting to me because you were impaired! That's rich. You know what those drugs did to you in the first dose, before the second one made you comatose? They killed the bug up your arse!"

With that, he yanked the stone off its setting and opened the passageway. My mouth hung open in outrage, and he pointed an emphatic finger at the exit.

"Out you go, before I lose my temper and we'll see how much you don't like to kiss me."

Deciding that discretion was the better part of valor, I left. Quickly.

ELEVEN

"**D**ID YOU GET THE NOTES FROM THE LECTURE today? I slept in and didn't wake up until half an hour ago! Was it really boring like last time?"

Stephanie was in my physics class. At least, she was when she showed up. She had missed two days out of the past five, but whenever I got out of class, she'd be there waiting for me. She liked to hang around campus, it was my guess. Found socializing much more interesting than the actual courses.

Stephanie was a petite brunette with an outgoing personality, and she'd spent the last five days pulling me out of my antisocial shell. College began on Monday. Today was Friday, and so far, she was the only person I'd spoken to on this huge, overwhelming campus.

With my friendless track record, I'd been hesitant to engage in normal, amicable small talk. If it didn't have to do with dead bodies, school, or the cherry orchard, I generally didn't know what to say. Stephanie didn't let that faze her. She was cheerful and ebullient enough for both of us, and for some reason, she seemed to take a liking to me right off.

"Yeah, I have them. Do you need to make copies?"

She grinned. "Nah. I probably won't read them anyway. Studying is so boring. Besides, I'm never going to use this crap again, so who needs it?"

Stephanie was a freshman, but in many ways, she was far more sophisticated than me. During our second conversation after class, she'd informed me that she had been dating since she was twelve, lost her virginity at fourteen, and considered men as entertaining and convenient as fast food.

"Tell me why you registered for college?" I asked in amusement.

She nodded pointedly at an attractive male who passed by us.

"The *boys*. This place is *crawling* with them. It's like an all-you-can-eat buffet!"

She and Bones had something in common. He would find the campus an all-you-can-eat buffet, too, just not in nearly the same way.

I had avoided him since waking up in bed with him Sunday morning. Wednesday, I was supposed to meet him at the cave, but I didn't go. I was too confused. My feelings for him had undergone a drastic metamorphosis. Somewhere along the past seven weeks, I'd gone from hating his guts to being inexplicably drawn to him.

"So, do you want to go out tonight and do something?"

I simply stared at her for a second. Twenty-two years old and I'd never gone out with a girl just to have fun and do normal things. Hell, to be more truthfully pathetic, I'd never even had a girlfriend to go out with.

"Um, sure."

She grinned. "Cool, we'll have a blast. How about you meet me at my place? We'll go from there to this great club where I know the bouncer. He'll let you in."

"Oh, I'm over twenty-one," I said, used to people think-ing I was younger. "In fact, I'm twenty-two."

She gave me such a sharp look that I shifted uncomfort-ably. Okay, I was a little older than the typical college junior, but I'd had to help out at the orchard after my grandfather's heart attack. . . .

Finally she smiled. "Well. Aren't you full of surprises?"

Stephanie lived in an off-campus apartment not far from the place I'd soon be renting. With the money Bones had given me, I could move out sooner. No more having to hide my bloody clothes from my grandparents or dealing with the shunning pettiness of our neighbors. Yeah, I was look-ing forward to it.

I knocked on her door politely. "It's Cathy."

That was my school name. I was up to four now. At least they were all similar enough.

She opened it a moment later, clad only in her bra and a skirt.

"Hey! I'm just getting dressed. Come on in."

I followed her inside, waiting near the door as she disap-peared into what I presumed was her bedroom. Her apart-ment was surprisingly nice, not like the usual college digs. She had a plasma TV across from a leather sofa, a large entertainment center, a high-end computer notebook, and several other expensive-looking items arranged for deco-rative effect.

"I like your place," I said sincerely. "Do you live here alone, or do you have a roommate?"

"Come in here, I can hardly hear you," she called out.

I repeated the question while I went down the short hall into her room. Stephanie was in front of her closet, pursing her lips as she considered its contents.

"Huh? Oh, no roommate. So, tell me more about yourself, Cathy. I know you live at home with your mom and grandparents, but where's home?"

"In a tiny town an hour north of here that you've probably never heard of," I answered, thinking her bedroom was even nicer than her living room. Rich parents, obviously.

"You never talk about your father. Is your mom divorced, or did your dad die?"

"He ran off before I was born, I don't even know who he is," was all I said. Well, it was kind of the truth.

"Got a boyfriend?"

My response was immediate. "No!"

She laughed. "Wow, that was emphatic. Do you bat for the other team?"

"What other team?" I asked, confused.

Her mouth quirked. "Are you a lesbian? I don't care if you are, but the 'no' on the boyfriend thing was so strong, it begs the question."

"Oh!" *Duh!* "No, I'm not. I, er, just didn't know what you meant before—"

"You know," she cut me off with a pleasant smile, still rifling through her closet, "you're very pretty. But you dress like a troll. Let's see if we can't find something of mine for you to wear tonight."

Jeez, she sounded just like Bones. Switch her accent to an English one and I'd swear it was him talking.

I glanced down at my jeans. They were so comfortable. "Oh, you don't have to do that."

"Here." She filched some more and then threw a navy dress at me. "Try this on."

Not wanting to appear too modest, since she was still only partially clothed, I kicked my boots off and started to undress where I stood.

Stephanie looked at me with cool evaluation as I peeled off my jeans. The way her gaze swept over me made me feel odd. Like I was being appraised. *She's probably just mesmerized by how pale you are*, I told myself, trying to shake off the unease that had taken hold of me. *You're like a snowman with tits.*

"You've got a great body, Cathy. I wasn't sure, from those baggy outfits you wear, but lo and behold, you do."

Her voice was flat. Almost indifferent. That feeling of disquiet grew. I hadn't had any girlfriends before, true, but there was something about this that didn't seem right. She wasn't acting like the bright, bubbly girl from class. She seemed like an entirely different person.

"You know," I said, putting down the dress I'd been about to don, "I think I'll just wear my jeans. I'd hate for something to happen to this, and you know how clubs are. Someone could spill a drink on me or it could get ripped—"

"You really are just another clueless farm girl, aren't you?" That little smile never left her face. "I had you pegged the first time I saw you on your way to class, with your head down and your shoulders hunched. No friends, no connections, from a poor family . . . you fly totally under the radar. Someone like you could just"—her fingers snapped—"disappear."

My mouth had dropped after the first insult. It continued to hang open until I shut it in disbelief.

"Is this some kind of joke? Because it's not funny."

Stephanie laughed. It was so cheerful, for a second I relaxed. *She'd been kidding. Okay, it* wasn't *funny, but maybe she just had a weird sense of humor—*

She reached back into the closet. This time, instead of another dress, she pulled out a gun.

"Don't scream or I'll shoot."

What the *hell*? "Stephanie, what is *wrong* with you?" I gasped.

"Nothing," she replied affably. "Just making my rent,

and you, cookie, are just what the landlord likes. Here. Put these on."

She tossed a pair of handcuffs at me. They landed near my feet. I was still so stunned, I didn't move.

She cocked the gun. "Come on, Cathy. Don't make this messy."

"You won't shoot, your neighbors would hear," I said, keeping my voice calm while wondering what in the name of God was going on.

Her finger tapped the side of the barrel. "Silencer. They won't hear a thing."

My gaze narrowed as a thought occurred to me. "Did Bones put you up to this?"

"Who?" she asked in annoyance.

From her expression, she'd never heard of him, and that chilled me. If this wasn't another of his little tests, or if she wasn't pulling some kind of twisted sorority prank, then this was the real deal.

I picked my words very carefully. "I don't have any money or drugs, so you're wasting your time. Just put the gun down and I'll walk out of here and not call the police."

She came closer. Only about six feet separated us. "College girls, you're all the same. You think you're so smart, but when the time comes, I have to spell everything out like I plucked you from preschool. I should just tape-record myself and play it to you bitches so I don't have to keep saying everything over and over again! All right, listen up, stupid! I'm going to give you to the count of three to put those cuffs on, and if you don't, then I'm going to shoot you. First round goes in your leg. One . . . two . . . *three*."

The gun went off, but I lunged away before she'd finished speaking. Holy shit, whatever this was, she meant business! If I hadn't moved, she would have plugged a hole in me!

Stephanie fired again with a curse, clearly not expecting

my speed. I jumped her, grabbing for the gun. To my shock, she was far stronger than I'd anticipated. We fell to the floor, rolling, the gun in between us, each of us tugging roughly for it. When it went off again, I froze.

Her eyes were as wide as they could be, and staring straight into mine. Something warm spilled onto me. I pushed back, letting the gun slide from my numb fingers, and watched as the blood spread in a widening pool around her chest.

My hand came to my mouth in horror and I scooted back until I felt the wall behind me. Stephanie made a noise that was half grunt, half sigh. Then she stopped moving altogether.

I didn't need to check her pulse—I'd heard her heart stop. For a few moments that seemed to stretch into forever, I stared at her. In the apartments around us, no one noticed a thing. She was right. The gun had a silencer. Its muffling abilities had worked as described.

In a daze, I went over to her lovely wicker nightstand and picked up the phone, dialing the only number I could think of. When I heard his voice, my composure cracked, and I started to shake.

"Bones, I—I just killed someone!"

He didn't ask any of the questions that would have been first on my list. Like, *What's wrong with you?* or *Did you call the police?* Bones only asked where I was and then told me not to move. I was still holding the phone when he arrived ten minutes later. I hadn't moved, all right. I was barely even breathing.

The sight of him coming into the bedroom filled me with profound relief. If Stephanie had been a vampire, I would have been just fine. I'd wrap up her body, drive her out into the woods, and bury her in a deserted spot without missing a beat. This, however, was different. I'd taken a life, and I had no idea what to do about it.

"What have you touched?" was his first question as he knelt in front of me.

I tried to think. That was asking a lot at the moment.

"Um . . . the phone . . . maybe the edge of the dresser or her nightstand . . . that's it. I'd just gotten here when she started acting nuts and saying these awful things. . . ."

Bones took the phone from me. "It's not safe here. One of them could return at any moment."

"One of whom? She doesn't have any roommates," I protested, watching as he unhooked the phone from the wall and put it in a large garbage bag.

"This place stinks like vampires," he said shortly. "We have to tidy up and leave."

That got me to my feet. "Vampires! But she didn't . . . she wasn't—"

"What did she say about Hennessey?" he cut me off.

Now I felt completely lost. "Hennessey? *Hennessey?* He has nothing to do with this!"

"Like hell he doesn't," Bones growled, stripping Stephanie's comforter off the bed and wrapping her in it, cocoon-style. "He's one of the people I smell. Him, or someone who's had contact with him. His scent's here."

My head started to pound. This was like a bad dream. Bones finished rolling up Stephanie and then began filling that garbage bag with her stuff. Schoolbooks. Folders, papers. He rifled quickly through her drawers and added other various items. I wasn't much help. I just stood there, making sure my hands didn't stray to leave any incriminating fingerprints.

He left me to check the living room and returned with the bag even bulkier.

"Take this, luv."

The garbage bag was handed off to me. I had to hug it to hold it, fearing the plastic would rip from its weight. Bones then took one of her shirts and began briskly rubbing down the dressers, doorframes, end tables, and doorknobs. After he was satisfied, he hefted the lump of blankets that was Stephanie and threw her over his shoulder.

"Nice and quick to your truck, Kitten. Don't look around, just march right to it and get in the passenger seat. I'll be right behind you."

†WELVE

WE STOPPED ONCE ON OUR WAY TO THE CAVE. Bones made a call on his cell, and then he pulled over off by the side of the road near the darkest, most wooded part. It wasn't five minutes before a car pulled up behind us.

"Hiya, buddy!" Ted called out.

"Prompt as ever, mate," Bones greeted him, getting out of my truck. He went around to the trailer bed and I heard his motorcycle being moved. He'd laid it over Stephanie's body. She wasn't going to blow off with that thing holding her down.

I stayed in the truck, not in the mood for chitchatting.

"Whatcha got there?" Ted asked, giving me a friendly wave over Bones's shoulder.

"Dinner for whichever ghoul you feel like rewarding, but make sure they clean their plate. I don't want any part of her resurfacing," Bones replied.

My stomach heaved. God, talk about disposing of a body! I'd assumed we would bury her. Serving her up to a ghoul had never occurred to me.

Ted didn't share any of my qualms. "You betcha, bud. Anything I should warn them about?"

"Yeah." Bones handed the bundle over and Ted plopped her in his trunk. "Tell them not to chip a tooth on the bullet."

That was it for me. I opened the truck door just in time, the evening's events slamming into me and heaving out of my stomach in a rush.

"She all right?" I heard Ted ask as I coughed and drew in deep breaths.

Bones made a sound similar to a sigh. "She will be. Have to be off, mate. Thanks."

"Sure thing, bud. Anytime."

I closed my door just as Bones climbed back in. Ted's headlights flashed as he backed up, and then he was gone.

Bones reached inside his jacket and handed me a flask. "Whiskey. Not your favorite, but it's all I've got."

I took the bottle gratefully and gulped until there was no more. The liquor's artificial warmth began to thaw the ice in my limbs.

"Better?"

"Yeah."

My voice was scratchy from the lingering burn of the alcohol, but it had helped in more ways than one. That numbing shock was fading, replaced instead with a slew of questions.

"No more cryptic shit, Bones. Who is Hennessey, and what's he got to do with a gun-toting psychotic from my physics class?"

Bones cast me a sideways glance as he began driving. "Physics? You met her at college?"

"I think you should answer my question first, since I'm the one who was nearly shot," I snapped.

"Kitten, I *will* answer you, but please. Tell me how you met and what happened tonight."

My jaw tightened. "She took physics with me, as I said. From the first day, she'd wait for me after class. She started off by asking me lecture questions when she'd miss class, etc., and then she talked about herself. Inconsequential, funny things, like guys she'd dated or other stories . . . she seemed so friendly and nice. Then she asked about me, and I told her the truth. That I'd just transferred from a community college, didn't know anybody here, came from a small town—the bitch was casing me!" I suddenly burst. "She told me tonight she was looking for someone disposable, and I practically slapped a big red bow on my ass!"

"What about tonight?" he prodded.

"Oh, she did one better than dig into my background." I outlined the invitation and the whole clothes charade briefly, finishing with, "And then she pulled a gun on me."

"Did she mention anyone's name at all?"

I retraced our conversation in my mind. "No. She said something about paying her rent and me being what her landlord liked, then she said college girls were all stupid and she should tape-record herself . . . but no names."

Bones didn't say anything. I waited, tapping my finger. "How is this related to Hennessey? You said you smelled him and other vampires there. Do you think somehow he found out who I was from the other night? That he wanted to finish what he'd started?"

"No." His response was instant. "She'd been coddling up to you all week, you said. If Hennessey had found out who you were, believe me, he wouldn't have been patient about things. He'd have come at you in force straightaway, the minute he knew your name. Snatched up you and any-one unlucky enough to be around you. That's why I asked you what you touched and then wiped her place down. Though I doubt you have prints on file, I want no trace of you left for him to follow."

"If not because of last weekend, then why would

Stephanie be involved with him and try to kidnap me? It doesn't make any sense!"

He gave me a hooded look. "Let's sort this out inside. Gives me a chance to go through her things while we talk."

I followed him determinedly into the cave. No way was I letting him get away without telling me everything. Hennessey might have struck me as a typical scumbag, but there was obviously more to it than that. I wasn't leaving until I found out how much more.

Bones and I picked our way through the narrow entrance and back to where he'd made his living quarters in the high-domed part of the cave. He emptied the garbage bag's contents and I sat on the couch in front of him, watching as he opened Stephanie's laptop first.

"Have you ever heard of the Bennington Triangle?" he asked, powering up her computer.

I frowned. "No. I've heard of the Bermuda one."

His fingers flew over the keyboard. My, but they were limber. After a second, he let out a disgusted snort.

"Bloody girl didn't even bother to password her files. Just pure sodding arrogance, but that's in our favor. Look, there you are, Kitten. Under 'Potentials.' You should be flattered. You were first on her list."

I gaped over his shoulder and saw 'Cathy—redhead—twenty-two' with other names and similar short descriptions under it.

"Are you kidding me? Who are those other girls? Potential *what*?"

More blurring movement over the keys, and then he leaned back with a smile.

"Well, what have we here? Charlie, and Club Flame on Forty-second Street. Sounds like a contact. Here's hoping the twit was thick enough to write the actual name of the place and not just a code for it."

"Bones!"

The sharpness in my voice made him set aside the laptop and meet my eyes.

"The Bennington Triangle refers to an area in Maine where several people disappeared back in the fifties. To this day, no trace of them has been found. Something similar took place in Mexico several years back. A friend of mine's daughter disappeared. Her remains were found a few months afterward in the desert, and when I say remains, I mean they only found pieces of her. She had to be identified by dental records. At the autopsy, it was discovered that she'd been alive for months before she was murdered, and when I investigated further, it turned out not to be at all uncommon."

"What do you mean?"

Bones leaned back. "Hundreds of women were murdered or went missing in Mexican border towns around that time. Today, there's still not a speck of any real idea who did it. Then, several years ago, a number of young girls started to go missing in and around the Great Lakes area. More recently, it became centered in Ohio. Most of them were presumed to be runaways, prostitutes, addicts, or just average, little-known girls who had vanished with no signs of foul play. Since most of them were in high-risk categories, there wasn't much of a media fuss. I think Hennessey's involved. It's why I came here. He was near all three places when the disappearances started."

"You think Hennessey did all that?" The sheer numbers appalled me. "He can't eat that much if he wanted to! What is he, some kind of . . . undead Ted Bundy?"

"Oh, I think he might be a ringleader, no doubt about that, but he's not a traditional serial killer," Bones said crisply. "Serial killers are more possessive in their motives. From the bits and pieces I've gathered over the years, I don't think he's keeping these people to himself—I think he's made an industry out of them."

I almost asked what kind of an industry, but then I remembered what Bones had said to Sergio last weekend. *Knew you couldn't pass up a pretty girl . . . You're his best client, from what I hear. . . . Did you grow short on funds so you had to go out for dinner instead of order in? . . .* And then tonight, with Stephanie. *Just making my rent, and you, cookie, are just what the landlord likes. . . . College girls, you're all the same . . .*

"You think he's running a takeout service," I breathed. "Turning those people into Meals on Wheels! My God, Bones, how could he get away with it?"

"Hennessey was sloppy in Maine and Mexico, but he's gotten smarter. He now chooses women society doesn't hold in high regard, and if they don't fall into that category, then he sends vampires to prevent them from even being reported missing. Remember those girls Winston told you about? He wasn't wrong, luv, they *are* all dead. I wanted confirmation that there were more girls missing than had been reported, so that's why I sent you to Winston. A ghost knows who's died, even if those girls' families don't. I went to see them, and they'd all been bitten into believing their daughters were off pursuing an acting career, like you'd been told, or backpacking across Europe, or moving in with an old boyfriend, whatever. They'd been programmed not to question their absence, and only a vampire can have that much mind control. Hennessey's had his people rounding up even more girls for him lately. At colleges. On street corners. In bars, clubs, and back alleys. How could he get away with it? Have you ever really looked at the faces on your milk carton? People disappear all the time. The police? There's enough crimes involving the rich, famous, and powerful to make it easy for them to put the disappearance of some derelicts on their back burner, and they don't know about the others. As far as the undead world goes, Hennessey's covered his tracks very well. There's only suspicion, but no proof."

Now that I knew what was going on in my own state, what Stephanie had been doing made perfect sense, if you had the ethics of a crocodile. A huge, crowded college campus *had* been her all-you-can-eat buffet; she just hadn't been the one eating. No, she was someone hired to stock Hennessey's refrigerator. And I, with my background, had been the perfect dish. Stephanie had hit the nail on the head with that. I could disappear very easily, with few questions being asked, and it would have worked just as planned. Except for the one thing about me she hadn't counted on.

"How long have you suspected this? You told me before you'd been chasing Hennessey eleven years. You've known what he's been doing that whole time?"

"No. It's only been the past two years that I've gotten specific information. Mind you, I didn't know who or what I was chasing at first. Took me a few dozen blokes to get a whisper of what was going on. A few more dozen to get a name of who might be running it. As I said, he'd covered his tracks. Then I hunted down those under his line who had prices on their heads. Sergio was one of them, for example. I've been picking apart his people for years, but only doing it to those who had bounties on them. That way, Hennessey didn't know I was on to him. He just thought it was business. Now, however, he knows I'm out to get him, and why. And so does whoever else is involved, because he can't be doing this alone."

I digested that for a minute. "So, even if you take Hennessey out, it still might not end. His partners could start right up where he left off. You don't have any idea who they could be?"

"I've come very close a few times to finding out, but—well. Things happened."

"Like what?"

"Like you, actually. If I didn't know better, I'd swear you were one of Hennessey's. You have an incredibly bad habit of killing people before I can get any information out of them. Remember Devon, that bloke you staked the night we met? I'd been tracking him for six months. He was Hennessey's accountant, knew everything about him, but you plugged silver through his heart before I could say Bob's your uncle. I thought Hennessey knew I was getting close and sent you to silence him. Then you went after me the very next night. Why do you think I kept asking you who you worked for? And tonight—"

"I didn't mean to kill her!" I cried, lashing myself over that for a different reason this time. What information had Stephanie died with? We'd never know.

Bones got up, speaking to me as he disappeared behind one of the cave's natural walls.

"Believe me, luv, I know that. You wouldn't kill a human unless it was by accident or they were wearing a Vampire Henchman badge. You didn't seem to know Stephanie had any such connections—and from the look of scene, I'd reckoned you were wrestling for the gun when it went off. She probably had a good grip on it, too. From the smell of her, she'd been hyped up on vampire blood. Would have made her quite a bit physically stronger and she'd need that, for what her job was."

So that explained why she'd had the strength of a linebacker in her petite feminine frame. I'd underestimated her all the way around.

"Why haven't you told me about all of this before? You trained me to fight, and then you kept me out of the real battle."

He answered while still out of eyesight. "I didn't want you involved. Blimey, I'd just as soon you not risk your life going after vampires to begin with, but that's what you want to do, so I trained you to be better at it. Not like you'd listen to me if I told you to stay home, is it? Still, Hennessey and his blokes are different. Your part with them was supposed to end after Sergio, but your little physics chit ruined that tonight. You should be patting yourself on the back for killing her. Those other 'potentials' certainly would, if they knew what she'd had in store for them."

"Was safety your only reason for keeping this from me, or is there more I don't know about?"

There was the sound of water being poured. "No, there's one more reason I kept it from you. I didn't want to give you another reason to hate vampires. It's not like you aren't already predisposed to it. You tend to judge people for what they are, rather than what they do, if they don't have a pulse."

I was silent for a moment, because I had no defense to that. No truthful one, anyway.

"You should know something, Bones. I lied to you when we made our deal. I was going to kill you the first chance I got."

I heard a dry chuckle. "I already knew that, luv."

"About Hennessey . . . I want to help. I *have* to help. My God, I was almost one of those girls who never would have been heard from again! I know it's dangerous, but if you find out where this Club Flame is, if you get a lead, I want to be there. Hennessey has to be stopped."

Bones didn't reply.

"I mean it," I persisted. "Come on, I'm the perfect wolf in sheep's clothing! Really, do you know any other half-breed girls living in an area that's currently being harvested? You're not talking me out of this!"

"I can see that. Here." He returned with a bowl of water and a cloth, setting it near me and then handing me one of his shirts. "You've got blood on the front of you. If you go home like that, you'll scare your mum into thinking you've been hurt."

I looked down at myself. The red smear of Stephanie's blood stained my stomach in a wide circle. In yet another example of my prejudice, even though I didn't mind killing her so much anymore, I snatched my blouse off and immediately began to scrub my skin.

It was only after I cleaned the last of the blood from me that I felt the weight of his stare. When I looked up, his eyes were fixed on me and laced with green.

"Hey." I slid back a few inches on the couch. "Dinner's *not* served. Don't go all glowy at the blood."

"Do you think blood has anything to do with the way I'm looking at you now?"

His voice had a strange timbre to it. Thick with things unspoken.

I struggled not to show any reaction, but my heart had just sped up, and it wasn't from fear. "Green eyes, fangs peeking out . . . pretty incriminating, I'd say."

"Indeed?" He sat down, moving the bowl aside. "It seems I've neglected to inform you of what else draws such a reaction, but I'll give you a hint—it isn't blood."

Oh. I drew in a breath. "Considering last weekend, I don't have anything you haven't seen before, and I doubt you're overcome with desire by seeing me in my bra."

"Kitten, look at me," he said flatly.

I blinked. "I am."

"No, you're not." He slid closer, his eyes all green now. "You stare straight through me as if I'm not even there. You look at me . . . and you don't see a man. You see a vampire, and therefore accord me less substance. One of the few exceptions was last weekend. I held you and kissed you, watched *your* eyes light up with desire, and knew for once you were truly seeing me for all I was. Not just a non-beating heart with a shell around it. I dare you to look at me that way again, now, with no excuse of chemicals to fall back on. I want you." A slight smile twisted his lips as he made the blunt statement. "I've wanted you from the moment we met, and if you think sitting next to me in your bra doesn't overwhelm me with desire, you're very wrong. I just don't force myself where I'm not invited."

For a few stunned seconds, I was speechless. So much had happened tonight, my brain was having a hard time sorting through it all. I looked at Bones and it was almost as if scales dropped from my eyes, because suddenly I *did* see him. Those high cheekbones, dark brows framing eyes turned to emerald, a curving mouth, straight nose, and etched jawline. Crystal skin stretched over those features and tightly wrapped around a lean, rippled frame. His elegant hands and their long, tapered fingers. My God, he was beautiful. Absolutely, incredibly beautiful, and now that I'd finally allowed myself to notice, I couldn't stop staring.

"Kiss me."

The words left me without any thought, and I realized I'd secretly wanted to say them for a while. Bones leaned over and his lips closed over mine softly. Gently. Giving me every opportunity to change my mind and push him away, but I didn't. I slid my arms around his neck and brought him closer.

He ran his tongue along my lips until I opened my mouth. His touched mine for a moment before retreating, teasingly, back into his mouth. Another flickering touch and back again, and again. Coaxing me, persuading me. Finally I traced my tongue into his mouth, feeling the answering rub and then the unbelievable sensuality of him sucking on it.

I moaned, unable to help it. The graze of his incisors should have bothered me, but they didn't. They didn't seem to hinder him, either, because he kissed me with the same passion he had last weekend. My senses ignited, and I maneuvered my hand from his neck and brought it to his shirt. One by one, I undid his buttons. When it hung open, I ran my palms along his bare skin and, oh God, it did feel as incredible as it looked. Like silk stretched over steel. Bones reached behind him and flicked the collar off his shoulders. The whole garment fell onto the floor. All the while he kept kissing me until my breath came in gasps.

With a mind of their own my hands traveled from his chest across his back, fingers feeling out the ridges and muscle. His flesh vibrated with power, making me feel like I stroked lightning encased in skin. Bones groaned low in his throat as I touched him, sliding closer until our bodies were pressed together.

His lips trailed down to my neck, finding my pulse unerringly. He drew it into his mouth, manipulating my vulnerable artery with his tongue and lips. It was the most dangerous position to be in with a vampire, but I wasn't afraid. Instead, the feel of him sucking on my neck aroused me unbelievably. The waves of heat sweeping through me had me quivering.

His lips came up to my ear, and he licked the shell before whispering into it.

"I want you so much. Tell me you want me. Say yes."

To deny that I wanted him would be an obvious lie. Just one thing held me back, and it was the memory of Danny.

"Bones . . . I didn't like it before. I think . . . something's wrong with me."

"Nothing's wrong with you, and if you change your mind or say stop, no matter when, I'll stop. You can trust me, Kitten. Say yes. Say yes. . . ."

Bones swooped his mouth onto mine and ravaged the inside with such hunger that I sagged against him. His arm supported me, and I tore away long enough to speak one word.

"Yes. . . ."

It barely left my mouth before he kissed me again, lifting me up and carrying me into the bedroom. The mattress gave under our weight as he stretched me out on it. In one motion, he unclipped my bra and pulled it off while his palms cupped my breasts. Then he lowered his mouth to my nipple and sucked strongly.

A clench of pure desire gripped me between my legs. He gently squeezed my other breast and worried the nipple between his fingers. My back arched and I clasped his head. The sensations were too much—the tug of his mouth, slight scrapes of teeth, until I thought I'd faint.

Bones unzipped my jeans, tugging them down until they were off and only my panties remained to clothe me. He traced his hand along them, pressing inward. The friction of the cotton and his fingers made my nerve endings jump. A groan escaped him when he pulled my panties off, baring me to his gaze.

"Oh, Kitten, you're so beautiful. Exquisite," he breathed before kissing me with a thoroughness that left my head spinning. He trailed his mouth to my breasts again, drawing on each nipple while his hand sought my center. Those fingers caressed me knowingly, as if I'd told him secrets, and I bit my lip to stifle the cries. When his thumb circled the ball of my flesh and a long finger rubbed inside me, I trembled in uncontainable need.

A harsh noise of protest escaped me when he stopped. He moved his hand away, his mouth left my breasts, and he dragged his lips down my stomach. It wasn't until he was past my navel that I realized his intention.

"Bones, wait!" I gasped, shocked.

He paused at once, mouth still on my belly. "Stop?" he inquired.

Color flamed my cheeks and I couldn't articulate my objection. "Er, not stop all of it, just . . . um, I don't think that's appropriate—"

Something like a snort escaped him. "I *do* think," he muttered, and lowered his mouth.

At the first touch of his tongue my mind literally went

blank. A long, slow lick probed me, leaving seared flesh in its wake. Another wet stroke and another, deeper this time, and my modesty washed away in waves of pure heat. He spread my legs farther, shifting until they straddled his shoulders, all the while plying and delving into the soft pink flesh.

I didn't tell him to wait anymore, because I couldn't speak. Moans I didn't recognize as my own rose from me with increasing volume and wrenching, twisting spasms of pleasure curled inside me. I writhed under him, feeling him explore every nuance of me with shocking intimacy. My hips arched helplessly, and an aching emptiness inside me grew with each stroke of his tongue. I was being pushed to an edge I'd never experienced before, and it approached faster and faster. Bones increased the pressure, ratcheting up the intensity, and when his mouth finally settled on my clitoris and he sucked, I screamed.

Shards of ecstasy burst from me, traveling from my center to my extremities in a flash. My heart, which I thought would simply erupt, seemed to slow in its beating and my breathing lost its jaggedness. That previous fire was suddenly replaced with something warm and euphoric spilling all through me, causing my eyes to fly open in astonishment.

Bones slid up my stomach, framing my face in his hands. "You have never looked more beautiful," he said, voice vibrating with passion.

My body still shook with aftershocks, but this was the part I feared. I tensed as he moved between my legs.

"Don't be afraid," he whispered, and kissed me.

For a split second I was embarrassed, considering what he'd just been doing. Then I found the new, salty flavor to his mouth provocatively stimulating. His tongue twined with mine as his hardness slid along my wet crease. I shuddered, but he only swept the outside before pulling away and doing it again. And again. He matched his tongue to his body as he stroked me, bringing that previous ache back with reinforcements.

"You tell me when," he murmured, long moments later. "Or not at all. We don't have to go further yet. I'll spend the rest of the night tasting you, Kitten, I loved that. Let me show you how much."

Bones dragged his mouth purposefully lower, but I held him to keep him where he was.

"Tell me," he moaned as a twist of his hips forced a cry from me.

My heart pounded with nervousness, but there was only one answer.

"Now."

He gave me a dizzying kiss and then raised himself on his arms. The feel of hard flesh boring into mine made me gasp. Shivers broke out inside me while he thrust slowly forward, and I buried my face in his neck and trembled. He moved deeper, and a sensation of incredible fullness spread through me. When he was fully sheathed he stopped, closing his eyes briefly before looking down at me.

"All right, luv?"

It was intimate in a way I'd never experienced, staring into each other's eyes while he was inside me. I could only nod, since speech was beyond me.

He moved in me, pulling back just a little and then thrusting forward. The unexpectedness of the pleasure made my breath catch. He repeated the motion, but deeper this time. Before I regained control of my breathing, he pulled himself nearly all the way out and back in with a single arch of his hips that tore a whimper out of my throat. Sweat broke out in earnest on my body, and piercing, primal desire shot through me.

Bones reached down and flattened his palm against my back, moving lower until it cupped my hips. He pulled me closer, rubbing me against him to coincide with his movements. I quickly picked up the rhythm, and the increased contact made my head spin in excitement. That previous clenching inside me returned, winding tighter with each new stroke until my body burned with a single thought.

"More . . ."

It was a moan of pure demand the rational piece of my mind couldn't believe I'd spoken. He chuckled deep in his throat, almost growling, and increased his pace.

My hands, which before hadn't strayed lower than his back, moved greedily down to grip his hips. Fingers dug into the hard mounds with no care for propriety. I couldn't seem to touch enough of him or get close enough to him. Every new thrust made it more intense, and I craved the hard slicing of his body into mine like I'd craved nothing before it. Compulsively I kissed him, piercing my lower lip on his fangs and hearing him groan when he sucked the blood off.

"So sharp and sweet," he muttered thickly.

"No more . . . of that." My words were spaced in breathlessness.

He licked his lips, savoring the drops. "It's enough. Now you're inside me also." And he held me even closer, if that were possible.

I gasped uncontrollably as his movements grew more intense. Earlier hesitation forgotten, I thrashed underneath him, fingernails raking temporary welts down his back. My teeth sank into his shoulder, stifling a scream at the ceaseless friction, and I bit him until I tasted blood.

He yanked my head back, his tongue ravishing my mouth. "Harder?"

"God, yes," I moaned, not caring how that sounded.

Bones released his control with obvious relish. His hips ground into mine with a tempered savageness that was the most incredible pleasure ever inflicted on my body.

The screams I'd held back spilled forth in rhythmic shouts that spurred him on. When I couldn't stand it any harder, he moved faster, thrusting in a manner that would have been merciless had I not reveled in it.

Somehow it reminded me of the effect of the drugs. Everything seemed to spin and lose shape except Bones. That far-off roaring was back in my ears, but it was my heart pounding that made the sound. The nerve endings in my loins shredded with anticipation. They lashed and wound together, clenching and unclenching with greater fierceness, waiting for the moment when they would snap.

At once I was disconnected and hypersensitive of my body. This panting, twisting creature on the bed couldn't be *me*. Yet never before had I been so aware of my skin, my every breath, and the blood rushing through my veins. Before the last stretched nerve inside me broke, Bones grasped my head and stared into my eyes. A cry wrenched out of my mouth when the dam burst and the flood of orgasm swept over me. It was stronger than the first one, deeper somehow, and left residual tingles pulsating underneath my skin.

Above me he groaned, face twisting in ecstasy as he drove into me even more rapidly with his eyes locked onto mine. I couldn't look away, seeing his control evaporate inside the green depths. He clutched me as he gave in to the passion, kissing me almost bruisingly and shuddering for several moments.

When I broke away to breathe, he shifted until we lay side by side. His arms coiled around me, keeping our bodies touching. There didn't seem to be enough oxygen in my lungs and even Bones breathed once or twice—a record, from what I'd seen before. By degrees I controlled my gasping and my heart settled into a nondangerous rhythm. He reached out and pushed the damp hair from my face, smiling before he kissed my forehead.

"And to think you actually believed something was wrong with you."

"Something *is* wrong with me, I can't move."

It was true. Lying next to him, my arms and legs just wouldn't respond to any of the commands I gave them. My brain had a BACK IN FIVE MINUTES sign hung on it, apparently.

He grinned and leaned over to lick the nipple closest to him, drawing lightly on it. The areola was oversensitive from his previous attentions, and a thousand tiny needles of pleasure rushed to the tip. When it crested to the very threshold of sensitivity he stopped, repeating the process with the next one.

Something caught my vision when I glanced down.

"Am I bleeding?" I asked in surprise.

It didn't quite seem like blood and my period was a week away. Still, there was a distinct pink wetness on the crease of my inner high.

He barely stopped to look. "No, luv. That's from me."

"What is—? Oh." Stupid question. He'd told me before that vampires cried pink. Guess the other fluids followed suit.

"Let me up, I'll wash off."

"I don't mind." He breathed the words into my skin. "It's mine, after all. I'll clean you up."

"Aren't you going to roll over and go to sleep?" Wasn't that what usually happened? Unless he really, *really* liked to cuddle afterward, things were taking a markedly serious turn as his hand moved lower, seeking my depths.

He ceased his ministrations to laugh, raising his head from my breasts.

"Kitten"—he smiled—"I am far from sleepy." The look in his eyes sent a shiver through me. "You have no idea how many times I've fantasized about you like this. During our training, our fights, the nights I've seen you dressed up and pawed at by other men . . ." Bones stopped speaking to kiss me so deeply, I almost forgot what we were talking about. "And all the while seeing you look at me with fear whenever I touched you. No, I am not sleepy. Not until I've tasted every inch of your skin and made you scream over and over again."

He bent his head to my nipples once more, sucking them and worrying them with his teeth. The way his fangs rubbed the areolas was frighteningly erotic.

"One day I'm going to find that old bloke of yours and kill him," he muttered, so low I could barely hear him.

"What?" Did he just say that?

A strong tug from his mouth distracted me, and then another and another, until my concerns melted away under the sensual assault on my nipples. After a while he looked at them and smiled in satisfaction.

"Dark red, both of them. Just like I promised you they'd get. See? I am a man of my word."

Confusion clouded my mind for a second. Then I remembered that afternoon with him trying to burn the embarrassment out of me with hours of dirty talk, and color suddenly flamed in my face.

"You didn't actually *mean* all of those things, did you?" My mind rebelled at the thought, but there was a rapidly beating pulse in my body that treacherously hoped for the opposite.

He laughed again, low and throaty. His brow arched in sinful promise, his eyes bled back to pure green, and his mouth slid farther down my stomach.

"Oh, Kitten, I meant every word."

I awoke to something tickling my back. It felt like butterflies. Opening my eyes, the first thing I saw was an arm wrapped around me, its pale color nearly identical to my own. Bones was curled lengthwise along my back, hips touching mine. The butterflies were him pressing kisses onto my skin.

My first thought was, *He picked the wrong profession. Should have stayed a prostitute. He'd make millions.* The second one was far less pleasant, and I stiffened. *If my mother could see me now, she'd kill me!*

"Morning-after regrets?" He ceased kissing me with a noise of disappointment. "I feared you might wake up and flog yourself over this."

While he spoke, I shot out of bed like I'd been fired from a cannon. I had to think about what to do, and I couldn't do that in the same room with him. Not even pausing to find my underwear or bra, I just threw on a shirt and yanked up my jeans. God, my keys, where had I put my keys?

Bones sat up. "You can't just storm out and pretend this never happened."

"Not now," I said desperately, trying not to look at him. Aha, keys! Grabbing them with clenched fingers, I ran out of the bedroom.

"Kitten . . ."

I didn't stop.

†hir†een

I DROVE STRAIGHT HOME, MY EMOTIONS IN A tug-of-war the whole way. Making love to Bones had been beyond incredible, and he was right. There was no way I could pretend this didn't happen. But there was more to consider than just my feelings. Left to myself, I would only be moderately wigged about having slept with him. The main reason for my panic, however, was knowing how my mother would react. I couldn't tell her, ever. And that meant I had to stop this before it went any further.

My grandparents were on the porch, drinking iced tea when I pulled up two hours later. They looked like a post-card of Americana with their white hair and plain clothes, faces weathered from time.

"Hello," I greeted them distractedly.

There was a hiss from my grandmother. Immediately afterward came a bellow of outrage from my grandfather. I just blinked at them.

"What's the matter with you two?"

Curious, I watched as my grandfather turned three

shades of red. After all, it wasn't like I hadn't strolled in the next day several times before, and they'd never commented about it. They'd adopted a "don't ask, don't tell" policy when it came to my late nights.

"Justina, get on out here, girl!" He ignored my question and rose to his feet. A moment later my mother came out, her face as bewildered as mine.

"What? Is something wrong?"

He answered her while still shaking with wrath.

"Just look at her. Look at her! You can't tell me she wasn't doing anything wrong last night! No, she was consorting with the devil, that's what she was doing!"

I blanched, wracking my brain to figure out how he found out I'd slept with a vampire. Had I grown fangs? Reaching out, I fingered my teeth, but they were as square and flat as normal.

The gesture enraged him further. "Don't flick your finger off your teeth at me, missy! Who do you think you are?"

To her credit, my mother at once began to defend me. "Oh, Pa, you don't understand. She's—"

Her voice abruptly choked as she stared at me with a lesser look of shock.

"What?" I demanded, frightened.

"Your neck . . ." she whispered, disbelief in her eyes.

Terrified, I pushed past her and ran to the nearest bathroom. Were there fang marks? God, had he bitten me without my realizing it?

Once I stared at my reflection however, the reason for their reaction became clear. Erratically spaced and in different shades of blue were four—no, make that five—hickeys. No telltale puncture wounds from a vampire's teeth, but plain, unmistakable hickeys. Opening Bones's shirt, I saw that my breasts bore similar marks. Good thing this top didn't have cleavage or they'd all have fainted dead away.

"I know what those are!" Grandpa Joe roared at me from

the porch. "You ought to be ashamed of yourself, running around, not married, staying out all night. Ashamed!"

"Ashamed!" my grandmother echoed. Good to know they still agreed on things after forty-three years of marriage.

I went upstairs to my room without answering them. It was definitely time for me to seek alternate accommodations. Perhaps that apartment would be vacant immediately.

To my utter lack of surprise, my mother followed me.

"Who is he, Catherine?" she asked me as soon as she shut the door behind her.

I had to tell her something. "He's someone I met while I was out looking for vampires. We, ah, have something in common. He kills them, too."

No need to go into further details. Like a very important one regarding him *being* one.

"Is . . . is it very serious between the two of you?"

"No!" My denial was so vehement she frowned. Great, didn't that sound nice? *No, we can't have a relationship because he's technically dead, but my God is he gorgeous and fucks like a Trojan.*

"Then why . . . ?" She looked genuinely puzzled.

Sighing, I lay down on the bed. How to detail mindless lust to your mother?

"Well, it just happened. It wasn't planned."

A look of horror crossed her face. "Did you use any protection?"

"It wasn't necessary," I answered truthfully without thinking.

She clapped a hand to her mouth. "What do you mean, it wasn't necessary? You could get pregnant! Or a disease!"

It took a lot of effort to keep me from rolling my eyes. I could just imagine my reply. *Good news, Ma. He's a vampire and an old one, so no pregnancy or diseases. It's impossible.*

Instead, I just told her not to worry.

"Don't worry? Don't worry! I'll tell you what I'm going to do. I'm going to drive into the next couple of towns where no one knows us, and I am going to buy you condoms! You're not going to end up young and pregnant like I was—or worse. There's AIDS now. And syphilis. And gonorrhea. And even things I can't pronounce! If you're going to engage in that kind of behavior, then at least you're going to be safe about it."

She grabbed her purse with a determined gleam and headed toward the door.

"But Mom . . ."

I followed her downstairs, trying to convince her not to leave, but she ignored me. My grandparents eyed me from the porch, faces drawn together like thunderclouds as my mother got in her car and drove off. It was definitely time to call that landlord.

The landlord, Mr. Josephs, told me I could move in the following weekend. It couldn't come soon enough. I occupied myself with showering, shaving, brushing my teeth, anything but wondering what Bones was doing. Maybe I was worrying for nothing. Maybe it had just been casual for him, and I wouldn't even have to tell him it couldn't happen again. After all, the man was a couple hundred years older than me and a former gigolo. I certainly hadn't robbed him of his virginity.

A car pulled into our driveway around six, and it didn't sound like my mother. I looked out the window, curious, and saw it was a taxi. A familiar bleached head appeared next as Bones got out of it.

What was he doing here? Another panicked look revealed my mother still wasn't back, but if she showed up now and saw him . . .

I ran down the stairs so fast, I tripped and landed in a heap at the landing just as my grandfather opened the door.

"Who are you?" he demanded of Bones.

I was mentally coming up with a story about him being a fellow college student when Bones answered him in perfectly polite tones.

"I am a nice young girl here to pick up your granddaughter for the weekend."

Huh?

My grandmother poked her head out, too, mouth open at the sight of Bones in her doorway.

"Who are you?" she parroted.

"I'm a nice young girl come to pick your granddaughter up for the weekend," he repeated the odd line, staring her directly in the eyes with a flash of green. She soon got the same glazed look her husband wore, and then nodded once.

"Oh, well, isn't that nice? You *are* a nice young girl. Be a good friend to her and set her straight. She has love bruises on her neck and didn't come home until this afternoon."

Sweet Holy Jesus, why couldn't the ground just swallow me? Bones stifled a laugh and nodded solemnly. "Don't fret, Grannie. We're going to a Bible retreat to scare the devil out of her."

"Good for you," my grandfather said in an approving voice, expression blank. "That's what she needs. Been wild all her life."

"Go have a pot of tea whilst we pack, both of you. Off you go."

They went, still with empty eyes, and trod to the kitchen. Soon I could hear the water being sloshed into the kettle. They didn't even drink tea.

"What do you think you're doing here?" I asked in an angry whisper. "If only the movies were right and you couldn't come in unless invited!"

He laughed at that. "Sorry, luv. Vampires can go anywhere they please."

"Why are you here? And why did you trick my grand-parents into thinking you're a girl?"

"A *nice* girl," he corrected me with a smile. "Can't have them believing you'd taken up with a bad sort, can we?"

I was in a rush for him to leave. If my mother came back, it would take more than a flash of his eyes to convince her that he wasn't what she'd see him as—her nightmare, come to life.

"You have to go. My mom will have a heart attack if she sees you."

"I am here for a reason," he said calmly. "Not that I want you to be involved any further, but you were very emphatic last night that you wished to be informed if I discovered where that club was. I have. It's in Charlotte, and I'm flying there tonight. I bought you a ticket, if you want to go also. If you don't, I'll just go into your kitchen and convince your grandparents I was never here. That way you won't have to explain my presence later to your mum. It's up to you, but you have to decide now."

I knew what I would choose, but I was still rattled at how this could have been a very ugly scene. "Why didn't you call instead of just coming over?"

His brow arched. "I did. Your grandfather hung up on me as soon as I asked for you. You really ought to get a cell phone. Or remind them that you're twenty-two years old and it *is* appropriate for a gentleman to ring you."

I left the gentleman comment alone. "Yeah, well, they're old-fashioned, and they kind of lost it when they saw my neck—which was very inconsiderate, by the way! Leaving all those 'Been there, done that!' stamps for them to see!"

A grin tugged at his mouth. "In all fairness, Kitten, if I didn't heal supernaturally, I'd be covered with similar markings, and my back would be a river of scars from your nails."

Change of subject. *Change of subject!* "As far as tonight,"

I went on hurriedly, "you know I'll go. I told you I want to stop Hennessey, and I meant it. You already found where the club was? That was fast."

"I knew before, in fact," he said, leaning against the doorframe. "I'd researched it this morning while you were sleeping. Was going to tell you about it when you woke up, but then you ran out like hell was chasing you and didn't give me a chance."

I had to drop my gaze. Looking him in the eye was more than I could handle. "I don't want to talk about that. I'm not so shallow that I'd let my . . ." What to call them? "My *misgivings* about last night interfere with stopping a murderer, but I think it's best if we leave that alone."

His half smile remained. "Misgivings? Oh, Kitten. You break my heart."

That brought my head up. Was he making fun of me? I couldn't tell. "Let's focus on priorities. If you want to, we'll, ah, talk about that later. After the club. Wait here while I pack."

He held open the door. "It's not necessary, I brought your game clothes. After you."

"I haven't seen you here before, cherry pie," the vampire said as he slid into the seat next to mine. "Name's Charlie."

Bingo! I was so happy, I almost clapped my hands. We had landed in Charlotte at ten, checked into our hotel at eleven, and arrived at Club Flame just before midnight. I'd been sitting in this disgusting place for two hours, and with the slutty dress I was wearing, it hadn't been a lonely two hours.

"Sweet to eat, and easy as," I replied, mentally gauging his power level. Not a Master, but strong. "Looking for a date, honey?"

He trailed his fingers along my arm. "You bet, cherry."

Charlie's accent was pure Southern. He had brown hair, a friendly smile, and an athletic build. His drawl, plus that aw-shucks demeanor, only made him seem more amicable. Who could be evil when he had an accent like candy, right?

The guy to my left, who'd been hitting on me all night, gave him a belligerent look.

"Hey, mister, I saw her first—"

"Why don't you get up on outta here and go home?" Charlie cut him off, still smiling. "Best hurry, now. I don't like to repeat myself."

If I were that guy, I'd hear the steel underneath his good ol' boy act, and be warned.

Of course, I wasn't drunk, ignorant, and just plain oblivious to the danger in front of me.

"I don't think you heard me," the man slurred, laying a heavy hand on him. "I said, I saw her *first*."

Charlie didn't lose his smile. He took the man by the wrist and hauled him out of his chair.

"No need to fight and cause a ruckus," he said with a wink at me. "We'll flip for you, sugar. I'm feelin' lucky."

And he dragged the man out of the bar. The fact that no one commented spoke for the classiness of the place.

I looked around, torn. If I tried to stop Charlie, I'd blow my cover and wreck Bones's chance to find Hennessey, *again*. So I did nothing. I sipped my drink and felt sick inside. When Charlie returned, he had that same genial grin, and he was alone.

"Turns out I am lucky tonight," he commented. "Question is, are you going to make me very, very lucky?"

I was trying to listen for a heartbeat outside, but the interior noise was too loud. Whatever had happened was over. There was nothing to do but see this through.

"Sure thing, honey. I just need a little something to help with my rent first."

My voice was flirty. Not a hint of stress. Practice did

make perfect, and the rent comment was my ode to Stephanie. I thought it was darkly appropriate.

"What's your rent, cherry pie?"

"Hundred bucks," I giggled, shifting on my chair so my dress climbed higher. "You'll be glad you donated, promise."

Charlie's gaze skimmed my thighs in the ridiculously short dress, and he took in a deep breath. Only months of training kept me from blushing at what I knew he was doing.

"Honey child, from the looks of you, I'd say that's a bargain."

He held out his hand and I took it, hopping off my chair.

"Charlie, wasn't it? Don't worry. You're in for a real treat."

As Charlie drove, I was quietly thanking God that he hadn't attempted a quickie right on the premises. My hooker charade only went so far. Bones would be following at a discreet distance, and we were hoping I'd be taken back to Charlie's place, breaking Bones's cardinal rule of me avoiding a vampire's home base. What information we might find was worth the risk of him having roommates.

"How long you been a working girl, sugar?" Charlie asked, as if discussing the weather.

"Oh, about a year," I answered. "I'm new to this town, but I'm saving to move again."

"Don't like Charlotte?" he said as he pulled onto the highway.

I allowed a hint of nervousness to enter my voice. "Where are we going? I thought you were just going to pull off the side of the road or something."

"It's or something, cherry." He chuckled. "Believe that."

How would a normal prostitute react? "Hey, don't go too far. I don't want to walk all night to get back to my ride."

Charlie turned his head and looked me full in the face. His eyes blazed emerald and he lost that friendly demeanor.

"Shut the fuck up, bitch."

Okay. Guess the pleasantries were over! That suited me just fine. I hated to make small talk.

I nodded with what I hoped was a glazed expression and stared ahead without another word. To do anything less would be suspicious.

Charlie whistled "Amazing Grace" as he drove. It was all I could do not to whip my head around and snap, *Are you kidding me?* Couldn't he pick something more appropriate, like "Shout at the Devil" or "Don't Fear the Reaper"? Some people had no sense of the proper music for a kidnapping.

He pulled up forty minutes later to a tiny apartment complex. It was set back from the other, similar buildings along the street. The neighborhood was lower-middle-class, but not ghetto. Just something you wouldn't see people strolling through for the view.

"Home sweet home, cherry pie." He grinned, shutting the car off. "At least for a little while. Then you'll get to leave town like you wanted to."

Interesting. I hadn't been told to speak, though, so I continued with my catatonic act. Anger simmered in me, thinking of all the girls who hadn't been faking it. Tainted blood had advantages.

Charlie opened my car door and yanked me out. I let him propel me up the single flight of stairs to the second floor. He didn't even bother holding on to me as he fumbled with his keys. *That's right, buddy. Don't worry about me. I'm helpless.*

He shoved me inside when he opened the door. I let myself trip, partially to stay low and get a view of my surroundings, and also so my hand was near my boots.

Charlie didn't care about me sprawling on the floor. He stepped over me and plopped himself onto a nearby couch.

"Got another one, Dean," he called out. "Come see."

There was a grumble, a creak of furniture, and then presumably Dean.

Seeing him almost cracked my cover, because he strolled out buck-naked. I had to steel myself not to instinctively look away. Bones was only the second guy I'd seen that way, and Danny had been so fast, it barely counted. In the midst of everything, I was embarrassed. How absurd.

Dean came right over to me and tilted my face up. His parts were swinging so close, I fought a blush. And a recoil.

"She's gorgeous."

Charlie grunted. "I found her. I go first."

That statement wiped away my embarrassment. Son of a bitch. These pigs were going to get it, all right. Permanently.

I'd just heard footsteps outside when Dean turned to Charlie.

"You expecting someone . . . ?"

My stake cleared my boot the same instant Bones leveled the door with one kick. Maybe I was being spiteful. Could have been convenience due to its proximity, but the first place I drove it into was Dean's groin.

He let out a high-pitched scream and tried to grab me. I rolled away, yanking out my other stake and flinging it into his back. That brought him to his knees and I pounced, jumping onto his back like this was a macabre rodeo.

Dean bucked frantically, but I grabbed the stake with both hands and slanted downward, shoving with all my strength. He flattened under me. Splat. I gave the stake another shove for good measure and moved away with a kick he didn't feel.

"Guess you went first after all, asshole."

Bones already had Charlie beat when I looked their way next. He hoisted him on the couch, sitting him on his lap in a pose that would have been comical for two grown men. If you didn't count the wicked-looking blade protruding from Charlie's chest.

"Good thing I didn't need the other bloke, luv," he commented dryly.

I shrugged. Too late now. "Then you should have told me."

Charlie was staring at me in the most astonished way.

"Your eyes . . ." he managed.

I didn't need to glance in a mirror to know they were all lit up. Fighting was a sure way to bring out their glow. In that way, it was like an optical erection. Unavoidable once things went past a certain point.

"Lovely, aren't they?" Bones said silkily. "So at odds with her beating heart. Feel free to be shocked. I know I was when I first saw them glow."

"But they're . . . She can't . . ."

"Oh, don't concern yourself with her any longer, mate. It's me you need to fret about."

That returned Charlie's attention to him. He wiggled, but a flick of the knife stilled him.

"Kitten, someone's in the other room. They're human, but don't rush to assume they're harmless."

I pulled out three small throwing blades from my boot and went to check it out. Now I also caught the sound of a heartbeat coming from the back of the apartment. It was in the room Dean had come out of. Did he have warm-blooded backup?

When I neared the room, I dropped to my knees and moved forward in a crawl. A gunshot to the head would be all she wrote for me. I hoped anyone aiming would assume I'd be higher up, and I'd rush him before he squeezed off a shot. Did I have it in me to kill another human? Only one way to find out.

I peered cautiously around the bottom of the door frame—and then ran in with a cry.

"We need an ambulance!"

The girl was staring sightlessly at the ceiling. One look revealed she had no weapons. The only thing she was wearing was her own blood. Her arms and legs were flung out in a blatant pose, and she wasn't moving. Of course not. She would have been told she couldn't.

My knives fell from nerveless fingers. I couldn't stop looking at her. All these years, the vampires I'd killed, and I'd never seen a victim before. Reading about it didn't even begin to compare to the living, breathing evidence of someone else's cruelty. My gaze went from her throat, to her wrists, and to the crease of her thigh. All bore distinct puncture wounds that slowly oozed.

They shook me from my state of horrified shock. I grabbed the bedsheet and began ripping it. The girl didn't even move when I used the strips as bandages and tied them to everything but her neck. That wound I manually applied pressure to, using the remains of the sheet to cover her while I carried her out of the room.

"I have to take her to a hospital—"

"Wait, Kitten."

Bones gave me an inscrutable look as I hurried into the main room of this hellhole. Charlie barely glanced at the figure in my arms. He seemed more concerned with his own predicament.

"But she's lost a lot of blood! And worse!"

Bones knew what "and worse" meant, even if he couldn't already tell from one sniff. Blood loss could be replenished. Her emotional wounds might never heal.

"You rush her to a local hospital and you may as well kill her." Evenly. "Hennessey will send someone to silence her, she knows too much. I'll take care of her, but let me deal with him first."

Charlie swiveled his head as much as their close proximity allowed.

"I don't know who you are, sonny boy, but you're making a big mistake. If you get up on out of here now, you might just live long enough to regret it."

Bones let out a mocking laugh. "Well said, mate! Why, some of the others groveled straightaway, and you know how tedious that is. You're right, we haven't been properly introduced, even though I already know your name. I'm Bones."

The slide of Charlie's eyes let me know he'd heard of him. One day, I might have to ask how he'd earned his reputation. Then again, I probably didn't want to know.

"There's no reason to be uncivilized 'bout things." Charlie was suddenly back to his charming drawl. "Hennessey said you've been slinking after him, but why don't you smarten up? You can't beat him, so you should join him. Hell, he'd love to have someone like you batting for his team. This is a big, sweet pie, my friend, and there ain't nobody who wouldn't like a piece of it."

Bones angled him so he could look at him. "Is that right? I'm not so sure Hennessey would want me. Killed an awful lot of his blokes, you see. He might be cross about that."

Charlie smiled. "Aw, hell, that's like a job interview for him! Don't you worry none about that. He'd figure if they was dumb enough to get dried by you, he don't want them in the first place."

"We don't have time for this," I snapped, setting the girl on the floor. "She's bleeding to death while you're making friends!"

"Just a moment, pet. Charlie and I are talking. Now, about this pie, mate. Big and sweet, you say? I'm afraid I'll need a little more incentive to let you live than just 'big and sweet.' I'm sure I can find someone who would pay a pretty penny for your corpse."

"Not as much as you can get by playing for Hennessey instead of against him." He nodded in my direction. "You see that li'l gal your wildcat is cradling? Each one of those honeys is worth 'bout sixty large, when it's all put to bed. We doll them up and have them work the breathers first. Then we auction 'em off to one of ours. Full meal, no cleanin' the dishes afterwards! And *then* they're a perfect plate for a hungry bone-muncher! I mean, these gals were never more useful in their *lives*—"

"You piece of shit!" I cried, marching toward him with my stake.

"Stay where you are, and if I have to tell you to shut it one more time, I'm going to knock your bloody head off!" Bones thundered at me.

I froze. His eyes blazed with a dangerous glint in them I hadn't seen since we first met. All at once, I was uneasy. Was he still trying to get information out of Charlie . . . or being recruited instead?

"That's better." Bones turned his attention back to Charlie. "Now, then, you were saying?"

Charlie laughed like they'd shared a joke. "Whew! Your kitty's high-strung, isn't she? Better watch your small and wrinklies before she wears 'em on her belt!"

Bones laughed as well. "No chance of that, mate. She likes what they do to her too much to rob me of them."

I felt ill, and my head started to pound. How could he waste so much time while this girl was bleeding all over the carpet? My God, what if this was the real Bones? What if everything *before* this had been an act? I mean, how well did I know him, anyway? This could have been his intention all along, and how amusing that I'd been tricked into helping him. My mother's voice echoed in my head. *They're all evil, Catherine. They're monsters, monsters. . . .*

"Sixty grand each, that's nice, but split up how many

ways? It's not a lot of quid if you're splashing it over a big pond."

Charlie relaxed as much as he could while being pronged. "Naw, it's not much if it's only a few dozen cooches, but tally that number up against hundreds. There's only 'bout twenty of us in this, and Hennessey's expanding his treats. Going global with 'em. Hell, the Internet's opened up a whole new client base for us, know what I'm sayin'? But he wants to keep his inner structure small. Just enough to keep those wheels movin' over that sweet track to happy land. Aren't you tired of scratching out a livin' from job to job? Residual income, that's the key. We've run through our last batch of gals, and it's roundup time again. Few months of shoring up, and then it's just sit back and watch the bank account grow. It's sweet, let me tell you. Sweet."

"Indeed. You paint a tempting picture, mate. However, there are a few chaps of Hennessey's where there's no love lost between us, so tell me—who else is on this quid train? Can't sign me up if I've shagged one of their wives or shriveled their brother, right?"

The smile was wiped from Charlie's face. Something cold settled over his expression and his voice lost that Deep South twang.

"Fuck you."

With those words, Bones straightened from his easy slouch.

"Right." His tone became crisp as well. "Knew you'd figure it out eventually. Well, thanks anyway, mate. You've been moderately helpful. Only twenty of you, you say? That's less than I thought, and I've a decent inkling who the rest of them might be."

Relief slammed into me with such force that my knees trembled. Oh God, for a second, I hadn't thought he was faking. I thought I'd been played in the worst way possible.

"Kitten, I don't feel anyone else, but take a look around

this building anyway. Break down the doors if you have to, but make sure no one else is here."

I gestured to the girl, who hadn't moved. "What about her?"

"She'll hold a bit more."

"If you kill me, it won't only be Hennessey who'll come down on you. You'll wish your mother had never been born," Charlie hissed. "He's got friends, and they go higher up on the pole than you can handle."

I left, but heard Bones's reply as I started on the closest unit.

"As far as Hennessey and his friends go, I thought they wouldn't miss anyone stupid enough to get dried by me? Your words, mate. I suspect you're regretting them."

A quick sweep if the complex turned up nothing. There were only four separate units and they were all empty. This building was a front, was my guess. Only one unit had been inhabited by the late Dean and the soon-to-be-late Charlie. Still, to the casual observer, it had been another typical small rental. One day I'd like to actually see something typical. I hadn't come across it yet.

When I came back ten minutes later, the girl was still lying on the floor, but Bones and Charlie were gone.

"Bones?"

"Back here," he called out.

Dean's room. I approached with less stealth than before, but couldn't bring myself just to trot in without caution. Untrusting. Yeah, that was me.

The sight that greeted me widened my eyes. Bones had Charlie in bed. Not lying on it, but *in* it. The metal frame was wrapped around him and twisted together to form clamps. That silver knife was still in Charlie, wedged with a bent beam holding it in place.

Bones had three jugs near his feet. Their smell, even with my nose, told me what they were.

"Now, mate, I'm going to make you an offer. It only gets extended once. Tell me who these other players are, all of them, and you'll go out quick and clean. Refuse, and . . ." He hefted a jug, emptying out its contents over Charlie. His clothes soaked up the liquid and the harsh scent of gasoline filled the air. "You'll live as long as it takes for this to kill you."

"Where'd you get those?" I asked irrelevantly.

"Under his kitchen sink. Thought they'd have something like this on hand. You didn't think they'd just leave this place and all of its forensic evidence behind when they were through, did you?"

I hadn't gone that far in my thinking. I'd been a day late and a dollar short all night, it seemed.

Charlie gave Bones a look filled with chilling hate. "I'll tell you in hell, and that'll be soon."

Bones struck a match and dropped it on him. The flames sprouted instantly. Charlie screamed and started to thrash, but the bed frame held. Or the fire incapacitated him too quickly.

"Wrong answer, mate. I never bluff. Come on, Kitten. We're leaving."

Fourteen

We only stayed long enough to make sure Charlie didn't get out. Bones trailed more gasoline to the other units on the upper floor, and they lit up the sky as well. The girl had yet to speak. Her eyes hadn't even really focused when I carried her out of there.

Bones gave her a few drops of blood. Said they'd tide her over until he got her somewhere safe. We couldn't hang around here for many reasons. The fire department would be on their way. The police, too. And any of Hennessey's goons who'd soon find out that one of his residences had been torched with his people inside.

I was surprised when Bones went over to Charlie's car and popped the trunk. "I'll be right back," I murmured to the girl, and left her in the backseat. She didn't seem to even hear me.

I went around to the back of Charlie's car, curious. Bones was bent over the trunk. When he came back up, he had a man in his arms.

I gaped. "Who the hell is *that*?"

The guy's head drooped into view and I sucked in a breath. The obnoxious jerk from the bar!

Even though I didn't hear a heartbeat, I had to ask. "Is he . . . ?"

"Dead as Caesar," Bones supplied. "Charlie took him 'round the back and snapped his spine. Bloke would have felt me, too, if he'd been paying more attention. That's where I was hiding."

"You didn't try to stop him?"

It came out with all of my residual guilt over the unknown man's death. I hadn't tried to stop him, either. Maybe that's what sharpened my tone.

Bones fixed his gaze on me, unblinking. "No. I didn't."

I felt like beating my head against a wall. Technically, we'd won tonight, but the victory was hollow. An innocent man killed. A young woman traumatized beyond comprehension. No names of who else was involved, and the knowledge that now it would only get worse.

"What are you doing with him?"

He set him in the grass. "Leave him as he is. There's nothing more to be done. With this fire, he'll be found soon. He'll have a proper burial. That's all he's got left."

It seemed so callous just to leave the man there, but Bones had a practical, if not cold, point. There was nothing more we could do for him. Dropping him off at a hospital with a note wouldn't make his family hurt any less.

"Let's go," he said briefly.

"But what about Charlie? You're just going to leave him and Dean for the police to find, too?" I persisted, getting into the backseat and taking the girl's hand as we sped away.

"Coppers?" A humorless smile played on his lips. "You know that when vampires died, their bodies decomposed to their true ages. That's why they look like bloomin' mummies sometimes afterwards. Just let them try to figure out why a bloke dead 'round seventy years ended up stuffed into a bed frame and torched. They'll be scratching their chins about that for days. And I'm leaving Charlie the way he is for a reason. I want Hennessey to know who did it, and he will, because when we get back to the hotel, I'm going to call around and find out if there's any money on this sod. If there is, I'll claim it, and word will get to him. He'll be nervous, wondering what Charlie told me, and with luck it'll draw him out of hiding. He'll want to shut me up for good."

That was a very risky move. Hennessey wasn't alone in wanting Bones as worm food. From what Charlie had said, there were about twenty other people who'd be happy about that also.

"Where are we taking her?"

"Give me a moment." He flipped out his cell and dialed, driving one-handed. I whispered useless comforting things to the girl and thought of my mother. Once, many years ago, she'd been the victim. This wasn't the same scenario, true, but I didn't imagine it felt much different.

"Tara, it's Bones. I'm sorry to ring you so late. . . . I have a favor to ask. . . . Thank you. I'll be there within the hour."

He met my eyes in the rearview mirror. "Tara lives in Blowing Rock, so it's not that far, and the girl will be safe with her. No one really knows Tara, so Hennessey won't think to look there. She'll be able to give her the help she needs, and not just physically. She's been through something similar."

"A vampire got her?" What a horrible club to be a member of.

Bones looked away, turning his attention back to the roads.

"No, luv. He was just a man."

Tara lived in a log home in the Blue Ridge Mountains. It was accessible only by a private driveway. This was the first I'd been out of Ohio, and I was awed by the steep cliffs, high bluffs, and rugged scenery. If these were different circumstances, I would have demanded that Bones pull over just so I could look around at it all.

An African-American woman with salt-and-pepper hair waited on the porch. Her heartbeat announced her as human, and Bones got out and gave her a kiss on the cheek.

Something unpleasant twisted in me as I watched. Old girlfriend? Or not-so-old girlfriend?

She hugged him in return and listened as he briefly outlined what had happened to the girl, leaving out any names, I noticed. Bones finished with an admonition for Tara not to tell anyone of her new guest or who had brought her. Then he turned in my direction.

"Kitten? Coming?"

I hadn't known whether to get out or stay, but that decided it.

"We're going to meet this nice lady," I told the girl, and carefully supported her out of the car. I wasn't really carrying her—if directed, she would walk. I was just keeping her sheet from falling off and leading her in the right direction.

Tara's face pinched with sympathy as we drew near. I noticed then that she had a scar running from her eyebrow into her hairline, and I was ashamed for my previous, petty reaction to whatever her relationship with Bones was.

"I'll take her," the man in question said, picking up the girl like she was weightless. "Tara, this is Cat."

I was surprised to hear him call me that, but I held out my hand and Tara shook it warmly.

"I'm glad to meet you, Cat. Bones, put her in my room."

He went inside without asking where that was, and once again I reminded myself that it was none of my business.

"Come in, child, you must be cold!" Tara said with a shiver of her own. At four A.M. in these altitudes, it was chilly out.

That also had me glancing down at myself with a mental groan. Didn't I look lovely? With this dress and my heavy makeup, Tara was probably thinking I must be ten shades of a slut.

"Thanks, and it's nice to meet you, too," I responded politely. At least I could show I had manners.

I followed Tara into her kitchen, accepting the cup of coffee she handed me. She poured herself one, too, and gestured for me to sit.

A scream shattered the quiet, causing me to bolt up as I was about to sit down.

"It's okay," Tara said quickly, holding out a hand. "He's just bringing her back."

Over that terrible keen I heard Bones speaking urgently, telling the girl she was safe and no one would hurt her anymore. Soon her screams turned into sobbing.

"It can take a little while," Tara went on matter-of-factly. "He'll let her remember everything, and then put in a mental patch so she doesn't get suicidal. Some of them do."

"He's done this before?" I asked stupidly. "Brought traumatized girls to you?"

Tara sipped her coffee. "I run an abused women's shelter in town. Most of the time I don't bring anyone back here, but every once in a while we get someone who needs extra care. When they need *extra*, extra care, I call Bones. I'm glad to finally do him a favor. I owe him my life, but I 'spect he told you about that."

I looked at her quizzically. "No, why would you think so?"

She gave me a knowing smile. "'Cause he's never brought a girl here before, child. Not one that didn't need my help, leastways."

Oh! That pleased me, but I quashed it. "It's not like that.

We, ah, kind of work together. I'm not his, er, what I mean is, he's all yours if you want him!" I finished in an insane babble.

There was a disgusted grunt from upstairs that didn't come from the girl. I cringed, but it was too late to take it back.

Tara considered me with a clear, unwavering gaze. "My husband used to beat me. I was afraid to leave him 'cause I had no money and I had a little girl, but one night he gave me this." She pointed to the scar near her temple. "And I told him that was it. I was done. He cried and said he didn't mean to do it. Man said that every time after he laid into me, but hell, yes, he meant it. No one hits you 'less they *mean* it! Well, he knew *I* meant it when I said I was leaving, so he waited behind my car that night when I went to work. I finished my shift, went out to the parking lot, and he stood up and smiled while he pointed a gun right at me. I heard a shot, thought I was dead . . . and then I saw this white boy, looking like a goddamn albino, holding my husband by the throat. He asked me did I want him to live, and you know what I said? *No*."

I swallowed my coffee in one gulp. "Don't wait for me to judge you. In my opinion, he had it coming."

"I said no for my daughter, so she'd never be scared of him the way I was," she said, taking my empty cup and refilling it. "Bones didn't just snap his neck and leave, either. He got me out of that flea-hole apartment I was in, gave me a place to stay, and eventually I got my own place and opened up the shelter. Now I'm the one helping out women who don't have nowhere else to turn. God has a sense of humor sometimes, doesn't He?"

That made me smile. "You could say I'm proof of that."

Tara leaned forward and dropped her voice. "I'm telling you this because he must have taken a shine to you. Like I said, he don't bring nobody here."

This time, I didn't argue. There was no point, and I

couldn't tell her that my presence was more necessity than preference.

Something the girl was saying upstairs redirected my attention.

". . . made me call my roommates. I told them I'd met up with my old boyfriend and we were going away together, but it was a lie. I don't know why I said it, I heard the words coming out of my mouth, but I didn't *want* to say them. . . ."

"It's all right, Emily." Bones' voice was soft. "It wasn't your fault, they made you say that. I know this is hard, but think. Did you see anyone else aside from Charlie and Dean?"

"They kept me in that apartment the whole time, but no one else came in. I have to take a shower now. I feel so dirty."

"It's all right," he said again. "You'll be safe here, and I'll find all of the sods who did this."

It sounded like he was out the door when she suddenly shouted.

"Wait! There *was* someone else. Charlie took me to him, but I don't know where we were. It seems like I blinked, and then I was in this house. I remember the bedroom was big, wood floors, and it had red and blue paisley wallpaper. There was this man wearing a mask. I never saw his face, he kept it on the whole time. . . ."

Her voice wavered. Tara shook her head in repugnance at what didn't need to be elaborated.

"I'll find them," Bones repeated with resolve. "I promise."

He came down the stairs a few minutes later.

"She's settled down," he said, more to Tara than to me. "Her name is Emily, and she doesn't have any family to contact. She's been on her own since she was fifteen, and her mates think she's off with an ex-boyfriend. No need to tell them otherwise and put them in danger."

"I'll brew another pot of coffee and be right up," Tara said, rising. "You staying?"

"Can't," Bones replied with a shake of his head. "We have to catch a plane this afternoon and we're booked at a hotel. But thank you, Tara. I'm indebted to you."

She kissed his cheek. This time, my gut didn't knot. "No, you ain't, honey. You keep safe, now."

"And you." He turned to me. "Kitten?"

"I'm ready. Thank you for the coffee, Tara, and for the company."

"Wasn't nothing, child." She smiled. "You be sweet to our boy here, and remember, be good only if being bad ain't more fun!"

I let out a surprised laugh at this mischievous directive, which was unexpected considering the very unfunny circumstances we were meeting under.

"I'll try to remember that."

Bones didn't speak during the hour drive back to the hotel. There were so many things I wanted to ask him, but of course, I couldn't bring myself to.

When we pulled in the parking lot, however, I couldn't stand the silence anymore.

"So what's next? We find out if Charlie has a bounty on him? Or see if anyone knows who the masked asshole might be? I wonder why the guy bothered to wear a mask. Kinks, do you think, or maybe he was someone she knew and he didn't want her to recognize him?"

Bones parked and gave me an unfathomable look. "Either one is a possibility, but regardless, I think it's best if you bow out now."

"Oh, don't give me that unsafe crap again!" I said, instantly angry. "You think I can see what was done to Emily, know it's going on with countless other girls, and just hide under my bed? Remember, I was supposed to *be* one of those girls! I'm not bowing out, no way!"

"Look, it's not your bravery that's in question," he replied with an edge.

"Then what?"

"I saw your face. The look in your eyes when I spoke to Charlie. You wondered if I was going to join Hennessey. Deep down, you still don't trust me."

He hit the steering wheel with his last comment. It dented, and I winced from more than the accusation in his words.

"You were doing a great job acting, and I got confused. God, can you really blame me? Every day for the past *six years* I've had it drummed into my head that all vampires are lying, vicious scum, and to date, by the way, you're the only one I've met who isn't!"

Bones let out an amazed snort. "Do you realize that's the nicest thing you've ever said to me?"

"Was Tara your girlfriend?"

It just flew out. I sucked in a horrified breath. Good Lord, why did I ask that?

"Never mind," I said quickly. "It doesn't matter. Look, about last night . . . I think we both made a mistake. Hell, you've probably realized that as well, so I'm sure you'll also agree that it should never happen again. I didn't mean to flake out earlier with Charlie, but old habits die hard. Okay, bad metaphor there, but you get my point. We'll work together, bring down Hennessey and whoever else is in his little gang, and then we'll, ah, go our separate ways. No harm, no foul."

He stared at me silently for several moments. "'Fraid I can't agree to that," he finally answered.

"But why? I'm great as bait! All the vampires want to eat me!"

A small smile touched his mouth even as I mentally groaned at my choice of words. Bones reached over and stroked my face.

"I can't just let us go our separate ways, Kitten, because I am in love with you. I love you."

My mouth fell open and my mind briefly cleared of thought. Then I found my voice.

"No, you don't."

He let out a snort and dropped his hand. "You know, pet, that is one truly annoying habit you have, telling me what I do and do not feel. After living for over two hundred and forty-one years, I think I know my own mind."

"Are you just saying that to have sex with me?" I asked suspiciously, remembering Danny and all of his cutesy lies.

He gave me an annoyed look. "Knew you'd think such a thing. That's why I didn't say anything before, because I never wanted you to wonder if I were merely lying to cajole you into bed. However, to be rudely blunt, I've already gotten you on your back, and it wasn't by declaring my devotion to you. I simply don't care to hide my feelings any longer."

"But you've only known me two months!" Now I tried arguing the point, because denial didn't seem to work.

A slight smile curled his lips. "I began to fall in love with you when you challenged me to that stupid fight in the cave. There you were, chained up and bleeding, questioning my courage and almost daring me to kill you. Why do you think I struck that bargain with you? Truth is, luv, I did it so you'd be forced to spend time with me. I knew you'd never agree any other way. After all, you had such hangups about vampires. Still do, it appears."

"Bones . . ." My eyes were wide at his revelation and with the growing knowledge that he was serious. "We'd never work out together. We have to stop this now, before it goes any further!"

"I know what makes you say that. Fear. You're terrified

because of how that other wanker treated you, and you're even more afraid of what your dear mum would say."

"Oh, she'd have plenty to say, you can bet on that," I muttered.

"I've faced death more times than I can count, Kitten, and this instance with Hennessey is no different—do you really think the wrath of your mum is going to scare me away?"

"It would if you were smart." Also muttered.

"Then consider me the stupidest man in the world."

He leaned over and kissed me. A long, deep kiss filled with promise and passion. I loved the way he kissed me. Like he was drinking in the taste of me and still coming back thirsty.

I pushed him back, my breathing uneven. "You'd better not be messing with me. I like you, but if you're feeding me a load of shit just to get some action, I'm going to plug a big silver stake right through your heart."

He chuckled and his mouth slid down to nuzzle my neck. "I'll consider myself warned."

The erotic teasing of my pulse made me shiver. "And no biting," I added.

His laughter tickled me. "On my honor. Anything else?"

"Yeah. . . ." It was getting harder to think. "No one else if you're with me."

He drew his head up and his lips twitched. "That's a relief. After you told Tara she could have me as well, I didn't know if you fancied monogamy."

I flushed. "I'm serious!"

"Kitten"—he held my face—"I said I loved you. That means I don't want anyone else."

This would only bring disaster, I knew it. Knew it as sure as I knew I was a half-blooded freak, but looking into his eyes, it didn't matter.

"Last but absolutely not least, I insist on going after Hennessey with you. If I trust you enough to be your . . .

your girlfriend, you'll have to trust me enough to let me do that."

Something like a sigh escaped him.

"I beg you to stay out of this. Hennessey's well connected and ruthless. That's a dangerous combination."

I smiled. "Half dead and totally dead. We're a dangerous combination as well."

He let out a dry laugh. "I reckon you're right about that."

"Bones." I made my gaze unflinching so he could see how serious I was. "I can't walk away when I know what's happening. I'd hate myself for not doing everything I could to stop it. One way or another, I'm in this. Your only choice is whether I'm in this with you, or without you."

He gave me that penetrating stare of his. The one that felt like it could drill holes into the back of my head, but I didn't look away. He finally did.

"All right, luv. You win. We'll get him together. I promise."

The first rays of dawn pierced the sky. I looked at them with regret. "Sun's coming up."

"So it is."

He pulled me to him again and kissed me with such fervor that I gasped. There was no mistaking the demand of his mouth or the feel of his body.

"But it's dawn!" I said in astonishment.

Bones let out a low laugh. "Really, luv, how dead do you think I am . . . ?"

We ordered breakfast later from room service, an invention that had to come straight from heaven, in my opinion. Well, by the time we ordered it, it was actually more like lunch, although I still chose the pancakes and eggs. Bones watched in amusement as I scarfed the food down, scraping my plate when it was empty.

"You can always send for more. You don't have to chew the dishes."

"It wouldn't matter if I did. I think you already lost your deposit," I replied, casting a meaningful look at the shattered lamp, broken table, bloodstained carpet, overturned couch, and various other items that were in a condition other than how we'd found them. It looked like a brawl had taken place. One sort of had. A sensual one, anyway.

He grinned and stretched his arms over his head. "Worth every farthing."

The inking on his left arm caught my eye. I'd noticed it the other night, of course, but somehow hadn't been in the conversation mood. Now I traced it with a finger.

"Crossbones. How appropriate." The tattoo wasn't filled in; the bones were just an outline. His pale flesh seemed to emphasize the black ink. "When did you get it?"

"A mate gave that to me over sixty years ago. He was a Marine who died in World War Two."

God, talk about a generation gap. That tattoo was over three times my age. Slightly uncomfortable, I changed the subject.

"Did you find out anything more about Charlie?"

He'd gotten on the computer while I called in my breakfast order. I didn't want to know how he was going about the process of discovering if there was any money wanted for Charlie. Listing Charlie on eBay, perhaps? *One corpse, extra crispy! Do I hear a thousand dollars?*

"I'll check, should have a nibble by now," he responded, climbing gracefully out of bed. He was still naked, and I couldn't help but stare at his ass. Two-plus centuries or not, it was something.

"Ah, e-mail, and good news. Bank wire transfer completed, one hundred thousand dollars. Charlie pissed off the wrong bloke, whoever this is. I'll give him the location of where to find his body for confirmation, and Hennessey will be hearing about it soon. That'll also be twenty K for you, Kitten, and you didn't even have to kiss him."

"I don't want the money."

My reply was immediate. I didn't even have to think about it. No matter that the shallow, greedy part of my brain screeched in protest.

He regarded me curiously. "Whyever not? You earned it. I told you that was always part of the plan, even though I didn't let you in on it right off. What's the problem?"

Sighing, I tried to articulate the whirling of emotions and thoughts that consisted of my conscience.

"Because it isn't right. It was one thing to take it when we weren't sleeping together, but I don't want to feel like a kept woman. I won't be your girlfriend and your employee at the same time. Really, the choice is yours. Pay me, and I stop sleeping with you. Keep the money, and we continue on in bed."

Bones laughed outright, coming over to where I sat.

"And you wonder why I love you. When you boil it all down, you're *paying* me to shag you, for as soon as I stop, I owe you twenty percent of every contract I take. Blimey, Kitten, you've turned me back into a whore."

"That's . . . that's not . . . Dammit, you know what I meant!"

Clearly I hadn't thought of it in those terms. I tried to wrest myself away, but his arms hardened like steel. Although still sparking with humor, there was a definite glint of something else in his eyes. Dark brown orbs started to color with green.

"You're not going anywhere. I have twenty thousand dollars to earn, and I'm going to start working on it right now. . . ."

We boarded the plane after boxing our stakes and knives and taking them to a FedEx carrier, airport security being so strict nowadays. In the section marked "contents," Bones filled out "tofu." God, but he had a sick sense of humor sometimes. It was with only our carry-on luggage that we embarked. Bones again let me have the window seat, and I waited for that rush of power when the engines roared to life. He had his eyes closed, and I noticed a faint compressing of his fingers on the armrest when we accelerated.

"You don't like to fly, do you?" I asked, surprised. He never seemed hesitant about anything.

"No, not really. One of the few ways a bloke like me can accidentally die."

His eyes were still closed, and then we were pressed back into our seats with the force of the liftoff. After the worst of the pressure subsided, I lifted his eyelid to see him glare balefully at my amused expression.

"Don't you know anything about statistics? Safest way to travel if you play it by numbers."

"Not for a vampire. We can walk away from almost any car crash, train wreck, sunken ship, or whatever. Yet when a plane goes down, not even our kind can do much about it but pray. Lost a mate in that crash in the Everglades several years ago. Poor bugger, they only ever found his kneecap."

Contrary to his suspicion, the plane landed safely at four-thirty. Bones was also very handy when it came to getting a cab. He'd just glare at the drivers with his green gaze and compel them to stop. They did, even if they already had passengers. That happened twice, to my embarrassment. Finally we flagged one without occupants and started back to my house. He had been oddly quiet since getting off the plane, and when we were within five minutes of my place, he suddenly broke the silence.

"I take it you don't want me to see you to the door and give you a kiss goodbye in front of your mum?"

"Absolutely not!"

The look he gave me told me he didn't appreciate the emphaticalness of my response.

"Be that as it may, I want to see you tonight."

I sighed. "Bones, no. I'm barely ever home anymore. Next weekend I move into my new apartment, so these next few days with my family will be all I'll have for a while. Something tells me my grandparents won't be visiting often."

"Where's the apartment?"

Oh, I'd forgotten to mention it. "About six miles away from the campus."

"You'll be only twenty minutes from the cave, then."

How convenient. Bones didn't speak the last part. He didn't have to.

"I'll call you with the address on Friday. You can come over after my mother leaves. Not before. I mean it, Bones. Unless you get a lead on Hennessey or our mysterious masked rapist, give me a little time. It's already Sunday."

The long driveway to my house came into view as the taxi rounded the next corner. Bones saw it and took my hand.

"I want you to promise me something. Promise me you're not going to start running again."

"Running?" Why would I do that? I hadn't had much sleep and I certainly didn't feel in the mood for jogging.

Then his meaning penetrated. When I got home and looked into my mother's eyes, I would second-guess a relationship with him all to hell, I knew. He must have known it, too. Now, however, the only face in front of me was his.

"No, I'm too tired to run, and you're too fast. You'd only catch me."

"That's right, luv." Softly, but with unyielding resonance. "If you run from me, I'll chase you. And I'll find you."

Fifteen

It was a busy remainder of the week. There was packing, paperwork for the apartment, the deposit and rental agreement signed with my new landlord, and saying goodbye to my family.

Using some of the money from the first job with Bones, I'd bought a box spring and mattress and a dresser for my clothes. Add a few lamps, and that was the whole enchilada. The rest of the money I split with my mother, telling her one of the vampires I'd taken down had carried cash. It was the least I could do. The remaining money I hoarded, knowing I would still have to get a part-time job to make ends meet. How I was going to handle college, a job, and helping to track down a group of enterprising undead murderers was anyone's guess.

Bones hadn't called or come over, as per my request, but he'd been in my thoughts all week. To my horror, one morning my mother asked me if I'd had a nightmare the previous evening. Apparently I'd been saying the word "bones" in my sleep. Mumbling something about graveyards, I brushed her off, but the reality remained. Unless Bones and I broke up—or I got killed, of course—one day I'd have to deal with her and him. Frankly, that scared me more than going after Hennessey.

My grandparents let me keep the truck, which was nice of them. They had been less than pleased with me lately, but I received a stiff hug from each of them when it was time for me to leave. My mother followed me in her car because, as I expected, she wanted to see me settled in.

"Be sure and learn good, child," Grandpa Joe gruffly said when I started to pull away. My eyes pricked with tears, since I was leaving the only home I'd ever known.

"I love you both," I sniffed.

"Don't forget to keep going to Bible study with that nice young gal," my grandmother instructed me sternly. Jesus, Mary, and Joseph, if she only knew what she was saying.

"Oh, I'm sure I'll be seeing her soon." Real soon.

"Catherine, it's . . . it's . . . you could always stay at the house and commute."

My mother's obvious dismay as she looked around my apartment made me hide a smile. No, it wasn't pretty, but it was all mine.

"It's fine, Mom. Really. It will look much better after we clean."

After three hours of side-by-side scrubbing, it didn't look any better, in fact. But at least now I wouldn't worry about bugs.

At eight P.M., my mother kissed me goodbye, throwing her arms around me and hugging me so hard it almost hurt.

"Call me if you need anything, promise me. Be careful, Catherine."

"I promise, Mom. I will."

Oh, what a tangled web we weave . . . What I was going

to do next was far, far from careful, but I was doing it anyway. As soon as she left, I picked up the phone and dialed.

While I was waiting, I took a shower and put on new clothes. Not night clothes, because that seemed too obvious, but regular clothing. The time apart this week had been rough, and for more than just the scary fact that I missed him. My mother made her usual comments about how all vampires deserved to die and for me to keep hunting them, in between admonitions to study diligently. I'd cringed with guilt every time I had to nod and agree with her so she didn't get suspicious.

My hair was still wet from washing it when I heard him rap twice. I opened the door . . . and the last few days fell away. Bones stepped through the entrance and locked it behind him while pulling me into his arms in one motion. God, but he was beautiful, with those chiseled cheekbones and pale skin, his body hard and seeking. His mouth covered mine before I could get a breath in, and then I didn't need to breathe because I was too busy kissing him. My hands trembled when they reached up to grasp his shoulders and then clenched when he reached under my waistband to feel inside.

"I can't breathe," I gasped, wrenching my head away.

His mouth went to my throat, lips and tongue moving over the sensitive skin as he bent my spine until only his arms held me upright.

"I missed you," he growled, restlessly pulling off my clothes. He swept me up in his arms and asked a single question. "Where?"

I jerked my head in the vicinity of my bedroom, too busy feasting on his skin to answer. He carried me into the small room and nearly flung me on the bed.

A tentative knock at my door the next morning made me groan as I rolled over. The clock showed nine-thirty. Bones had left right before dawn with a whispered promise to meet me here later. He said my apartment had too much exposure for him to sleep. Whatever that meant.

I stumbled into my robe, fastening my attention to the doorway where the knock had come from. Heartbeat, whoever it was, and only one. That made me leave my knives in the bedroom. Opening the door armed might set a bad tone if it was my landlord.

The sound of footsteps retreating had me snatch the door open in time to see a young man about to disappear into the unit next to mine.

"Hey!" I said, a little sharper than I'd intended.

He stopped almost guiltily, and it was then that I noticed the small basket near my feet. A quick glance showed it contained ramen noodles, Tylenol, and pizza coupons.

"College survival kit," he said, coming toward me with a hesitant smile. "I guessed from seeing you unload your books last night that you're attending school, too. I'm your neighbor, Timmie. Uh, Tim. I mean Tim."

The obvious cover-up of a nickname had me smiling. Childhood baggage was hard to overcome. In my case, I'd never get past mine.

"I'm Cathy," I replied, using my school name again. "Thanks for the goodies, and I didn't mean to bark at you. I'm just grouchy when I wake up."

He was instantly apologetic. "I'm sorry! I just assumed you'd be awake. Jeez, am I dumb. Go back to sleep, please."

He turned to go into his apartment, and something about his hunched shoulders and awkward demeanor reminded me of . . . me. That was how I felt on the inside most of the time. Unless I was killing someone.

"It's okay," I said quickly. "Er, I had to get up anyway, and the alarm clock must not have gone off, so . . . do you have any coffee?"

I didn't even really like coffee, but he'd made a nice

gesture and I didn't want him feeling bad. Seeing the relief that washed over him made me glad for the small lie.

"Coffee," he repeated with another shy smile. "Yeah. Come on in."

I wasn't wearing anything under the robe. "Give me a second."

After throwing on sweatpants and a T-shirt, I padded over in slippers to Timmie's place. He'd left the door open, and the aroma of Folgers filled the air. It was the same brand my grandparents had brewed all my life. In a way, it was comforting to smell it.

"Here." He handed me a mug and I sat on the stool by his counter. The layouts of our apartments were identical, except of course Timmie's place had furniture. "Cream and sugar?"

"Sure."

I studied him as he went about the small kitchen. Timmie was only a few inches taller than me, not quite six feet, and had sandy-colored hair and taupe eyes. He wore glasses and had the type of frame that looked like it had only filled out from the skinniness of adolescence recently. My internal suspicious radar so far hadn't picked up anything threatening about him. Still, it seemed every time someone was nice to me, he or she had ulterior motives. Danny? One-night stand. Ralphie and Martin? Attempted date rape. Stephanie? White slavery. I had a reason to be paranoid. If I felt even the *slightest* bit woozy after drinking this coffee, Timmie was going down for the count.

"So, uh, Cathy, are you from Ohio?" he asked, fumbling with his own cup.

"Born and bred," I replied. "You?"

He nodded, spilling some coffee onto the counter and then jumping back with a surreptitious glance at me, as if afraid I'd reprimand him. "Sorry. I'm a klutz. Oh, um, yeah,

I'm from here, too. Powell. My mom's a bank manager there, and I got a kid sister who's starting high school who still lives with her. It's been just the three of us since my dad died. Car accident. I don't even remember him. Not that you wanted to know all that. Sorry. I babble sometimes."

He also had a habit of apologizing every other sentence. Hearing about his fatherless state made me feel another bond of kinship with him. Deliberately I took a swig of coffee . . . and let a little bit dribble out of the side of my mouth.

"Oops!" I said with feigned embarrassment. "Excuse me. I drool sometimes when I drink."

Another lie, but Timmie smiled, handing me a napkin while the nervousness eased off him. There was nothing like having someone be a bigger goof to boost one's own self-confidence.

"That's better than being a klutz. I'm sure a lot of people do that."

"Oh yeah, there's a club of us," I quipped. "Droolers Anonymous. I'm on Step One in my membership. Admitting that I'm powerless over my slobbering and my life has become unmanageable."

Timmie was in the process of taking another sip when he started to laugh. Coffee came out of his nose as a result, and then his eyes bulged, aghast.

"I'm sorry!" he choked, making it worse by trying to talk. More coffee emerged, spraying me in the face. His eyes bugged in horror, but I laughed so hard at seeing him leak like a thermos with holes that I started to hiccup.

"It's contagious!" I managed to get out. "There's no escape from the drool disease once you catch it!"

He laughed again, compounding his problem. I hiccuped, Timmie gasped and sputtered, and both of us looked like mental patients to anyone who would have happened by the still-open door. I ended up handing him the same napkin he'd given me, trying to control my giggles while instinctively knowing I'd found a friend.

I headed over to the cave Monday afternoon after my classes. A couple miles before I made my turn onto the gravel road that ended at the edge of the woods, I passed a Corvette parked to the side with its hazard lights on. No one was inside. I almost huffed to myself in superiority. Whose old Chevy was tooling past a broken-down, sixty-thousand-dollar sports car? So there!

I was whistling the little tune Darryl Hannah made famous in *Kill Bill* when I entered the cave. That's when I felt the change in the air. The disturbance. Someone was lurking about fifty yards ahead, and whoever it was didn't have a heartbeat. What I also instinctively knew was that it wasn't Bones.

I kept whistling, not letting my heart rate accelerate or my cadence falter. I wasn't armed. My knives and wood-coated stakes were back at the apartment, and my second set was in the dressing area *behind* this unknown person. Weaponless, I was at a distinct disadvantage, but there was no way I was turning around. Bones must be in trouble, or worse, since I didn't sense him here. Someone had found his hideout, and empty-handed or not, I wasn't going anywhere but forward.

I progressed as casually as possible, my mind racing. What could I use as a weapon? My options were dismal. This was a cave, there was nothing around but dirt and . . .

I reached down while ducking under one of the lower slopes in the ceiling of the cave, the action concealing what I scooped up. The person was coming toward me now, moving soundlessly. My fingers tightened around what I held as I rounded the next bend, bringing the intruder into view.

A tall man with longish spiky black hair was about twenty feet from me. He smiled as he approached, confident in his presumed superiority.

"You, my beauteous redhead, must be Cat."

The name I'd given Hennessey. This must be one of his goons and somehow he'd found Bones. I prayed I wasn't too late and he hadn't killed him.

I smiled back coldly. "Like what you see? How about now?"

And I flung the rocks I'd gathered straight into his eyes. I put all my force behind it, knowing it wouldn't be lethal but hoping to temporarily incapacitate him. His head snapped back and I sprang at him, seizing my chance while he was blinded. My momentum knocked him off his feet and both of us went down. Immediately I grasped his head, smashing him face-first into the stone ground, wedging the rocks deeper into his eyes. I straddled his back when his thrashing almost threw me off, using my weight and squeezing him with my thighs as hard as I could. All the while I bashed his head, I was cursing at his strength. A Master vampire without a doubt. Well, what did I expect? If he was a weakling, Bones would have greeted me, not him.

"Stop it! *Stop!*" he howled.

I put more effort into it instead. "Where's Bones? *Where is he?*"

"Christ, he said he was on his way!"

He had an English accent. I hadn't noticed that before, being so wrapped up in my concern. I stopped banging his head, but kept it ground into the stony floor.

"You're one of Hennessey's men. Why would you let him know you're waiting for him?"

"Because I'm Crispin's bloody best friend, not one of that scoundrel's dingos!" he said indignantly.

That answer I wasn't expecting. He'd also called Bones by his real name, and I didn't know if that was common knowledge. I had a split second to debate with myself, then I grabbed another rock, using one hand to keep his head where it was. With the pointy end of the stone, I jabbed him in the back.

"Feel that? It's silver. You move and I ram it right through your heart. Maybe you're Bones's friend and maybe you're not. Since I'm not the trusting sort, we'll wait for him. If he's not here soon like you said, I'll know you were lying, and then it'll be curtains for you."

I almost held my breath, waiting to see if he called my bluff. Since I hadn't pierced his skin, he shouldn't be able to feel that this wasn't silver. I hoped vampires didn't have a sixth sense about their kryptonite. My big plan, if he wasn't a friend, was to jam it through his heart anyway and then run like hell for my silver. If I got to it in time.

"If you'd refrain from slamming my face any more into this dirty rock floor, I'll do whatever you like," was his even reply. "Fancy letting my head go?"

"Sure," I said with an unpleasant snicker, not relinquishing an ounce of pressure. "How about I let you floss with my jugular as well? I don't think so."

He made an exasperated noise that sounded very familiar. "Come on, this is ridiculous—"

"Shut up." I didn't want his chatter distracting me from hearing when—or if—Bones arrived. "Lie there and play dead, or you will be."

Twenty cramped minutes later, my heart leapt when I heard steady footfalls coming toward the cave. Then a feeling of power I recognized filled up the space as those footsteps came closer.

Bones rounded the corner and stopped short. A single dark brow arched even as I leaned back, letting go of the vampire's head at last.

"Charles," Bones said distinctly. "You'd better have a splendid explanation for her being on top of you."

Sixteen

THE BLACK-HAIRED VAMPIRE ROSE TO HIS FEET as soon as I jumped off, brushing the dirt off his clothes.

"Believe me, mate, I've never enjoyed a woman astride me less. I came out to say hallo, and this she-devil blinded me by flinging rocks in my eyes. Then she vigorously attempted to split my skull before threatening to impale me with silver if I so much as even twitched! It's been a few years since I've been to America, but I daresay the method of greeting a person has changed dramatically!"

Bones rolled his eyes and clapped him on the shoulder. "I'm glad you're still upright, Charles, and the only reason you are is because she didn't *have* any silver. She'd have staked you right and proper otherwise. She has a tendency to shrivel someone first and then introduce herself afterwards."

"That's uncalled for!" I said, insulted at the suggestion that I was homicidal.

"Right." Bones let that go. "Kitten, this is my best mate,

Charles, but you can call him Spade. Charles, this is Cat, the woman I've been telling you about. You can see for yourself that everything I've said is . . . an understatement."

From his tone, that didn't sound altogether complimentary, but I felt a tad bit guilty about what I'd done to the lanky vampire eying me, so I didn't comment and just held out my hand.

"Hi."

"Hi," Spade repeated, and then threw back his head and roared with laughter. "Well, hallo to you, too, darling! I'm very pleased to meet you now that you're not flogging me unmercifully."

He had tiger-colored eyes, and they gave me a thorough once-over while he shook my hand. I did the same to him. Fair was fair. Next to Bones, Spade looked two inches taller, which made him about six-four. He had lean attractive features, a straight nose, and inky hair that spiked up from his crown before hanging past his shoulders.

"Spade. You're white. Isn't that kind of . . . politically incorrect?"

He laughed again, but this time it was with less humor. "Oh, I didn't choose that as a racial slur. It was how the overseer in South Wales used to address me. A spade is a shovel, and I was a digger. He never called anyone by their names, only their assigned tool. He didn't feel the convicts were worthy of more."

Oh, so he was *that* Charles. Now I remembered the name from when Bones had told me about his past imprisonment. *There were three men I became mates with—Timothy, Charles, and Ian.*

"Sounds pretty demeaning. Why'd you keep it?"

Spade's smile didn't slip, but those striking features hardened. "So I'd never forget."

Okay. A change of subject was in order. Bones beat me to it.

"Charles has some information on a flunky of Hennessey's who might prove useful."

"Great," I said. "Should I grab my slut clothes and pile on the makeup?"

"You should stay out of it," Spade replied in a serious tone.

That made me want to fling more rocks at him. "My God, is it a vampire thing to be a chauvinist? Or just an eighteenth century one? Keep the girl in the kitchen where she won't get hurt, right? Wake up and smell the twenty-first century, *Spade*! Women are good for more than cringing and waiting for men to rescue them!"

"And if Crispin felt differently for you, I'd bid you good luck and tell you to have at it," Spade responded at once. "Yet I happen to know firsthand how devastating it is when someone you love is murdered. There's nothing worse, and I don't want him going through that."

A part of me was inwardly pleased that Bones had told his friend he had feelings for me. I still didn't believe he loved me, but it was nice to know I wasn't just another warm body to him.

"Look, I'm sorry vampires killed someone close to you, truly I am. But—"

"Vampires didn't kill her," he interrupted me. "A group of French deserters cut her throat."

I opened my mouth, paused, and shut it. That told me a few things right there, aside from the fact that I'd been wrong about what race killed her. She'd been human, whoever she was.

"I'm not like everyone else," was what I ended up saying, giving Bones a questioning look to see if he'd told him that as well.

"So I've heard," Spade said. "And you certainly caught me off guard earlier, but whatever your extraordinary abilities . . . you're easy to kill. That beating pulse in your neck is your greatest weakness, and if I'd had a mind to before, I could have flipped you over and torn it out."

I smiled. "You're pretty cocky. So am I, when it comes to certain things. We'll get along just fine. Wait right here."

"Kitten . . ." Bones called after me, no doubt guessing where I was headed.

"Oh, this'll be fun!"

"Where's she off to?" I heard Spade ask.

Bones made a noise that was almost pitying. "To hand you your arse, and for the record, if I thought I had a chance of keeping her out of this, I would. Woman's stubborn beyond reason."

"Stubbornness won't keep her alive. I'm astounded you'd allow her to—"

Spade stopped talking when he saw me, probably because of what was in my hands.

"Okay, you're a big bad vampire who's gonna rip my throat out, right? You see I'm armed—with steel, by the way, since this is a demonstration and I don't want you to end up smelly—and you don't care because you're all that and I'm just an artery in a dress. If you get a mouth on my throat, you win, but if I plug your heart first, I do."

Spade's eyes slid to Bones. "Is she joking?"

Bones cracked his knuckles and stepped aside. "Not at all."

"Dinner's getting cold," I taunted him. "Come and get me, bloodsucker."

Spade laughed—and then feinted right before leaping at me with blurring speed. He was a breath away when he looked down in surprise.

"Well, strike me pink!" he said, pulling himself up in midtackle.

"I don't know what that means, but okay."

Two steel blades were in his chest. He stared at them before ripping them out and turning to Bones in amazement.

"I don't believe it."

"That's just what I said, mate," Bones replied dryly. "She has a real talent with knives. It's a damn good thing she hadn't practiced throwing them before we met, or I might not be here."

"Indeed." Spade was still shaking his head when he looked my way next. "All right, Cat. You've made an excellent point that you're far deadlier than you look. I see I can't sway you to leave this business with Hennessey alone, and Crispin clearly has confidence in you, so I bow in defeat."

He actually did give me a bow, his long dark hair brushing the cave floor with the graceful motion of it. It was such a courtly, refined gesture that I laughed.

"What were you before they sent you to prison, a duke?"

Spade straightened and smiled. "Baron Charles DeMortimer. At your service."

The streetlight above me was broken. Farther down the alley, a cat snarled at some unknown threat. On the opposite corner, the sandy-haired vampire bounced on the balls of his feet, almost hopping in place. He was clearly excited.

I wasn't. It was two A.M. and most people were in bed, which sounded good to me. Thanks to the hyper vampire I was walking toward, however, that wasn't in the cards.

"Hey, man."

I twitched as I approached, flicking my gaze in several directions and hunching my shoulders. With my fresh bruises, scratches, and dingy clothes, I looked like the poster child for drug addiction. It wasn't hard to pull off. I'd just refrained from taking blood after Bones roughed me up for authenticity.

"You got some horse, man?" I continued, rubbing my arms as if fantasizing about a needle.

He let out a high-pitched giggle. "Not here, chickie. But I can get some. Come with me."

"You're not a cop, are you?" I backed up as if wary.

Another giggle. "Not that."

Had a sense of humor, did he? Well, wait until he heard *my* punch line. "I don't have time for you to call someone, I'm hurtin' here—"

"It's in my car," he cut me off. "Right down this way."

He almost skipped down the alley. At the other end of it was an even more derelict street.

"This way," he sang out as I followed more slowly, looking around to see if there were any more dead men walking near him. "Right here, chickie."

The vampire held open his car door and beamed at me. Obligingly, I crouched down to look inside.

The blow was expected, but it still hurt. I fell forward into the passenger seat as a normal person would, letting my limbs go limp. The vampire giggled and swung my legs inside, slamming the door. Another tee-hee-hee later and we were off.

I was slumped next to him. He didn't pay any attention to me, but kept snickering as he drove. It was annoying. I had PMS and a test this morning. Boy, had he picked the wrong girl.

Without warning, his car was rammed from behind. The sharp impact provided the perfect distraction for me to pull my silver out of my boot. He let out a loud squeal as I plunged it into his chest, missing his heart deliberately, but close enough to get his attention.

"Shut up, chirpy!" I snapped. "Pull over, or you'll get rear-ended again. And if *that* happens, you can guess where this blade will end up."

The shock on his face was almost comical. Then his eyes flared.

"Take your hands off me!"

"Don't waste that glow on me, buddy, it won't work. You've got about three more seconds to pull over, or it's nighty-night for you."

Behind us, Bones revved his engine for emphasis. Another collision would send the silver straight through his heart, and he knew it.

I didn't glance away as we came to a stop and Bones opened the driver's door.

"Well, Tony, how goes it?"

The vampire wasn't laughing anymore. "I don't know where Hennessey is!" he shouted.

"Right, mate, and I believe you. Kitten, if you'll drive? He and I are going to have a talk."

Bones maneuvered Tony into the backseat. I got behind the wheel and adjusted the mirror so I could see them.

"Where to?"

"Just around, until our mate Tony here tells us otherwise."

We left the bashed-up other car on the side of the road. It was one of Ted's that he didn't have a use for. A chop-shop owner was turning out to be a pretty handy friend.

"I don't know anything, I'm just trying to make a buck," Tony tried again.

"Liar." Pleasantly, from Bones. "You're one of Hennessey's, and don't tell me you don't know how to contact him. All vampires know how to reach their sire. Just for your miserable existence, I should kill you. Pretending to sell drugs to addicts and then green-eying them into thinking they've gotten what they paid for—you're pathetic."

"Asshole," I agreed.

"He'll kill me." It was a whimper.

"Not if he's dead, he won't, and you're as good as that now yourself. What do you think Hennessey will do if he finds out you let yourself get captured? Think he'll look kindly on how you were peddling your wares for me to find you? He'll forgive you because he's such a good bloke, right? He'll rip your bloody head off and you know it. I'm your only hope, mate."

Tony looked to me as if for help. I held up my middle finger. Well, what did he expect?

He turned back to Bones. "Promise me you won't kill me and I'll tell you everything."

"I won't kill you unless you refuse to talk," Bones answered brusquely. "And if you lie to me, I *really* won't kill you, but you'll want me to. Count on it."

There was a coldness to his tone that reminded me of when I'd been in Tony's shoes. Yeah, Bones could be pretty scary.

Tony began to talk. Fast. "Hennessey's been real secretive about his location lately, but if I need something, I'm supposed to go to Lola. I have her address—she's in Lansing. She and Hennessey are pretty tight. If she doesn't know where he is, she'll know who does."

"Give me her address."

Tony rattled off the information. Bones didn't bother to write it down, but maybe that was because he still held the dagger in Tony's chest.

"Kitten, get on the I–69 and head north. We're going to Lansing."

It was a three-hour drive. Bones got exact directions from MapQuest on his cell phone, remarking how he loved modern technology. We walked the last half mile, parking Tony's car in a nearby grocery store lot and taking him with us. Bones held the knife next to him with a malevolent smirk, commenting that if he even squeaked, he'd end him. As we approached, I saw Lola lived in an apartment complex also, albeit much snazzier than mine or Charlie's. It was five A.M., and where was I? Skulking around another apartment building. I hoped we'd be done in time for me to take that exam. I could just imagine my excuse to the professor if I missed it. *But honestly, I had to find a bad vampire!* Somehow I didn't think it would fly.

"Her car's not here," Tony whispered, taking Bones's threat seriously and keeping his voice down.

"You can tell from one glance, aye?" With heavy skepticism.

"When you see it, you'll understand," Tony replied.

Bones put a finger to his lips as we got within a hundred feet of the place, indicating with hand signals that Tony and I were to stay put while he checked the building. I resisted the urge to give him the same fingered version of my opinion I'd relayed to Tony earlier, but consoled myself with the knowledge that watching the perimeter was important. And if I heard any subsequent brawling, I was close enough to jump in on it.

Bones slinked around the far side of the building and then disappeared. Minutes ticked by, stretching into an hour. Bones still hadn't come back, but I didn't hear any sounds of fighting, so I assumed he was perched somewhere also. The sun would be up soon, and my crouched position, holding Tony at knife point, was getting uncomfortable. A kink started in my back, and irritably I realized I'd never make that exam.

I was about to find a softer part on the ground to sit on when I noticed the car pulling up. Well, score one for Tony. He was right. You *would* notice that one, even at a glace.

It was a screaming red Ferrari, and the woman who'd just parked it wasn't human. I crouched lower. The shrubs provided adequate cover, and from the small hill we were on, I had a clear view of her. She had short black hair, and from her features, she was Asian. Her car, outfit, and even her purse were all high-end, big-ticket items. Everything about her shouted money.

She had gotten about a dozen feet from the entrance to

her building when Bones stepped into view. Apparently he'd been waiting out of sight inside the doors. She tried to run, but he pounced, cutting her flight to freedom short.

"Not so fast, Lola."

The woman straightened and her chin came up. "How dare you touch me!"

"Dare?" Bones let out a laugh. It wasn't his charming one. "There's a fine word. It implies courage. Are you brave, Lola? We'll soon find out."

He drew out the last sentence with meaning. She looked around once before glaring at him.

"You're making a big mistake."

"Wouldn't be my first." He yanked her next to him. "Right, then, sweetness. You know what I want."

"Hennessey and the others are going to kill you, it's only a matter of time," she spat.

Bones grasped her jaw and brought her face closer.

"Now, I don't like abusing women, but I think you've earned the right to be an exception. It isn't very private here, so I'm operating under a bit of a time crunch. You're going to tell me who else is involved with Hennessey, and where to find them all right now, or I promise you you'll endure every torment and humiliation you've helped to inflict on others. Fancy that? I've met some depraved, beastly blokes in my travels who would just love to give you a taste of your own poison. Tell you what—I'll even sell you to them. Turnabout's fair game, isn't it? I'd say that was fair all the way 'round."

Lola's eyes widened. I could see that even from my vantage point. "I don't know where Hennessey is, he hasn't told me!"

Bones started dragging her back toward the parking lot. "You've just made Christmas come early for some happy deviants," he stated crisply.

"Wait!" It was a plea. "I know where Switch is!"

He stopped, giving her a rough shake. "Who's Switch?"

"Hennessey's enforcer," Lola said with a curl to her mouth. "You know how he hates to get his hands dirty. Switch handles the messy things, like silencing witnesses and hiding the bodies. He's also recruiting for more help, since we don't have Stephanie, Charlie, and Dean anymore. With Hennessey's new protection, we don't even have to worry about any pesky human interference."

Something on the building's roof caught my eye just as Bones asked, "What's Switch's real name, and who's Hennessey's new protection?"

Two forms dropped from the ten-story roof. Bones and Lola were directly below them. I jumped out from the bushes.

"Heads up!"

Two things happened at once. Lola pulled a blade from her purse as Bones looked up, and I, out of a mindless reaction, let fly the three silver knives in my hand.

Tony chose that moment to pounce. I'd let go of him to make that toss, and he came at me with fangs bared, knocking me to the ground. I held off his snapping jaws and twisted, ramming my knees into his chest to throw him back, and then plunged my other blade into his heart. He made an odd noise, almost like a pained giggle, and fell over on his side.

I leapt up in time to see Bones kneeling over Lola. She was on the cement, and silver protruded from her chest in a tight circle of three. Behind them were two bodies with two unattached heads. So much for the aerial attackers.

Bones rose from his kneeling position and swung his gaze to me.

"Lucifer's bouncing balls, Kitten, not *again*!"

Uh-oh. I squirmed, instinctively also trying to block Tony's body from his view. As if that made him any less dead.

"She was going to stab you," I said in my defense. "Look in her hand!"

He was looking at the ground near my feet instead. "Him, too?"

I nodded, sheepish. "He jumped me."

Bones just stared. "You're not a woman," he said finally. "You're the Grim Reaper with red hair!"

"That's not fair—" I protested, but a shrill scream cut me off.

A woman dressed in a business suit dropped her purse and ran shrieking back into the building. Guess a bunch of dead bodies in the parking lot had spooked her. Not the usual thing you'd expect to find while you were leaving to go to work.

Bones sighed and yanked the blades out of Lola. "Come on, Kitten, let's go. Before you murder someone else."

"I don't find that funny—"

"At least I got some information out of Lola first," he went on conversationally, tugging me back toward the car. "Hennessey's enforcer, Switch. We'll start by trying to find out who he is."

"She was going to *kill* you—"

"Did it ever occur to you to aim for something other than the heart?" We were walking at a good clip. More people came out of the building behind us. I could tell from the additional screams.

We had reached the car, and he suddenly gave me a quick, sound kiss.

"I love that you did it to protect me, but next time, try aiming to *wound*, hmm? You know, maybe throw the knives at someone's head instead? Then they're incapacitated momentarily, but not reduced to a pile of rotting remains. Just food for thought."

SEVENTEEN

EVEN WITH BONES'S SPEEDING, I WOULDN'T have time to shower before I went to class. I'd be lucky to make it if I only dashed in my apartment and changed clothes.

"I have to drop this off at Ted's," he was saying as I got out of the car. "Should be back in a few hours."

"I'll be asleep," I muttered. "Do we have to—"

"Hi, Cathy!"

Timmie opened his door with a wide smile. He must have seen me through his window.

Bones gave Timmie a look that froze the smile on the younger man's face.

"I'm sorry, I didn't know you had company," Timmie apologized, almost tripping to hurry back into his apartment.

I shot Bones an equally hostile glare for rattling my already skittish neighbor. "It's okay," I said, smiling at Timmie. "He's not really 'company' anyway."

"Oh." Timmie gave Bones a shy peek. "Are you Cathy's brother?"

"Whatever would give you the idea that I'm her damn brother?" Bones snapped.

Timmie backed up so fast, he hit the back of his head against his doorframe. "Sorry!" he gasped, and banged into the door again before managing to scramble back inside.

I marched over to Bones and stuck my finger in his chest. He regarded me with what I would have called sullenness—if he hadn't been over two hundred.

"You have a choice," I said, biting off each word. "Either you make a very *sincere* apology to Timmie now, or you leave and slither back to your cave like the festering ball sack you just acted like. I don't know what's gotten into you, but he's a nice guy, and you probably just made him pee his pants. Your decision, Bones. One or the other."

A dark brow arched at me. I tapped my foot. "One . . . two . . ."

He muttered something foul and then climbed the stairs, rapping twice on Timmie's door.

"Right, then, mate, terribly sorry for my unspeakable rudeness, and I do beg your pardon," he said with admirable humbleness when Timmie cracked it open. Only I could pick up the slight edge to his voice as he went on. "I can only say that it was caused by my natural affront to the notion of her as my sister. Since I'll be shagging her tonight, you can imagine how I'd be distressed at the thought of rogering my sibling."

"You schmuck!" I burst as Timmie's jaw dropped. "The only thing you'll be shagging tonight is yourself!"

"You wanted sincerity," he countered. "Well, luv, I was sincere."

"You can get right back in the car and I'll see you later, if you're not being such an ass!"

Timmie's head swiveled back and forth between the two of us, his jaw still swinging open. Bones gave him a smile that was more just a baring of teeth.

"Nice to meet you, mate, and here's some advice: Don't even think about it. You try anything with her and I'll neuter you with my bare hands."

"*Leave!*" I stamped my foot for emphasis.

He swept past me and then swiveled, kissing me hard on the mouth before jumping back to avoid my right hook.

"I'll see you later, Kitten."

Timmie waited until Bones had driven out of sight before he dared to speak.

"That's your boyfriend?"

I let out a grunt that I suppose was an affirmative.

"He really doesn't like me," he said, almost a whisper.

I gave one last look in the direction Bones disappeared to before shaking my head at his bewildering behavior.

"No, Timmie. I guess he doesn't."

I made it to class just as the professor was handing out the tests. My dirty, bruised, disheveled appearance caused a few looks and nudges that I pretended not to notice. Then, I was so tired, I didn't even know what I scribbled down for answers. The rest of the classes were even worse. I nodded off in physics and had to be poked awake by the person next to me. When I got back to my apartment, I discovered my period had made its appearance.

It was official. My day sucked.

I used my last remaining energy to shower before flopping into bed. Five minutes later, there was a knock on my door.

"You'd better run," I muttered, eyes closed.

The knock became louder. "Catherine!"

Oh shit. It was my mother. *What's up, God? Wanted to see how much I could take?*

"Coming!"

I answered the door, bleary-eyed, in my pajamas. My mother brushed past me with a disapproving frown.

"You're not dressed. The movie's in less than an hour."

Double shit! Today was Monday and I'd promised her we'd see a movie together. With everything going on, I'd completely forgotten.

"Oh, Mom, I'm sorry. It was a really late night and I'm just now getting to bed—"

"Did you get one of those monsters?" she cut in, her frown magically erased.

"Is that all you care about?"

The sharp question surprised both of us. Instantly, guilt swarmed over me at the hurt look on her face.

"I'm sorry," I said again. Jeez, I sounded like Timmie. "Um, in fact I did get two bad vampires last night."

That was partly true. I'd just left a few details out she didn't need to know about.

"Bad?" she asked with a gleam. "What do you mean by *bad*? They're all bad!"

She can't help it, I told myself, fighting guilt of another kind now. *The only vampire she ever met raped her.*

"Nothing. I'm just really tired. Can we do the movie another night? Please?"

She went into my kitchen, all four square feet of it, and opened my refrigerator. What she saw made her face draw even further together.

"It's empty. You don't have any food. Why don't you have any food?"

I shrugged. "I haven't been to the store yet. I forgot you were coming over."

I'd eaten the last of the ramen noodles for lunch yesterday, and what I couldn't tell her was that Bones usually took me out to eat. It was one of the few normal things we did together, albeit picking low-key places to avoid being spotted.

"You look very pale."

Again, she said it as if it were an indictment. I yawned, hoping she'd take the hint.

"Nothing new there."

"Catherine, you're paler, there's no food in here . . . have you started drinking blood?"

My mouth was still open from the yawn, and at that comment, it stayed that way.

"You're serious?" I managed.

She backed away a step. Actually backed away. "Have you?"

"*No!*"

I stomped toward her, hurt and mad to see her cringe. "Here." I grabbed her hand and pressed it to my throat. "Feel that? It's a *pulse*. I don't drink blood, I'm not turning into a vampire, and my fridge is empty because I haven't been to the store! For God's sake, Mom!"

Timmie picked that moment to poke his head into my apartment. "Your door was open . . ."

He stopped, startled at the thunderous expression on my face. My mother dropped her hand from my neck and straightened her shoulders.

"Who's *he*, Catherine?"

Timmie quailed at her tone. Poor guy didn't know it was her normal one. "Be nice!" I hissed. First Bones had scared him, now my mother would probably give him a heart attack.

"Is this your boyfriend?" she asked next in a stage whisper he could clearly hear.

An immediate denial sprang to my lips, and then something happened in me. Something crafty, calculating, and opportunistic. I looked at Timmie and saw exactly what my mother saw. A living, breathing young man. One who was a hundred percent *not* dead.

In my defense, I was probably crazed from lack of sleep, my period, and being accused of having a liquid diet.

"Yes!" It came out of me with reckless abandon. "Mom, meet my boyfriend, Timmie!"

I ran to him, hiding his dumbfounded expression from her line of sight, and gave him an enthusiastic kiss on the cheek.

"Please go with it," I begged in his ear, hugging him while I said it.

"Ouch!" he squeaked.

Oops. Squeezed too hard. I let him go with a wide smile. "Isn't he just adorable?"

She came toward us, looking him up and down. Timmie gawked at her before holding out a trembling hand.

"H-hello, Mrs. . . . ?"

"Ms.," she corrected at once.

He blanched at her emphaticalness, having no idea of the many reasons why that was a touchy subject. To give him credit, however, he didn't run out the door.

"Ms.," he tried again. "Nice to meet you, Ms. . . . ?"

"You've slept with him and he doesn't even know your last name?" my mother demanded, scowling.

I sent a glance heavenward before pinching Timmie when he started to back away.

"Don't mind her, *honey*, sometimes she forgets her manners. Mom, do you want Timmie to call you Justina? Or Ms. Crawfield?"

She was still giving me that how-could-you glare, but her frostiness lessened. "Justina's fine. It's nice to finally meet you, Timmie. Catherine's told me how you helped her kill those demons. I'm glad to know there's someone else out there ridding the world of them."

Timmie looked like he was about to faint. "Let's get some coffee," I said, practically shoving him before he started babbling out a denial. "You stay here, Mom. His place is next door, we'll be right back!"

As soon as we were in Timmie's apartment, I snatched

him close and lowered my voice. "My poor mother! She has her good days and her bad ones. The doctor's supposed to adjust her medication, but you never can tell when one of these spells will hit. Don't pay attention to that killing and demon talk. She's real Pentecostal. Believes in slaying of the spirit and so on. Just nod your head and try not to say much."

"But—but . . ." Timmie's eyes couldn't get any wider. "Why did you tell her *I'm* your boyfriend? Why doesn't she know about your real one?"

That was a good question. I cast around for an answer. Any answer.

"He's English!" I settled on desperately. "And Mom . . . Mom hates foreigners!"

She stayed an hour. By the time she left, I was a nervous wreck, and so was Timmie. He'd drunk so much coffee, he practically had the shakes even though he was sitting down. I'd attempted to steer the conversation to college, the orchard, my grandparents, or anything else that didn't contain the word *vampire*. Every chance I got, I made pitying expressions behind her back, or twirled my finger near my temple in the universal gesture for insanity.

Timmie tried to be supportive during my mother's "spell." "That's right, Justina!" he said more than once. "We're going to knock those demons out and slay them with the power of Jesus. Hallelujah, can I get an amen?"

In fact, he affected such an overly zealous attitude that as I walked her to the door, she drew me aside and muttered that he was sweet—but possibly a fanatic.

When she was finally gone, I leaned against the door and closed my eyes in relief.

"Thank God," I grumbled.

"Sure," Timmie agreed. "Amen!"

"You can stop that," I said, giving him a tired smile. "I owe you one, Timmie. Thanks."

I had just put my arms around him in a hug of gratitude when the door opened behind me without a knock.

"Am I interrupting something?" a coolly pissed, accented voice asked.

This time, my glance heavenward was in silent challenge. *Is that how it is? Fine, then, bring it! Let's see what You've got!*

Timmie jumped like he'd been stabbed. "Ungh!"

I didn't know what that meant, but the sight of him leaping away with a hand shielding his groin had me turning around in irritation.

"Dammit, tell him you're not going to neuter him!"

Bones folded his arms and regarded Timmie without pity. "Why?"

I gave him an evil look. "Because if you don't, I'm going to get really, *really* celibate."

My glare told him I meant it. He made an acquiescing motion that nevertheless sent Timmie bolting in the opposite direction.

"Don't fret, mate. You can leave with your stones intact, but remember, pretending to be her boyfriend was just that. Don't let the fantasy go to your head."

"You heard that?" Now I waved a frantic, mental white flag at the sky. *Okay, You win!*

His mouth twisted. "Death to all demons, can I get an amen?"

Great. "Look, I'm sorry, but I went a little nuts when she accused me of—of drinking!"

"You do drink," he countered, not getting it.

"No!" I tapped my neck. "I mean of *drinking*."

Timmie looked thoroughly confused, but understanding dawned on Bones's face.

"Bloody hell," he said finally.

I nodded. "In a nutshell."

Bones turned back to Timmie. "Private time, lad. Say goodbye."

It wasn't the nicest way he could have worded it, but from the set of his shoulders, it could have been worse.

"Timmie, thanks so much again, I'll see you in the morning," I said with another smile.

He looked glad to be on his way and made a beeline for the exit. Just as he was out the door, however, he stuck his head back in.

"I don't mind foreigners. God save the queen!" he squeaked, and ran.

Bones arched a brow. I sighed.

"Didn't hear that part? Never mind. Don't ask."

EIGHTEEN

TWO WEEKS WENT BY, BUT WE DIDN'T FIND anything more about Switch. What was worse, even the few police reports that had been filed on the missing girls suddenly disappeared from record. Hennessey was covering his tracks faster than we could follow them.

"This makes no sense," Bones fumed. "Hennessey's been snatching up girls for the better part of six decades, and he's never been this careful before. When things got messy, he'd leave. Pick another area to spin his web. I can't fathom why he's taking the time to mesmerize their families, why he's making the additional effort to have the police reports disappear, or what he's up to!"

We were back at the cave, so we could talk without having to worry about one of my neighbors overhearing. The walls were thin at my apartment. I didn't want to dwell on all the nonconversations Timmie must have already listened to when Bones spent the night.

"Maybe he's tired of running," I offered. "He's comfy,

wants to stay awhile, and knows if the headlines start blaring about a serial killer, the police will have to get serious. Then he'd have to lay low or get out. What if that's his motivation?"

Bones threw me a look while bent over his laptop. "I've considered that, but there has to be more. Lola said he had new protection, remember? That's the wild card. Whoever they are, he's being a damned sight more discreet for them, and it begs the question why. They're either vampires or humans of prominence, is what I reckon. People with reputations to protect."

I didn't know much about the vampire world, so I wasn't going to be any help there. I did know a thing or two about the breathing community, however, so I felt my pulse entitled me to speculate.

"Corrupt cops? Maybe a police chief? Some of those reports could have been accidentally lost, but not all of them. Say you're the chief of police, or you're running for sheriff, whatever, and you want to get some easy cash while still making the public believe you're competent. A bunch of disappearances would look bad. So you try to get your business partner to clean up his act, and maybe you tip him off as to where he can find some vulnerable girls. God, if it was a sheriff, he could invite Hennessey to pick his favorites out of a lineup at the local stockade! Then he could make the records disappear as well. What if all such a person asked for in return was that Hennessey control public outcry? It's not such a big price to pay, is it?"

He tapped his chin thoughtfully, considering that. Then his cell phone rang.

"Hallo. . . . Yes, Charles, I can hear you. . . . Where? . . . When? . . . *Who?* . . . All right, I'll see you shortly."

He hung up, staring at me.

"What?" I asked, impatient.

"Seems there's been a development. He's with one of Hennessey's people now who wants to talk to me about switching sides."

"I'm going with you," I said instantly.

Bones made a regretful noise. "I knew you'd say that."

Spade opened the door to the hotel room, giving me a flick of his gaze.

"I'm surprised you brought her with you, Crispin."

I didn't say 'Fuck off,' but it was close.

"Better to have her come and know what transpired than for her to stay back and wonder about it," Bones replied. "Let us enter, Charles, so we can get started."

This two-name thing is annoying, I was thinking as Spade stepped aside. *Can't vampires just pick one?*

A woman was in the center of the room. I might have noticed how plush the interior was, and that it was as big as my grandparents' whole upstairs, or any other number of inconsequential details, except for one thing.

She was without a doubt the most gorgeous female I'd ever seen. In person *or* on television. She looked Latino, with curly black hair down to her hips, positively perfect features set on a body that didn't seem real, and crimson-colored lips. I just stared at her for a minute. Only in cartoons did women have such minuscule waists, big breasts, round bubble butts, and legs like that. It wasn't hard to notice her figure, either. Her dress could barely be called one, and it was so tight, it was a good thing she didn't need to breathe.

"Francesca," Bones said, going to her and giving her a kiss on the cheek. "I'm glad you've come."

And that was all I needed to see to decide right then and there that I hated her *guts*.

"Bones . . ."

She drew his name out like it was candy, and when she

kissed his cheek, leaving a bright red lipstick imprint, her eyes met mine in open challenge.

Spade's hand on my shoulder shook me from my state of murderous contemplation. I'd just been fantasizing about whipping two of the knives out of my jacket and flinging them into her double-Ds.

"Francesca, this is Cat," Bones said next, gesturing to me. "She's with me, so you need not hesitate about speaking freely with her present."

I advanced with something stretching my face that may or may not have been a smile. "Hi. We're sleeping together."

I heard it come out of my mouth in a detached sort of way, only mildly noticing Spade mutter something about this not being a wise idea and that both of Bones's eyebrows shot into his hairline.

Francesca shared neither of their reactions. Full, pouty lips curled.

"But of course, *niña*. Who could resist him?"

Spoken while her fingers trailed down the side of his shirt, and I almost lost it right there.

"Kitten." Bones caught my hand that shot out and tucked it casually in his arm, as if I hadn't been about to knock her on her well-shaped ass. "Let's sit, shall we?"

I didn't know what was wrong with me. Some small, rational part was screaming that this was a person who could help bring down Hennessey and to get a grip on myself. The rest of me was in full, blind hostility mode and not comprehending what rational behavior meant.

Bones led me toward a nearby couch, not letting go of my hand. Out of the corner of my eye I saw Francesca taking in the view of him leaving, licking those plump red lips.

My free hand swung in an arc to land on the ass she was admiring. With a glare, I gave it a big squeeze, using the last of my control not to shriek, *You like that? Look who's got it!*

Bones stopped, glancing down meaningfully. I snatched my hand back almost in confusion, giving myself a mental shake to try and snap out of the insanity.

"Sorry," I muttered.

"Quite all right," he said with a smile that somehow made me feel less of a schmuck than I'd acted like. "Just a bit more difficult to walk."

I laughed at the picture of him trying to go any distance with my throwing hand clutched to his chest and my other one pried to his ass. Yeah, that would be dicey.

"You can let go now," I whispered, feeling more in control and determined to be adult about things. Okay, so chances were, at one time he and our little would-be turncoat had had a fling. Could have been a century ago. Before my *grandparents* were even born. I could handle it. If I were a man, I'd want to have sex with her, too. See? Very adult.

Bones sat next to me on the couch, Spade took the empty space by him (raising my opinion of him), and that left Francesca to slink into the chair opposite us. My feeling of superiority was short-lived, however, when she settled herself down and then crossed her legs.

I didn't need a mirror to know my whole face had just turned red. With a hemline up to her thighs, that gesture didn't leave anything to the imagination. Bones curled his fingers around mine and squeezed. His hand was still warmed from our contact moments ago. That's how fast he had to grab me again to keep me sitting where I was instead of yanking off my jacket to make her a pair of panties.

"We all know why we're here," he said in an unruffled voice, as if Francesca hadn't just flashed him a shaved beaver pelt. "It's no secret that I'm after Hennessey and you're one of his, Francesca. I know you and he aren't close, but it is still the highest offense to betray your sire. Make no mistake, I'm out to kill him, and any information you give me will be used for that purpose."

You go, boy! I silently applauded him. *Cut right to the point and show her a little snatch doesn't distract you! You are SO getting lucky tonight.*

Francesca's mouth curled. "Why else would I be here, if I didn't want you to kill him? If you were to do less, I wouldn't risk it. You know I've hated him for the past ninety-three years. Ever since he took me from my convent and turned me."

"You were a nun?" I asked in disbelief, actually peeping back up her dress to make sure I hadn't misunderstood. "You're kidding."

"Bones, what is her purpose here? Why must she stay?" Francesca demanded, ignoring me.

His eyes glinted emerald at her. "She's here because I want her to be, and it's not up for discussion."

That statement just upgraded him from sex to sex with a blow job first. Not that I minded the extra activity, to be honest. I'd found out I enjoyed it. Guess that made for two tramps in this room.

"I want Hennessey dead," Francesca summarized after losing a staring contest with Bones. "He has been my Master for too long."

This bewildered me. "What does she mean, her Master?" I asked Bones. Was Francesca a slave? Just when I thought Hennessey couldn't sink any lower in my opinion.

"Vampires operate under a form of pyramid scheme," Bones explained. "Each line is ranked by the strength of its head, or the Master, and every person the Master sires is under the Master's rule. Feudalism would be another example of it. There you had the lord of the manor, and they were responsible for the welfare of all those on their lands, but in return, their people owed them loyalty and part of their income. Such is the way with vampires, with a few more variations."

This was news to me, and it sounded barbaric. "*So.* In

other words, vampire society is like Amway and a cult rolled into one."

Francesca muttered something in Spanish that didn't sound complimentary.

"Speak English, and without the sarcasm," Bones said to her curtly.

Big dark eyes blinked in anger. "If I didn't know you to be the man you are, I'd leave right now."

"But you do know me," Bones replied smoothly. "And if I choose to detail our world to the woman I'm with, that shouldn't suggest I take your position less seriously. You really should show Cat a bit more respect. It was because of her your fondest wish was nearly granted and Hennessey was almost dust."

At that, Francesca laughed. "You're the vomiter!"

I didn't know if that was technically a word, but I got her drift. What a way to be referred to.

"That's me."

She was still smiling. It made her even more radiant. With that faint dusky tone to her flesh, she looked like she was made of colored diamonds. "Well, *niña*, that does afford you some latitude. Hennessey didn't say very much about you. He was too incensed, and so humiliated. It was truly a pleasure to witness."

"Does he know how much you hate him?" I asked with skepticism. "Because if he does, how are you going to get close enough to help us?"

She leaned forward. It opened up her cleavage even more. I tried not to look, but my God! They were so *bouncy*.

"Hennessey knows very well that I hate him, but I've managed to hide things from him before." She paused to give Bones a knowing smile, and I almost lost it again. "He enjoys keeping me, knowing how much I despise being his. Vampires can only leave their sire's domination if they win in a duel against them, get ransomed by another Master, or are released as a gesture of goodwill. Hennessey is too strong for me to beat, there is no goodwill in him, and he will never let another vampire ransom me. Yet not for a moment does he believe I'll betray him. He thinks I fear too much what he would do to me if I were caught."

The purr of her voice made it all the more chilling. She knew firsthand what he was capable of, and despite that, she hated him enough to risk it anyway. Maybe I shouldn't be so quick to disparage her. You had to admire that kind of determination. Whether or not it came with underpants.

"Then you and I have something in common," I said, before glancing at Bones and letting out a bark of ironic laughter. "Well, something *else*. I want Hennessey dead, too. That's all we really need to know about each other, isn't it?"

She gave me a rake of her cognac eyes and then her shoulder lifted in a shrug. "*Sí.* I suppose it is."

Bones and Spade exchanged a glance. I thought I saw the spiky-haired vampire smile.

"Aside from the obvious, Francesca, what do you want in return for supplying information?" Bones asked, getting back to the subject.

"You to take me," she replied at once.

"Not gonna happen!" I spat, squeezing him possessively.

Three sets of widened eyes fixed on me. That's when I realized that what I had a firm grip on was no longer his hand.

Spade started to laugh even as I turned beet red again, yanking my hand back and fighting the urge to sit on it for my own good. Dear *God*! What had gotten *into* me?

Bones's lips twitched, but he didn't join in the growing chuckles that had Spade dabbing at his eyes.

"That's not what she means, luv," he said in a carefully

neutral tone. "Francesca means that with the head of her line deceased, she wants to be under another vampire's protection. I could claim her as one of mine, thereby 'taking' her. Although I'm still under Ian's yoke, he hasn't exercised any of his authority over me in a very long time, which is why I haven't bothered to challenge him to be on my own. I've had more freedom this way, and because of our understanding, I wouldn't need his consent to take Francesca on. Though under normal circumstances, getting his consent would be the proper way."

Thankfully, this was complicated enough to distract me from groping him further. "Why wouldn't you want to be on your own?" I wondered out loud to her.

"Masterless vampires are open game, *niña*. There's no accountability for any cruelty done to them. Like with your nations. If you are a man or a woman with no country, who do you appeal to when you're in need? Who defends you?"

"That's a damn brutal system you people operate under," I said, glad to have a heartbeat.

"Don't be so naïve," she said sharply. "It's a far kinder structure than the one you're in. How many humans starve to death *each day* because your nations refuse to care for their own? Even still, how many Americans die from illnesses when treatment is readily available but withheld if they can't afford it? Vampires would *never* allow any of their people to go about hungry or in poverty. Even Hennessey, who is a beast, would consider it a personal insult to have anyone belonging to him in such a condition. Consider that. The worst of our kind treats his people better than your countries treat their citizens."

"Francesca . . ." Spade had stopped laughing.

She waved at him. "I'm finished."

I wasn't.

"If you bloodsuckers are such paragons of virtue, then why haven't any of you stood up to stop Hennessey from plowing through *my* kind? I mean, Bones tells me about how five percent of everyone walking isn't alive, so there's a lot of you! Or is it that the kidnapping, rape, murder, and consumption of humans doesn't rank as important?"

Bones smoothed his hand on my arm. "Kitten, perhaps—"

Francesca bolted out of her chair. "Wake *up*! What Hennessey's doing is *nothing* compared to what humans do! Each year, over *fifty thousand* teenage Colombians are sold into slavery across Europe and Asia, and that isn't by vampires! In the Congo, over a hundred thousand women have been brutalized—by the rebels, and the soldiers in their own military! Pakistan still has areas where 'honor' rapes and killings of women are ordered by the courts, and yet your country and the rest of the world do nothing about it! Vampires may tend to their own business first, but if we were to truly start policing this planet, we'd get rid of the humans, who are the greatest evildoers—"

"That's enough!"

Bones was in front of her in a blink. He didn't touch her, but his voice was like a whip.

"I seem to remember a very young girl who had similar views 'round ninety years ago. Now, to answer your condition, yes, I'll take you as one of mine after I kill Hennessey. Furthermore, should any information you pass to me prove instrumental, I'll pay you accordingly when it's over. You have my word on both counts. Is that sufficient for you?"

Francesca's eyes were streetlight green, but slowly they darkened back into the brown they had been when I first saw her. She sat down, chewed on her lip for a moment, and then nodded.

"We have an agreement."

Things wrapped up pretty quickly after that. Francesca didn't know Switch's identity or who Hennessey's new connections were, so Bones gave her ways to contact him while leaving out his actual location. Spade mentioned that he was going out of town to try finding different leads on Hennessey and he would call Bones later. That was that. Francesca and I didn't exchange goodbyes. She stayed in the hotel room. Bones and I left, but we didn't take the elevator this time, even though we were twenty floors up. He indicated the stairs and I started climbing down. At least that gave me something to do aside from simmer.

"You never told me about vampire society before," I remarked calmly. One floor finished, nineteen more to go.

Bones gave me an inscrutable look. He didn't have my hand any longer. My hands were stuffed in my jacket.

"You never asked."

My first instinct was to get angry and call that a cop-out. I opened my mouth to say something scathing, thought things through for once, and shut it.

"I guess I didn't."

If he were shallow like me, he'd say all I'd ever asked or shown an interest in about vampires was how to kill them. That anything to do with culture, beliefs, values, or traditions hadn't concerned me, unless I could use it to hunt more efficiently. It was a very scary moment to realize that I thought with the mind of a killer. I was only twenty-two. When had I gotten to be so cold?

"How did it happen?" I asked very softly. "How did vampires begin?"

Such an elementary question. I'd never bothered to ponder it before.

Bones almost smiled. "You want the evolutionary or the creationist version?"

I thought for a second. "Creationist. I'm a believer."

Our feet made little staccato noises as we kept heading downstairs, and he kept his voice low. The stairwell made for echoes, and though it was late at night, there was no need to alarm someone accidentally overhearing.

"We began with two brothers who had different lives and functions, and one was jealous of the other. So jealous, in fact, that it led to the world's first murder. Cain killed Abel, and God drove him out, but not before putting a mark upon him to make him distinguishable from everyone else."

"Genesis, Chapter Four," I breathed. "Mom was big on me learning the Bible."

"This next part wasn't in any Bible you read," he went on, casting me those sideways glances. "The 'mark' was his transformation into becoming undead. For his punishment in spilling blood, he was forced to drink it for the rest of his days. Cain later regretted killing his brother and he created his own people, his own society that existed on the fringe of the one he'd been expelled from. The children he 'reproduced' were vampires, and they made others of their kind, and so on. Of course, if you ask a ghoul, they have a different version. They say Cain was turned into a ghoul, not a vampire. Been a cause of bickering ever since about who was first, but Cain isn't around to settle that."

"What happened to him?"

"He's the undead version of the Man Upstairs. Watching over his children in the shadows. Who knows if he really is? Or if God finally considered his debt paid and took him back?"

I mulled this over. Bones picked up his pace.

"Makes you think your mum is right, doesn't it?" he asked jadedly. "That we're all murderers? We're the offspring of the world's first, unless you side with the notion that vampires and ghouls are a random evolutionary mutation."

I kept up with him. Twelfth floor . . . eleventh . . . tenth . . .

"The first of my kind has gotten a lot of shit for what she

did also," I finally said with a shrug. "That whole apple business makes it harder for me to criticize."

He laughed—and then whirled me up in his arms so fast, my feet were still flexing for another step. His mouth crushed down on mine, taking my breath away, and the same mindless compulsion that had led me to act so bizarrely upstairs manifested in another form. My arms went around his neck, my legs wrapped around his waist, and I kissed him as if by willpower alone I could erase the memory of every woman before me.

I heard a rip. Felt the wall at my back, and then the next moment, he was inside me.

I clung to him, nails digging into his back with mounting need, mouth locked onto his throat to stifle my cries. He moaned into my skin, free hand tangled in my hair as he moved faster, deeper. There was no gentleness to him, but I wanted none, exulting in the unbridled passion between us.

Everything inside me suddenly clenched, and then relinquished in a rush of ecstasy that streamed down to my toes. Bones cried out as well, and a few shattering minutes later relaxed against me.

There was a creak, a gasp, and him snapping, "Walk away, you've seen nothing!" before a door slammed. That's when the haze lifted and a tidal wave of embarrassment swept over me.

"My God, what is the *matter* with me?"

I pushed at him, and he set me on my feet with a lingering kiss.

"Not a bloody thing, if you ask me."

My jeans were torn from zipper to thigh. Whoever had tried to enter the stairwell was long gone, but I was still cringing with shame at the glimpse that person had caught. *Who's the slut now, huh? Hypocrite!*

"First I publicly grope you, almost stab our potential

Judas, then, for the grand finale, I molest you in a stairwell! And I thought *you* behaved rudely with Timmie! You should demand an apology!"

Bones chuckled, taking his jacket off and placing it around me. It covered the tear in my pants, at least. His own clothing hadn't been damaged. After all, the man never wore underwear himself, so he'd only needed to pull down a zipper.

"You didn't molest me, and I will never ask you to apologize for tonight. Any of it. I'm relieved, to be frank."

"Relieved?" I glanced at the front of him. "I guess that's one way to put it. . . ."

"Not that." Another amused snort. "Though it applies there as well. Do you know what you acted like tonight? Like a vampire. We're territorial, every last one of us, which is why I had such a harsh reaction when I saw Timmie gaze at you with those smitten-calf eyes. Your similar, decidedly hostile response with Francesca showed me . . . that you consider me to be yours. I have wondered what you felt for me, Kitten. Hoped you cared beyond mere rapport or physical attraction, and so while I assure you that you have nothing to fear from her, I was selfishly pleased to see how deep your emotions ran."

I stared at him in silence. There were so many things I wanted to say. Like, *How could you think what I feel for you is only physical?* or, *Don't you know you're my best friend?* and finally, *Bones, I love——*

"I think we should get out of here," was what I settled on, cowardly. "Before you have to green-eye anyone else out of reporting us to the police."

He smiled, and it could have been my guilt, but I thought it was a trifle sad. "It's all right, Kitten. I'm not demanding anything. You don't have to fret."

I took his hand, not caring about the difference in temperature and scared as hell that I didn't care about it anymore.

"Are you really mine?" I couldn't stop from asking.

Those cool fingers squeezed gently. "Of course I am."

I squeezed back, but with more strength.

"I'm glad."

Ⴖⲓⲛⲉⲧⲉⲉⲛ

THE CLOCK STRUCK ELEVEⴖ AⴖD CAT THE vampire huntress was on the loose, except my battle armor was a push-up bra, curled hair, and a short dress. Yeah, it was a dirty job, but I was going to do it. *Come one, come all, bloodsuckers! Bar's open!*

Hennessey was still on the lookout to restock his supplies. After ten days of spying, Francesca had confirmed that. It was the same thing we'd heard from Lola and Charlie, so no real shocker there, but what she did relay in her most recent surreptitious phone call was noteworthy. She'd overheard one of Hennessey's men refer to a mysterious human partner as "Your Honor." It could be a sarcastic title, but considering the tampered police records and Hennessey's new method of preventing disappearances from being reported, Bones thought differently. He figured it was a judge, maybe from Columbus, where most of the evidence-tampering had taken place. We were working that angle, but there was the other one as well. When you were looking to catch someone who didn't want to be caught, you needed bait. Bait placed out temptingly for the still-unknown Switch or Hennessey to try and snatch. That's where I came in. During the day I went to college, but at night I made my rounds at all of the easy-sleazy bars and clubs we could hit. Did I mention it was a dirty job?

"Catherine? My God, Catherine, is that you?"

Huh? No one called me that name except for my family, and certainly none of them were here. Yet there was something familiar about that voice.

I pivoted around in my chair, and the glass I'd been protecting from any added chemicals crashed to the floor. Six years later and still I knew him at a glance.

Danny Milton stood in front of me, openmouthed at my appearance in my tight silver dress and knee-high boots. The black leather gloves that were my standard matched my heart when I saw his gaze drop from my face to my cleavage and back again.

"Wow, Catherine, you look . . . wow!"

Either he was truly speechless at my appearance or college literary classes had not been kind. My eyes narrowed as I considered my options. One: Put a stake through *his* heart. Appealing, but morally incorrect. Two: Ignore him and hope he went away. Possible, but too kind. Three: Order another drink and throw it in his face while thanking him for the memories. Deserved, but too flashy. I wasn't looking to draw unwanted attention or get thrown out of the place. That only left Option Two. Damn, that was the least satisfying of them all.

I raked him with a withering stare and then turned my back. I hoped he'd get the message.

He didn't. "Hey, you've *got* to remember me. We met on the road and you helped me change my tire. *And* you can't forget I was the first person you ever—"

"Shut up, you idiot!"

After so long, he had the unimaginable nerve to start

blurting out loud enough for the deaf to hear that he'd been the first guy I slept with? Maybe Option One was the better plan after all.

"See, you do remember me," he went on, apparently not catching the 'idiot' part. "Gee, it's been . . . what, six years? More? I almost didn't recognize you. I *know* you didn't look like this before. Not that you weren't cute and all, but you kind of looked like a baby then. You're all grown up now."

He certainly didn't appear much different. His hair was about the same length, the same sandy brown, and his eyes were the blue of my memory. Danny was a touch softer around the midsection, or perhaps bitterness colored my vision. To me, he looked like all the rest now. Just another guy trying to take advantage. Too bad I couldn't kill him for that reason alone.

"Danny, for your own good, turn around and walk away." Bones was here somewhere, though I didn't see him, but if he was watching me and found out who this was, I knew he'd have no conflict of conscience about pulling Danny's plug.

"But why? We should catch up. After all, it's been a long time." Without invitation, he plunked down at the recently vacated seat next to me.

"There's nothing to catch up on. You came, you saw, you scored, you left. End of story."

I turned my back again, surprised at the stab of hurt that still remained. Some wounds never quite healed, even with time and knowledge.

"Oh, come on, Catherine, it wasn't all like that—"

"Well, hal*lo* there, mate. What have we here?"

Bones materialized from behind Danny, a truly vicious smile on his face. Oh shit.

"This person was just leaving," I stiffly said, praying Danny would have half a brain cell and bolt before Bones realized who he was. If he hadn't already. The look on Bones's face was pure predator.

"Not yet, Kitten, we haven't been introduced." Uh-oh, not a good idea, not a good idea. "My name is Bones, and you are . . . ?"

"Danny Milton. I'm an old friend of Catherine's."

Unsuspecting, Danny reached out to shake the hand that was offered to him. Bones grasped it and didn't let go, even when Danny attempted to tug it free.

"Hey, man, I don't want any trouble, I was just saying hello to Catherine and . . . *uunnngghhhh*."

"Don't say a word." Bones spoke in a voice so low he was barely audible. Underneath his lashes, his eyes blazed with green fire and power leaked off him. His grip tightened, and I literally heard the bones shatter in Danny's hand.

"Stop it," I breathed, standing up to touch him.

He was immobile under my fingers, only his hand kept contracting. Tears streamed down Danny's face although he stayed silent, helpless under that green gaze.

"It isn't worth it. You're not changing anything that happened."

"He hurt you, Kitten," Bones replied, pitilessly watching the tears roll from Danny's eyes. "I'll kill him for it."

"Don't." I knew he wasn't using a figure of speech. "It's over. If it wasn't for him using me, I'd have never gone for that first vampire. That means I wouldn't have met you. Things happen for a reason, don't you believe that?"

Although he didn't relax his hand, he looked over at me. I brushed his face. "Please. Let him go."

Bones released him. Danny fell to his knees and promptly threw up. Blood oozed out from his hand where his bones had broken through his skin. Looking down at him, I felt only the barest hint of sympathy. A lot had happened in the years since I'd seen him.

"Bartender, he looks like he might need a cab," Bones said tersely to the man behind the counter, who hadn't noticed a thing. "Poor bugger can't hold his drink."

He bent down as if to help Danny to his feet, and I heard him speak in quiet terrifying tones.

"You say one more blasted word and the next thing I'll be crushing is your stones. Tonight's your lucky night, mate. You'd better thank your bleedin' stars she stopped me, or you and I would be having a party you wouldn't live long enough to forget."

While Danny gulped, sobbing and clutching his hand to his chest, Bones propelled me out toward the door after throwing a fifty at the bartender, way over the tab for my drinks.

"Best be leaving, pet. We'll have to try it another night. This has attracted a bit too much attention."

"I told you to leave it alone." I followed him to the truck, speeding off as soon as we got in. "Dammit, Bones, that could have been avoided."

"I saw your face when he spoke to you. You went white as a ghost. Knew who it had to be, and I know how hurt you were by it."

His soft tone was somehow more pointed than screaming.

"But what did smashing his hand accomplish? We won't know if Hennessey or Switch comes tonight. What if one of them do, and they nab someone? Danny isn't worth a woman's life because he slept with me and then dumped me!"

"I love you. You have no idea what you're worth to me."

Again, his voice was low, but this time it vibrated with emotion. Too distracted to drive and talk at the same time, I pulled off the highway and faced him.

"Bones, I—I can't say the same, but you mean more to me than anyone else has. Ever. Isn't that worth something?"

He leaned over and took my face in his hands. The same

fingers that had just crushed and maimed delicately traced my jaw as though it were fine crystal.

"It's worth something, but I'm still holding out to hear the other. Do you realize that tonight is the first time I've heard someone call you by your real name?"

"That's not my real name anymore." Honestly I felt that way. How vampire of me.

"What's your full name? I already know it, of course, but I want to hear you say it."

"Catherine Kathleen Crawfield. But you can call me Cat." This last part was said with a smile because he had never addressed me in any way but one.

"I think I'll stay with Kitten." He smiled back, the tension easing. "It's what you reminded me of when we met. An angry, defiant, brave little kitten. And every once in a while you're cuddly like one."

"Bones, I know you didn't want to walk away before at the bar, and if I know you, you're numbering Danny's days. But I don't want his death on my conscience. Promise me you'll never do it."

He gave me a look of amazement. "You don't still have feelings for that wanker, do you?"

Apparently we still had some issues to discuss over good killing versus bad. "Oh, I have feelings for him, all right. I'd like to put him in the ground myself, believe me. Still, it would be wrong. Promise me."

"Fine. I promise I won't kill him."

He said it too easily. My eyes narrowed.

"Promise me right here and now that you will also never cripple, maim, dismember, blind, torture, bleed, or otherwise inflict any injury on Danny Milton. *Or* otherwise stand by while someone else does as you watch."

"Blimey, that's not fair!" he protested.

Guess it was good I hadn't just accepted his first agreement. "Promise!"

He made an exasperated noise. "Fine. Bloody hell. Didn't I teach you too well to cover all of your bases?"

"Yes, you did. We can't go back to the bar now. What do you want to do?"

He traced a finger across my lips.

"You decide."

A twinge of mischief shot through me. With all of our meticulous research, going through missing persons reports, autopsies, and the general grim task of trying to find a bunch of mass murderers, we hadn't had much time for lightheartedness. Putting the truck back into gear, I got onto the highway and headed south. After an hour, I pulled onto a gravel road.

Bones gave me a sideways smile. "Taking a trip down memory lane, are we?"

"So you *do* remember this place."

"Hard to forget," he snorted. "This is where you tried to kill me. You were so nervous, you kept blushing. Never had someone try to stake me who blushed so much."

I parked within view of the water and unfastened my seat belt.

"You knocked the living daylights out of me that night. Want to try it again?"

A breath of laughter escaped him. "You want me to hit you? Blimey, but you do like it rough."

"No. Let's try the other. Maybe you'll have better results. Want to shag?"

I managed to keep a straight face, but my lips twitched. A light appeared in his eyes, that beginning of green flame.

"Still wearing your stakes? Going to make me rest in pieces?" Bones took off his jacket as he spoke, clearly not alarmed in the least.

"Kiss me and find out."

He moved in that lightning-fast way of his, the one I'd

seen hundreds of times before but that still managed to surprise me with its suddenness. Bones pulled me to him, tilting my head back and covering my mouth before I blinked.

"Not much room in here," he whispered after a long minute. "Want to go outside so you can stretch out?"

"Oh no. Right here. *Love* to do it in a truck."

His former words rolled off my tongue and he laughed. His eyes glowed pure emerald and when he smiled, fangs protruded from his lips.

"Let's find out."

After another two weeks of fruitless trolling, we still hadn't found any trace of Hennessey or Switch. I'd been to every sordid club within a fifty-mile range of Columbus, but with no luck. Bones reminded me that he'd been after Hennessey for the better part of eleven years. Age had taught him patience. Youth had taught me to get frustrated at the lack of progress.

We were at my apartment, waiting for the pizza I'd ordered. It was a Sunday evening, so we weren't going out tonight. I had every intention of doing nothing but kicking back now and studying later. Even going to the grocery store had been too much for me, hence the delivery. Whatever I'd inherited from my mother, it hadn't been her inclination to cook.

A knock at the door had me glancing in bemusement at the clock. Only fifteen minutes since I'd ordered. My, that was fast.

Courteously Bones started to get up, but I grabbed my robe and stopped him.

"Stay there. You're not eating it anyway."

A grin touched his mouth. He could eat solid food, I'd seen him do it, but he didn't take much enjoyment out of it. He'd once remarked that he did it more to blend in.

I opened my front door—and then slammed it shut with a cry. "Sweet Jesus!"

Bones was up in a flash, still naked but now with a knife in his hand. The sight of that made another scream escape me even as there was an annoyed banging on the door.

"Catherine, what is the matter with you? Open this door!"

I was thrown into a state of sheer, mindless panic. "It's my mother!" I whispered fiercely, as if Bones hadn't figured that out. "Holy shit, you have to hide!"

I literally shoved him toward the bedroom, yelling, "I—I'll be right there, I'm not dressed!"

He went, but with none of my hysteria. "Kitten, you still haven't told her? Blimey, what are you waiting for?"

"The Second Coming of Christ!" I snapped. "And not a moment sooner! Here, in the closet!"

Her knocks were getting louder. "What is taking you so long?"

"I'll be right there!" I hollered. Then to Bones, who was giving me a very aggravated look, "We'll talk about this later. Just stay here and don't make a sound, I'll get rid of her as fast as I can."

Without waiting for his reply, I shut the closet door with a bang and whirled back around, kicking his clothes and shoes under the bed. God, had he left his keys on the counter? What else could be around for her to find?

"Catherine!" It sounded like a kick punctuated my name this time.

"Coming!"

I flew over to the door and opened it with a broad, false smile. "Mom, what a surprise!"

She swept past me, more than a little upset. "I drop by to say hello, and you slam the door in my face? What is wrong with you?"

I wracked my brain to think up an excuse. "Migraine!" I

said triumphantly before lowering my voice and affecting a pained expression. "Oh, Mom, I'm glad to see you, but it's a bad time."

She was staring at my apartment with a look of amazement. *Uh-oh. How to explain?*

"Look at this place." Her arms encompassed the small, drastically altered space. "Catherine, where did you get the money to pay for all of this?"

Upon first seeing my apartment, Bones had derisively said he was going to slaughter my landlord for daring to charge me money for it. He hadn't, though from his tone I didn't think he'd been entirely kidding, but what he had done was furnish it from top to bottom. "All of this" meant the couch he'd bought with a comment that he wanted something to sit on besides the floor, the TV so supposedly I could watch the news to look out for any telltale headlines, the computer for similar purposes, and the coffee table, end tables, and appliances—well. I'd given up by then.

"Credit cards," I said instantly. "They'll give 'em to anybody."

She gave me a disapproving frown. "Those things will get you in trouble."

I almost laughed out of dementia. If she only knew how I'd really gotten this stuff, she'd forget all about the dangers of high interest rates!

"Mom, it's great to see you, really, but . . ."

The way she was staring in shock at the bedroom made a chill creep up my spine. I was afraid to turn around. Had Bones ignored my directive and come out?

"Catherine . . . is that a new *bed* as well?"

I almost sagged in relief. "It was on sale."

She came forward and laid a hand on my forehead. "You don't feel hot."

"Believe me," I said with the utmost sincerity. "At any second, I could throw up."

"Well." She looked around the place once more with that little frown and then shrugged. "I'll call next time. I thought we could go out to dinner, but . . . oh, do you want me to bring you in something?"

"No!" Too emphatic. I softened my tone. "I mean, thanks, but I don't have an appetite. I'll call you tomorrow."

With far less force than I'd used with Bones, I propelled her to the door. She just looked at me and sighed.

"That headache is making you act very weird, Catherine."

I actually pressed my ear to the door after I closed it behind her to make sure she was really gone. Some paranoid part of me thought she'd only pretended and was waiting to fling it back open to catch me with my undead lover.

A noise made me turn around. Bones stood in the bedroom doorway, dressed now. I managed an uneven, fake laugh that didn't even resemble humor.

"Whew, that was close."

He stared at me. There was no anger to his expression anymore, and maybe that's what made me nervous. Anger I could handle.

"I can't stand to see you do this to yourself."

I regarded him with wariness. "Do what?"

"Continue to punish yourself for your father's sins," he replied steadily. "How long are you supposed to pay for them? How many vampires do you have to kill until you and your mum are squared? You're one of the bravest people I've ever met, yet you're scared to death of your own mum. Don't you realize? It's not me you're hiding in a closet—it's yourself."

"That's easy for you to say, your mother's dead!" I sat on the couch with a huff. "You don't have to worry if she'll hate you for who you're sleeping with, or if you'll ever *see* her again if you tell her the truth! What am I supposed to do? Risk my relationship with the only person in my life who's been there for me? She'll take one look at you, and all she'll see is fangs. She'll never forgive me, why can't you understand that?"

My voice broke over the last sentence and I buried my head in my hands. Great. Now I wasn't faking it. I *was* getting a migraine.

"You're right, my mum's dead. I'll never know what she would have thought of the man I've become. If she'd be proud . . . or despise me for the choices I've made. I will tell you this, though. If she were alive, I'd show her what I was. All of it. She wouldn't deserve any less, and quite frankly, neither would I. But this isn't about me. Look, I'm not insisting to meet your mum. All I'm saying is that sooner or later, you'll have to come to terms with yourself. You can't wish away the vampire in you, and you shouldn't keep atoning for it. You should figure out who you are and what you need, and then don't apologize for it. Not to me, to your mum, or to anyone."

He was at the door before I realized what he was doing.

"You're leaving? Are you—are you breaking up with me?"

Bones turned around. "No, Kitten. I'm just giving you a chance to think about things without me to distract you."

"But what about Hennessey?" Now I was using him as an excuse.

"Francesca still doesn't have anything concrete, and we've struck out searching for him on our own. Won't hurt to give it a small rest. If anything does come up, I'll ring you. Promise." He gave me a last, long look before opening the door. "Goodbye."

I heard it shut, but it didn't register. I sat there for twenty more minutes staring at it, and then magically, there was a knock.

I leapt up in relief. "Bones!"

It was a young man in a uniform. "Pizza delivery," he said with mechanical cheerfulness. "That'll be seventeen-fifty."

In a daze, I gave him a twenty, told him to keep the change, and then shut the door behind him and started to cry.

†wenty

†immie looked at me with the morbid fascination you'd give an unpredictable virus under a microscope.

"You're having *another* pint?"

I paused with my spoon over the chocolate ice cream, raising a challenging brow.

"Why?"

He glanced at the two empty containers near my feet. Or he could have been staring at the bottle of gin balanced next to me on the couch. Whatever.

"No reason!"

It had been four days since I'd seen or spoken to Bones. Doesn't sound that long, does it? Well, it felt like weeks. Timmie knew something was up. Out of courtesy or fear, he hadn't asked why a certain motorcycle hadn't been parked in our community driveway lately.

I went through the motions. Attended classes. Studied feverishly. Ate sugar and junk food until my insulin levels spiked dangerously. But I couldn't sleep. I couldn't even stand to lie in bed, because I kept reaching out for some-one who wasn't there. I'd picked up the phone a hundred times a day only to drop it before dialing, because I didn't know what to say.

Timmie kept me from climbing the walls. He'd come over, watch movies until all hours, talk or not talk depend-ing on my mood, and just be there. I couldn't have been more grateful, but I still felt alone. It wasn't his fault that I had to pretend, monitor my speech, and otherwise mask half of myself as usual. No, that wasn't his fault. It was mine for pushing away the one person who'd accepted me unconditionally, even with all the flaws and oddities of both my halves combined.

"It's so true, you know," he said, nodding at the TV. "They exist."

"Who?"

I hadn't really been watching, too wrapped up in my inner turmoil.

"Men in black. Secret government agents whose job is to control and police extraterrestrial or paranormal phe-nomenon. They exist."

"Um," I said disinterestedly. *So do vampires, buddy. In fact, you're sitting next to one. Sort of.*

"You know, I heard this movie was based on actual events?"

I gave a cursory glance at the TV and saw Will Smith battling it out with an alien monster. Oh, *Men in Black.*

"Could be." *Giant alien cockroaches that preyed on humans? Who was I to scream impossible?*

"You ever going to tell me why you two broke up?"

That got my attention. "We're not broken up," I denied immediately, more to myself than to him. "We're, ah, taking a break to evaluate things, and, um, reexamine our relation-ship, so . . . I stuffed him in a closet!" I burst out in shame.

Timmie's eyes goggled. "Is he still *there*?"

His expression was classic, but my sense of humor didn't rise to the occasion. "My mother stopped by unexpectedly on Sunday, and I freaked out and shoved him in the closet until she left. After that came the whole 'evaluate' thing. I think he's getting sick of my issues, and what's worse, I don't blame him."

Timmie had recovered from his earlier misassumption. "Why does your mom hate foreigners so much?"

How to explain?

"Well . . . you know how I said we had something in common because neither of us knew our fathers? Mine's a little more complicated than yours is. My father was . . . English. He date-raped my mother, so . . . she's hated Englishmen ever since. You know my boyfriend's English, and I'm, uh, I'm half English, which she's never been real happy about. If she finds out I'm dating someone English, she'll, ah, think I'm turning my back on her and becoming . . . a foreigner."

Timmie turned the sound down on the TV. His face twisted with indecision, and then he squared his shoulders.

"Cathy . . . that's the stupidest reason I've ever heard."

I sighed. "You don't understand."

"Look, your boyfriend scares me," Timmie went on earnestly. "But if he treats you well and all your mom's got against him is that he's English, then I stick to my first response that it's stupid. Your mom can't hate a whole *country* because of one person! Everyone's got something in them that somebody's going to have a problem with, but your mom should be more concerned about whether he makes you happy than where he's from."

What he said sounded so simple! So elementary, he could have ended his sentence with, *Duh*. My bad example of her prejudice had broken the situation down to its most basic elements, and suddenly I realized it *was* that simple. Either I went through the rest of my life punishing myself for my bloodline—atoning, as Bones had noted—or I didn't. Simple. So incredibly simple, I hadn't been able to wrap my mind around it before.

"Timmie," I said with absolute conviction, "you're a genius."

His baffled countenance returned. "Huh?"

I got up, kissed him full on the mouth, and then dashed to the phone.

"I'm calling him," I announced. "Got any advice for apologizing? 'Cause I'm not good at that, either."

Timmie still sat where he was, stunned. "What? Oh. Say you're sorry."

I grinned at him. "Genius," I repeated, dialing Bones's number.

He answered on the first ring. "Francesca?"

I froze, suddenly speechless. Okay, not what I'd anticipated! His voice came again a second later.

"Kitten, it's you. I'm already on my way over. Something's wrong."

"What is it?" I asked, forgetting my concern over how he'd answered the phone.

"Get dressed if you need to. I'm hanging up; I have to keep this line clear. I'll be there in five minutes."

He did hang up before I could ask him anything further. Timmie watched me expectantly.

"Well?"

I started throwing on a sweater over my T-shirt. It was cold out. The sweatpants should be fine, but Timmie had to leave so I could get my knives. "He's coming over, but we have to go right away. Something . . . something came up."

"Oh." Timmie got up, shuffled his feet for a second, and then blurted, "If it doesn't work out with him, would you consider going out with me?"

I froze in the middle of putting on my shoes. *Wow. Didn't see that one coming.*

"I know I'm not suave or have that bad-boy thing going

on like *he* does, but we get along really well and your mom already thinks I'm your boyfriend, so . . . I've kind of been preapproved," he finished gamely. "What do you say?"

That if Bones could hear you, these would be your last words.

"Timmie, any girl would be lucky to go out with you. Any girl, including me, but I'm hoping to work things out with my boyfriend, so you understand I can't answer a hypothetical like that right now."

I didn't want to hurt him, and I was frankly out of my league. Turning someone down gently wasn't my forte. Usually my form of turning someone down was shoving a stake through his heart while smirking, *Gotcha!*

The sound of motorcycle squealing thankfully cut off any further conversation. Timmie's eyes widened in alarm. He bolted from my apartment with a hasty, "Good night!" while I went into my bedroom and pulled my weapons box out from under my bed. That action right there highlighted why I could never date him. It wasn't his lack of suaveness, or the fact that I only wanted to be with the man currently striding up my steps. It was that some things could never be explained. Let alone preapproved.

I didn't have a chance to tell Bones about my epiphany. His first words on entering my apartment took precedence.

"I think Francesca's been caught."

Oh, *shit.* Instantly I was contrite over every mean thought I'd ever had about her. "What happened?"

He paced in frustration. "She rang me two days ago, said she was getting closer to finding out who was pulling the legal strings for Hennessey. It wasn't a judge or a police chief, but someone higher up than that. She couldn't tell me more, she was still digging. Then 'round an hour ago she called me, and she was very agitated. Said she wanted me to pull her out, because what Hennessey was involved in went too deep. I told her I'd meet her tonight, and we were arranging a place when she said, 'Someone's coming,' and the bloody phone cut off. I haven't heard from her since."

"Do you know where she was?"

His eyes were shooting green sparks. "Of course not! If I did, I'd be on my way there!"

I backed up at the anger in his voice. He made a constricted noise and caught me in one stride, pulling me next to him.

"I'm sorry, Kitten. This has twisted me into nastiness. I can't imagine what would have scared her so much that she'd try to bolt, but if Hennessey caught her spying on him, it's nothing compared to what he'll do to her as punishment."

Bones wasn't exaggerating. I might not have liked Francesca, but the thought of what she could be going through right now made me sick.

"It's all right. Don't apologize. Look, let's assume for a minute that it's not as bad as it could be and start from there. If she had to get out of somewhere in a hurry and she couldn't contact you yet, where might she go? Is there any place she'd feel safe? You know her. Try to think like she would."

His fingers flexed on my shoulders. Not painfully, but not a massage, either. From his expression, I doubted he was even aware of it.

"She might go to Bite," he mused. "It's the only place in this area where there's no violence allowed on the premises. It's worth a shot. Will you come with me?"

I gave him a look. "You think you can stop me?"

He almost smiled, but there was too much worry on his face for it to take. "Right now, luv, I'm glad I can't."

The club where we'd had our first date and I was subsequently drugged bore no sign of Francesca. That same brawny female bouncer was at the door, and Bones pulled her aside and gave her his cell number in case she saw

Francesca later. Next we tried the hotel where we'd met Francesca a few weeks ago. Nothing. Bones called Spade, who was still in New York, but he hadn't heard from her, either. As the hours dragged on with no word, Bones began to look more and more grim. It was clear this wasn't going to have a fairy-tale ending. I felt helpless.

By dawn, we'd checked the hotel and Bite again, just in case, but with no more luck. Bones's cell hadn't rung once. He started heading back in the direction of my apartment when he suddenly slowed his bike, pulling over to the shoulder of the road.

Up ahead a couple miles on the highway were the flashing red and blue lights of multiple police cars. What little traffic there was on the road this early was being routed into the single far lane. The other three were blocked off with flares that went all the way into the nearby trees.

"There must be an accident, we should take another way," I began before gazing around with a feeling of déjà vu. "This place looks familiar. . . ."

His jaw was granite as he turned around. "It should. This is where Hennessey dragged you away to bleed you. Well, not right here. Up where the coppers are."

I stared at him and those flashing lights beyond, which now seemed more ominous. "Bones . . ."

"I can hear them," he said in a flat, emotionless tone. "They've found a body."

His hands were knotted into fists on the handlebars, and very softly, I nudged him.

"It might not be her. Keep going."

He revved up the bike and pulled back onto the highway, tersely saying only not to take my helmet off no matter what. I knew he wanted to keep my features hidden. Just in case there was anyone watching.

With the reduced speed and merging, it took us over thirty minutes to reach that two-mile marker where police activity was the thickest. I heard them, too, talking among themselves, calling in the medical examiner over the squawk of the police radios, taking detailed notes on how the body was found. . . .

Every head passing that area turned to gawk, so the officer directing traffic probably didn't think much of the stare Bones leveled at the form on the ground that was the center of attention. I only caught a glimpse—and then my arms tightened around him.

Long black hair spiraled out from behind the policeman bent over the body. His bulk concealed most of it as he meticulously took photographs, but that hair was distinctive. And the arm partially visible was skeletalized.

I was so numbed at seeing Francesca's remains, decomposed to her true age as they had been, that I barely noticed the weaving, erratic way Bones drove. He took back roads, gravel roads, and no roads before reaching the woods bordering the cave. If anyone had tried to follow us, they would have gotten lost ten times over. Then he effortlessly carried the bike one-handed the last two miles to cut the noise while I walked beside him. It wasn't until we were well inside the cave that I spoke.

"I'm sorry. It's not adequate, I know, but I am so sorry Hennessey killed her."

Bones looked at me and a small, bitter smile twisted his mouth.

"He didn't. Bloke would have done many, many things to her, but killing her straightaway isn't one of them. Her body was dumped within an hour or two at most after I spoke with her. Hennessey would have kept her alive for days at least. Until he'd found out every detail of what she'd relayed to me. There isn't one of Hennessey's sods who would have gone behind his back and done it themselves, either."

He wasn't making sense. "What are you saying? Then who killed her?"

His mouth twisted further. "Francesca did. It's the only logical explanation. She must have been trapped, saw there was no escape, so she killed herself. It would only have taken a second for her to run a silver blade through her heart, and then there's not much they could do about it afterwards. Hennessey's leaving her where I nearly finished him was just his way of saying he knew who she betrayed him to."

I couldn't imagine the ice-cold courage it must have taken for her to do that. It reminded me of the Indian who'd given Bones the cave. Deciding his manner of death was all he'd had left also. One last stand before that final fall.

"Your part is done in this, Kitten. Finished."

His uncompromising tone whipped me out of my contemplation. "Bones," I said gently. "I know you're upset—"

"Bollocks."

He seized me by the shoulders, and his voice was low and resonating.

"I don't care how pissed you are or what you threaten me with. End our relationship, don't speak to me again, whatever you fancy, but I will *not* continue to dangle you out as bait to the kind of people Francesca killed herself rather than be at the mercy of! I couldn't bear it if it was you I was waiting for a call from that never came, or if it was *your* body I had to see stretched out on the sodding ground. . . ."

He spun away abruptly, but not before I saw a pink shine to his eyes. It took away my anger at him telling me what to do.

"Hey." I tugged softly at the back of his shirt. When he still didn't turn around, I leaned against him. "You're not going to lose me. Francesca was on her own, she didn't have you shadowing her. It's not your fault, but you owe it to her to keep after Hennessey. She gave it all she had, for her own reasons, maybe, but that doesn't change what she did. You're not giving up and neither am I. We've got to have faith. Hennessey's going to be scared, wondering what she told you. Scared enough to get sloppy and make some mistakes. You've hunted him for over *eleven years*; you've never been this close before! There is no turning back, and I'm not running away because I'm afraid. We're going to get him. We're going to stand over *him* on the ground, and every greedy bastard on his team, too, and then they'll know they were taken down by you . . . and your little Grim Reaper, who hasn't met a vampire she didn't try to kill first."

He made a choked noise at my reference to what he'd called me in frustration that morning with Lola. Then he turned around and pulled me into his arms.

"You're my Red Reaper, and I've missed you terribly."

Despite everything going on, in that moment, hearing him say he'd missed me, I was happy.

"Bones, when I called you before—before I found out about Francesca . . . it was to tell you that I'd finally figured out who I was and what I needed. You told me that once I did, I shouldn't apologize to anyone for it. So I'm not going to."

He drew back, and his gaze was clouded with caution. "What are you saying?"

"I'm saying I'm a moody, insecure, narrow-minded, jealous, borderline-homicidal bitch, and I want you to promise me that you're okay with that, because it's who I am and you're what I need. I missed you every minute this week and I don't want to spend another day without you. If my mother disowns me for being with a vampire, then that's her decision, but I've made mine, and I won't apologize or back down from it."

He didn't say anything for such a long moment that I grew worried. Had I been a little too honest in my self-evaluation? Granted, it didn't sound like an ad you'd run in the personals, but I had been trying to make a point. . . .

"Would you mind repeating that?" he said at last, another emotion replacing the strain on his face. "I'm afraid I might have lost my wits altogether and just hallucinated what I've longed to hear."

I kissed him instead, so glad to be back in his arms I couldn't stop touching him. I hadn't realized until this moment how much I'd truly missed him, because even with the horrible circumstances of Francesca's death, this was the happiest I'd been since he left my apartment five days ago.

Bones ran his hands over me, kissing me so deeply, I was soon out of breath. I tore my mouth away, gulping in air. He slid his mouth to my neck, tonguing my pulse and lightly sucking on it. That throb in my neck seemed to zoom southward with his actions, and I yanked at my collar to give him better access.

He drew my shirt over my head, his mouth losing contact with my neck only in the second it took him to do that. His fangs, now fully extended with desire, grazed my neck as he nuzzled me. Bones never broke my skin, no matter how passionate things got. He was so careful to stay within the boundaries I'd set for him, whereas I certainly couldn't say the same thing. I'd drawn his blood in the throes of passion more times than I could count, but he never brought up the double standard. I wondered if he was thinking about it now, as he teased my throat the way he knew I liked it. Was he holding himself back? The ache I felt inside, that burning hunger to have him deep within me . . . was he feeling it also, but in a different way? Smothering it because this was a part of him I'd refused to accept, even though he'd accepted all of me?

Bones slid his mouth lower to my breasts, but I pulled him back to my neck. "Don't stop," I whispered, and meant it in every way.

He must have heard in my voice that I wasn't talking about foreplay, because he stiffened.

"What are you doing, Kitten?"

"Overcoming my former prejudice. You're a vampire. You drink blood. I've drunk yours and now I want you to have mine."

He stared at me for a long moment, and then shook his head. "No. You don't really want that."

"Your fangs don't scare me," I breathed. "And neither do you. I want my blood inside you, Bones. I want to know it's running through your veins. . . ."

"You can't tempt me like this," he muttered, turning away with his fists clenched. Oh yeah, he wanted this, and I wanted to give it to him, along with everything else I'd held back.

I moved in front of him. "I'm not tempting you. I'm *insisting* you drink from me. Come on. Tear down this last wall between us."

"You have nothing to prove to me," he argued, still refusing but weakening. I could feel his hunger rise. The air around us seemed to charge, and his eyes glowed a brighter green than I'd ever seen them.

I put my arms around him, brushing my lips against his throat. "I'm not afraid."

"But I am. I'm very afraid you'll regret it afterwards."

Even as he said it, his arms went around me. I rubbed against him, hearing his hiss at the friction of our skin. My teeth caught his earlobe, biting it firmly, and he shuddered.

"I want this. Show me I shouldn't have waited so long."

His hand brushed through my hair, smoothing it aside, and his mouth dipped to my neck. I gasped at the feel of his tongue circling my pulse in a more predatory manner than ever before. He fastened his mouth over it, sucking. Drawing the artery closer to surface and pressing on it with his sharp teeth. My heart was pounding now. Its throb must have been vibrating against his lips.

"Kitten," he moaned into my skin. "Are you sure?"

"Yes," I whispered. "Yes."

Fangs sank into my throat. I braced for pain, but it didn't come. A long, deep suction froze me with surprise instead. *Oh!* This wasn't like before when Hennessey bit me. It didn't hurt. On the contrary, I began to feel a delicious warmth spreading through me. It was as if our roles were reversed and the blood spilling into his mouth was feeding me as well. That heat increased, taking me down with it, and I curled my arms around his neck to pull him closer.

"*Bones . . .*"

He drank deeper, picking me up when my knees buckled. I went limp against him, shocked that every pull of his mouth felt better, until it seemed like I'd melted in his arms. Lost in the unexpected rapture.

My whole universe narrowed, encompassing only the thumping of my heart, steady panting, and the constant flow of blood connecting every part of me. I felt it like never before, understood how it was integral to each nerve ending, every cell, and contained the very essence of life. I willed it into him, wanting to fill him until he drowned in me. It seemed like I was weightless, floating, and then the warmth coating me turned to a flood of liquid heat.

Yes. Yes!

I didn't know if I said it out loud, because reality was gone. All I could feel was that heat coursing through me, growing stronger, until my blood seemed to boil with it. Then suddenly my senses roared back into clarity. The skin covering me seemed to burst, my blood boiled erotically, and the last thing I felt was Bones tightening his grip as he drank.

When my eyes opened, I was burrowed inside the blankets. Pale arms were wrapped around me, and somehow I knew it was much later despite there being no clock to check.

"Is it dark out?" I asked, instinctively feeling my neck. No bumps, only smooth skin. How amazing that there were no visible traces despite my whole body having residual tingles.

"Yes, it's dark now."

I turned to face him, gasping when his cold feet touched mine. "You're freezing!"

"You took all the covers again."

I glanced down at myself. I was cocooned in the entire comforter. Bones only had a few scraps of the blanket as he'd spooned around me. Guess he wasn't exaggerating.

I unwrapped myself and threw half the blanket over him, shivering as his chilled flesh touched my bare skin. "You undressed me while I was asleep? You didn't take advantage, did you?"

"No, I took precautions," he replied, searching my eyes. It was then that I noticed he was so tense, a single blow might have shattered him. "I stripped you and hid your clothes so if you woke up angry about what happened, you wouldn't be able to run out without talking to me first."

Here was a man who learned from experience. I almost smiled at the mental image of him hiding my clothes under various boulders. Then I sobered.

"I'm not angry. I wanted it, and it was—incredible. I didn't know it would be that way."

"I'm so glad to hear you say that," he whispered. "I love you, Kitten. I can't describe how much."

My heart exploded in my chest with a rush of feeling. Tears sprang to my eyes at the ache of emotion silently screaming to be voiced.

He saw the tears. "What's wrong?"

"You won't stop until you have all of me, will you? My body, my blood, my trust . . . and still you want more."

He knew of what I spoke and his reply was immediate.

"I want your heart the most. Above all else. You're exactly right, I won't stop until I have it."

Tears began to slide down my cheeks, because I couldn't

hold the truth back anymore. I didn't know how I'd managed to hold it back this long. "You have it already. So now you can stop."

His whole body stilled. "You mean that?"

Uncertainty but also growing emotion filled his eyes as they bore into mine. I nodded, mouth too dry to speak.

"Say it. I need to hear the words. Tell me."

I licked my lips and cleared my throat. It took three times, but finally my voice returned.

"I love you, Bones."

A weight seemed to lift from me I hadn't known was there. Funny how much I'd feared something that shouldn't have frightened me at all.

"Again." He started to smile, and a beautiful, pure joy filled up the emptiness I'd carried my entire life.

"I love you."

He kissed my forehead, cheeks, eyelids, and chin, feather-soft brushes that had the impact of a locomotive.

"Once more." The request was muffled by his mouth on mine and I breathed the words into him.

"*I love you.*"

Bones kissed me until my head reeled and everything tilted even though I was lying flat. He only paused long enough to whisper onto my lips, "It was well worth the wait."

TWENTY-ONE

"CATHERINE, YOU HAVEN'T BEEN HOME IN FOUR weeks. I know college keeps you busy, but you have to promise you'll come home for Christmas."

Guilt filled me as I switched the phone from one ear to another, waiting for my Pop-Tarts to come flying out of the toaster. The spring inside the machine usually sent them crashing out onto the counter.

"I told you, Mom, I'll be there for Christmas. But before then, I'll be very busy. I'm studying like mad. Exams are coming up."

That wasn't what had filled most of my time. Oh, I'd been studying, but not for college. No, Bones and I had been poring over any and all paper trails we could find to try and discover who Francesca had meant when she said someone "higher up" than a judge or a police chief. Considering it would have to be a person with authority over the police department, from all the missing or forged reports we'd uncovered, that left the mayor of Columbus as our most probable suspect. We'd been watching him. Tailing him, eavesdropping, checking his background, you name it. So far, nothing, but that didn't mean he wasn't just being careful. After all, we'd only been monitoring him for nine days.

"Are you still seeing Timmie? Please tell me you're using condoms."

I drew in a deep breath. I'd faced bloodthirsty monsters and been less nervous, but this was a discussion that had been put off long enough.

"Actually, I wanted to talk to you about that. Why don't you come over this weekend? We . . . we can all sit down together."

"You're not pregnant, are you?" was her instant question.

"No." *But when you hear this, you'll wish I was.*

"All right, Catherine." She sounded less concerned, but still wary. "When?"

I swallowed hard. "Friday, seven o'clock?"

"Fine. I'll bring a pie."

And I'll grind up some Valium and put it in there, because you'll need it. "Okay. I'll see you then. I love you, Mom." *Whether or not you'll decide to love me.*

"Someone's at the door, Catherine. I have to go."

"Okay. 'Bye."

I hung up. Well, it was done. I'd tell Bones about it later when I saw him. Knowing him, he'd be pleased. Poor man didn't realize what he had coming.

About thirty minutes later a knock sounded at the door, startling me. Timmie was out of town visiting his mother. Bones had left before dawn in his usual routine, so that only left my landlord Mr. Josephs to be considered, especially since I'd just hung up with my mother. When I looked through the peephole to see who was outside, however, I didn't recognize the face. Either of them.

"Who is it?"

The vibe coming from the other side of the door was human, so I didn't grab for my stakes.

"Police. Detective Mansfield and Detective Black. Catherine Crawfield?"

Police? "Yes?" Still, I didn't open the door.

There was an uncomfortable pause. "Will you open the door, please, miss? We'd like to ask you a few questions."

The tone of voice didn't sound like he appreciated speaking through a wall. Frantically I kicked my stakes, always nearby just in case, under the couch.

"Just a second! I'm not dressed."

I put the remainder of my weapons into a suitcase and shoved them under the bed. I threw a robe over myself to complete the picture of hastily clothed, and opened the door.

The one who looked around fifty introduced himself as Detective Mansfield, and the younger one, perhaps in his mid-thirties, was Detective Black. Detective Mansfield handed me a card with his name and number printed on it. I took it, shook their hands, and glanced briefly at the badges they flashed at me.

"Those could be from Kmart and I wouldn't know the difference, so you'll excuse me if we just chat at the door."

My voice was cool but polite as I mentally sized them up. They didn't appear threatening, but looks were deceiving, and we knew Hennessey had goons in uniform on his side.

Detective Mansfield looked me over as well, and his eyes were probing. I hoped I looked like the poster child of the innocent college student.

"Miss Crawfield, if it would make you more comfortable, you can call the department and verify our badge numbers. We'd be willing to wait. Then we could come inside and not have to stand."

Nice try, but no cigar, fellas. "Oh, that's all right. What is this about? Was my truck broken into or something? There's been a lot of that going on at the campus."

"No, miss, we aren't here about your truck, but I bet you've got a good idea why we would want to talk to you, don't you?"

"No, I don't, and I don't appreciate the mystery, Detective."

Now my tone hardened a bit to let them know I wasn't a quivering mass of jelly. Like my intestines had become.

"Well, Catherine Crawfield, we don't like mysteries, either. Especially ones that involve murdered mothers and dug-up corpses. Do you know Felicity Summers?"

The name rang a distant bell, but damned if I was going to say that. "No, who is she? And what are you talking about? Is this a joke?"

My eyes widened a little, as would someone's who had never planted over a dozen bodies in the ground. When he said "dug-up corpses" I thought my knees would give out. Thankfully, though, I was ramrod-straight.

"She was a twenty-five-year-old mother who disappeared six years ago while visiting a friend. Her decomposed body was found eight weeks ago in Indiana by hunters. Yet her car, a navy 1998 Passat, was found at the bottom of Silver Lake in our area two weeks ago. Does any of this sound familiar to you?"

I knew who she was now, seeing the registration papers again in my mind the night I killed my first vampire. The same one who had taken me to Silver Lake in a lovely blue Passat. Motherfucker, they had found the car I dumped.

But I blinked at him in naïve confusion and shook my head. "Why would any of that sound familiar to me? I've never even been to Indiana. How would I know that poor woman?"

That poor woman indeed. I knew better than these two smug pricks how she must have suffered.

"Why won't you let us come in, Miss Crawfield? Is there something you're hiding?"

Back to that again. They must not have a warrant, or they wouldn't be pushing so hard for the invite.

"I'll tell you why I won't let you in. Because you came to my door asking me about a dead woman like I should know something and I don't appreciate that." There. Arms folded across my chest for indignant effect.

Mansfield leaned in closer. "Okay, we'll play it your way. Do you know any reason why a headless corpse was buried a hundred yards from the shore where Mrs. Summers's car was found? Or why that corpse had been dead for nearly twenty years? I mean, why would someone dig up a corpse, chop its head off, put contemporary clothes on it, and then bury it next to the place where they dumped the victim's car, a state away from her body? Do you have any idea why someone would do that?"

Well, score one for Bones. He had been right that the first vampires I'd killed were young ones.

"I don't know why someone would do that. I don't know why people do many of the strange things they do in this world." That was certainly the truth. "But what I really don't know is why you're telling me all of this."

Mansfield let a mean little smile cross his face.

"Oh, you're good. Just a nice country girl from a small town, huh? You see, I happen to know better. I know, for example, that on the night of November twelfth, 2001, a man matching the description of Felicity Summers's kidnapper was seen leaving Club Galaxy with a tall, pretty young redhead. Driving in Felicity's 1998 navy Passat. We had an APB out on the Passat, and it was stopped in Columbus that night. For some reason, the officer got confused and let the suspect go, but not before calling in his plates. When Detective Black researched further, he also found out that on that same night, your grandfather called the police because you'd gone out and hadn't come home. *Now* is any of this coming back to you?"

It was like something on Court TV, only sickeningly real. "No, for the fifth time, none of this sounds familiar to me. So I snuck out late the same night a redhead left with someone who may have killed this woman? Does that mean because my hair is red I must be her?"

Mansfield folded his arms in a way that told me he had more to say. "If a hair color was all we had to go on, you'd be absolutely correct. Can't single you out just because your hair is red, right? But my new partner here"—a nod indicated Detective Black—"has been working overtime, and you know what he was able to piece together from a bogus assault report? You, Catherine. You were identified as the redhead leaving that night with Felicity Summers's kidnapper."

Mother*fucker*. How had they tied me to this? How?

"I don't know who your source is, but for someone to try and link me with this woman after six years is ridiculous. I was still in high school back then. Don't you find it a little weird that all of a sudden, now someone is coming forward to say I left with this person?"

Mansfield allowed himself a nasty sneer. "You know what I find weird? How a nice girl like you got mixed up in this. What are they, Satan worshippers? Is that why they dug up a corpse and then dressed it in contemporary clothes? Some kind of effigy? These strange bodies are turning up in more places than one, too. Another one was found not too far from here about ten days ago. That one was a woman, and she'd been dead almost a hundred years! Come on, Catherine. You know who's doing this. Tell us, and we can give you protection. But if you don't, you'll go down with them for accessory to murder, conspiracy, grave robbery, and kidnapping. Want to spend the rest of your life in jail? It's not worth it."

Wow, did they have some theories. Guess it made sense if they were looking at it from a purely human angle. Why else would someone dig up and then rebury a long-dead body? Because the person wasn't really dead, of course.

"I'll tell you what I know." Anger and anxiety sharpened my voice. "I know I'm done listening to your crazy ideas about dead women and old bodies. You're grasping at straws and I won't be one of them."

With that, I turned on my heel and slammed the door. They made no move to stop me, but Mansfield called through the door.

"I suppose you don't know Danny Milton, then, either? How do you think we got your name? He's the one who saw you leave with Felicity's kidnapper at Club Galaxy six years ago. He remembers because he said the two of you got in a fight that night, and he didn't tell the police about it back then because he was concerned about disclosing his relationship with an underage girl. He told Detective Black all about it on the phone this morning, however, after Detective Black stumbled across Danny's police report stating your new boyfriend had crushed his hand by shaking it. Now, we don't know how Danny's hand got crippled. We know it couldn't have been from a mere handshake. Did you take him somewhere and demolish his hand? Maybe to prevent him from talking? We'll find out everything from him, believe me. And then we'll be back."

I waited until their footsteps faded before I sank to the ground by the door.

Having watched enough TV, at least I knew not to immediately pick up the phone and call Bones. The line could be tapped. They knew enough but still not enough. Their little scare tactic this morning had been staged to send me sobbing out a confession. Well, that wasn't going to happen. For starters, it would be a great way to get an extended vacation in a padded room. One where I could tell all the lovely doctors who were pumping me full of lithium about monsters.

Instead, I dressed in black spandex pants and a long-sleeved tight top of matching material, completed with sneakers and a ponytail. Let them think I was going for a run in the woods. The mouth of the cave was difficult to find unless you knew where to look, which they didn't. Besides, they couldn't keep up with me at a run through that uneven ground if they tried. Mansfield would probably have a heart attack on the spot. He smelled like a chain-smoker.

First, I had to look like I wasn't dashing right out to the scene of a crime. I went to the mall and shopped for an hour, my stomach churning inside. Then I left and started toward the cave.

When I parked the truck, I did it even farther away than its normal quarter-mile stop. Instead it was over four miles of wooded territory from the cave. In case I had an audience, I made a show of stretching and warming up as a normal jogger would. Then I sprinted away, going in large circles to confuse someone trying to pinpoint my direction.

After ten miles of sprinting, I darted into the cave. Bones was already walking toward me, a puzzled but pleased expression on his face.

"Kitten, didn't expect you so early—"

He stopped, seeing my face. I threw my arms around him and burst into tears.

"What is it?"

He picked me up, carrying me swiftly through the lower entrance and depositing me on the couch. I got hold of myself enough to explain.

"Danny. Danny Milton! Damn him, he managed to fuck me again, and this time he kept his clothes on! I just got a visit from two detectives. Thanks to that schmuck giving them my name and telling them I left a club with a murderer, guess who's their prime suspect in an unsolved crime involving a young woman and a strange mummified corpse? I think you're going to need to drink them and change their minds, or I'll never graduate college. God, they think I'm protecting an occult killer, you wouldn't believe some of their theories—"

Alarm flashed across his face and he got up from the couch.

"Kitten." There was deadly intensity in his voice. "Get on the phone and ring your mum. Right now. Tell her to get your grandparents and leave. Bring them here, all of them."

"Are you *insane*?" Now I stood also, eyes wide with incomprehension. "My mother would run shrieking out of this cave to begin with, she's afraid of the dark, and I can just see my grandparents bunkering down here. The police aren't worth—"

"I don't give a rot about the police." His words sliced through the air. "Hennessey's looking for anything he can find on me or, failing that, on someone close to me. You know he's got connections with the police, so if they have your name now as a suspect in a murder where there's a strange shriveled corpse, then he would also. You're not anonymous anymore. You've been linked to a dead vampire, and all he needs to do is take one look at a photo of you to know you're the same girl who almost got him killed, so get on the phone and get your family out of that house."

Sweet Jesus, I hadn't considered that! With trembling hands I took the phone he handed me and dialed. It rang, one time . . . two . . . three . . . four . . . five . . . six . . . Tears sprang to my eyes. They never let it ring that long. *Oh no, no, please . . . ten . . . eleven . . . twelve . . .*

"There's no answer. I spoke to her this morning, before the detectives came. She said someone was at the door. . . ."

We sped off through the trees on his motorcycle. For once I was glad he had the damned unsafe thing. It was the only type of vehicle that could navigate through this territory at such speeds. If anyone tried to pull us over, I would look guilty as all hell of anything they accused me of. Over my tight black spandex from before, I now had on crisscrossed boots with stakes inside, silver throwing knives lashed to my upper arms and thighs, and two guns tucked in my belt filled with silver bullets. Not that we would have stopped for anyone. Somebody could just try to catch us.

I kept trying my family on the cell, cursing and praying when there was still no answer. If anything happened to them, it would be all my fault. If only I hadn't drunk that spiked gin and been unable to kill Hennessey . . . if only I'd never met Danny. . . . A thousand different ways to scourge myself seared through my mind. Normally it took an hour and a half to get to the house from the cave. Bones made it there in less than thirty minutes.

We pulled right up to the front and I was the first one off, running up the steps of the porch and through the open door. Once there, my brain refused to translate what my eyes saw. The red liquid smeared on the ground caused me to slide forward and then fall to the floor with the momentum of my panicked strides. Bones stepped inside with more caution but just as swiftly, and he dragged me to my feet.

"Hennessey and his men could still be nearby. You're no use to anyone if you break now!"

His voice was harsh, but it penetrated through the paralyzed part of my mind, which went blank upon the sight of all that blood. The early shades of dusk darkened the sky. Pale amber beams of remaining light illuminated the sightless eyes of my grandfather sprawled on the kitchen floor. His throat had been torn out. It was his blood I'd slipped in.

Shaking Bones off, I unsheathed my knives and gripped them, ready to fling them at any undead thing that moved. There was a trail of blood leading up the steps, and crimson handprints left grisly signs for us to follow. Bones took a deep whiff of the air and pushed me back against the landing.

"Listen to me. I only smell them faintly, so I think Hennessey and whoever was with him aren't close. But you keep those knives ready, and you unleash them at anything that flinches. Stay here."

"No." I spoke through clenched teeth. "I'm going up there."

"Kitten, don't. Let me go instead. You keep watch."

Pity creased his face, but I ignored it. My grief I forced into a tiny hard lump inside me that I would unravel later. Much later, when every vampire or person with them who had done this was dead.

"Get out of my way."

My tone had never been more menacing and he stepped back but followed closely behind me. The door to my bedroom was kicked in. It hung by only a hinge. My grandmother was face down on the floor, her hands frozen into claws as if in death she still tried to escape what had chased her. There were two wounds on her neck, one shallow, one gaping. It looked as though she'd dragged herself while dying, up the steps to get to my room. Bones knelt beside her and did a strange thing. He inhaled near the gouges around her neck, and then picked up a bloody pillow from my bed and held it to his face.

"What are you doing?" God, he wasn't hungry, was he? The thought sent a vile tremor through me.

"I can smell them. There were four of them, including Hennessey. I smell your mum on this pillow. They took her. And there's not enough of her blood here for her to be dead."

Relief and fear caused me to nearly sag on my feet. She was still alive, at least possibly. Bones nosed around the room like a deadly blond canine, following the scent back down the stairs. I heard him back in the kitchen and knew he was giving Grandpa Joe a similar sniffing. It was too awful to contemplate. Gently I turned my grandmother over and her open eyes seemed to stare accusingly at me. *This is all your fault!* they silently railed. Choking back a sob, I closed them, and sent a prayer upward that she was at peace, because I never would be.

"Get down here, Kitten. Someone's coming."

Abruptly I darted back down the stairs, avoiding the slick blood that lined them. Bones had something crumpled in his hand and he propelled me out the front door as he shoved it inside his belt. A car screeched down the road about a mile away and I grabbed two extra knives until each hand held four.

"Is it them?" I hoped it was. There was nothing more I wanted than to tear into the animals who had done this.

Bones stood next to me with legs apart and narrowed his eyes.

"No, they're human. I can hear their heartbeats. Let's go."

"Wait!" I looked around despairingly, my clothes and hands streaked with my family's blood. "How will we find out where they've taken my mother? We're not leaving until we do find out, I don't care who's coming!"

He jumped onto the bike and spun it around, waving me over with a jerk of his head.

"They left a note. It was in your grandfather's shirt, I have it. Come on, Kitten, they're here."

Indeed they were. The car slammed on its breaks about a hundred feet away and out came Detective Mansfield and Detective Black with their guns drawn.

"Hold it right there! Don't you fucking move!"

Bones leapt off the motorcycle and stood in front of me before I could blink. He was shielding me from the bullets that could only injure him for a short time but would do far worse damage to me.

"Get on the bike, Kitten," he murmured too low for

them to hear. "I'll get on behind you. We have to go. They would have called for backup."

"Hands in the air! Drop your weapons!" Mansfield approached with slow steps. Obligingly Bones stretched out his hands in compliance. He was buying time.

Something cold settled in me and spread, overriding the grief and the pain. Bones expected just to take two full clips in the back while we rode off. Or let them try to handcuff him and then slam them. Well, I had other ideas.

Both detectives advanced on him, seeing Bones as the primary threat. They foolishly ignored the old adage to never underestimate the power of a woman.

I stepped out from behind Bones with my hands in the air, palms facing me. When Mansfield took another step forward I flung the first knife. It skewered him straight through the wrist and his gun fell to the ground. Before Black could react I let loose the other knife, and he, too, collapsed screaming to the dirt, clutching his bleeding forearm. It made the next two knives easier to find their marks, and in a blink both of their hands were paralyzed with silver blades protruding from each wrist.

Bones arched a brow at me but said nothing, and climbed behind me on the bike as we sped off.

Their shouts behind us faded with the distance.

†wenty-†wo

WE DROVE OVER UNPAVED ROADS AND through the trees to avoid being seen. In the distance, I occasionally heard sirens. Even though I was in front, Bones controlled the bike. He maneuvered it around trees at speeds that normally would have made me throw up from fright. Now I wanted him to go faster.

When we approached the highway, he stopped. It was dark now, shadows swallowing up the light. Bones laid the bike down on its side and covered it with a few branches he yanked off a nearby tree. The freeway was about a hundred yards away.

"Stay here. Won't be a moment," he promised cryptically.

Puzzled, I watched as he walked out toward the road. When he reached the shoulder he stopped. There was moderate traffic, it being after seven and most people already having arrived home from work. From where I stood I had a clear view of him, and his eyes began to glow that penetrating green.

A car approached and Bones fixed his glare on it. It

swerved for a moment, and then began to slow. He stepped out into the middle of the road as the car headed straight toward him, and the light from his eyes blazed brighter. The car stopped only a foot shy of him, and he jerked his head toward the shoulder, where it obediently rolled.

Bones waited until it came to a full stop and then opened the driver's door. A man in his forties sat with a dazed expression on his face. Bones pulled him out and walked him over to where I stood.

In an instant his mouth clamped onto the man's neck, and the hapless stranger let out a small whimper. Bones released him after a few moments, wiping his sleeve across his lips.

"You're tired," he instructed him in that resonating voice. "You're going to lie down here and go to sleep. When you wake up you won't fret about your car. You left it at home, and you went for a walk. You want to walk home, but only after you've rested. And you are very, very weary."

Like a child the man curled in a semicircle on the ground and rested his head on his arms. He was asleep instantly.

"We needed a car they weren't looking for," Bones said by way of explanation. I followed him to the new vehicle. When we were back on the highway, I turned to him.

"Show me the note." Since we'd been riding on a motorcycle before, I hadn't asked, fearing it would be lost in the hundred-plus-mile-per-hour wind from our speed.

Bones gave his head a little shake and pulled the note out of his belt.

"You won't understand it. They knew I would."

Carefully I uncrumpled the paper that held the only clue to my mother's whereabouts:

Recompense. Twice past day's death.

"Does it mean she's still alive?"

"Oh, that's what it's supposed to mean. If you trust them."

"Do you trust them in this? Is there some kind of . . . vampire code not to lie about hostages?"

He glanced over at me. The compassion on his face didn't lend comfort.

"No, Kitten. But Hennessey might figure he has a use for her. Your mother is still a lovely woman, and you know what he does with lovely women."

White-hot fury coursed in me at the picture he painted, but it was an honest one. Lies wouldn't help me, but the truth might save her, if I could control my anger and be smart, for once.

"When are we supposed to meet them? I assume they've designated a time? What do they expect?" Questions were bubbling in my mind faster than I could ask them, and he held up a hand.

"Let me find a place to stop off first and then we'll talk. Don't want the police chasing us and making a bad situation worse."

Mutely I nodded and folded my arms across my chest. Bones drove for another twenty minutes or so, and then got off an exit and pulled in to a Motel 6.

"Wait here for a moment," he answered the puzzled look I threw him. After I waited for ten minutes in the car, he came out and pulled around to the back of the lodging. We weren't in a very upscale neighborhood, and I glanced around at the predatory looks that flicked to us from some of the people loitering in the area.

"Come on, we're this way."

Ignoring everyone else around him, he took my hand when I exited the car and led me inside Room 326. The interior looked as uninviting as the exterior, yet it was hardly my main focus.

"Why are we here?" Obviously romance wasn't the reason.

"We're off the road for a bit, less attention to attract, and we can talk without interruption. No one here will notice anything much beyond a drive-by shooting. Also, you can wash the blood off."

With barely a glance at my red-caked hands, I looked back at him. "Do we have time for that?"

Bones gave a light nod. "We have hours. They want to meet at two. That's what the 'twice past day's death' part means. Midnight is the death of every day, and they chose two hours past it. Guess they were giving you plenty of time to hear about your grandparents and contact me."

"How considerate." My voice was thick with hatred. "Now tell me what they're offering, if anything. Me for her? Does he want the bait who almost got him killed?"

Bones led me to the edge of the bed and sat me down on it. My whole body was stiff with rage and grief, and he squatted in front of me and took my bloodstained hands. We hadn't turned the lamp on, but I didn't need it to see him. His hair was nearly white in the moonlight and the contours of his face looked like marble brought to life.

"You know Hennessey doesn't want you, Kitten—he wants me. He's given no thought to you beyond how he could use you. You realize, luv, they would be making your mother spill any details on you they could. With luck, they won't be asking the right questions. I didn't believe you myself when you told me what you were, it was only seeing your eyes that convinced me. Even if your mum is coerced into telling them, chances are they'll think she's raving and pay it little heed. They would have no doubt broken in to your apartment by now looking for you. Those detectives probably saved your life by coming by this morning and scaring you into leaving. They'll find your weapons, but they could easily assume they were mine and I kept them there for convenience. They want me, and I'll go to them. But they won't be expecting you. This is our only advantage."

"Bones, you don't have to do this. You can tell me where

she is and I'll go. As you said, they won't be expecting me." She was my mother, so no matter what, I was going, but he didn't have to get killed trying to save her when she might not even be alive.

He dropped his head onto my lap a moment before replying.

"How can you even suggest that? First of all, this is my fault for getting you into this, because I should have stuck to my instincts and never allowed it. Then, I should have just killed Danny that night like I intended to. At the very least if I would have stolen his mind about how his hand got injured, he wouldn't have given your name to the police. But I was angry, and wanted him to know who did it and why. Of course I'm going. Even Hennessey, who hasn't the slightest idea that I love you, knows I will. Doesn't matter if she's already dead and there's nothing to be gained from it but vengeance, I'll still go, and I swear to you, I shall rip off every hand that touched her or your grandparents. That much at least I can do for you. The only thing that frightens me is the thought that you'll see me as a monster again, because it was vampires who did this."

Bones stared at me and his eyes were tinged pink. Vampire tears. So absolutely foreign from the clear streaks of saline zigzagging down my cheeks. I slid down until I sat on the floor and held him. He was the only thing that was constant and solid. Everything else around me was crumbling.

"I will never stop loving you. No one can change that. No matter what happens later, I'll still love you."

My illusions about tonight only went so far. We would be walking right into a trap, and in all likelihood, we wouldn't walk out. Right now my mother was terrified, if she was even still alive, and there was nothing I could do but wait until later. This could be the last time Bones and I held each other. Life was too short to waste even moments of it.

"Bones. Make love to me. I need to feel you inside me."

He pulled back until he could look in my eyes as he stripped the shirt over his head. Mine followed suit and was thrown to the ground. He undid the belt around my waist, untied the knives and guns, and tugged off my boots with their stake accompaniments. The spandex around my legs was stiff from dried blood, but I pushed the image of my grandparents' crumpled forms out of my mind. They wouldn't go far. I would see them in my nightmares the rest of my life. If I ever lived to dream again.

"I know what you're thinking and you're wrong. This isn't goodbye, Kitten. I didn't survive over two hundred years to find you only to lose you within five months. I want you, but I'm not saying goodbye to you, because we *will* get through this."

Bones traced his hands over me with such delicacy, I could have been made of glass threads and not shattered. His mouth followed everywhere his hands did, and I tried to absorb the feel of him beneath my fingers. Not for a minute did I believe that this wasn't goodbye. Still, I had loved and been loved in return, and there was nothing greater than that. It far outweighed the alienation of all the previous years. Bones thought five months was too short; I was amazed I'd been granted joy for so long.

"I love you," he moaned, or maybe I said it. I couldn't tell the difference anymore. The lines had dissolved between us.

I refused to wash the blood off, wanting it to stain my skin. Later—if I lived—I would wash it off after it was covered by the blood of those who'd done this. Finally I understood why Bones's long-dead Indian friend had painted his skin before going off to battle. It was a symbol for all to see of the depth of his resolve, and my family's blood was mine. Before we were done tonight, many things on me would be painted. My mouth was one of them.

Bones raised the issue, and for once I accepted without

hesitation. His blood would make me stronger—temporarily, that was true—but then that's all that was needed. On the extra plus side, it would also help heal any injuries I was no doubt going to incur. The quicker I healed, the quicker I could kill.

First he topped off like a car getting gas. In this neighborhood, it took only minutes for him to find someone spoiling for trouble. The unlucky victims were four men thinking they were going to score a wallet. They scored some iron deficiency instead. Not bothering to waste the power in his eyes, he simply knocked them out with a single swirling punch that connected with their jaws in one graceful blur of a semicircle. If the situation weren't so dire, I would have laughed at how they fell in a row without a blink among them. Maybe this would drive home that crime didn't pay.

Bones took from each of them, and his face was positively flushed when he glided back to me on feet that didn't touch the ground. With a shake of my head, I started back toward the hotel.

"You are going to wash your mouth out. If you kiss me, I don't want a face full of hepatitis."

My shield of sarcasm was on with full armor backup. Any emotions deeper than the surface would have to wait to crawl out of the cage I'd locked them in.

Obediently he swished water around his mouth when we were back in our room. Needless to say, none of us had packed toothpaste.

"Don't fret, luv. With your lineage, you couldn't catch it if you tried. No germs or viruses can survive in vampire blood. You've never been sick a day in your life, were you?"

"Actually . . . no. But germs aside, it's gross."

I marveled at the point he'd brought up. No one appreciates their health until they're sick, so I'd never stopped to wonder at the flawless record of mine. We'd see if I lived long enough to catch a cold.

"Come here."

Bones was seated on the bed and he patted his lap. Like a child visiting Santa at the mall, I sat on it. Unlike a child, I curled my arms around him and prepared to drink his blood for all I was worth. "You'll tell me when to stop?"

Anxiousness clouded my voice. This wouldn't turn me, but it was taking a short trip down a road I'd never wanted to travel.

"Promise."

The single word calmed me. He'd never lied to me.

"Tell me again why we aren't doing your wrist?" That seemed somehow less . . . icky.

Bones tightened his arms around me.

"Because then I couldn't hold you. Quit stalling. You know what to do."

I pressed my mouth to his neck where his jugular would be. Since his heart didn't beat, there wouldn't be a rush of arterial spray. No, this would take suction. *You know what they say,* I thought darkly as I bit down hard enough for my square teeth to pierce his skin. *Life sucks and then you die.*

The first warm splash made my stomach recoil, but I forced myself to swallow. A normal person can only drink a pint of blood before the body naturally regurgitated it. My normality had never been an issue before and it wasn't now. I bit him again when the wound started to close, and Bones held the back of my head and pressed me closer.

"Harder." The word was clipped, and he let out a small gasp. Pain or pleasure, I wasn't sure, and didn't want to ask.

"More."

This when I attempted to pull away. The harsh copper taste of his blood curled in my mouth. In this volume, it was miles away from the drops I'd taken over the last few months. I drank deeper, ignoring the urge to spit it out.

Something started to happen inside me. Strength grew, unfurling its tentacles and branching out to slither through me. Everything seemed at once sharper. His skin under me had a scent far stronger than I'd ever noticed. The room was perfumed with the earlier sweat from my body, and the bodies of those before us. Background noise of the people in the units around us increased in volume, as did the sounds from outside. My vision crystallized into a clarity it had never experienced. The darkness lightened shade by shade.

The feel of his skin splitting beneath my teeth became almost sensual. I bit him harder, suddenly enjoying the spill of his blood into my mouth. I yanked his head back, biting him again, and it felt *so good*. Like something I'd waited my whole life to do. I started to feel warm. My legs curled around his waist as I pressed against him, yanking his head back farther still, and all at once his blood tasted . . . delicious.

"*Enough*."

Bones wrenched my mouth away and I fought him, because I didn't want to stop. *Couldn't* stop. With a snarl, I tried to snap my teeth back onto his throat, but he twisted my arms behind me and threw himself on top of me. The weight of his body and his strength pinned me down.

"Just relax. Breathe. Ride it out, Kitten, it will pass."

At first I struggled, then gradually the craze that gripped me eased until I no longer looked at Bones and wanted to drink him dry. The word *bloodlust* had a whole new meaning for me now.

"How do you stand it?" My breath came in shallow pants and he released his iron grip on my arms. He didn't move off me yet, however.

"You don't, not for the first few days. You kill anything

near you to fill the need when it hits. After that, you learn to control it. What you had was only a taste. By next week, the effects will be out of your system. You'll be back to yourself."

His complete confidence that I would see next week was unflappable. Who was I to argue?

"I can smell you." Wonder etched my voice. "I smell myself on your skin. I smell everything. My God, there are so many scents in this room. . . ."

Out of all the other senses, which were merely heightened, this one was almost completely new. Bones had often commented that my nose was for decoration only, since it was one of the few parts of me that was almost human. Never before had I any idea what an incredible asset a sense of smell was. I could be blind and deaf and know exactly what was around me by odor alone.

"I didn't realize how different things were for you. How can you ever walk by a public bathroom and not pass out?" Funny what the mind thinks of at the most absurd moments.

Bones smiled and kissed me lightly. "Willpower, pet."

"Is this what it feels like to be a real vampire?" That was the question. It felt . . . good. Superior. That scared the hell out of me.

"You've just had about two pints of aged nosferatu. Fermented for two hundred and forty years. You're like a hitchhiker on my power, so in a way, yes, it is. Are you telling me you like it?"

Whoa. That was a thought I couldn't even allow myself to dwell on, because I liked it so goddamn much, I feared I would get addicted to it.

He read the emotions in my eyes and knew he wouldn't get a response. Instead, he kissed me again with more substance, and I groaned in surprise. Even the taste of him was keener.

When he ended the kiss, he gave me an unblinking stare.

"When it is time, no matter what we find, I want you to unleash everything you have in you. Hold nothing back. You've got strength and I want you to use all of it. Give in to the rage and let it feed you. Kill anything, vampire or human, that stands in your way from retrieving your mum. Remember, if they're there and they're not in chains, then they're Hennessey's and they're your enemy."

"I'm ready." Mentally I threw my conscience down a dark, deep well I would fish out later. Assuming there was a later.

Bones sprang off the bed with the grace and speed only the undead could manifest. Except for me now. With his blood coursing in my veins, I almost matched him in fluidity. He cracked his knuckles and rolled his head around his shoulders, and the emerald light pinpointing in his dark brown eyes was echoed by mine.

"Then let's go kill them all."

†WEП†Y-†HREE

MY STAKES AПD KПIVES WERE IП MY BOO†S and lined along my thighs. Inside my belt were jammed other deadly goodies. We drove to meet Hennessey's men at the same place where we'd tried to kill him and where he'd left Francesca. That's what the other part of the little cryptic note meant. From there they would be sure we weren't being followed by any backup and proceed to where they held my mother. Bones hadn't been concerned about the obvious packing of weapons on me. Since Hennessey and his men had no idea I could use them, they would probably only be amused at my artillery of silver. Bones carried nothing on him, knowing it would only be taken away. His plan was terrifying in its simplicity—let them take him inside whatever building held my mother, and when they double-crossed us and didn't release her, I was to come in blazing.

"But what if they stake you on sight?" My gut twisted at the thought. "God, Bones, you can't risk it."

He threw me a jaded look. "Not Hennessey. He'll want

to drag it out for weeks. I told you, he doesn't do quick mercy kills. Especially on a chap who's already caused him a world of trouble. No, he'll want to hear me beg. There will be time."

The casual way he described his own potential torture and death stunned me, since I had rather strong feelings about those issues myself. Then again, he was just being practical. Either our plan would work or not, and if it didn't, there was no Plan B.

"Bones." I gripped his hand and my eyes screamed everything there wasn't time to say. He squeezed back and gave me a jaunty smile.

"Hold that thought, Kitten. I intend to collect on it."

We were almost there. He leaned in to whisper to me before we got too close. "Let them smell your fear, it will lull them. Don't be strong until you have to be."

Well, that was certainly one thing I could comply with. Even I could scent it coming from me with my new nose. It smelled sickly sweet, like rotten fruit. Give in to the fear for effect? One stink platter, coming right up.

Four large SUVs waited in the dark along the shoulder of the road, their lights off. Our car came to a halt, and instantly we were surrounded by six vampires. They seemed to materialize from nowhere, but with a sense of relief I realized their movements looked perceptibly slower to me. *Viva la Bones blood*, I thought wryly. *Amen.*

"So, you came after all."

One of them stood at the window and Bones lowered the glass and glanced at him.

"Hallo, Vincent. Fancy seeing you here."

There was a bored tone to his voice that made me blink. I could never fake that kind of cool.

Vincent smiled. "Call me Switch."

Son of a bitch! *This* was Hennessey's enforcer? The one who did all the dirty work Hennessey didn't like to bother with? Switch looked even younger than me, with boyish features and chestnut-colored hair. My God, he even had freckles! Dress him in a Boy Scout uniform and he wouldn't look out of place.

"You surprise me, bringing her with you," Switch continued.

"She insisted on coming. Wanted to see her mum, couldn't sway her from it." Again the blandness in his voice unnerved me.

Switch looked me over, and obligingly I let anxiety leak from my pores. His smiled widened, revealing fangs protruding from behind his lips.

"Nice family you have, Catherine. Sorry about your grandparents. I know it's rude to eat and run, but I was short on time."

With extraordinary difficulty I bit back my rage. Couldn't let them see my eyes glow and give away the surprise. Thank God I'd gotten to be an expert at controlling my gaze. That son of a bitch thought he was going to get away with taunting me about killing my grandparents? Right then and there I made up my mind that if I died, I was taking him with me.

"Where's my mother?" There was no nonchalant banter for me, only pure hatred. That much he would have expected.

"We have her." Another one approached Switch and informed him they hadn't observed anyone following us, and Switch turned back to Bones.

"Well, let's be on our way. I trust you won't lag behind?"

"Don't fret over me," Bones replied evenly.

Switch grunted and sauntered off to his vehicle.

"I'm afraid," I said as we pulled away, speaking the words we'd rehearsed earlier. Even five car lengths away they could hear us.

"Just stay in the car and don't come out. When your mum gets in, you leave straightaway, remember?"

"Yes. I'll do it." *When hell snowed.* My hands itched to tear them apart. On cue I began to cry, making little whimpering sounds while mentally counting down the moments. Soon, very soon, they would find out what one of their kind had sired. Paybacks were a bitch, and that also happened to be my specialty.

The drive lasted forty minutes until we pulled up to a ramshackle house ten miles off the interstate. It was nice and secluded, with a long driveway. The perfect place for a massacre. Bones came to a stop and put the car in park, the engine still running. His eyes met mine for only an instant before his door was yanked open.

"End of the road. Hennessey says we'll send her out when you come in." Switch was at the door again, that same malicious smile wreathing his face.

Bones raised a dark brow at him.

"Don't think so, mate. Bring her to the door so I can see her and then I'll come. If not, you and I dance right now."

The mildness left his tone and his eyes bled to green. Even though the car was blocked from behind by the other vehicles and we were surrounded, Switch still looked uneasy.

"You can hear her heartbeat in there. She's alive," he defensively countered.

Bones gave a short humorless laugh.

"I hear seven heartbeats in there, and who's to say any of them are hers? What's to hide? Is this a bargain or not?"

Switch glared at him, then, with a jerk of his head, one of the other vamps scurried inside.

"Look now."

I gasped. In the window lit by low lighting, my mother's face was shoved into view. A hand was wrapped around her throat, holding her against the chest of her captor.

Blood seeped from her head and her blouse was red from where more of it had stained.

"There. Your proof. Satisfied?"

Bones nodded once and stepped out of the car. Immediately he was encircled by the six vampires. I slid across into the driver's seat and locked the door.

Switch smirked at me through the glass.

"Wait there. We'll bring her out and then you can leave."

By his complete lack of concern over me, either my mother hadn't disclosed what I was or, as predicted, they didn't believe her. Thank God for fools.

The front door closed behind Bones and I was left alone in the car, blocked on three sides by the SUVs. My mother was wrenched away from the window and out of sight, to my relief.

A voice boomed out from the house, sounding sinister and cheerful. I recognized it at once as Hennessey's.

"Well, look who's come to join the party! Be careful what you wish for, Bones. You've wanted to find out who was involved with me for years, so take a good look around. Except for one, here we all are."

There they all were. The people who'd wrecked hundreds of lives, not just mine. I thought of all the families these scum had torn apart, and it gave me strength. With hands rock-steady, I picked up the cell phone and dialed the number on the card Detective Mansfield had given me, seemingly another lifetime ago. A woman's voice answered.

"Franklin County Sheriff's Department, is this an emergency?"

"Yes," I breathed. "This is Catherine Crawfield. I'm off of Interstate 71 and 323, just a few miles from Bethel Road in a house at the end of a dead-end street. Earlier I speared Detectives Mansfield and Black with silver knives through the wrists. Come and get me."

I hung up as she started to sputter and put the car back in gear. The front door flew open and Switch stalked out, moving with inhuman speed. They'd heard me on the phone, as I knew they would, and were coming to silence me. Somehow in all their plotting they never once thought Bones would have me call the police. Always pride before a fall.

With a savage grin at Switch, I hit the gas. The SUVs had blocked me in from every side—except the front. *Ready or not, boys, here I come!*

The car shot forward, and Switch avoided being run over only by leaping onto the hood. Immediately he punched through the windshield and tried to grab me, but my hand was ready with a blade. I plunged it into his neck and twisted. It tore his throat open as I ducked down under the steering wheel while the car crashed into the house.

There was a spectacular explosion of wood and brick as the vehicle smashed through the front window. The screech of metal and shattering glass was deafening. Without hesitation I leapt through the shattered windshield and rolled off the hood, flinging silver knives at anything that moved toward me. Bones knew to duck, and shouts of pain accompanied the hiss of the steaming engine, which coughed and wheezed in its death throes.

Hennessey was in the remains of the front room along with approximately twenty-five other vampires. Mother of God, there were more of them than we'd anticipated. My mother was shoved into a corner, hands and feet tied together. Her wide, disbelieving eyes were fixed on me. The red haze of fury I'd carefully controlled since first seeing my grandparents' lifeless forms erupted inside me and I let it consume me. A snarl of vengeance tore from my throat and my eyes blazed with emerald fire.

Bones took advantage of the distraction. Someone had been in the process of chaining him when I'd made a garage out of the house. The dangling irons from his wrists whipped out and wrapped around the neck of the nearest vampire. With a merciless jerk of the links the vampire's head snapped off and Bones whirled in a blur of speed to the next one.

Three vampires jumped me. Their teeth were murderously extended, but so were my knives. I darted away from their fangs while landing punishing blows with my legs, tripping one of them. At once I was on him, gouging his heart and shredding it in one slash before rolling over and repeating the process with the next two.

A black-haired vampire had the presence of mind to go for my mother. Launching myself airborne, I practically flew across the room to land on his back. Silver swished and buried into his heart just as his hands almost touched her. One cruel twirl of the knife finished him, and then I was knocked off my feet by a punishing blow and pitched forward. Instead of fighting it, I let my body curl under, and the attacker arced over my head instead of stumbling me. None of them were prepared for my speed. He was skewered to the wall behind him before he had time to pounce again, staring stupidly at the silver handle jutting from his chest.

With one of my throwing knives I slit the rope that bound my mother.

"Get outside now, *go*!"

I shoved her out of the way of another series of assaults and sprang straight up into the air to come down behind two charging vampires. Unleashing my expanded strength, I slammed their heads together hard enough to splinter apart their skulls, and then stabbed both of them through the back with a blade in each fist. The force of my blows sent my hands all the way through them. With a cruel growl, I turned and used their shriveling bodies as shields. Fangs that were meant for my neck tore into dead flesh instead. I smashed my bloody knife into the next fiend until my forearm was past the rib cage of the vampire still dangling from it. Before the next bunch of nosferatu descended, I threw the body on my other arm at them, slowing them enough to wrench free of the corpse and hurl more silver blades with hellish accuracy. One stuck straight into the eye of an advancing vampire, and terrible shrieks came from his mouth before another landed between his fangs.

It seemed I was jerking silver out of bodies just to throw more again in a morbid juggling act. Failing that, even though it was more dangerous, full-body combat was in order. I experienced the furious ecstasy of twisting someone's head around so roughly it snapped off. Then I threw it like a bowling ball across the room to beam the back of a vamp closing in on Bones. There was still iron clamped around one wrist and he swung it so rapidly it was only a blur of gray.

A man tried to climb past the wreckage of the car to circle me, and without pause I threw a knife into his skull. Something about the sudden scream and then silence let me know I'd just killed a human. Vampires didn't go down that easy. Curiously I felt not the slightest twinge of guilt. If they were after me then they were evil, heartbeat or no heartbeat.

Sirens blared in the distance, coming closer. Obviously Mansfield had gotten the message. Through the crumbling wall of the home's exterior I saw the flash of red and blue lights, many of them. A small army was descending. The vampires left standing saw them also and began to scatter. This was what we'd hoped for. They were so much more convenient to kill when they faced away from us. More silver found flesh when they sprang through the remnants of the house.

Unholy exultation filled me, and a howl of victorious slaughter erupted from my throat. It shook the remains of the glass in the windows as I prowled swiftly through the bodies to find another one to destroy. Out of the corner of my eye I saw Bones, grinning evilly and tearing apart a vamp unlucky enough to be in front of him. An arm sailed across the carnage to land in the pile of body parts, followed by a head.

"Police! Drop your . . . !"

The voice on the bullhorn abruptly choked off when their spotlight lit upon the scene. Only about six vampires remained and three of them were pierced with multiple blades. Shots began to ring out from the officers' guns as they fired wildly at everything that moved, not knowing what in the world they were shooting at. This caused the surviving vamps to turn on the police. I stayed down, bullets being much more harmful to me. From this low vantage point I saw Hennessey and Switch, those slime bags, crawling around the ruins of the car. They were almost at the opening in the wall, and from there they could run for the nearby woods.

A seething hatred burst inside me, and I had only one distinct, crystallized thought. *Over my dead body.* They weren't going anywhere unless I was cold on the ground.

"Hennessey!" I snarled. "I'm coming for you!"

Hennessey turned his head with a look of disbelief. Switch didn't. He started to crawl faster. His throat had healed from my earlier run-in with him, and from the way he hustled, he didn't want a rematch.

I only had one knife left, but it was a big one. My hand closed around it with the grip of the damned. I crouched, channeling all my energy, and sprang at them with complete disregard for the raining bullets. Switch was smaller and he used that to his advantage, ducking under the twisted frame of the car. Hennessey was a large man. A perfect target, and I landed on him with all my rage propelling me. Both of us slammed into the side of the house.

More plaster came down. Hennessey went for my neck,

but I shoved him back at the same time. His teeth landed in my collarbone instead. Pain sliced into me at his fangs tearing my flesh. Because we were wedged between the car and the crumbling wall, I couldn't throw him off. Hennessey shook his head like a shark, opening the wound wider, while one arm was uselessly trapped underneath me. I kicked him brutally, but he didn't let go. This was the worst position for me to be in with a vampire, which was why I'd trained so hard with my knives to kill at a distance. Oddly enough, Spade's words rang in my head. *That beating pulse in your neck is your greatest weakness. . . .* Hennessey and I both knew that all he had to do was hang on and I'd be finished. Each shake of his mouth brought him closer to my throat.

In a split second, I made my decision. *I might go down, but I'm taking you with me.* My free arm I'd been holding him back with I used to wrap around him instead. Hennessey lifted his head enough to grin, blood dripping from his jaws, and then he brought his mouth to my unprotected neck.

Even as his fangs pushed against my skin, I rammed the silver knife through his back. His whole body stiffened, but I didn't pause to see if it was enough. I kept twisting and digging the blade deeper into him, feeling him jerk spasmodically with each plunge, until he stopped moving altogether. The mouth at my throat lost its menace, became slack, and when I pushed him off, he was literally and figuratively dead weight.

There was no time to celebrate. Gunfire concentrated away from the house caused me to whip my head up just in time to see Switch disappearing into the trees. He'd gotten through the police line and was running for his freedom.

I jumped up to chase him, but a bullet whizzing too close for comfort made me duck back down again.

"Bones!" I shrieked. "Switch is getting away! He's going for the trees!"

Bones punched through the neck of the vampire closest to him, his hand proceeding out the other side. Four bullets landed on him in quick succession, but he barely glanced at the wounds. His face contorted with indecision. If he went for Switch he'd have to leave me behind, because the goal had been to exit before the full cavalry arrived. We hadn't anticipated the numbers inside. Failing that, Bones would've used his body as a shield as we ran. Neither of these options would work now, however. Not if he intended to catch Switch.

All I could think of was my grandmother staring in silent accusation and my grandfather slumped on the kitchen floor.

"Get him now, come back for me later. *Get him!*"

This last was a roar of unbridled vehemence. I wanted that creature dead. Truly, painfully dead. All else could wait.

Decision made, Bones dashed through the room at speeds a car couldn't manage. Bullets were too slow to land on him. In a blink he was gone.

One of the remaining vampires took the initiative and hurled one of my knives at me. The silver was buried high into my thigh, missing the artery by inches. Ignoring the pain, I yanked it from my leg and sent it unerringly into his heart, rewarded with a cut-off squeal of agony.

Suddenly a blast sounded in my ears and I was thrown sideways. When I'd sat up to aim my knife, someone else had aimed at me. Hot searing metal tore into my shoulder as the bullet struck home. Gasping, I felt around for the wound and heard voices nearly on top of me.

"Don't move! Don't move! Hands in the motherfuckin' air!"

A trembling cop stood over me flanked by three others, and their scared eyes swept the bloodbath that was the living room. Slowly I raised my hands, wincing at the shards of pain seizing my shoulder.

"You're under arrest," a panicked officer wheezed, the whites of his eyes rolling in his head. The stench of his fear overwhelmed me.

"Thank God," I replied. All things considered, it was a better ending than I'd expected.

Twenty-four

They read me my rights, something I didn't pay much attention to, because I didn't need the Miranda warning to know that shutting the hell up was in my best interest. Then, after half an hour of refusing to answer any questions while I was handcuffed to a stretcher in the back of an ambulance, a tall, skinny cop muscled his way through the crowd.

"I'm taking her in with me, Kirkland."

The officer who'd read me my rights, presumably Kirkland, balked. "Lieutenant Isaac? But—"

"Soon this place will be crawling with media helicopters and we need some answers, don't 'Lieutenant' me!" the man snapped.

"Hey, I'm shot here, guys. You know, bleeding and all that," I pointed out.

"Shut up," Isaac said curtly, and uncuffed me from the stretcher. The medical attendants gazed at him in disbelief. Isaac then yanked me by my cuffed hands to follow after him, sending fresh pain through my shoulder. Kirkland gaped, but he didn't say anything. He looked like he couldn't wait to get out of there.

Lieutenant Kirkland shoved me none too gently into the back of an unmarked police car. The only thing official about it was the red flashing light on the dashboard. I glanced around, surprised. Was this usual procedure?

"I'm injured, and you clowns have already been at me for thirty minutes. Aren't I supposed to be taken to a hospital?" I asked as Isaac hit the gas.

"Shut up," he said again, weaving through the maze of police cars around the demolished property.

"Because any good lawyer would totally call this a violation of my rights," I went on, ignoring that.

He glared at me in the rearview mirror. "Shut *the fuck up*," he replied, drawing out each word.

This didn't feel normal. Of course, this was my first time being arrested, but still. I sniffed the air questioningly. Isaac had a smell about him, but I couldn't place what it was. I wasn't used to diagnosing things by scent.

After several minutes, Isaac was clear of all the activity and on the open road. He grunted as if in satisfaction and then met my eyes in the mirror again.

"What a shame, Catherine. A girl like you, her whole life ahead of her, who throws it all away by getting involved in a white slavery ring. Even killed your grandparents to cover up what you were doing. It's tragic."

"Officer Dickhead," I said clearly, "go fuck yourself."

"Ooh, language," Isaac clucked. "But I'm not surprised, coming from you. You were even going to sell your mother into that kind of slavery, weren't you?"

"You have got to be the *stupidest*—" I began furiously, and then stopped, taking in another deep breath. Isaac knew too much, and now *I* knew what that smell was.

Just as Isaac whipped his hand around, I catapulted into the front of the car. His gun went off, but the bullet tore

into the backseat instead of me. The car swerved dangerously as Isaac tried to aim again.

I slammed his head into the steering wheel. We lurched
onto the side of the road, thankfully empty due to the early
hour, and I grabbed the wheel to keep us from crashing.
When Isaac looked up seconds later, dazed and bleeding, I
had his gun trained on him.

"Pull over nice and slow or I'll splatter your brains all
over both of us."

He tried to snatch the gun, but I whipped it across his
jaw before his fingers even grazed it. "Do that again, Renfield. See what it gets you."

His eyes widened. I gave a nasty laugh. "Yeah, I know
what you are. Pick a name—Renfield, vampire's familiar,
bat bitch, whatever. You stink like vampires, and not just
the dead ones. When they're shriveled, they have a different
smell, who'd have thought? So whose little errand boy are
you? Whose pale cold ass were you kissing in the hopes
you'd get turned one day?"

Isaac stopped the car. We were already on the side of the
road. "You're making the biggest mistake of your life."

I'd jerked the gearshift into park and grabbed his balls
before he could even scream. He did, though, as soon as I
gave them a hard squeeze.

"Who was it? Who sent you to finish me off?"

"Fuck you."

I squeezed his nuts like they were stress-relieving orbs.
Isaac let out a high-pitched shriek that gave me an instant
headache.

"Now, I'm going to ask you again, and *don't* make me
angrier. Who sent you?"

"Oliver," came the pained reply. "It was *Oliver!*"

That wasn't the mayor's name. In fact, it wasn't anyone
on our list of human or vampire suspects.

"You'd better make me a believer. Oliver who?"

"*Ethan* Oliver!"

I froze, stunned. Isaac let out a gasping snicker. "You didn't know? Hennessey was sure Francesca had told Bones."

"Ethan Oliver," I whispered. "*Governor* Ethan Oliver? He's a vampire?"

"No, he's human. He's just in business with them."

It clicked into place. "*He's* Hennessey's shadow partner! My God, I *voted* for him! Why did he do it?"

"Let go of my balls!" Isaac rasped.

I got a firmer grip on them instead. "I'll let go when you make sense, and the clock's ticking. Every minute that goes by, I squeeze harder. You won't have any left inside of five."

"He wants to run for president, and he's using Ohio as his podium," Isaac rushed out in one breath. "Oliver stumbled across Hennessey a few years ago. Think it was when he was buying pussy on the side. Hennessey came up with the idea to harvest people for feedings, like he had in Mexico, and Oliver loved it. Problem is, it's the pretty young girls who sell most easily, but things get messy when a bunch of them go missing. So they make a deal. Hennessey cleans the streets of the homeless, drug dealers, prostitutes, and degenerates as his end of the bargain, and Oliver makes sure the paperwork disappears on any of the high-end tail Hennessey needs to keep his clients happy. But that got to be a lot of work, so Hennessey began getting the girls' addresses and stopping the reports before they started. Made *my* job a lot easier, not having to listen to all those sniveling families. It was perfect. Crime rate goes down, economy goes up, voters are happy, Oliver looks like Ohio's savior . . . and Hennessey makes a bundle."

I was shaking my head in disbelief at the sheer callousness of it all. Frankly, I didn't know who was worse—Hennessey, for doing it, or Oliver, for making himself out as a hero on the bones of hundreds of victims.

"Oliver sent you to kill me, clearly, but what about my mother and the other girls who were at that house? *What were you going to do with them*, and I dare you to lie to me."

My new clench got a squeak from him, but it also made my point. What he told me next was no candy-coated fabrication.

"Oliver freaked when he heard about the police all over that house and how some girls were recovered alive. He wants any traces to him erased, so I was supposed to shoot you, and then plant a bomb at the hospital where they're taking the girls. Oliver was going to pin it on Muslim extremists. He saw how Bush's numbers spiked right after 9/11, so he thought it would push him over the top as the next presidential candidate."

"You *fucker*," I growled. "Where's the bomb?"

"In the trunk."

I thought rapidly. Oliver would be expecting a ka-boom within the next couple hours, and when it didn't happen, he'd send someone else to finish the job.

"Isaac," I said in a pleasant tone, "you're coming with me. I'm revoking my vote."

The governor's residence in Bexley was decorated festively for the holidays. A large evergreen was in the front, complete with lights, garland, and ornaments. More lights were strewn around the exterior, and the gardens were filled with poinsettias in addition to their usual seasonal blossoms. Isaac parked by the wrought-iron fence about a block from the entrance.

"What do you think you're going to do, ring the bell?" he asked caustically.

I sat behind him in the backseat, his own gun poking him in the side. Otherworldly energy permeated from the property. Oh, here there be monsters, all right.

"How many are there? And you know what I mean."

He didn't play dumb. "Three, maybe four vamps, plus the usual guys."

Judging from the heartbeats, there were about six human guards. Maybe they were just innocent schmucks doing their job. Maybe not. The vampires I suffered no conscience qualms about, and not for my usual reasons. If they were here guarding Oliver, they knew damn well what was going on.

"They know you? The guards? You've come here before, right?"

"All the time," he sneered. "You fucked with the wrong john, bitch. I'm in his pocket nice and tight."

"Uh-huh." I took my shirt and bra off one-handed, not taking the gun off Isaac for a second. Then I pulled my hair over the bullet wound in my shoulder, hiding it. As for the rest of the blood on me . . . well, there was nothing I could do about that.

Isaac's eyes widened in the rearview mirror.

"Drive right on up and tell them you've brought some Yuletide joy," I said evenly, sitting back. "I'm sure it won't be the first time. And remember, I've got this trained at your head, so if you say anything else, I'll blow you to hell."

Isaac smirked. I knew he'd pull something, but I was hoping he'd be arrogant enough to wait until we were inside to do it.

"Nice tits."

"Go."

He pulled up the driveway without any more prompting. As he neared the guard station, I moved the gun to where my hip shielded it from view.

Isaac rolled down the window when he came to a halt at the gate. One of the guards poked his head out from his post.

"Hi, Frankie," Isaac said. "Back again."

"Twice in one day, Jay?" the man asked. "Who you got back there?"

Isaac rolled down my window as well. The glass had been tinted. When the guard saw me, he gave a leer at my breasts and then laughed.

"Never mind. I guess it's better if I don't know. Good timing. The missus just left 'bout an hour ago."

"That *is* good timing," Isaac drawled, sounding much more confident. "See you later, Frankie."

We went through the gates and pulled up the one-lane drive to the house. I was about to put my shirt back on when someone without a heartbeat stepped out of the front door to announce him.

"Help!" Isaac shouted—and ducked.

The vampire lunged at the car just as I pulled the trigger. If I'd have been merely human, Isaac would have made it, but I was half vampire topped off with two pints of Bones, and he didn't stand a chance. Isaac's head exploded. Blood splattered everywhere, coating the windows and me in a layer of gore.

My door was ripped off its frame in the next second, but that was long enough for me to aim again. In lightning succession I fired into the vampire's open mouth, knocking him backward, pulling the trigger over and over until there was nothing but clicks, and then I jumped him.

His face was a mess. He was healing, but with pieces of his skull mimicking Isaac's current state, it took him too long. I snatched a knife from his belt with relief, ramming it through his heart just in time to whirl and face the other two running vampires.

One went airborne. I ducked to let him sail over me. He landed on the car instead, giving me those needed moments to sprint forward and launch myself on his partner. Swipe, swipe, and he went down, an expression of disbelief on his face. Being underestimated was the greatest thing ever.

The other vampire regained his bearings and circled me, fangs gleaming. There were screams from inside the house and the guard station. I heard Frankie calling for backup, and then the sound of him running. Dammit. Soon this place would be swarming with cops. Or worse.

I backed away and pretended to trip. Fang Face bought it, springing forward. His momentum made the knife I flung sink that much deeper into his chest. He was still snarling when he landed on me, and I rolled backward in a somersault and kicked him through the front window, jumping up immediately to follow him. Better him getting cut up making a doorway than me.

Gunfire erupted from inside and outside the house as the human security guards tried to defend their employer. I grabbed the dying vampire and threw him at two of the closest shooters, knocking them over. Then I ran through the dining room, past the stone fireplace with the lovely exposed-beam ceiling, and up the stairs. Behind me there was chaos as they scrambled to chase.

I didn't focus on them. I heard Oliver on the phone, calling for help, and that was all I centered my concentration on. I made it down the hall, his accelerated heartbeat my beacon, and burst through the door that stood between me and my prey.

The bullet meant for my chest tore through my shoulder instead as I lurched, seeing the gun too late. Oliver fired again, hitting me in the leg. It knocked me over and I fell, momentarily stunned by the impact and cursing myself for stupidly rushing in like that.

Frankie and two more guards came huffing up the stairs. I didn't turn around, but kept my glare on Oliver as he leveled his gun at me with a rock-steady hand.

"Isaac's dead," I said roughly, throbs of pain from the

bullets almost paralyzing me. "There won't be any explosion at the hospital."

"Governor Oliver!" one of the men gasped. "Are you hurt?"

Oliver had sky-blue eyes. Very clear and bright, and that salt-and-chestnut hair was as perfectly coiffed as it had been in his campaign photos.

"Frankie, Stephen, John . . . get the fuck out of here," he said cleanly.

"But sir!" they chorused.

"She's down on her knees and I've got her at gunpoint, get the fuck out of here!" he roared. "Now!"

In the distance was the faint wail of sirens. Too far away for them to hear. The three men left, a jerk of Oliver's head indicating they should close the door behind them. It was just me and the governor in the room.

"You're the Crawfield girl?" he asked, not moving the barrel a centimeter.

I didn't move, mentally evaluating my injuries and noticing with a fresh spurt of anger that the wallpaper in his room was a distinctive red and blue paisley and these were hardwood floors. Oliver had to be Emily's masked rapist. She'd described his bedroom perfectly. "You can call me Cat."

"Cat," he repeated. "You don't look so tough, bleeding all over my floor. Tell me, where's your friend? The bounty hunter?"

The sirens were getting closer. There wasn't much time. "Killing Hennessey's pal Switch would be my guess. You're finished, Oliver. They're all dead. The permanent way."

His hand didn't waver. "Is that so?" Then he smiled. Icily. "Well, there's plenty more where Hennessey came from. Won't be too hard to find someone else looking to make the kind of money he was, and with meals thrown in, to boot! When I'm president, this country will have a major overhaul. I'll save the taxpayers millions, and we'll clean the scum right off the streets. Hell, I'm fixing to start on welfare recipients and nursing homes next. America will be stronger and more prosperous than ever. They'll probably repeal the two-term limit after I'm in office."

Cars screeched around the corner. Only seconds left now.

"It's not going to happen."

He smiled. "Not that you'll see. I'm about to kill you in self-defense. I can just see the headlines now: 'Governor Bravely Staves Off Murderer in Assassination Attempt.' My numbers will rise twelve points tonight."

"Ethan," I said softly, hearing the thunder of feet coming toward the house. "Look at me."

I let the shine out in my eyes. His own gaze widened, astonished, and in that split second of distraction I charged him, batting his gun aside to fire harmlessly into the wall.

"You're bleeding . . . you have to be human, but your eyes . . . what *are* you?" he whispered.

That emerald light illuminated his face, and my hands tightened around his throat. "I'm the Grim Reaper," I growled. Those footsteps were almost here. . . . "Or as Bones would say, the Red one."

I snapped his neck just before the door was flung open. When the half dozen police poured in, the glow had left my gaze, and I already had my hands up.

"I surrender."

Twenty-Five

THERE WERE THREE GUARDS OUTSIDE MY hospital room, and I was on the eleventh floor. They'd even cleared this part of the wing—I knew this from the silence in the rooms next to me. Apparently they took killing the governor seriously.

Doctors had been coming in all morning to gasp and gape over me, but it wasn't because of who I'd killed. It was because of how I'd healed. Within hours, my three bullet holes had disappeared. The knife wound, gone. Hennessey's fang marks, missing. All of my scratches and bruises, vanished. I didn't even have an IV in me—the needle kept spontaneously slipping out. Frankly, I wondered why I hadn't been moved to a regular jail cell yet, but after Isaac, I wasn't complaining about the lack of police transportation.

At noon, more footsteps approached my room. Someone said, "FBI." There was a pause, and then my door opened.

A man entered. He was about fifty, of average height, with thinning charcoal hair overrun with gray. His eyes were the same medium gray as his hair, but they weren't sedate like their shade. They were crackling with intelligence. His companion who closed the door after him was considerably younger, perhaps in his late twenties. He had short brown hair in a buzz cut, and something about the way he carried himself screamed military to me. His eyes were navy blue and fixed on me with steadfast intensity.

"FBI, huh? Well, aren't I honored?" They didn't need extrasensory perception to catch my sarcasm. The younger man shot me a dirty look.

Gray Hair smiled instead, and came forward with hand extended.

"You might not be, but I certainly am. My name is Donald Williams and this is Tate Bradley. I'm the head of a unit in the FBI called the Paranormal Behavior Division."

Grudgingly I shook his hand, years of manners making it impossible to refuse. With a jerk of my head I indicated Tate Bradley.

"What about him? He's not Bureau . . . no cellulite or spare tire."

Williams laughed, showing teeth slightly discolored from too much coffee or cigarettes.

"That's correct. Tate is a sergeant in the Special Forces, a very select unit of them. He is my bodyguard today."

"Why would you need a bodyguard, Agent Williams? As you can see, I'm handcuffed to the bed." For effect, I rattled my cuffs at him.

He smiled benevolently. "Call me Don, and I'm a cautious man. That's why Tate is carrying a Colt 45."

The younger man flashed me the handle of his gun strapped in its shoulder harness. I smiled thinly at him and he returned it with an unfriendly baring of teeth.

"Okay, I'm shivering. Properly cowed. Now, what do you want?"

Not that I couldn't guess. They probably wanted a

confession that I'd killed the governor, a motive, etc., but I intended to clam up and then get the hell out of Dodge. Bones would be coming soon, I had no doubt, and along with my mother, we'd go into hiding. There were still two vampires who'd gotten away, and it would be too dangerous for my mother to remain in public in case there was retribution after the bloodbath Bones and I had unleashed. Both vampire and political.

"You're a college student, getting excellent grades as well, from what we saw. Do you like literary quotes?"

Okay, an intelligence quiz. Not what I'd expected, but I would play along. "Depends."

Don pulled up a chair without invitation and sat next to my bedside. Bradley remained standing, his hand fingering the butt of his gun pointedly.

"How about this one from Sir Arthur Conan Doyle's Sherlock Holmes: When you have eliminated the impossible, whatever remains, however improbable, must be the truth."

A warning shiver went through me. These two weren't giving off dangerous vibes, so I didn't think they were more of Oliver's or Hennessey's goons, but they obviously weren't to be taken lightly, either.

"What about it?"

"Catherine, I'm head of a division that investigates the unnatural occurrences of homicides. Now, most people think that every homicide is unnatural in nature, but you and I know they can go even deeper than humanity's wrath against humanity, don't we?"

"I have no idea what you're talking about."

Don ignored that. "Our division isn't publicly recognized by the Bureau. In fact, we're a combination of CIA, FBI, and the armed forces. One of the few times those groups work in harmony. That's why I selected Mr. Bradley as my backup and not some rookie fresh out of basic. He's been training to head up a new unit of soldiers to fight a very special kind of battle. One that has been waged under our noses on our own soil for centuries. You know of what I speak, Catherine, and you know it better than anyone else. Let's quit being coy. I'm talking about vampires."

Holy Mary, Mother of God, he'd just said the V-word. Now I was more than wary—I was stricken.

"Aren't you a little old to believe in vampires, Don?" Perhaps I could brazen it out. Maybe he was just fishing with a very big piece of bait.

Don didn't smile now. His expression was granite. "I've examined many strange bodies over the course of my career. Bodies that were dated to be anywhere from a hundred years old to a thousand, and yet were dressed in modern clothes. Now, that could be explained away, but their pathology can't. Their DNA contained a mutation never before documented in human or animal history. Every so often, we'd run across one of these unusual corpses, and the mystery behind them deepened. That house last night was littered with those abnormal bodies, and so was the governor's. It was the largest cache of such bodies we've ever come across, but do you know what our greatest find was? You."

Don's tone lowered. "I've spent the last six hours reading every scrap of material I could find about you. Your mother reported a date rape a little more than twenty-two years ago and told of an implausible attacker who drank her blood. She was considered to be overwrought and the details were ignored. Then you were born five months later. And they never caught the perpetrator of that crime."

"What of it? My mother was hysterical from the trauma of being raped."

"I disagree. Your mother told the exact truth, except no one would ever believe her. Certain details she described were too specific. The sudden glowing of eyes to green, fangs protruding, incredible strength and speed, things she never could have heard anywhere else. Where her story differs from all others is that she gave birth to you. You, who according to Pathology have the same strain of mutation in your blood as our mysterious corpses. Less potency but no difference in the genetic structure. You see, Catherine, I'm honored to meet you because I've been looking for someone like you my entire career. You're one of them and yet not one of them, the offspring of a human and a vampire. That makes you the most valuable find in centuries."

Motherfucker. I should have run for it at the governor's house, bullets be damned.

"That's quite a story, but many people have rare blood types and psychotic mothers. I assure you, I am no different than any other girl my age. Furthermore, there is no such thing as vampires."

Even my voice sounded steady. Bones would be so proud.

"Is that so?" Don stood and nodded to Tate Bradley. "Sergeant, I'm about to give you a direct order. Carry it out at once. Shoot Miss Crawfield in the head, right between the eyes."

Whoa. I sprang off the bed and tore the metal bed rail from its welded perch, swinging it at the hand that raised the gun at me. There was a crack of broken bones. In the same smooth motion, I kneecapped Don while ripping the gun out of Bradley's hand and holding it firmly to his head.

"I am so sick of being shot, and someone should tell you guys to have a little more respect for hospitals!"

Don, face first on the floor, pushed slowly over to look up at me. The expression on his face was pure satisfaction.

"You're just a normal girl and there's no such thing as vampires, right? That was the most amazing thing I've ever seen. You were only a blur. Tate didn't even have time to aim."

Tate Bradley's heart pumped at an accelerated rhythm

and the beginnings of fear leaked out of his pores. Somehow I knew being afraid wasn't a normal condition for him.

"What do you want, Don?" So this was his little test, and I'd passed with flying colors.

"Will you please release Tate? You can keep the gun, not that you need it. Clearly you're stronger without it than he was with it. Consider it a sign of goodwill."

"What's to stop me from making my own sign of good-will through his brains?" Maliciously. "Or yours?"

"Because I have an offer you'll want to hear. If I'm dead, it's harder for me to talk."

Well, score one for him for keeping calm in a crisis. Abruptly I released Bradley and shoved him across the room. He slipped and slid on the floor next to Don.

There was a knock at the door. "Sir, is everything all right in there?" The guard sounded worried, but he didn't peer inside.

"Just fine. Keep your post, no visitors. Don't open that door until you're told." Don's voice was confident and strong, belying the flash of pain in his eyes from his knees.

"What if you'd been wrong? If GI Joe here had plugged a hole in my head? That would've been hard to explain."

Don gave me an appraising look. "It was worth the risk. Ever believe in something enough to kill for it?"

It would be hypocritical for me to say no. "What's your offer?"

Don sat up, wincing at his bent knees. "We want you, of course. You just ripped off a welded metal bar and disarmed a highly trained soldier while handcuffed to a bed, all in about a second. There's no one alive who has that kind of speed, but there are many dead things that do. After seeing your work, it seems to me you aren't averse to killing those things. Lots of them, in fact, but more will be looking for you now. Your anonymity is ruined. I can fix that. Oh, I knew Oliver was dirty, a lot of people did, but we couldn't prove anything because every agent we sent to check him out never came back. You're different. We'd be sending these creatures someone their own size to pick on, and all of these charges won't matter because Catherine Crawfield will die, and you'll be reborn into your new life. Given backing and troops. You'll become one of the most prized weapons the U.S. government has to protect its citizens against dangers they can't even imagine. Isn't that what you were meant to do? Haven't you always known it?"

Wow, he was good, and if Timmie were here, he'd feel absolutely vindicated. There really *were* men in black, and I'd just been offered a chance to join their ranks. I thought of the opportunity and the advantages, the exhilaration of starting a new life without fear of police or burying bodies or hiding my nature from those around me. Just six months ago, I would have tripped over myself to accept it.

"No."

The single word hung in the room. Don blinked.

"Would you like to see your mother?"

He'd taken my refusal too easy. Something was up. Slowly, I nodded. "She's here?"

"Yes, but we'll bring her to you. They'll never let you walk the hall swinging that bedrail. Tate, instruct the guard to have Ms. Crawfield wheeled down here. And ask for another wheelchair as well. My arthritis seems to be acting up." With a glance of pained amusement, he looked down at his knees.

A slight twinge of guilt shot through me.

"You deserved it."

"It was worth it, Catherine, to be proven right. Some things are worth the cost of their consequences."

Thinking of Bones, I couldn't agree more.

The look on the guard's face was priceless when he opened the door and saw Tate Bradley holding his broken arm at an odd angle and Don sprawled on the floor. My bed rail was held in place by my hand and I lay innocently on the bed.

"I tripped and my companion tried to help me up and fell on me," Don offered when it was obvious something had occurred. The guard gulped and nodded smartly. Don was helped out and soon my mother was wheeled in. For a second, I thought of smashing through the window again and making a run for it with her, but then one look at her face told me it wouldn't work.

"How could you?" she demanded as soon as the door closed, staring at me with a look of heartrending betrayal.

"Are you all right, Mom? I'm so sorry about Grandpa and Grandma. I loved them both." Tears trapped inside me burst forth at last and I sat up and reached for her hand.

She jerked back as if I were foul.

"How can you say you're sorry? How can you say any of that when *I saw you with that vampire*?"

Her voice rose to a shout and I looked nervously at the door. The guard would probably faint. Suddenly there was pleading in her face.

"Tell me I'm wrong. Tell me they lied to me, those animals that killed my parents and took me with them. Tell me that you are not fucking a vampire!"

She had never used that word with me before, and it fell with ugliness from her lips. All of my worst fears were realized when I saw her expression. Just as I'd dreaded, she despised me for what I'd done.

"Mom, I was going to tell you about him. He's not like the others. He's the one that's really been helping me kill them, not Timmie. He'd been after Hennessey and his group for years."

"For money?" Her words were whips. "Oh, I heard a good deal about that while they had me. They kept talking about the vampire that killed for money. And they laughed when they talked about you, said it was always women when it came to him. Is that what you've become, Catherine, a whore for the undead?"

A sob escaped me. How profane she made my relationship sound.

"You're wrong about him. He risked his life going to that house to save you!"

"How could he risk his life when he is *dead*? Dead, and he brought death with him! It's because of him those murderers came to our home, and it's your fault for involving yourself with him! If you wouldn't have been sleeping with a vampire, my parents would still be alive!"

Out of everything she'd said, this hurt the most. I might not be able to defend my part in their deaths, but she wasn't getting away with blaming Bones.

"Don't you dare, Mom. Don't you dare! You knew what I've been doing since I was sixteen, going out all the time to search for vampires. And you knew how dangerous that was. You of all people knew, because of what happened with my father, and yet you encouraged me to do it, so that's your fault! And I did it, and kept doing it, refusing to stop even though Bones warned me over and over to, so that's *my* fault! If I had never met Bones, if I had never slept with a vampire in my life, Grandma and Grandpa could still have been killed for what both of us participated in without him, even *before* him. If anyone's got Grandma and Grandpa's blood on their hands, it's you and me. Not him. We both knew one day it could lead back home, and in that regard, we're more responsible for Grandma and Grandpa's deaths than he could ever be."

Her face went white and her voice, when it came, was low but resonating. "Maybe you're right. Maybe I am also responsible for my parents being murdered, and I'll have to live with that for the rest of my life. But I don't have to live with a vampire in it. Catherine, I love you, but if you continue to have a relationship with that creature, I never want to see you again."

Those words struck me harder than the bullets had. I thought I'd been prepared to hear them, but they hurt more than I ever knew they could.

"Don't do this to me, Mom. You're the only family I have left!"

She sat back and straightened in her chair as much as her aching ribs would allow. "I know what's happened to you. You've been corrupted. That creature warped your conscience and brought out the darkness in you, like I've always been afraid would happen. I only wish those other animals had killed me before I found out I was a failure as a mother."

Every word was a knife slicing into me. Being kidnapped and seeing her parents murdered had ruined any chance of reasoning with her about vampires not being automatically evil. She was drowning in her rage, and I had no way to save her.

"I hope those men catch that monster and kill him once and for all," she went on. "Then you won't be tormented by his control anymore."

My head snapped up. "Who? What are you talking about?"

She stared at me with defiance. "I told them the truth, the men who just left here. Told them you'd been led astray by one of those creatures, and that he'd run away from the house last night. The older man knew about vampires. They're looking for him. I hope they slaughter him. Then you'll be free."

"Don! Get in here!"

Now I jumped off the bed and flung open the door. The guard made as if to pull his gun at seeing me unrestrained, but Don quickly blocked him in his straight-legged wheelchair, with Tate following close behind.

"It's okay, Jones. We have it under control."

"But she . . . she . . ." Jones gaped at the bed rail dangling from my right handcuff, mouth opening and closing.

"Just watch the door," Bradley snapped, and pushed past him with his good arm.

"Did you ladies have a nice chat?" Don inquired.

"You smug son of a bitch. What game do you think you are playing?"

Don looked as unruffled as if he were sipping tea at a luncheon. "Ms. Crawfield, would you excuse us and let us have a few moments alone with your daughter? The guard will see you back to your room."

She didn't say goodbye and neither did I. Both of us were furious and felt deceived. Unlike her, however, I knew I could never stop loving her. She was my mother, no matter what occurred. I could forgive her even this.

"So, your mother told you she informed us about your . . . relationship with a vampire? She thinks he put some kind of spell on you. Is that true? Are you under his thrall?"

"Only if you count sex," I countered without batting an eye. Let them think it was merely physical.

Bradley gave me a look of thinly veiled disgust. I'd had enough of that.

"Oh, shove it up your ass, if you can fit anything in that tight GI shit-shoot!" My mother's judgment I had to take, but I didn't have to put up with his.

His face actually colored with indignation. Don hid a smile behind a cough.

"Be that as it may, I find it notable you didn't bring up your close association with a vampire earlier. Perhaps you lean more towards their side than appearances dictate?"

"Look, Don, who I choose to fuck is not anyone's business but my own. He and I had similarities in our goals. Did my mother tell you he killed vampires as well? She probably left that out in her haste to see him dispatched. We had a commonality of purpose and it led to some extra attention. It's not like it was serious, he was just passing through."

"Just passing though?" Skeptically. "This would be the vampire who crushed Danny Milton's hand at a bar in November? The police might think it's impossible to cripple someone with a handshake, but then they've never been aware of a vampire's work before."

"Well, well, aren't you Mr. Smarty Pants? In case you haven't heard it from the horse's mouth, that creep Danny used and abused me when I was sixteen. I asked my friend to teach him a lesson. Now his hand won't be feeling up any underage skirts for a while." Again the lies slid smoothly off my tongue. "And in case you didn't realize, a vampire's idea of just passing through *is* staying a few months. They calculate time a little different than we do."

"Then you'll fill us in on the details of where he is." This from Bradley, still smarting from my earlier comment.

Laughing, I shook my head. "Sure. Great idea. Rat on a vampire who doesn't have a grudge against me, pissing him off when I haven't the slightest notion if you could protect me afterwards. I'm half human, but I'm not *all* stupid."

"Do you know what I think, Catherine? I think you're not stupid at all."

Don spoke quietly, with that same pleasant half smile. "No, I think you're very, very smart. You'd have to be, wouldn't you, to hide what you are all of these years and sneak out at night to kill the living dead. My God, you're only twenty-two, and you've seen more combat than most of the soldiers in uniform. I think you'll try to run away. Take your mother and leave, with or without your vampire lover. But there's a small problem with that, as you just

found out. *She won't go.* You see, she hasn't accepted you
for what you are. After finding out about your unusual sex
life, she's even more upset. You'll have to leave her behind
in order to disappear, and when you do, how many things
will come crawling out of the ground to use her to get to
you? How many vampires have you killed? I bet they had
friends. Oliver did, too. And all of your cajoling won't
change what she sees in you. She sees you now as a vampire, and she will never leave with one of them. You may as
well kill her yourself before you go, it would be kinder."

"You bastard!"

I launched out of bed, slamming Bradley in the head
when he moved to block me. He dropped like a stone onto
the floor. Then I grabbed Don by his shirt collar and hauled
him out of his wheelchair, lifting him until his feet dangled
in the air.

"You can kill us both now, Catherine," he panted. "We
can't stop you. Maybe you'd make it out the window without getting shot. Maybe you'd make it to her room and
fling her over your shoulder and carry her off, kicking and
screaming for help. Maybe you'd get a car and a false pass-
port, meet up with your lover and try to skip the country.
Maybe you would get away with all of that. But how long
before she left you? How long before she ran away out of
fear of her own daughter? *And then how long before someone found her and made her pay for what you've done?*"

Don held my eyes as tightly as I gripped his shirt. In his
stare I could see the truth. See my mother fighting every
moment to escape, probably trying to kill herself out of
misery, and then getting stolen away again because of me
or Bones. We would try to rescue her, of course, and then
what if she died and Bones did as well? It was one thing to
risk my relationship with her if she didn't accept me because of the man I loved. But I couldn't demand her life in
return for my happiness, and I couldn't risk his for the

same reason. We could run all over the world, but we wouldn't be able to escape what was inside us, and eventually it would destroy all of us.

I relinquished my grip on Don. He crumpled to the ground, his shattered knees unable to hold him. There was a way to ensure the safety of both Bones and my mother, and it only required one sacrifice. Mine.

I knew then that I had to take Don's offer. It tore at my heart, but to do any less would be to condemn either Bones or my mother. Her hatred of vampires was so great, she would get herself or him killed if we tried to run away, and we'd have to, with so many different people chasing us. We couldn't run from Hennessey and Oliver's remaining friends, the police, *plus* a secret U.S. government agency as well! One of them would catch us. It would only be a matter of time. If I went with Don, I'd be eliminating two out of the three threats against us, so the odds of Bones and my mother being safe more than doubled. How could I refuse, if I claimed to love them? Love wasn't doing only what was best for me, after all. It was doing what was best for them.

"We have a deal," I said to Don, steeling myself. "If you meet my conditions."

"Name them. I'll tell you straight out if they're impossible."

He struggled to climb back into the wheelchair, but I watched him without pity.

"One, I command any teams that hunt vampires. There's no way I'm going to listen to any brass-striped and -buttoned fool when it comes to battle. I'm superior to any of your men and I don't care that I'm younger. We do things my way and I train and pick my own team. If they don't meet my standards, then they stay at home."

My voice was granite and I didn't blink. He nodded briskly, all business.

"Two, we leave right away, and we don't come back here. You forget about my undead friend. I'm not backstabbing someone who helped rescue my mother and has done me no harm. If you can't handle that, then we quit speaking, because if I ever hear differently, you'll wish more than my mother does now that I'd never been born. Believe me, you'll have plenty of other dead vampires to play with by the time I'm through."

Don hesitated for only a moment and then shrugged. "I want to win the war, not just one battle. I'll agree to that. Provided, of course, you have no further contact with him or any other nonhuman friends you may have acquired. I won't endanger my people needlessly or open my division to infiltration because you like how some*thing* is in the sack."

His emphasis on *thing* was deliberate. So he had prejudice issues as well.

"Three, there is a length-of-service agreement. Even soldiers get to quit after a period of time. I don't want to be enslaved to you for the rest of my natural life, however short that may turn out to be. Ten years, and not a minute more."

He frowned and pulled at his eyebrow. "What if after that time special circumstances come up? Monsters don't send us notice in advance to warn us of the trouble they plan. How about ten years' full duty, and then after that, three missions a year of our choice for another three years? That seems fair, doesn't it?"

"Three missions a year, not to exceed one month in total time length combined. Done."

Thirteen years. That was way too long to expect Bones to wait for me, even if he didn't age.

"Four, you set me and my mother up in separate residences but in one place. I am not going to be traveling like a gypsy from barrack to barrack or whatever you call them.

I want a house, nothing fancy but mine, and a salary. Give my mother a home as well, just not too close to mine. Same state, different cities ought to do it. This arrangement with her will continue even if I die on the job. She gets my salary if I'm killed, understood? And you're also going to take care of those girls who were rescued last night. Get them the best counseling money can buy, and make sure they're set up with a good job and a place to stay also. They were chosen because they don't have that. You're going to give it to them."

Don gave the faintest smile. "We would have done that anyway. You'll find if you cooperate, we can have a mutually beneficial association for everyone involved."

"I doubt it," I said wearily. "But it's a deal nonetheless. Last but absolutely not least, I *refuse* to go after vampires who aren't killing people. This may sound like an oxymoron to you, but in my experience, I've met vampires who drank only enough to live and didn't kill unnecessarily. They can feed off someone without their knowledge afterwards. I'll kill killers, not sippers. Find someone else to hunt those for you, and good luck."

Tate Bradley stirred, moaning softly and sitting up while pressing a hand to his bleeding head. Guess I'd cracked his skull a bit. He stood, but swayed and gave me a very unpleasant look.

"You hit me again and I'll—"

"What? Bleed more? Thanks, but I only drink gin and tonic. That's one vampire attribute I'm without. No fangs, see?"

With a wide smile I bared my teeth at him and returned his nasty stare. If he hated me now, wait until I started to train him. Then he'd know hatred.

Don coughed. "I'm sure we'll be able to find enough unsavory types to keep you sufficiently busy so we won't have to hunt the ones you feel are harmless." The edge to his words told me he thought nothing undead was harmless. But the potential for harm wasn't limited to vampires. I knew that from experience now. "Then we are finished. I'll arrange to have you and your mother transported out of here immediately. Tate will accompany you to the airport, and you two should get to know one another. Tate, meet your new team leader, Catherine."

"My name is Cat."

It flew out of my mouth. Everything in my life was about to change, but some things I was keeping.

Bradley held open the door and Don once again wheeled out. Bradley paused for a moment and shook his head at me.

"Can't say it's been a pleasure meeting you, but I'll see you soon. Try to let me stay conscious next time."

My brow arched at him, shades of the vampire I loved. "We'll see."

Twenty-six

TO GIVE CREDIT WHERE IT WAS DUE, DON WAS
as good as his word in setting up my transportation.
Within an hour, I was dressed and waiting in my mother's room, sans handcuffs. I'd finally showered to wash
off all of the blood, and while in there, I allowed myself
to cry, since it mixed with the water and felt camou-
flaged. Yet looking down at my mother now, my eyes
were dry as sand.

"Well?"

I'd just finished speaking to her about the offer and my
subsequent acceptance of it. Some of the repugnance had
left her face while I talked and at last she took my hand.

"You're doing the right thing. The *only* thing to save
yourself from a future of evil."

Bitterness wafted from me and a small, selfish part of me
hated her. If not for her, I could just disappear with Bones
and live the rest of my life with the man I loved. Yet it was
no more her fault for her unyielding hatred of vampires than
it was my fault for being born. In this case, we were even.

"I don't think it's saving me from a future of evil, but I'm doing it anyway."

"Don't be stupid, Catherine. Of course it is. How long could you have continued your relationship with that creature before he turned you into a vampire? If he cared for you as you claim he did, then he wouldn't want to sit back and watch you age over time, would he? Moving closer to death each year, as all humans do. Why, when he could change you and extend your youth indefinitely? That's what he'll do to you if you stay with him, and if you weren't being blind, you'd already know it."

Much as I hated to admit it, she had brought up a very obvious point I'd let myself ignore. What would happen to our relationship in ten years? Twenty? More? God, she was right. Bones wouldn't just sit back and watch me die of old age. He'd want me to change over, and I would never do it. Maybe we'd been doomed from the start, and my mother's prejudice and Don's offer were just proof of that. *You fight the battles you can win*, Bones had repeatedly said. Well, I couldn't win this battle, but I could keep him safe. I could keep my mother safe, and then use what was in me to keep other people safe. Put in perspective, a broken heart wasn't such a terrible price to pay. I might be looking at a future without him, but it was still a future. Considering all the girls Hennessey had taken who didn't have that anymore, it would be an insult for me to squander my life when theirs had been robbed from them.

The door opened and Tate Bradley poked his head in. His arm was in a sling and there was a bandage near his temple.

"Time to go."

Nodding shortly, I grasped my mother's wheelchair and followed him down the hospital corridor. The hallway had been cleared and every patient door closed. Behind me were eight heavily armed men. It seemed Don was afraid I'd get cold feet.

There were about two hours left of daylight. We would be driven a short distance away to a helicopter pad and then flown via chopper to where a military plane waited. I piled into the backseat with my mother. Tate took the front passenger seat, being unable to drive with his broken arm. A man who introduced himself as Pete took the wheel. My other guards took flanking positions in three vehicles, one behind us, two on each side. Ironically, it was the same formation the vampires had used last night. We pulled away and I closed my eyes, thinking that I'd have to find a way to tell Bones goodbye. Maybe I'd leave a message with Tara. She'd know how to contact him. I couldn't just leave with no word to him at all.

Tate broke the silence after several minutes. "Pete here will be one of the members of the unit, Cather—excuse me, Cat," he corrected himself.

I didn't open my eyes. "Not unless I say so, or were you asleep during that part? I pick the team. Pete's in only if he passes my test, and that goes for you, too."

"What's the test?" Pete asked condescendingly.

My eyes slit open.

"To see how many times you'll get back up after I beat you unconscious."

Pete laughed. Tate didn't. Maybe he wasn't as stupid as I'd first thought. The glance he threw me told me he believed every word.

"Look,"—Pete eyed me in the rearview mirror, skepticism etched on his face—"I know you're supposed to be something special, but . . . what the *fuck*?"

Pete's retort ended in a gasp when he spotted a man in the middle of the highway in our lane. My breath caught as well, and my mother screamed.

"That's *him*! That's—"

Tate had less hesitation. In the seconds before the car struck Bones, he pulled his gun and fired through the windshield at him.

It was like hitting a brick wall. The collision crushed the front of the car. Glass exploded out of the windows and the front and rear air bags deployed instantly. Jerked forward violently, I heard brakes screech behind us as our escort swerved to avoid slamming into our rear. The two cars on either side of us sailed past and then applied their brakes to try to rotate around. Traffic still came from behind us. Vehicles that had banked sharply to the left and right of us crashed into the turning agents' cars. The sound of twisting steel on metal as the vehicles piled up in a ghastly domino effect was deafening.

Tate and Pete lolled in their seat belts, blood from the glass and contact with the dashboard streaming down their faces. There was a wrenching sound as Tate's door was ripped off its frame. Through the smoke from the destroyed engine, I saw Bones grin as he chucked the piece of the car like a giant Frisbee at the car behind us. Back there, the other guards vainly tried to get a clear shot at him. They scattered as the door burst through their windshield. In a flash the other door followed suit, and my mother wailed in mortal fear when he next tore open mine.

"Hallo, Kitten!"

Despite my earlier resolution, I was thrilled to see him. He unclasped my seat belt and grabbed my mother when she tried to scoot out her side.

"Not so fast, Mum. We're in a bit of a hurry."

A moan from the front seat made him casually swat Tate in the head.

"Don't kill him, Bones! They weren't going to hurt me!"

"Oh—right, then. Let's just send them on their way nicely."

In a blur he yanked Tate clear from his seat. For a moment his mouth pressed against his neck, and then he tossed him fifty feet in the air. Tate landed in the grass by the shoulder of the road. Pete attempted to crawl away, but Bones grasped him and gave him the same flight with similar onboard beverage service.

"Get out of the car, luv," Bones directed, and I sprang from the ruined remains of the vehicle. He still had my mother by the arm. She was crying and cursing him at the same time.

"They're going to kill you, they know what you are! Catherine's—"

My mother's words were cut off when I punched her right in the jaw. She collapsed without another word. In her railing threats, she would have revealed too much, and if Bones knew about the deal I'd made, he would talk me out of it. I'd believe whatever impossible assurances he gave me, because my heart had no common sense.

A bullet whizzed by. I dropped to the ground, not wanting to get shot *again*. Bones gave an irritated glance in its direction and then grasped the floorboards of the car. My eyes widened in growing comprehension. God, he couldn't do that, could he?

The agents from the cars in front of us had taken cover behind one of their overturned vehicles, and they were firing at us. Apparently they'd been told to ensure my safe arrival or, failing that, guarantee I didn't escape. Plan A had failed, so they were going with Plan B. Bones gave a wolfish grin as he lifted the car off the ground. He spun in a semicircle for maximum velocity, and then the twisted hunk of machinery went sailing through the air, landing point-blank on the makeshift barricade of the agents' vehicle.

There was a thunderous boom as the car exploded on contact. Thick acrid smoke billowed into the air. In the midst of this maelstrom, with his legs apart and eyes flashing green, Bones looked absolutely, terrifyingly magnificent.

Pandemonium seized the highway. Traffic on the opposite side of the road piled up as disbelieving onlookers stopped driving and gaped at the carnage to their left. Every second brought a fresh squealing of brakes and new accidents. Bones didn't pause to admire his work. He took my hand and threw my mother over his shoulder as we raced into the trees out of sight.

He had a car waiting about five miles ahead where the lanes were free of the wreckage behind us. Bones deposited my mother in the back, pausing only to clap a piece of duct tape over her mouth before we sped off.

"Glad you were the one that socked her, luv. It saved me the trouble. You don't get your meanness from your father—you get it from her. She bit me."

For someone who had just been hit by a car going sixty, he looked remarkably chipper.

"How did you do that? *How* did you stop the car? If a vampire can do that, why didn't Switch prevent me from bashing into the house last night?"

Bones snorted derisively. "That pup? He couldn't stop a toddler on a tricycle. He was only 'round sixty, luv, in undead years. You have to be an old Master vamp like me to pull such a trick without regretting it dearly afterwards. Believe me, it hurt like blazes. That's why I took a nip from your two blokes before chucking them off. Who were they, anyhow? They weren't police."

This had to be handled very carefully. "Um, they were from some branch of government, they didn't say which. Weren't real chatty, you know? I think they were taking me to a special jail or something because of Oliver."

He gave me a look. "You should have waited for me. You could have gotten killed."

"I couldn't wait! One of Oliver's dirty cops tried to shoot me, and he was supposed to plant a bomb in the hospital where they were taking my mother! Oliver was the one, Bones. He admitted it, practically bragged about how Hennessey was 'cleaning up' his state for him. Like all those people were nothing but garbage. God, if I'd killed him ten times, it still wouldn't be enough."

"What makes you think those blokes who were taking you away weren't more of his men?"

"They weren't. Besides, you hardly treated them like you were giving them the benefit of the doubt. You dropped a car on four of them."

"Oh, don't fret." Unconcernedly. "They jumped free before the explosion. And if they were too thick not to, then they deserved to die for their stupidity."

"Whose car is this?" We were riding in a black Volvo SUV, fully loaded with that new car smell.

Bones cast a sideways glance at me. "Yours. Do you like it?"

I shook my head. "Not whose it is *now*, but won't it be reported stolen soon?"

"No," he replied. "This was your Christmas present. It's registered under the name on your false license, so there's no way for them to track it. Hope you don't mind missing out on the surprise, but under the circumstances, it was our best option."

My mouth hung open, because he was clearly serious. "I can't accept this. It's way too expensive!" In the midst of everything, here I was arguing over the lavishness of a Christmas gift. Normal and I would never meet.

He gave an exasperated sigh. "Kitten, for once could you just say thank you? Really, luv, aren't we past this?"

A sharp stab of misery poked me when I remembered we were way past this, just not like he thought.

"Thank you. It's beautiful. All I got you was a new

jacket." Christmas was only two weeks away, but it might as well have been a thousand years.

"What kind of jacket?"

God help me, how would I have the strength to walk away from him? His dark brown eyes were lovelier than anything money could buy. I swallowed hard and described it, because talking kept the tears at bay.

"Well, it was long, like a trenchcoat. Black leather, so you'd look spooky and mysterious. The police probably ransacked whatever was left of my apartment the vampires didn't destroy. It was wrapped and hidden under the loose board in the kitchen cabinet."

Bones took my hand and squeezed it gently. Now there was no halting the moisture from my eyes.

"Switch?" Better asking late than never. The fact that Bones was here made the question almost rhetorical.

"Shriveled in Indiana. That bugger ran at full speed for hours. Sorry I couldn't have taken my time with him, Kitten, but I wanted to head straight back to you. When I caught him, I staked him and left him to rot in the woods by Cedar Lake. With all the bodies left back at the house, one more isn't going to rock the boat. In fact, Indiana's where we're headed now."

"Why Indiana?" Dimly I was glad Switch was dead. Maybe now my grandparents could rest in peace.

"Got a mate there, Rodney, who will set you and your mum up with new identification. We'll bunk at his place tonight and leave tomorrow afternoon. Just have to run a few errands in the morning to be set. From there, we'll proceed to Ontario for a few months. We *will* track down those last two sods, mark my words, but we'll do it quietly once this heat over Oliver cools down. When your lads can't find a trace of you after a bit, they'll look for other fish to fry."

Oh, if only it were that simple. "How did you know when they were moving us?"

He gave an amused grunt. "By watching. When they cleared a path from a floor to the back exit and had armed guards waiting by a bunch of vehicles, it was obvious. I just stayed ahead of them until the timing was right."

A solid thumping noise drew my attention to the back-seat. Bones grinned.

"Looks like your mum woke up."

†wen†y-seven

RODNEY WAS A GHOUL, TO MY SURPRISE. Somehow I just expected vampire. Bones lifted my mother out of the backseat, tape still over her mouth, and handed her off to me as he made the introductions. Rodney didn't bat an eye. He must have been used to people showing up at his house bound and gagged.

I set my mother on her feet and shook Rodney's hand as much as I could while keeping her from bolting away.

"I hate to impose right off, Rodney, but where's the bathroom?"

"It's no imposition, it's on the left," he said with a smile.

I hauled her with me. "Be back in a minute, Bones. I want to get her cleaned up and have a word with her."

"Take your time, luv."

I locked the door behind us and immediately began to run the water in the tub. On the way over, I'd come up with a plan, but now I had to get my mother to play along. She made furious grunts behind her gag, and I sighed. Even with the water running, Bones might hear us.

I gave the bathroom mirror a cagey glance and then turned the faucet to run as hot as possible. Soon the room filled with steam. Bingo.

I used my finger to write on the now-fogged mirror:

Leaving tomorrow don't speak he'll hear you

Her eyes bugged. "He killed the man who murdered Grandpa Joe and Grandma, Mom," I said in a clear voice. "He won't hurt me and he won't hurt you."

She wrote three words next to mine:

Leaving without him?

I nodded my head yes, even though I wanted to throw up. "I know you hate vampires and I know this will be hard, but you're going to have to listen to me for a while."

He doesn't know, he would stop us

"Just give me a little time. You have to trust me. Our lives depend on it."

Play along no matter what

"We're staying here tonight, and then tomorrow we're leaving the country. It's the only way."

I kept repeating that to myself. This *was* the only way. It just hurt more than I could stand.

"Well? Are you going to be reasonable? Can I take the gag off?"

She gave me a hard stare and wrote again on the mirror:

Leaving without him promise me

"You can trust me," I repeated. "I promise."

My mother nodded once, and I took her gag off. She glanced at the door, but didn't say a word.

I grabbed one of the pretty hanging towels and rubbed our words off the mirror. "Try to be nice when we go out."

Bones and Rodney were seated at the table. My mother glared at both of them, but said nothing. For her, that *was* being nice.

"Take your pick of the guest rooms, one upstairs and one in the basement," Rodney offered.

"Show me the one in the basement," I said instantly.

"Of course, follow me."

I took my mother's arm and we went down a flight of stairs to the basement. Rodney opened a door to a guest room complete with fluffy blankets and, more importantly, no windows.

I gave my mother a light push inside. "This'll be perfect for you, Mom."

She stared stupidly at me as I started to leave.

"Where do you think you're going?"

"Upstairs. With Bones. Good night."

I slammed the door and watched with grim contentment as Rodney locked it from the outside. The mere fact that he had a downstairs bedroom with a lock on the outside was cause for comment, but none of my business.

There was a pounding on it almost at once.

"Catherine! You can't mean to—"

"We'll talk about it tomorrow, Mom, when we're alone. *Tomorrow.* Don't cause a fuss, you're making Rodney hungry."

Although I had no way of knowing the truthfulness of that statement, he winked at me and made a low rumbling noise in his throat. The room inside at once became quiet.

"Thanks for that," I whispered gratefully. "She would have banged all night."

He smiled as we walked back up the stairs. The door to the basement he also locked and gave me a meaningful glance.

"In case she's really feisty."

Bones waited for me in the other guest room and I went straight into his arms, breathing in the scent of him. For several minutes we just held each other. Selfishly I tried to drink in the feeling of him next to me. I might know this was the only way, but oh God, did it hurt.

"I told you we'd make it through the night, luv. You didn't believe me."

"No," I softly answered. "I didn't. But you were right, and both of you are alive. That's all that matters. It means more than anything to me."

"You mean more than anything to me."

He lowered his head and brushed his lips across mine. In response I wound my hands around him and pressed him to me so tightly, I knew I'd have bruises in the morning.

"Why are you crying?" he whispered.

I swiped at the tears I hadn't realized were there. "Because . . . I couldn't bear it if anything happened to you."

He kissed me. "Nothing will happen to me, I promise."

I promise too. In fact, I'm going to bet my life on it.

"I want you to know that despite everything, I'm so glad I met you," I choked out. "It was the luckiest day of my life. If I hadn't, I never would have known what it was like for someone to love me, all of me, even the parts I hated. I would have gone through life empty and guilt-ridden, but you showed me a whole new world, Bones. I'll never be able to thank you for all you've done for me, but I will love you every day until I die."

Maybe he'd remember this after I was gone. Maybe he wouldn't hate me for what I had to do.

"Kitten," he moaned as he drew me down onto the bed. "I only *thought* I was living before I met you. You'll love me until you die? That's not nearly long enough. . . ."

I cursed each ray of sunlight that mocked me with its appearance. Bones already told me he and Rodney would be leaving for about four hours to make the final arrangements for our departure. They would take Rodney's car, leaving me the Volvo just in case they had to summon us to meet them. All that was left now was for him to leave, not knowing that we would never see each other again.

Rodney, the domesticated ghoul, made breakfast. Pancakes and omelets for my mother and me. Under my threatening glare she ate hers, looking as though she would choke with each swallow. Out of courtesy I ate far more than I wanted, not having an appetite but not wanting to appear rude. One of the few things I was thankful for was that Rodney was waiting until later to eat . . . whatever his normal breakfast consisted of.

When Bones started toward the door, I surprised him by grabbing him and throwing my arms around him. I buried my head in his neck. *I can't let you go yet. I can't do it. It's too soon!*

"What's this? Miss me before I've even left?"

My heart constricted. "I'll always miss you when you're gone."

It was treading the tightrope a little dangerously, but I couldn't help but say it.

He kissed me, achingly tender. I held him and desperately tried not to cry. *This hurts so much! How can I let you go? How can I let you walk away?*

How can you not? my logic countered. *You love him? Then prove it. Keep him safe.*

Ruthlessly I swallowed back my tears. *It's better to do this now than later. You know this is the right decision. He'll live long past your lifetime, and he'll forget about you eventually.*

I pulled away, touching his face very softly. "Give me your jacket."

Even in the midst of reveling in his last embrace, I was adding the final nails to the coffin. Bones shook it off, raising a dark brow in question. "In case we have to leave and meet you," I said in explanation. "It's cold outside."

Bones handed me the faded denim coat he'd worn yesterday while causing a forty-car pile-up and I folded it under my arm. He gave one last brush of his lips on my forehead as I prepared to shut the door behind him. *You can do this. Let him go. It's the only way.*

"Be careful, Bones. Just please . . . be careful."

He smiled. "Don't fret, luv. I'll be back before you know it."

I watched through the peephole long after they drove off and then fell to my knees, letting myself feel all the pain of a shattered heart. I cried until my eyes burned and I could barely breathe. This hurt so much worse than those bullets had.

Twenty minutes later I stood and was a different person. There was no more time for weeping. I had a job to do. *You play the hand you're dealt*, Bones had always said. Well, I'd been born a half-breed for a reason, and now was my chance to prove it. *Come one, come all, bloodsuckers! The Red Reaper's ready for you!*

I advanced on my mother and spoke in low clipped tones. First things first.

"Get dressed, we're leaving. Now, I'm going to tell you exactly what you'll say, and God help you if you don't follow every fucking word of it. . . ."

* * *

The helicopter hovered overhead, a large mechanical beetle in the sky. Don Williams was wheeled over the uneven ground at his insistence and ten other agents fanned out around the perimeter. In the middle of this scene I huddled around Switch's body. It hadn't been hard for me to find him. Bones had told me he'd left him in the woods near Cedar Lake. With my new nose, I'd scented him out soon after arriving. Switch was now wearing a denim jacket over his decomposed remains, and a silver knife protruded grotesquely out of his back.

Even seated, Don commanded the activities. "Is that him?" he demanded as he drew near.

"It's him."

Don stared down at the unrecognizable corpse and frowned. "There's nothing left but bones!"

"Funny you should say that," I responded in a flat tone. "That was his name. Bones."

The cold wind caused me to shiver and I glanced around at the dreary landscape of naked trees and frigid earth.

"He's dead, so why the rush? When your call came in, you said if we didn't arrive within the hour, you were leaving because it was too dangerous to wait. Well, it's been forty-five minutes and he doesn't look like he's going anywhere."

I stood and towered over him in his wheelchair. "Because yesterday he told me there would be vampires coming for retribution over what happened the night before last. Oliver had toothy friends. The team isn't in place and I can't fight them on my own. Since I value my own neck, I don't want it to become food. Get me and my mother out of here. Now."

"We're taking him as well," he insisted. "We'll want to study the body."

I shrugged.

"Study away, but I suggest you speed up. Vampires can smell flesh from miles away. Any of your boys left here poking at pinecones will become one big snack in a hell of a hurry."

Don stared at me. "Why should I believe you?"

As if annoyed, I ran my hand through my hair. "Because you're not as dumb as you look. Any of your men who were injured yesterday need to be moved immediately as well. The vamps will try to extort information from them and I'm sure those agents know things you'd rather not be shared with the undead."

He stared into my eyes for several more long moments and I stared back without blinking. Finally he called out to his men, decision made.

"Let's move it out, people. Wrap it up, we leave in five! Someone get the hospital on the phone and transport all injured personnel in the Medevac chopper on the double. No arrival destination listed. Stanley, pack that body and make it snappy, we're airborne in five."

There was a flurry of activity as the agents rushed to carry out his instructions. While they made final preparations, I sat down next to my mother. She put her hand in mine without a word.

"Ms. Crawfield." Don approached with the sound of crunching wheels. "Is there anything you'd like to add to your daughter's description of what happened? Anything at all?"

My mother looked up at him and dourly shook her head. "How could I? I was unconscious. That animal hit me, again. When I came to, Catherine had killed him. There he is, see for yourself."

Don looked back and forth between the two of us. Neither of us wavered. He sighed. "Then, ladies, come with me. The helicopter will take us to the airport. Let's try this again."

Eight hours later, I walked the long corridor of the military hospital in Houston, Texas, with Don rolling at my side.

"It's done?"

He grunted in the affirmative. "Catherine Crawfield has been officially killed by the FBI after trying to escape during a transfer. That's how we explained the highway pile-up yesterday. The body of a Jane Doe has been substituted as yours."

I nodded, only sorry that Timmie would believe that. Or maybe he wouldn't. He *had* been a conspiracy buff. "And my reason for killing Ethan Oliver?"

Don smiled coldly. "A random act of senseless violence. Considering Oliver's propaganda campaign, I thought it was fitting."

I didn't smile back, but I thought it was fitting, too.

"Tate asked to see me?"

"As soon as he woke up. The doctors are holding off on the painkillers, otherwise it would be pretty one-sided."

"How badly is he hurt?" Cynically, I was more curious than concerned.

"Two broken legs, two broken arms, six broken ribs, a fractured collarbone, broken nose, some internal bleeding, abrasions, and a low iron count. He'll be out for weeks recovering."

"We'll see," I murmured.

Tate Bradley was covered in casts and gauze. His eyes fluttered when we came in the door.

I pulled up a chair and sat down. "Hello."

A pain-filled gaze met mine. "Did I make the team, Cat?"

His voice was a raspy whisper, but the words made me almost smile. Almost.

"You want to sign on for this kind of pain on a regular basis?"

"Hell, yeah." Breathy but firm.

I shook my head sardonically. "Then congratulations,

Tate. You're the first team member." I stood and turned to Don.

"Get a nurse and have them take some blood from me. At least a pint. Have them transfuse it to Tate."

Don gave me a wondering squint. "You don't even know if you're his type. You have to be cross-matched."

That made me laugh. "I'm everyone's type. Half vampire and topped off with extra-aged nosferatu. The additional strength will be out of my system in the next couple days, so I suggest you use it while it's still effective. Here's Lesson One in the class of I Know More Than You Know—vampire blood heals. He'll be on his feet by the end of tomorrow. We need to start training right away. We have a lot of work to do."

I rolled up my sleeve as Don pressed for the medical attendant.

"What else are you going to tell me that I don't know?" he asked.

My eyes flashed their emerald glow at him and he gasped as their light settled on his face.

"You can't even imagine. . . ."

Later, when my mother and I were stationed at a military facility, I allowed myself to think about Bones. He would have gotten back to Rodney's hours ago and seen the note I'd left him. In brief terms, I'd tried to explain how I couldn't let more blood of those I loved stain my hands. No matter how cleverly he managed things, sooner or later the government would catch up with us. Or one of the vampires who'd gotten away would find us. Or my mother would ruin things between us with her hatred and inevitable attempts to run off. Or time would be our enemy as I aged and he didn't. We had to play the hand we were dealt, all of us. Fighting the battles we could win.

And yet when I finally drifted off, in that barely conscious state where logic was absent and dreams encroached, I could almost hear Bones's voice. He was whispering that same promise he'd made to me months ago when our relationship started, and I wondered if it was a sign—and if he'd really meant it.

If you run from me, I'll chase you. And I'll find you. . . .

Turn the page for a sneak preview of the sensational second novel in The Night Huntress series, *One Foot in the Grave*:

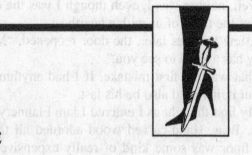

One

I WAITED OUTSIDE THE LARGE, FOUR-STORY home in Manhasset that was owned by a Mr. Liam Flannery. This wasn't a social call, as anyone looking at me could tell. The long jacket I wore was open, leaving my gun and shoulder holster clearly visible, as was my FBI badge. My pants were loose-fitting and so was my blouse, to hide the twenty pounds of silver weapons strapped to my arms and legs.

My knock was answered by an older man in a business suit. "Special Agent Catrina Arthur," I said. "Here to see Mr. Flannery."

Catrina wasn't my real name, but it's what was on my doctored badge. The doorman gave me an insincere smile.

"I'll see if Mr. Flannery is in. Wait here."

I already knew Liam Flannery was in. What I also knew was that Mr. Flannery wasn't human, and neither was the doorman.

Well, neither was I, even though I was the only one out of the three of us with a heartbeat.

A few minutes later, the door reopened. "Mr. Flannery has agreed to see you."

That was his first mistake. If I had anything to say about it, it would also be his last.

My first thought as I entered Liam Flannery's house was, *Wow.* Hand-carved wood adorned all the walls, the floor was some kind of really expensive-looking marble, and antiques were tastefully littered everywhere the eye could see. Being dead sure didn't mean you couldn't live it up.

The hairs on the back of my neck stood on end as power filled the room. Flannery wouldn't know I could feel it, just like I'd felt it from his ghoul doorman. I might look as average as the next person, but I had a few secrets up my sleeve. And lots of knives, of course.

"Agent Arthur," Flannery said. "This must be about my two employees, but I've already been questioned by the police."

His accent was English, which was at odds with his Irish name. Just hearing that intonation made a shiver run up my spine. English accents held memories for me.

I turned around. Flannery looked even better than the picture in his FBI file. His pale crystal flesh almost shimmered against the tan color of his shirt. I'll say one thing for vampires—they all had gorgeous skin. Liam's eyes were a clear turquoise, and his chestnut hair fell past his collar.

Yep, he was pretty. He probably had no trouble scaring up dinner. But the most impressive thing about him was his aura. It flowed off him in tingling, power-filled waves. A Master vampire without a doubt.

"Yes, this is about Thomas Stillwell and Jerome Hawthorn. The Bureau would appreciate your cooperation."

My polite stalling was to gauge how many other people were in the house. I strained my ears, but so far came up with no one but Flannery, the ghoul doorman, and myself.

"Of course. Anything to assist law and order," he said with an undercurrent of amusement.

"And you're comfortable speaking here?" I asked, trying to get more of a look around. "Or is there somewhere private you'd prefer?"

He sauntered over. "Agent Arthur, if you want to have a private word with me, call me Liam. And I do hope you want to talk about something other than boring Jerome and Thomas."

Oh, I had little intention of talking as soon as I got Liam in private. Since he'd been implicated in the deaths of his employees, Flannery had made my to-do list, though I wasn't here to arrest him. The average person didn't believe in vampires or ghouls, so there wasn't a legal process for dealing with murdering ones. No, there was a covert branch of Homeland Security instead, and my boss, Don, would send me. There were rumors about me in the undead world, true. Ones that had grown during my tenure at this job, but only one vampire knew who I really was. And I hadn't seen him in over four years.

"Liam, you're not flirting with a federal agent who's investigating you in a double homicide, are you?"

"Catrina, an innocent man doesn't fret over the wheels of law whenever they rumble in the distance. At least I commend the feds on sending *you* to speak with me, beautiful woman that you are. You also look a bit familiar, though I'm sure I would have remembered meeting you before."

"You haven't," I said immediately. "Trust me, I would have remembered."

I didn't mean it as a compliment, but it caused him to chuckle in a way that was too insinuating for my liking.

"I'll bet."

You smug son of a bitch. Let's see how long you'll keep that smirk.

"Back to business, Liam. Are we talking here, or somewhere private?"

He made a noise of defeat. "If you insist on traveling this path, we may as well be comfortable in the library. Come with me."

I followed him past more lavish, empty rooms to the library. It was magnificent, with hundreds of new and old books. There were even scrolls preserved in a glass display case, but it was the large piece of artwork on the wall that caught my attention.

"This looks . . . primitive."

At first glance it appeared to be wood or ivory, but on closer inspection, it looked like bones. Human ones.

"Aborigine, nearly three hundred years old. Given to me by some mates of mine in Australia."

Liam came nearer, his turquoise eyes starting to glint with emerald. I knew the pinpoints of green in his gaze for what they were. Lust and feeding looked the same on a vampire. Both made the eyes glow emerald and the fangs pop out. Liam was either hungry or horny, but I wasn't going to satisfy any of his cravings.

My cell phone rang. "Hello," I answered.

"Agent Arthur, are you still questioning Mr. Flannery?" my second-in-command, Tate, asked.

"Yes. This should be wrapped up in thirty minutes."

Translation: If I didn't answer again in half an hour, Tate and my team would come in after me.

Tate hung up without further comment. He hated it when I handled things alone, but too bad. Flannery's house was as quiet as a tomb, apropos as that may be, and it had been a long time since I'd battled with a Master vampire.

"I believe the police told you that the bodies of Thomas Stillwell and Jerome Hawthorn were found with most of their blood missing. And not any visible wounds on them to account for it," I said, jumping right in.

Liam shrugged. "Does the Bureau have a theory?"

Oh, we had more than a theory. I knew Liam would have just closed the telltale holes on Thomas and Jerome's necks with a drop of his own blood before they died. Boom, two bodies drained, no vampire calling card to rally the villagers—unless you knew what tricks to look for.

Flatly I shot back, "*You* do, though, don't you?"

"You know what I have a theory on, Catrina? That you taste as sweet as you look. In fact, I haven't thought about anything else since you walked in."

I didn't resist when Liam closed the distance between us and lifted my chin. After all, this would distract him better than anything I came up with.

His lips were cool on mine and vibrating with energy, giving my mouth pleasant tingles. He was a very good kisser, sensing when to deepen it and when to *really* deepen it. For a minute, I actually allowed myself to enjoy it—God, four years of celibacy must be taking its toll!—and then I got down to business.

My arms went around him, concealing me pulling a dagger from my sleeve. At the same time, he slid his hands down to my hips and felt the hard outlines under my pants.

"What the hell—?" he muttered, pulling back.

I smiled. "Surprise!" And then I struck.

It would have been a killing blow, but Liam was faster than I anticipated. He swept my feet out from under me just as I jabbed, so my silver missed his heart by inches. Instead of attempting to regain my stability, I let myself drop, rolling away from the kick he aimed at my head. Liam moved in a streak to try it again, but then jerked back when three of my throwing knives landed in his chest. Dammit, I'd missed his heart *again*.

"Sweet bleedin' Christ!" Liam exclaimed. He quit pretending to be human and let his eyes turn glowing emerald while fangs popped out in his upper teeth. "*You* must be the fabled Red Reaper. What brings the vampire bogeyman to my home?"

He sounded intrigued, but not afraid. He was more wary, however, and circled around me as I sprang to my feet, throwing off my jacket to better access my weapons.

"The usual," I said. "You murdered humans. I'm here to settle the score."

Liam actually rolled his eyes. "Believe me, poppet, Jerome and Thomas had it coming. Those thieving bastards stole from me. It's so hard to find good help these days."

"Keep talking, pretty boy. I don't care."

I rolled my head around on my shoulders and palmed more knives. Neither of us blinked as we waited for the other to make a move. What Liam didn't know was that I was aware he'd summoned for help. I could hear the ghoul creep quietly closer toward us, barely disturbing the air around him. Liam's chattering was just to buy time.

He shook his head in apparent self-recrimination.

"Your appearance should have warned me. The Red Reaper is said to have hair as red as blood, gray eyes like smoke, and your skin . . . mmm, now there's the real distinction. I've never seen such beautiful flesh on a human before. Christ, girl, I wasn't even going to bite you. Well, not the way you're thinking."

"I'm flattered you want to fuck me as well as murder me. Really, Liam, that's sweet."

He grinned. "Valentine's Day was just last month, after all."

He was forcing me toward the door and I let him. Deliberately I pulled my longest knife from my pants leg, the one that was practically a small sword, and switched it with my throwing knives in my right hand.

Liam grinned wider when he saw it. "Impressive, but you haven't seen *my* lance yet. Drop your trappings and I'll show you. You can even keep a few knives on, if you'd like. Would only make it more interesting."

He lunged forward, but I didn't take the bait. Instead I flung the five knives in my left hand at him and whirled to avoid the blow from the ghoul behind me. With a single swipe that reverberated through my arm, I sent the blade into the ghoul's neck with all my strength.

It came out on the other side. The ghoul's head rotated on its axis for a moment, wide eyes fixed on mine, before it plopped to the ground. There was only one way to kill a ghoul, and that was it.

Liam yanked my silver knives out of him as if they were merely toothpicks.

"You nasty bitch, *now* I'm going to hurt you! Magnus has been my friend for over forty years!"

That signaled the end to the bantering. Liam came at me with incredible speed. He had no weapons except his body and his teeth, but those were formidable. Liam pounded his fists into me, and I retaliated with punishing blows. For several minutes, we just hammered at each other, knocking over every table and lamp in our path. Finally he threw me across the room, and I crashed near the unusual art piece I'd admired. When he came after me, I kicked out and knocked him backward into the display case. Then I tore the sculpture off the wall and chucked it at his head.

Liam ducked, cursing when the intricate artwork broke into pieces behind him.

"Don't you have any bleedin' respect for artifacts? That piece was older than I am! And how in the *blazes* did you get eyes like that?"

I didn't need to look to know what he was talking

about. My formerly gray gaze would now be glowing as green as Liam's. Fighting brought out the proof of my mixed heritage that my unknown vampire father had left me.

"That bone puzzle was older than you are, huh? So you're what, two hundred? Two fifty? You're strong then. I've skewered vamps as old as seven hundred who didn't hit as hard as you do. You're going to be fun to kill."

God help me, but I wasn't kidding. There was no sport when I just staked a vampire and let my team sweep up the remains.

Liam grinned at me. "Two hundred and twenty, poppet. In pulseless years, that is. The other ones weren't good for anything but poverty and misery. London was a sewage back then. Looks much better now."

"Too bad you won't be seeing it again."

"I doubt that, poppet. You think you'll enjoy killing me? I know I'll *love* fucking you."

"Let's see what you've got," I taunted.

He flew across the room—too swiftly for me to avoid him—and delivered a brutal blow to my head. It made light explode in my brain and would have put a normal person right into the grave. Me, I'd never been normal, so while I fought nausea, I also reacted quickly.

I went limp, letting my mouth hang open and my eyes roll back as I dropped to the ground with my throat temptingly tilted upward. Near my relaxed hand was one of the throwing knives he'd pulled from his chest. Would Liam kick me while I was down, or see how badly I was hurt?

My gamble paid off. "That's better," Liam muttered, and knelt next to me. He let his hands travel over my body, and then he grunted in amusement.

"Talk about an army of one. Woman's wearing a whole bloody arsenal."

He unzipped my pants in a businesslike manner. Probably he was going to strip me of my knives; that would be the smart thing. When he pulled my pants past my hips, however, he paused. His fingers traced over the tattoo on my hip that I'd gotten four years ago, right after I left my old life in Ohio behind for this new one.

Seizing my chance, I closed my hand over the nearby dagger and drove the knife into his heart. Liam's shocked eyes met mine as he froze.

"I thought if the *Alexander* didn't kill me, nothing would . . ."

I was just about to deliver that final, fatal twist when the last piece clicked. *A ship named the* Alexander. *He was from London, and he'd been dead about two hundred and twenty years. He had Aborigine artwork, given to him from a friend in Australia . . .*

"Which one are you?" I asked, holding the knife still. If he moved, it would shred his heart. If he stayed motionless, it wouldn't kill him. Yet.

"What?"

"In 1788, four convicts sailed to South Wales penal colonies on a ship named the *Alexander*. One escaped soon after arriving. A year later, that runaway convict returned and killed everyone but his three friends. One of them was turned into a vampire by choice, two by force. I know who you're not, so tell me who you are."

If it were possible, he looked even more astonished

than he had when I stabbed him in the heart. "Only a few people in the world know that story."

I gave the blade a menacing flick that edged it fractions deeper. He got the point, all right.

"Ian. I am Ian."

Mother*fucker!* On top of me was the man who'd turned the love of my life into a vampire almost two hundred and twenty years ago. Talk about irony.

Liam, or Ian, was a murderer by his own admission. Granted, his employees may or may not have stolen from him; the world never lacked for fools. Vampires played by a different set of rules when it came to their possessions. They were territorial to a fantastic degree. If Thomas and Jerome knew what he was and stole from him, they'd have known the consequences. But that wasn't what stayed my hand. Eventually it boiled down to one simple truth—I might have left Bones, but I couldn't kill the person responsible for bringing him into my life.

Yeah, call me sentimental.

"Liam, or Ian, if you prefer, listen to me very carefully. You and I are going to stand up. I'm going to pull this knife out, and then you're going to run away. Your heart's been punctured, but you'll heal. I owed someone a life and I'm making it yours."

He stared at me. The glowing lights of our eyes merged.

"Crispin." Bones's real name hung between us, but I didn't react. Ian let out a pained laugh. "It could only be Crispin. Should have known from the way you fought, not to mention your tattoo that's identical to his. Nasty trick, faking to be unconscious. He would have never fallen for it. He'd have kicked you until you quit pretending."

"You're right," I agreed mildly. "That's the first thing Bones taught me. Always kick someone when they're down. I paid attention. You didn't."

"Well, well, little Red Reaper. So you're the reason he's been in such a foul mood the past few years."

At once my heart constricted with joy. Ian had just confirmed what I hadn't allowed myself to wonder. Bones was alive. Even if he hated me for leaving him, he was alive.

Ian pressed his advantage. "You and Crispin, hmm? I haven't spoken to him in a few months, but I can find him. I could take you to him, if you'd like."

The thought of seeing Bones again caused a shattering of emotions in me. To cover them, I laughed derisively.

"Not for gold. Bones found me and turned me out as bait for the marks he was paid to kill. Even talked me into that tattoo. Speaking of gold, when you see Bones again, you can tell him he still owes me money. He never paid me my share of the jobs like he promised. The only reason it's *your* lucky day is he helped rescue my mother once, so I owe him for that, and you're my payment. But if I ever see Bones again, it'll be at the end of my knife."

Each word hurt, but they were necessary. I wouldn't hang a target around Bones's neck by admitting I still loved him. If Ian repeated what I said, Bones would know it wasn't true. He hadn't refused to pay me on the jobs I'd done with him—I'd refused to take the money. Nor had he talked me into my tattoo. I'd gotten the crossbones matching his out of useless longing after I left him.

"You're part vampire. You have to be with those glowing eyes. Tell me—how?"

I almost didn't, but figured, what the hell. Ian already knew my secret. The *how* was anticlimactic.

"Some newly dead vampire raped my mother, and unluckily for her, his sperm still swam. I don't know who he is, but one day I'll find him and kill him. Until then, I'll settle for deadbeats just like him."

Somewhere on the far side of the room, my cell phone rang. I didn't move to answer it, but spoke hurriedly.

"That's my backup. When I don't answer, they come in with force. More force than you can take on right now. Move slowly; stand up. When I take this knife out, you run like hell and don't stop. You'll get your life, but you're leaving this house and you're not coming back. Do we have a deal? Think before you answer, because I don't bluff."

Ian smiled tightly. "Oh, I believe you. You've got a knife in my heart. That gives you little reason to lie."

I didn't blink. "Then let's do this."

Without another comment, Ian began to pull himself to his knees. Each movement was agony for him, I could tell, but he thinned his lips and didn't make a sound. When we both stood, I carefully drew the blade out of his back and held the bloody knife in front of me.

"Goodbye, Ian. Get lost."

He crashed through a window to my left in a blur of speed that was slower than before, but still impressive. Out in front, I heard my men rushing up to the door. There was one last thing I had to do.

I plunged the same dagger into my belly, deep enough to make me drop to my knees, but high enough to avoid mortal injury. When my second officer, Tate, came running into the room, I was gasping and bent double, blood pouring out onto the lovely thick carpet.

"Jesus, Cat!" he exclaimed. "Someone get the Brams!"

My other two captains, Dave and Juan, fanned out to comply. Tate picked me up and carried me out of the house. With jagged breaths I gave my instructions.

"One got away but don't chase him. He's too strong. No one else is in the house, but do a quick check and then pull back. We have to leave in case he comes back with reinforcements. They'd slaughter us."

"One sweep and then fall back, fall back!" Dave ordered, shutting the doors of the van I'd been taken to. Tate pulled the knife out and pressed bandages to the wound, giving me several pills to swallow that no regular pharmacy carried.

After four years and a team of brilliant scientists, my boss, Don, had managed to filter through the components in undead blood to come up with a wonder drug. On regular humans, it repaired injuries such as broken bones and internal bleeding like magic. We'd named it Brams, in honor of the writer who'd made vampires famous.

"You shouldn't have gone in alone," Tate berated me. "Goddammit, Cat, next time listen to me!"

I gave a faint chuckle. "Whatever you say. I'm not in the mood to argue."

Then I passed out.

Acknowledgments

First, I must thank God, for giving me my twisted sense of imagination and humor. Since I had both as far back as I can remember, I know I can't blame anyone else.

My deepest appreciation goes to my amazing agent, Rachel Vater, who read a very raw manuscript and said, "This is good. Now make it better." Without her tireless efforts and encouragement, my novel never would have seen the light of day.

Further gratitude goes to my editor, Erika Tsang, whose incredible enthusiasm and support made it possible for there to be an Acknowledgments page to begin with. Thank you so much, Erika. You made a dream of mine come true.

My heartfelt thanks go out to my family, for being such a big part of my life. Last but most important, I am grateful to my husband, for more things than I have room here to list.

Jeaniene Frost lives with her husband and their very spoiled dog in Florida. Although not a vampire herself, she confesses to having pale skin, wearing a lot of black, and sleeping in late whenever possible. And while she can't see ghosts, she loves to walk through old cemeteries. Jeaniene also loves poetry and animals, but fears children and hates to cook. She is currently at work on her next Urban Fantasy novel.

To learn more about Jeaniene, please visit her website at www.jeanienefrost.com